PRAISE FOR ROE

Praise for *The Watchmen*

"*The Watchman* came to life for me, because it is so well written and instills a sense of caution as you read.

I am delighted to have had the pleasure of discovering Robert Magarian and his talent."

—Bea Kunz, Amazon reviewer

Praise for *72 Hours*

"I was compelled to carry *72 Hours* around with me. It's a blend of trouble both personal and political, with an evil that will stop at nothing and a CDC that may—or may not—have found the only salvation. Here, also, is a family in pain. Suspenseful, timely, and breath-catching."

—Carolyn Wall, author of *Sweeping Up Glass*

Praise for *Follow Your Dream*

"In *Follow Your Dream*, Robert Magarian provides a template for turning a dream into reality, step-by-step. In 1987 Magarian created the first annual Norman Community Christmas Dinner, serving a free meal to individuals and family who would have been alone on Christmas Day. In the years hence, the event has grown to serve 1,600 people, with 200 volunteers. This is a remarkable story of what one person can do with a dream and how that dream can change many lives."

—Robert L. Ferrier, Amazon reviewer

"How does God want you to relate to Him? The same way you would to the least of our brethren. And that is what author Robert Magarian has done as so succinctly shared in this inspiring story, showing that the efforts of one mobilized an entire community to care for each other. THIS IS A MUST READ!"

—Mike Tomasco, Amazon reviewer

ALSO BY ROBERT MAGARIAN

Fiction

The Watchmen

72 Hours

Essays

Follow Your Dream

A Journey into Faith

YOU'LL NEVER
SEE ME AGAIN

A CRIME TO REMEMBER

A NOVEL

BY

ROBERT A. MAGARIAN

ISBN (print): 0-9973348-0-0
ISBN-13 (print): 978-0-9973348-0-7

Publisher's Note: This is a work of fiction. Names, characters, places, and incidents either are the product of the author's imagination or are used fictitiously. Any resemblance to persons, living or dead is entirely coincidental.

Cover design: Peter O'Connor
www.bespokebookcovers.com

Editing: Nancy Hancock

Print Formatting: By Your Side Self-Publishing
www.ByYourSideSelfPub.com

The path of the righteous is like the first gleam of dawn,
shining ever brighter till the full light of day.
But the way of the wicked is like deep darkness;
they do not know what makes them stumble.

Proverbs 4:18-19

DEDICATION

To Mary Shotwell Little and others who have disappeared and have never been found.

AUTHOR'S NOTE

A few years ago I read a couple of articles on the Internet, one by Gerdeen Dyer (1995) and another in the *Atlanta Journal-Constitution* by Jim Auchmutey, Gerdeen Dyer, and Pat Koester (2004) in which the authors report on the case of the *Missing Bride*. Reading their stories about the disappearance of Mary Shotwell Little, *a pleasant-faced, warm-hearted, loyal, punctual, and well-liked young brunette*, touched me so that I felt inspired to keep her memory alive by writing this novel. Therefore, I dedicate this novel to her and all the persons that have disappeared and have never been found. While some events in this novel are similar to those reported in the Mary Shotwell Little case, I remind the reader that this is strictly a work of fiction and in no way am I suggesting the events in *You'll Never See Me Again* solve the *Missing Bride* case.

CHAPTER ONE

She coughs hard; eyelids heavy like manhole covers. She struggles to open them. Her throbbing head feels locked in a vise. She remembers something: fingers at her throat, a wet cloth smothering her mouth and nostrils, a sickening smell, her burning lips, and then she journeys into darkness.

She licks her lips; a residue of sweetness turns her stomach. She twists her body. Feet shackled, hands tethered. Pain shoots through her with every wave of motion. Blinking hard now, she sees a glimmer of light. Her head, throbbing with pain can only move from side to side.

She wonders. *Is it night or day?* A tiny lamp on a nightstand provides faint light. Looking up at the ceiling, her senses heightened, she hears a ticking clock. She feels like screaming.

Where am I? Who did this to me?

She struggles to remember something, anything. An image pops into her mind—a grove of trees, a car. What else? *Come on, think.* She strains to know. *Someone has abducted me. Why? Oh, if only I could think straight.*

A thin sheet covers her naked body. She thinks about the animal that did this to her. A sound arises from across the room. Her pulse quickens.

Someone's in here. Her breathing becomes labored. She yanks on the restraints with as much force as she can muster. She wants to scream, but is afraid; instead, she turns an ear in the direction of the sound. A doorknob is yelping for a little oil as it turns. Suddenly, light explodes into the room like truck headlights. She blinks hard, trying to adjust her eyes. A giant silhouette looms through the doorframe, floating in like a ghost. She hears herself screaming, jerking, and crying as the figure bends over her. It has eyes, big ones. There's evil in them.

"Are you ready to cooperate now, my love?"

The voice is familiar. "Why are you doing this to me?" she says.

"Don't you know?" The cloud around the figure is shrinking and there's a face coming into view.

1

"You?"

"Of course, who else?"

"I told you I was married now, and wanted nothing to do with you."

"Doesn't matter, my love. You've always been mine. No one else will ever have you."

He disappears, but returns a moment later carrying folded clothes in his arms and sets them at the end of the bed. "If you behave yourself, I'll untie you and you can get dressed. We've got places to go."

"What do you mean? I'm not going anywhere with you."

He pulls several photos from his shirt pocket and says, "Before you say anything more, I'd take a look at these. If I were you, I'd think about cooperating. The Hamiltons wouldn't like these to get in the wrong hands."

He sets them on the tray next to the bed, unties her and disappears.

CHAPTER TWO

This Friday begins like any other day for Austin Payne at Citizens Bank in downtown Atlanta. The sun dawns in full view and the temperature is unusually warm for this October morning in 2011. Austin Payne, the bank's financial officer, greets the security guard with a smile, and waits until he unlocks the glass door. Payne, wearing a tailored gray suit, enters, smiles, and ambles to his left, carrying a leather satchel in his left hand as he makes his way through a hall with thick blue carpet, cream walls decorated with portraits of current and former members of the Board of Directors. The smell of the shampoo still lingers from the rug cleaning last evening. Payne heads down the corridor, passing several offices to reach his suite at the end. He opens the mahogany door and enters his domain, a sprawling room with wall-to-wall, vanilla-looking carpet, a secretary's desk in the center, chairs, and tables against the walls on which rest lamps. He proceeds to his office behind Ms. Eva Hamilton's desk, pulls out his keys from his coat pocket, rubs the gold metal plate on his door with the inscription, *Mr. Austin Payne, Chief Financial Officer*, with his elbow before turning the key in the lock. Once inside, he closes the door, moves to his desk and sets the satchel on the floor next to a dark suit case, removes his overcoat and hangs it on the hall tree in the corner, then eases into the leather chair, bending down to unzip the leather satchel and removing an important file for his eyes only. Next, he picks up a pen with his left hand, opens the folder, and ponders over the total dollar figures he had been working on last evening. His heart beats fast; blood is thundering throughout his body, and his ears are ringing. Money is his idol. He's making lots of it. "I'm becoming a rich man," he says in a whisper, glancing around the room like Scrooge, the cold-hearted miser who despises Christmas in Dickens' *A Christmas Carol. Have I become like him? Really?* He shakes off the thought. "Someday I'll leave this place," he tells himself. "Everyone goes to the Caymans, but not me; I'm too smart for that."

He returns to his calculations and forgets the time. The tick-tock, tick-tock, from the wall clock brings him out of his concentration. He glances up at it and realizes that he's been working for nearly two hours. It's ten-forty-five, and there's no movement in the outer office. He rises, moves around the desk and opens the door. He comes out of his office and looks around. The room is empty. *Where is Ms. Hamilton?* He frowns and returns to his desk, opens his personal directory next to the phone and calls her home. After four rings the answering machine picks up. Payne leaves a message in which he asks if she's okay, and for her to call him. He breaks the circuit and dials her cell phone number. It sends him to voicemail. "Ms. Hamilton. This is Mr. Payne. I'm checking to see if you're okay. I wasn't aware you'd be late this morning. Please call me." He sets the receiver in its base and looks at the wall. *This is not like her.* Minutes later, he jumps up, leaves his office and makes his way to the hallway. He sticks his head into the first office to his right. The ladies are close friends with Ms. Hamilton. Payne asks if they've seen her. They haven't. Did anyone know if she'd be coming in late this morning? She hadn't mentioned it to them. Mr. Payne is feeling isolated at the moment, which he doesn't like. He is a man with a code of behavior; always be prompt is his motto. He rushes back to his office, flops in one of the chairs facing his desk. Could she have gone shopping and forgotten the time? Certainly not; Ms. Hamilton is always very punctual. *Should I call her husband,* he thinks? *Don't want to worry him.* He gets up and goes round his desk, opens the directory again and looks up the number for Prestige Square Mall Security. The bank leases parking spots in the Mall area for their employees. The limited number of spaces around the bank is reserved for customers. He wonders if he's overreacting, but he's beginning to worry and his mind is beginning to play tricks on him. She could be dead on the side of the road. Ms. Hamilton has never been late, most mornings arriving before him. He makes the call and asks mall security to check Ms. Hamilton's parking spot number 1211 to see if her white Lexus is there. He gives security her license plate number.

Eva Hamilton has been with him for four years. She's thoughtful, competent and dedicated to her job. He doesn't really know her all that well, and less about her personal life, only that she's married to the only son of one of the richest banking families in Atlanta and that she's friends with most of the workers in this bank. While he has a good working relationship with her, he keeps up a professional persona as her boss. He has this other side that he hides from her, but suspects she might have caught him once or twice when he was out of character.

Payne resumes working his figures. The phone rings. The wall clock shows eleven-fifteen. It's mall security. He answers the phone and learns that Ms. Hamilton's Lexus is not in its spot. No car is in the space. Payne thinks it's time to call Eva's husband and looks in his registry a third time, this time for Dudley Hamilton's cell phone number. Ms. Hamilton gave Payne the number in case of an emergency. And Payne believes this is an emergency. He dials the number and waits. Dudley answers and it's obvious from the beginning that he doesn't want to be disturbed. "Who is this? I'm very busy. Can't this wait?"

4

"Sorry to bother you, Mr. Hamilton. This is Austin Payne at Citizens Bank. I'm your wife's boss."

"I know who you are. What do you want? I'm very busy."

Go to hell, asshole. Payne had never liked Dudley Hamilton since they met at one of the bank's Christmas parties. He's an arrogant imbecile and if it weren't for his family's money he'd be out on the streets.

"Again, I'm sorry, but I think this is important. Ms. Hamilton hasn't shown up for work. I called your home's landline and her cell and I couldn't reach her on either one. I wasn't aware that she wasn't coming to work this morning."

"She's out spending my money somewhere. No big deal. I wouldn't worry too much about it. She'll show up—"

"Wait just a minute," Payne interrupts. "This is not like her. She could be in trouble. She's always very prompt. I'm sure she wouldn't be shopping during working hours. Do you think I should notify the police if she doesn't show up after lunch?"

"You're overreacting, Payne. I'm in Athens, seventy miles away. When I left yesterday morning around five, she was fine. She may have decided to live it up while I'm away—"

He interrupts Dudley again. "Did you talk with her last night? She left here a little after five."

"No, and now I must go."

"But please listen. That makes it about eighteen hours since I saw her, and about thirty hours since you saw your wife last. Don't you think something should be done?"

Dudley Hamilton hangs up on Payne.

Living it up? You must be crazy as hell or you don't know your wife. Payne slams the receiver down and sighs. The husband would be the only one the cops would listen to, so Payne guesses he shouldn't report her missing to the police. He returns to his bank figures and loses track of time again. Payne is shaken out of his concentration when the phone rings close to the noon hour.

"This is Austin Payne."

"Mr. Payne? This is Josh Malone, mall security. I was making my rounds in the parking lot, and guess what? That white Lexus you called about earlier? Well, it's now in space 1211."

Payne jumps up. "Are you sure? Could it be someone else's?"

"No sir. It's got the license number you gave me. You'll want to come and look at this. Something's bad wrong."

Oh, my. "Please wait there. I'll be right over."

It takes Payne ten minutes to make his way to Eva Hamilton's parking space, pulling his egg-white Cadillac next to the Lexus and jumping out without closing the door. Josh Malone meets him by the trunk of the Lexus. They walk around the car and find no marks or dents in the body.

"Does it look like it's been cleaned to you?" Josh asks Mr. Payne.

"Sure does," Payne says.

5

"The doors are locked. But you need to look inside, sir," Josh says.

Payne cups his hands against the windows and peers in, then moves to the other side of the Lexus and does the same. He's startled at what he sees. On the front seat is ladies' underwear: panties, slip and bra, folded as if they had been washed and dried. On the driver's floor board is a pair of torn stockings. On the floor in the back are three brown paper bags filled with groceries.

"What do you make of it, sir?"

"I'm afraid to say."

"Do you think we should call 9-1-1?"

"You're security," Payne says, "and it's in your parking lot."

"Seeing that you're the lady's boss, I think you should call it in, sir."

Payne nods, reaches in his shirt pocket for his cell and dials 9-1-1.

"This is the 9-1-1 operator. What is your emergency?"

"This is Austin Payne, financial officer at Citizens Bank downtown. I'd like to report a missing person."

"Who's missing, sir?" the lady says.

"Ms. Eva Hamilton. She's one of our employees."

"Hamilton, you say?"

"Yes, of the Hamilton banking family."

"What makes you think she's missing?"

"She didn't come to work today. The security guard here at Prestige Square Mall where Citizens bank leases parking spaces for its employees is here with me. He located her car in its parking spot about thirty minutes ago. It hasn't been here all morning, but yet it turned up and Ms. Hamilton is nowhere to be found. Also, things in the car lead us to believe she might have been molested."

Payne describes to the operator what he saw in the car and gives her the address of the parking lot.

"Officers are on the way, sir. Please stay on the line."

Ten minutes later, two cruisers shoot into the parking lot with their light bars flashing, stopping behind Payne's Cadillac. Uniformed officers hop out. The taller one, closer to Payne, says "Are you Mr. Payne?"

"I am."

"Do you have the keys to the victim's car?"

"The victim's name is Ms. Eva Hamilton, and no, I don't have her keys. Why would I?"

The officer moves to Josh without answering. "You must be the one working security."

"I am."

"What's your name?"

"Josh Malone."

"You found the car?"

He nods. "And then I called Mr. Payne."

Both officers go to the Lexus and assess what's inside for several minutes, then confer with each other at the back of the car. The taller one comes over to

Payne. "There's definitely a possibility of foul play here. We'll have to call this one in. Detectives and forensics will take over. Just wait here." The shorter officer places rubber cone barricades at four corners of the vehicle and wraps yellow police tape around them, while the second officer returns to his cruiser and slides behind the wheel.

Josh turns to Payne. "How long do you think this'll take? I need to get back to work."

"Maybe you ought to call your supervisor."

"Sure. That's right. Thanks." He steps over to the side and makes the call. Seconds later he returns and says, "My boss wants to know if I will have to go to the police station to give a statement."

"I have no idea. You'll have to ask that big cop. They're sure taking their sweet time. They're pissed because they were called away from their favorite coffee shop."

Josh laughs. "That's a good one, sir." He heads over to the cruiser, and after a conversation with the officer, he pulls out his cell, then comes back to Payne. "The cop told me to sit tight and wait for the detectives. Maybe I should buy them some donuts." They laugh.

Twenty minutes later, an unmarked black Impala pulls in next to the uniforms' cruiser, and two men in suits step out. The driver's over six feet, wearing a tan suit, suede shoes, and has hair the color of walnuts with some gray on the sides, that hasn't been combed in some time. He doesn't look too happy (dour expression). The shorter guy is heavier, looks Hispanic, with a round face and pleasant smile and neatly trimmed hair the color of black shoe polish. He's wearing a gray suit. The detectives confer with the two uniforms before coming over to Payne and Malone.

The tall one introduces himself as detective Kramer and his partner, as detective Gomez. *These guys must buy their suits off the rack,* Payne thinks.

Kramer says, looking at the notebook he removes from his coat pocket, "You must be Josh Malone?"

Josh nods.

Kramer turns to Payne, looking at him with narrow eyes. "And you, sir, are Austin Payne from Citizens Bank, the one who called in the missing person." He's still looking at his notebook.

"I am Austin Payne."

"The missing person is Ms. Eva Hamilton, who works for you, is that correct?" Kramer says.

"That's right."

"How long has she been missing?" Gomez says.

"Close to eighteen hours, but take a look in her Lexus. Ms. Hamilton might have been molested."

Gomez nods. "The officers told us what's in the car. We'll have to wait for forensics. They're on the way."

Gomez turns to Payne. "Has Ms. Hamilton's husband been notified?"

"He has."

"Do you know where he can be reached?"

"He didn't say when he's coming back. He's at a bank in Athens, examining their books. I can give you his number."

Gomez frowns. "Why isn't the husband coming?" he says, "Isn't he concerned about his wife?"

Payne shrugs. "You'll have to ask him that. He doesn't seem too concerned to me."

"You'll have to come with us to the station; we'll need to take your statements."

"Me, too?" Josh asks.

"You, too," Kramer says.

At that moment, a black van with "Forensics, Atlanta PD" painted on the doors in white letters pulls in. A team of three—two men and one woman—hop out. They're dressed in white coveralls and caps. They stop to talk with the detectives before moving to the Lexus. They survey the ground around the vehicle. Minutes later, one man uses a tool to open the driver's side door. The second man dusts for prints outside and inside the car. The woman takes dozens of pictures and becomes interested in the inside. She places the clothing on the seat in evidence bags and removes the groceries on the back seat.

CHAPTER THREE

Lieutenant Noah McGraw leans back in his chair and releases a sigh of satisfaction. He has just successfully closed a case involving a guy who coldly and calculatedly murdered his wife and two children. The verdict was guilty. The judge socked it to the perp—three hundred years behind bars, no parole. This brings a smile across the cowboy detective's face as he reviews the disposition file. The chief had told him he did an exceptional job and McGraw had accepted the compliment with humility, brushing it aside, however, as more a snow job than the truth. But he did work very hard and once again had used the skills that made him one of the finest investigators in Atlanta, if not in the east. He shoots forward in his chair and closes the file on another evil perp when he hears the chief shout his name from across the squad room.

"McGraw?" Captain Norman Dipple, chief of detectives, calls out, walking into the squad room from his office. "McGraw?" he croaks a second time. Dipple, an ex-hockey player from Minnesota, could have played in the NFL, has come out of his office in shirt sleeves rolled up to his elbows, tie loosened enough to give relief to his bull-dog jowls, and heads straight to McGraw's desk with determination.

"Got one for yuh, cowboy," he says, throwing a folder on McGraw's desk. "You'll like this one. Right down your alley. Eva Hamilton, a cute number, has come up missing—only been married six weeks. Get out there, McGraw, you got the lead."

"Will do Capt."

"Another thing, the commish has gotten in on this one. Be extra careful how you handle the Hamiltons. They're big in this town."

Right down your alley? What does that mean? McGraw thinks. He never liked women beaten, molested or dead, or anybody else, as far as that goes. He's been the victims' avenging angel ever since he entered law enforcement. His mission had always been their advocate, and he never saw his job as just skill or craft.

9

He knows the chief really meant that McGraw loves the tough cases.

In the Sixth Precinct, the detectives work in an open area called the squad room or the bullpen. It is covered with bright ceiling lights that make it easy to see everyone—sitting, coming, or going. Desks are lined in rows separated with a center aisle, and have computers, printers, and a few have papers stacked on them a mile high. Drapes conceal what goes on inside the Capt.'s office, positioned across the room between two interview rooms along one wall, with a holding cell in the corner of the room.

The smell of hazelnut coffee brewing on a stand between the detectives' desks fills the room, and McGraw sidesteps detectives Kramer and Gomez to pour himself a cup, taking a drink before heading back to his seat. He opens the file labeled "Eva Bingham Hamilton" and finds the Officer Incident Report with summary notes from detectives Kramer and Gomez, newspaper clippings, pictures of Ms. Hamilton and another of her vehicle. She's married to Dudley Hamilton, the son of Atlanta's most famous banking family. He takes another drink of his coffee and stares at the innocence in the face of this beautiful woman with a natural, girl-next-door look. Her sunny eyes and movie-star smile remind him of the early Hollywood superstar from the Golden Age, Deanna Durbin. He scans the clippings and the detectives' report. Minutes later, he goes to the crime board in the corner, attaches the paper clippings and writes a few notes below them with a black marker. He places Eva's picture in the middle and writes her name below and *The Vanishing Bride* above. McGraw touches her photo, his fingers sliding over her smile. The innocence in her face grips him. Persons go missing for a couple of reasons: To escape the troubles in their lives or because they don't want to be found. Most others come up missing against their will and turn into homicides. His mission is to find Ms. Hamilton before the vanishing bride turns into a homicide.

Sergeant Holly Roark jars him out of his reverie. "Morning, McGraw," she shouts as she stops at her desk facing his and drops a heavy purse into one of the drawers. She is dressed in a two-piece blue suit and white blouse that accents her gleaming brunette hair combed to the right side and hanging down next to her face.

"Can I ask you something?" McGraw says.

She frowns as she approaches him. "What?"

"Hope you don't mind—just a simple question. Why do you always wear your hair pushed to one side, behind your right ear and down your right side?"

"I don't know; a habit, I guess."

He goes to her and says, "May I?"

"I don't know. What's up with you?"

He pulls her hair behind her, separates it and brushes it over her ears. "Now that's much better. Your brown eyes really stand out now."

"You think so?" She seems dazed. She goes to her desk, pulls a mirror from her purse and gazes at her new look. "I... I guess I like it." She pauses while looking in the mirror. "Yeah, I like it. Thanks."

"You're welcome."

"Whatcha got on the board?" she asks.

"A socialite came up missing Thursday night around eight."

"Lemme see," the sergeant says as she rounds McGraw's desk. Her thigh brushes against his white felt Stetson with its brim curled up on the sides, knocking it to the floor. "Oh my," she says, hands fly up against her chest in mock surprise. "I've committed a cardinal sin."

He stoops to retrieve it, turns the crown over, brushes the rim with his forearm and sets the hat on the other side of the desk, away from the aisle.

"Don't worry. I'm not going to damage your precious crown," she says, and laughs. She looks over at Kramer and Gomez, who are smiling but trying not to let on that they're interested in what has just happened. At the board, Roark takes her time reading the clippings and the notes. She says, "Eva Hamilton sure is pretty." Two breaths later, she says, "There's nothing here on the husband, Dudley Hamilton."

McGraw shouts across the room. "Kramer, Gomez. Get over here."

"Yeah, lieutenant," Kramer says with Gomez in tow. They crowd in behind him.

"I've read the OIR and your reports on what I am calling "The Vanishing Bride" case involving Ms. Eva Hamilton. There's not much on the husband."

"Know very little about him, lieutenant," Kramer says. "He was seventy miles away in Athens at the time examining bank books, and has a solid alibi."

"Mr. Hamilton doesn't seem too concerned about his wife's absence, either," Gomez says. "He's not home yet."

"What does he mean, 'absence'?" Roark asks, frowning. "Abduction is more like it. This note here from you guys," she says, pointing to the board, "indicates her boss Austin Payne reported her missing, not absent."

Gomez shrugs. "Her husband said she was just absent—"

"Whatever," McGraw interrupted. "The husband should tell us plenty about their relationship when he gets back." He grabs his Stetson and turns to Kramer. "You and Gomez, run him and find out all you can—where he goes, where he eats, when he sleeps and if he has another woman in his life." He turns to his partner. "Roark, let's hit it."

"Where to?" she says.

"The Hamiltons."

They head toward the exit. "Since the husband hasn't returned, we'll start with his parents."

The Capt. is standing outside his office talking with some handsome guy, well over six feet with dark hair, eyes visible through police sun shades that aren't completely darkened, white shirt collar open and strands of hair down on his forehead. His dark eyes blend in with his dark suit. *That smile seems more of a smirk of arrogance*, McGraw thinks.

"Who's the hunk?" Roark asks as they move closer. "He's some looker."

"I know you don't mean Dipple."

She laughs. "You're right. I don't mean the Capt."

11

"If you must know, he's Dipple's financial advisor, helping him with his investments and retirement plans. The boss thinks I should talk to him, but I'm not ready for that."

"It's never too early to plan for your financial freedom, McGraw. Maybe I'll talk to him," she says.

"I suspected you'd say that."

She scowls at him. "Whadda you mean?"

He shrugs. "It wouldn't be because he's good-looking, would it?"

"I may need some help with my investments," she says.

McGraw feels himself nodding and says, "I thought so."

Captain Dipple waves for the detectives to come over to them. "Like for you to meet a friend of mine, Max Kingston, my financial advisor."

Max removes his sun shades and shakes their hands, but he holds on to Roark's a little longer than he does McGraw's. Max's good looks seem to have her spellbound. When he releases her hand, he gives both detectives his card and invites them to call him at any time to discuss investments and their future retirement.

Turning to McGraw, Max says, "I understand they call you the Marlboro Man."

McGraw doesn't respond.

"Some do," Roark says, "but McGraw doesn't encourage it."

Kingston nods. "I understand, but I remember that guy on a horse in those billboard signs, and Detective McGraw, you sure look like him."

"I'll take that as a compliment, Mr. Kingston," McGraw says, adjusting his hat.

"Please do. And call me Max. Also, as a reminder, it's never too early to plan your future, detectives. Don't want to take a risk of not having enough when you retire," he says, keeping eyes fixed on Roark.

"Max's good and has really helped me a lot," Capt. says. "You might take him up on his offer."

Hmm, McGraw thinks. *So now you're big buddies with him?*

"Maybe later, Capt.," McGraw says, hurrying to the exit. He turns to Roark. "Macho man really got to you, didn't he?"

"Oh, I don't know. One thing for sure, though, I don't need a chaperone. I'm forty, daddy."

He nods, smiling.

They step outside and head to the unmarked Impala cruiser.

"Hey, I see you finally brought your Dad's bike to the station," she says, pointing at the blue motorcycle.

"It's a Harley, not a bike."

"Well, pardon me. Anyway, it's really pretty."

"It's my pride and joy."

"I thought cowboys rode horses," she says.

"I do that too; got two of 'em."

"Once a cowboy, always a cowboy, huh?" she says. "Guess you can't take

12

it out of you, as the saying goes."

McGraw tips his hat, opens the door of the cruiser and slides in behind the wheel and gazes at her. "Never," he says.

———— ◆ ————

The home of Douglas and Sophia Hamilton is a two-story white mansion with lots of windows and columns reminiscent of an antebellum home. Manicured hedges appear to stand at attention on both sides of the road leading up the driveway. The landscaping is picture perfect and inviting, so much so that one feels like rolling in the grass, or reading a book under the huge trees. McGraw rounds the drive and stops at the entrance.

"The rich have it all, don't they?" Holly Roark says before she climbs out on the passenger side.

"You think so? To me, folks with a passion for things (he emphasizes *things*) exhibit a symptom of longing for something more to fill the emptiness in their lives." He steps out.

Roark turns to him with a smile. "My, aren't you the cowboy philosopher. Oh, forgive me. I nearly forgot, the Harvard graduate," she says.

He overlooked the remark. "Okay. Here's one for you. When we come out, I want you to tell me what's missing in the lives of these Hamiltons." He pulls on the big golden knob in the center of the door.

A tall man in his early fifties with gray hair, thin, neat and straight as the front hedges, and wearing tails and white gloves, appears in the doorway. His brow rises when he faces McGraw.

"Atlanta PD, homicide detectives," McGraw says, holding up his ID. "We are here to see the Hamiltons."

He stares at McGraw again for a few seconds before saying, "They're expecting you. Please step in."

They follow him into the foyer, where he takes McGraw's Stetson, then leads them into a sitting room with oriental rugs and high-quality leather sofas and chairs. *The place is palatial,* McGraw thinks. *Is that cigar odor irritating his nostrils?*

Holly turns to her partner and says in a whisper, "The butler can't take his eyes off you, McGraw."

McGraw glances at the man. *He must not have seen a cowboy in person.*

"Please make yourself comfortable. May I bring you something, sergeant?"

"Nothing, thank you," she says.

"And you, cowboy?" That seemed to slip out.

"Dry soda, my good man," says McGraw.

"Very well, sir. On the rocks or neat?"

"Neat, my good man."

He bows. "Thank you, sir."

McGraw bows. "And you, sir."

The butler leaves.

13

"What the hell was that all about?" Roark says.

"Just wanted to let him know we cowboys can play his game, too."

"I thought I was back in grammar school."

Surprisingly, there were no Monets or Picassos on the walls in the room, just large paintings of hunters wearing black tails and red pants, on horses, with dogs leading the way. McGraw is drawn to them.

"Those pictures are right down your alley, aren't they?" she says, with glee in her voice.

"Make fun, city girl."

"Never saw a home like this outside of the movies," Roark says. "Guess I've hung out with the wrong crowd."

"Rich folks," he says with contempt in his voice.

No sooner have those words left his mouth then a couple in their sixties enters, dressed in their Sunday best. Neither one was smiling. Mrs. Hamilton looking like she just came from her hair stylist and her husband in an expensive tailor-made gray suit. Both Hamiltons are pudgy. McGraw thinks the wife looks like a dressed-up Marjorie Maine from the movies in the 50s, and the husband resembles the detective Hercule Poirot out of Agatha Christie's mystery movies, except he lacks the mustache and is a little taller.

The detectives rise. "I am Lieutenant McGraw and this is my partner Sergeant Roark." Both have their IDs out.

Mrs. Hamilton waves a hand, apparently trusting who they say they are. She studies McGraw for a few seconds before saying, "I am Sophia Hamilton and this is my husband, Douglas Hamilton, President of First Colonial Bank and its ten branches."

You had to get 'em all in, didn't you? McGraw thinks.

The butler enters and serves McGraw his soda with a napkin, all the while smiling. Mrs. Hamilton frowns. "Reginald, is there something wrong?"

"No ma'am," he says, all the while staring at the lieutenant.

McGraw reaches for the glass and napkin, and says, "Thank you."

The butler smiles, bows slightly, and takes his leave.

McGraw starts off by saying, "We're sorry to intrude, but as you know we're here to investigate the disappearance of your daughter-in-law, Eva Hamilton."

Mrs. Hamilton studies McGraw's seven-hundred dollar Lucchese boots with exotic square toes and frowns. The couple sits and the detectives are told to do the same.

"How did you learn of her disappearance?" Roark asks.

McGraw drinks half his soda and sets it on the napkin on the table next to his chair.

"Eva's boss, Austin Payne, from Citizens Bank, called us yesterday in the late afternoon," Sophia says. "Dudley, that's our son, Eva's husband, was in Athens. It's seventy miles away, you know."

We know how far Athens is, McGraw thinks.

"He goes out of town sometimes," Douglas says. "He's a part-time bank examiner, but mostly manages one of our branches. He called and should be

14

back today sometime."

"Yes, we know. We're awaiting his return."

"Do you know of anyone who would want to harm Eva?" Roark asks, retrieving a notebook and pen from her jacket pocket.

Mr. Hamilton shakes his head and his wife says she has no earthly idea.

"Have you received any notes or calls from anyone?" McGraw asks.

"You mean a ransom note or call?" Mr. Hamilton says.

McGraw nods.

"No we haven't," he says.

"Do Eva and Dudley have a good marriage?" McGraw asks.

"Oh, our son gave her everything. She didn't want for a thing."

"'Gave'?" McGraw says. "So you believe she's dead?"

"Oh my, no. Did I say gave? I meant gives."

He directs his next question to the husband. "Does your son have a temper, sir?"

"You're not suggesting...." His face becomes drawn. "Dudley would never harm Eva."

"Sorry. We have to ask."

"We'll need the names of Dudley's and Eva's friends?" Roark says.

"You'll have to get them from Dudley," Sophia says. "We know very little about their friends."

McGraw has been concentrating on Sophia's eyes. *The windows to the soul, they say. She's a tough bird,* he thinks.

"The kids have only been married six weeks," Mr. Hamilton says, his head tilted down toward the floor like he's about to cry, but Sophia shows no emotion.

"You didn't approve of the marriage, did you, Mrs. Hamilton?" McGraw says, turns to her husband. "But you did, Mr. Hamilton."

Roark shoots a furtive glance at McGraw.

A hand flips to Sophia's chest. "My word, lieutenant why would you say such a thing?"

Douglas' eyes are now a little glassy, but no tears.

"Because it's true," McGraw says. "Eva Bingham is a country girl from a small town in Oklahoma. I take it that that doesn't set well with you," he says.

"Detective, I find this line of questioning disrespectful and insulting. I may have to speak with your supervisor."

"That would be Captain Dipple, ma'am," he says.

She scowls at her husband. "Douglas, say something."

He grunts and says, "But dear, the detective is right. You never approved of Eva."

She swells like a bull-frog and says, "Well!" Fury fills her face. Her husband has said the wrong thing and may wish for the moment he could slide under his chair. Her eyes say she will deal with him later.

"What about Dudley's former girlfriends?" McGraw asks. "Was he involved with anyone before he married Eva?"

15

The Hamiltons look at each other, then the husband says, "Involved?" He pauses. "Our Dudley never went with anyone except on an occasional date. He went the longest with Eva."

Naw, because he's a snob like his parents, McGraw thinks.

"Does Dudley get along well with his employees?" Roark asks.

"He does," Mr. Hamilton says in a blunt manner.

"So, you know of no one who could have a vendetta against Dudley and would take it out on Ms. Hamilton?" McGraw asks.

Sophia looks as if she's about to faint.

"No, no, detectives," she says, "No one."

McGraw reaches for his drink, finishes it and stands. He pulls from his pocket a card and hands it to Mr. Hamilton and asks that he call him if either of them thinks of anything that might help.

The butler is standing in the threshold. "Reginald will show you out," Mrs. Hamilton says.

Before reaching the door, McGraw stops and turns back. "By the way, Mrs. Hamilton, why is it that Eva works for another bank and not in one of your branches, since you have so many?"

"Eva wouldn't have it any other way, detective," she says, without looking his way.

Her discontent with his line of interrogation is obvious in her tone and pouting. McGraw can expect to hear about this.

They follow Reginald to the front door. He hands McGraw his felt hat and bows.

McGraw reaches for it and returns the gesture.

"Nice hat, sir."

"You can't have it," he says, adjusting it on his head.

"I know, sir." They smile.

Outside McGraw and Roark amble to the cruiser.

"Well?" McGraw says.

"Well, what?"

"What's missing in their lives?" he says.

"What's missing in the lives of the Hamiltons?"

She pauses for a moment, looking directly at him. "I'd say it is love."

He nods. "You got it."

She shudders. "They're cold." Before she can elaborate her cell chirps, and she reaches for it on the side of her purse. "Detective Roark," she says. Her brow comes together. "How'd you get this number?"

McGraw opens the driver's side door of the Impala and waits for her to finish.

"I'll have to think about it," she says. "I'll get back with you." She closes her cell, climbs in and slams the door.

McGraw slides in. "Well?"

"You won't believe this," she says.

"You know how I feel about playing games."

16

"That was Max Kingston."

"The Capt.'s friend?"

"Yeah, he wants to take me to dinner tonight."

"He didn't waste any time."

"Hey, I'm flattered. But I don't like anyone giving out my cell number."

"I don't trust Pretty Boy," he says. "He's too much like Sylvester Stallone in those Rocky movies."

"I'll have my Glock with me."

"You better."

"Can I ask you a question, McGraw?" Roark says.

"Yes."

"You have this thing about matching people with movie stars. Why do you do that?"

He smiles. "It's a hobby of mine and it helps me to remember their faces."

"Do you have an actor icon picked out for me?" she says.

He hesitates. "Not for you to know."

"Why? Is she ugly?"

"No, far from it."

"Aw come on then, let's have it." She hits him on the shoulder. "I need to know."

"Sandra Bullock."

"Wow! You really mean that?"

"I never say anything I don't mean."

"Do you know who you remind me of?" she says.

"The Marlboro Man, I know."

"Well—not exactly. I saw him in old movies, but never saw those billboards Max mentioned. You and the Marlboro guy are clones of George Strait."

"Really? I am a big fan of his."

McGraw looks at his watch. "We have thirty minutes. Austin Payne and the girls at the bank have agreed to meet with us. The bank is open until one, this being Saturday."

CHAPTER FOUR

Citizens Bank is on the corner of Chelsea and Main, two blocks west of Prestige Square mall, downtown. Next door is Manhattan's, an expensive men's clothing shop. McGraw pulls the unmarked squad into the only empty space in front, next to a white Cadillac. The sun is bright and the wind is calm this late October day.

Inside, heads turn as the well-dressed customers gawk at McGraw— dressed in blue jeans; a jacket to match, starched white shirt, string tie, fancy boots and a white Stetson, which aren't common in this highfalutin part of Atlanta. A sexy looking brunette in her late twenties, slim, with shoulder-length hair and in high heels, could be thinking McGraw's a country-western singer. She is pointing at him as she tugs on another female's coat. They snap pictures of McGraw with their cell phones.

"Keep your eyes straight ahead, McGraw," Roark says as they walk into the lobby.

A man in his mid-fifties, round face, thin brown hair, gray on the sides, close to six feet and medium built, around 190 pounds, dressed in a suit that's definitely not off the racks, greets them. His face is filled with lots of lines; could be a sign of a worrier, or someone with something to hide. The guy's holding something in his hand.

"Lieutenant McGraw?" the man says. "I'm Austin Payne, Chief Financial Officer. We talked on the phone." McGraw nods and they shake hands. "This is my partner, Sergeant Roark."

Payne nods. This way, please," he says, as they move down a hall on the left. "I've gathered everyone who is a close acquaintance of Ms. Hamilton into our conference room."

Before entering, Austin hands McGraw a couple of sheets of paper. "As you requested, I've prepared a list of names, addresses and phone numbers of those in the room, and any phone calls Eva Hamilton received or made at the bank for the last two months."

Payne leads the way into the room. The same wide-eyed expressions that greeted McGraw in the bank lobby are seen on the faces of the three women seated around the long table. He and Roark move to the front. The women, wearing name tags, are fixed on McGraw. Austin introduces the two detectives.

McGraw asks Payne to begin by recounting the day Eva Hamilton didn't show up for work. He nods and begins reviewing the events that took place thirty hours ago: Eva didn't report to work at nine as she always had. This was unusual for her. She was never late. He called her home and her cell, but couldn't reach her. He left messages. Around eleven, he called her husband, Dudley, a bank examiner, who was working seventy miles away in Athens. After that, Payne called Prestige Square Mall Security to check Eva's parking spot. Citizens Bank leases parking spaces for its employees in an area in the posh mall, since parking around the bank is for customers only. Security reported that her white Lexus wasn't in its spot earlier, but then called back close to noon to report that it was there. That's when he left his office and met the security guard. When he pulled in a space next to it, he got out and looked inside. There were women's underclothes folded neatly on the passenger seat and three bags of groceries still in the back. He called the police.

"Did you try to open the car door?" Roark asks.

"No, I was afraid I'd be tampering with evidence."

"Good," she says. "Watching those police programs on TV helps, doesn't it?"

He nods, smiling. "Sure does."

"So what happened next?" McGraw asks.

"The police came first and then the forensic people, who shot dozens of pictures. Finally two detectives showed up and took my statement."

McGraw looks at Holly. "Gomez and Kramer," he says.

"I remember, yes, that was their names."

McGraw asks if anyone in the room was the last person to be with Eva Hamilton. They shake their heads and look at each other before Laura Cook speaks up.

"Not us, detective. But we know who was."

"Who would that be, Ms. Cook?" McGraw says, eyeing her name tag.

Her smile is extra friendly. "A friend of ours, Claire Dunbar, had dinner with Eva the night she disappeared. We all used to be roomies. Claire owns a home- decorating shop in Prestige Square."

Holly asks, "What restaurant?" She pulls out a small notebook from her pocket and makes a couple of entries.

Laura Cook continues. "They had dinner at Louie's in the mall, did some grocery shopping after, and Claire said Eva left the parking lot around eight."

The presence of Austin in the room seems to make the ladies uncomfortable, and they avoid eye contact with him.

Need to have them come to the station, McGraw thinks.

"What can you tell us about Dudley Hamilton?" Roark says.

The second woman Tammy Ingram speaks: "I never liked him." She eyes the other girls. "I believe I can speak for all of us. We thought he was distant, cold, and snobbish. He didn't treat Eva..." She doesn't finish.

"What were you going to say?" McGraw says.

Karen Harvey, the third woman, speaks in her place. "We feel he was rude to her, talked down to her, and very controlling. But Eva seemed okay with it and never complained, she is too—"

"Eva is a sweet girl," Laura Cook interrupts, "and can be a little naive at times, but is thoughtful and kind. She has made application to volunteer at Children's Hospital. She loves children."

Tammy Ingram reaches into her purse for a tissue and wipes her eyes.

"Do you know of anyone that would want to harm Eva Hamilton?" McGraw says.

Again, the ladies glance at Austin and then at each other. They shake their heads.

What is it about Austin that they fear? McGraw thinks.

"Is there anything else?" McGraw asks.

Laura raises her hand. "We didn't mention the telephone calls and the flowers."

Frowns appear on the detectives' faces. "What about them, Ms. Cook?" McGraw asks.

"Twice Eva received a dozen roses and each time someone called her right after."

"When was this?" Roark asks.

"A week before she disappeared," Tammy says.

"Anyone know who sent them?" Roark asks. "Could it have been her husband?"

Tammy shakes her head. "Someone just wrote, 'secret admirer' on the card."

"What about the telephone calls?" McGraw asks. "Did anyone hear what Ms. Hamilton said?"

"I heard one of the conversations," Karen Harvey says. "Eva's exact words were: 'I can't come over there anymore, I'm married now. But you can come to our place.'"

McGraw glances at Roark, who is staring at the girls. "Do you think it's someone she dated before Mr. Hamilton came into her life?" he says.

"At the time, we racked our brains to remember if she ever talked about any guys, but couldn't come up with anyone." She sighs. "We don't have any idea who he is. She never brought anyone to the apartment except Dudley."

"I see," McGraw says. He scans the room. "Anyone have anything else to add?"

They shake their heads.

"Well, we thank you all. You've been a big help."

Roark adds her thanks.

Outside the conference room, they followed Payne to Eva's desk in the Chief Financial Officer's suite. "I'll be in my office if you need me, detectives," he says.

They nod. McGraw mentions to Roark that Laura Cook wanted to say more, but apparently not in front of Payne.

Roark frowns. "I got that, too."

"It was her eyes that signaled to me," he says. "She knows a lot more. We need to get them to the station, away from him."

"Who does Payne remind you of?"

"I'd say he reminds me of Peter Lorre in the Maltese Falcon, except Payne is much taller."

"You scare me, McGraw. I was thinking the same thing."

He glances over the top of Eva's desk while Roark sits in the cushioned chair and begins opening and looking through the drawers.

"Nothing here," she says. "They've been cleaned out."

"You can bet Payne's taken anything important. Bag those pencils and pens," McGraw says. "Maybe Ms. Hamilton chewed on them."

Back at the cruiser, McGraw tells Roark to drive.

"Where to?" she says.

"Prestige Mall's security office, to review those tapes the day Eva left the mall and when her Lexus was returned."

A bulky, partially bald man in his forties is standing behind the counter in the security office. He smiles. A younger man, in his thirties, is sitting at a desk against the wall working a computer.

McGraw holds up his ID for the man to see. "I'm Lieutenant McGraw, Atlanta PD, homicide. This is my partner Sergeant Roark. We'd like to look at your security tapes for Thursday the 20th and for yesterday the 21st."

"Name's Will James, I'm in charge of security for the Mall. Is this about the lady that went missing night before last?"

"Yes," Roark says. "And her car was returned yesterday around noon. We need to see both tapes."

The young man at the computer jumps up. "I was with Mr. Payne from the bank yesterday when the police asked us all those questions. My name is Josh Malone."

Mr. James goes to a metal double-door floor cabinet, opens it and scans stacks of tapes.

McGraw turns to Malone. "I remember your name from the police report. Glad you're working today; we want to ask you a few questions."

"Anything I can do to help," he says.

"What was Mr. Payne's demeanor that day?"

Malone frowns.

"I mean, how did he act? Was he shaken or calm?"

Malone's brows come together as if he is concentrating on something. "He was very concerned about the lady."

"Did he say anything about her husband, or where he was?" Roark asks.

He shakes his head. "Naw, he didn't say much about him." Malone pauses. "He really got his shorts in a bind, though, when the cops asked him for the keys to the lady's car. I thought it was strange for the cops to ask that. Mr. Payne wouldn't have her keys unless he's the one that drove the car back."

21

Smart guy, McGraw thinks. "That's right," he says.

Mr. James turned from the cabinet. "I have both tapes," he says, holding them above his head. "You can sit over there at the computer desk and watch them. I'll join you; I haven't seen them, either."

Malone pulls up several chairs, and McGraw and Roark sit on either side of Mr. James, who inserts the first tape and it rolls. Malone stands behind his boss.

"Will this show the entrance closest to Ms. Hamilton's parking space?" McGraw says.

Mr. James nods. "Our system scans the entire lot."

The time on the tape begins ticking off, six-thirty, seven, and seven-thirty.

"Slow it down," McGraw says. "There," he says pointing, "that looks—"

Roark interrupts. "Stop it there. It's eight and that's her Lexus leaving. So the time reported is correct."

The Mall lights emit enough illumination in all directions to give a clear sighting of the parking lot.

"Back it up slowly, let's see if she's being followed," McGraw says.

"No one that we can see," Roark says.

"Let's look at the second tape," McGraw says, turning to Mr. James.

He shoves in the second tape.

The time line begins. The numbers, eleven, eleven-thirty, and twelve appear in the top right corner of the screen. Cars are streaming in and out of the mall.

"That's it," Malone says, pointing at the screen. "It's her Lexus pulling into the spot where we found it."

A young man steps out of the Lexus and locks the door. "He's looking around," Roark says.

"Stop it there," McGraw says, "where the guy is looking up."

"I know him," Malone says. "He's a valet driver for Armen's Steakhouse. It's just a few doors down from here. They have the best steaks in Atlanta."

"What's his name?" Roark asks.

Malone shakes his head. "Don't know, but I've seen him around here many times."

"Does he only work evenings?" McGraw says.

"Evenings and weekends," Malone says.

They rise. "We'll need these tapes for evidence," McGraw says to James. "Do you mind signing for them, detective?"

"Not at all," McGraw says.

James slips the cassettes into a manila envelope and McGraw signs the form.

"We'd like Mr. Malone to go with us to Armen's."

James looks at Malone and nods, his signal for giving him permission to go. Outside, they walk past several store fronts down to the red awning that extends over the sidewalk from Armen's to the curb. There's no one at the valet stand this afternoon.

"Looks like the place is closed," McGraw says. He tries the door. Locked. He cups his hands against the glass and looks in. "Someone's behind the bar," he says pulling out a ball point pen from his pocket. He taps on the door.

A guy comes from behind the bar and opens the door. McGraw introduces everyone. "Are you the manager?" McGraw says.

"I'm the owner. Harry Birch."

"We'd like to talk with one of your valet drivers," McGraw says.

"Is he in some sort of trouble?" Birch says.

Roark shakes her head. "Just want to talk to him, but we don't know his name. Malone here can describe him."

When Malone finishes describing the valet, Birch says, "That's Eaton Banks. He's supposed to be on duty this evening, but called in sick."

"Do you have an address for him?" Roark says.

"Sure, step in," he says, heading to the bar. He reaches under it for a ledger and opens it, then writes on a piece of paper. "Here's Eaton's address and phone number. He's one of our best. Hope he hasn't gotten himself into anything."

"We just need some information that we believe he can help us with," McGraw says.

"Has it anything to do with the lady that disappeared the other night?"

"Why do you ask?" McGraw says.

"Well, ever since that night, that's all Eaton's talked about."

"It sounds like he might be able to help us," Roark says, as she and McGraw head to the door. They step outside and McGraw reaches for his cell phone and calls the station and asks Kramer and Gomez to pick up Eaton Banks after giving the info on Banks. He pockets the phone and they head for the cruiser.

———— • ————

Back at the station, Kramer and Gomez are waiting.

"Got Eaton Banks the valet driver in one," Gomez says as McGraw and Roark come into the pit.

"He give you any problem?" McGraw says.

Kramer shakes his head. "He's scared to death, but came without a hitch."

McGraw watches Banks on the monitor for a few minutes; he's sitting next to the wall with his hands between his legs, rubbing the palms together, looking at the floor and rocking himself back and forth.

McGraw picks up a legal pad from his desk and turns to Roark, "Sergeant, let's go in." Kramer and Gomez gaze at the monitor.

Eaton Banks sits up straight in his chair when McGraw and Roark enter. They pull two chairs to the table across from him and sit. McGraw is closer to him. "I am Lieutenant McGraw, this is Sergeant Roark." Banks now is looking at the floor again.

"Would you like something to drink?" Roark says.

"No, ma'am." He sits up straight and stares at her. "Am I in trouble?"

"That depends," she says. "Before we get started, we want you to know

23

this conversation is being recorded."

"O-k-a-y," he says with suspicion in his eyes, as if he doesn't trust them.

"Do you know why you were brought in?" McGraw says.

"The cops said I had to come with them to headquarters for questioning, but didn't say why. I guess it's about that lady's Lexus."

"That's right," McGraw says. "Are you a valet driver at Armen's Steakhouse in Prestige Square Mall?"

"Yes, sir."

"You were identified from the mall security video tapes, pulling Mrs. Hamilton's Lexus into its parking spot on Friday, October twenty-first close to the noon hour. Then you got out, locked the car and left, wearing gloves and carrying a paper sack. Is that accurate?"

"Yes, sir."

"We need for you to tell us, from the beginning, how you got involved in this thing," McGraw says. "Remember your statements are being recorded."

Banks twists his hands. "I'll do my best, sir." He pauses for a moment. "Someone left a note Wednesday night—"

"That was two days before you brought the Lexus back, correct?" McGraw says, interrupting, "Just for the record."

"That's right."

"Go on."

"Like I said, someone left a note at the station with my name on it."

"So he must know you?"

He shrugs. "I guess you could say that. Maybe he saw my name tag when he came to the restaurant and I parked his car."

"What was in the note?" Roark asked.

"It had a number to call if I wanted to earn a hundred bucks. So I called it and this very nice guy answered. He said his wife was out of town and he was using her car and needed someone to drop it off at her parking spot in the mall by noon on Friday because he was flying out on Wednesday morning of that week for a business trip."

"Where was the car?" Roark asks.

"He left it at the airport when he took his flight."

"If she was flying in, why didn't she know her car was there?" Roark asks.

Banks shakes his head. "The man said his wife's sister was meeting her and bringing her back to town and dropping her off at the mall by one in the afternoon."

"Go on," McGraw says. "So you believed the guy?"

He shrugs again. "Yeah, why not? Anyway, do you know how many cars I have to park to make a hundred bucks in tips?"

"What were your instructions?" Roark says.

"He didn't give me any on the phone. He told me he'd be in touch and hung up. The next afternoon when I got to work, my boss told me someone left a package on the stand with my name on it."

"That was Thursday afternoon?" McGraw asks.

"Yes."

"Did your boss see the person?"

"No. He was away parking a car and when he got back to the stand it was there on top."

"What was inside?" Roark says.

"Two envelopes; the smaller one had a one hundred-dollar bill in it with directions to the car at the airport, and the second one was a little thicker 'cause it was padded. It was addressed to Mr. Dudley Hamilton."

"You put the car keys in and mailed them to Mr. Hamilton, correct?" McGraw says.

He frowns. "Yes, sir."

"So you didn't talk to the man again?"

"There was one more call. To this day, I don't know how he got my number. He told me he'd leave some money on the front seat for me to have the car washed and cleaned spotless and there would be a package there, too, with instructions. Before I could say anything, he hung up."

"In the video, you were wearing gloves. Why?"

"That was another thing. The guy told me his wife was pretty particular and didn't like finger marks from oily skin all over the car. I guess that's why he had me get it washed and cleaned." Eaton shook his head. "She must really be a neat freak."

"What about the undergarments you placed in the car?"

"He told me he wanted to play a little joke on his wife. He asked me to place the underclothes on the seat." He shrugs. "Guess they got some sex thing going." He sighs. "I don't know, detectives. I just did what he told me. All I could think about was the hundred dollars I had in my pocket."

"Do you still have it?" McGraw says.

Banks frowns. "Lord, no. I had bills to pay."

"That's unfortunate," Roark says. "There could have been prints on it."

"Didn't you think it unusual that there were three bags of groceries in the back?" McGraw says.

"No sir. I thought he bought them for her because he said they were out of food in the house. I thought that was kinda nice of him."

"What time did you pick up the car?" Roark says.

"I had a friend take me there around ten. I wanted enough time to get it cleaned and washed before I drove it to the mall."

McGraw rises. "Sit tight." He and Roark go to the pit and meet up with Kramer and Gomez. "What do you think?" McGraw asks.

"The kid is telling the truth," Kramer says.

"Yeah, boss," Gomez says.

"I'm a little surprised he wasn't more curious," Roark says.

"The kid just wasn't thinking straight," Kramer says. "As he said, he only thought about the C-note."

"What about the keys going to Dudley Hamilton?" McGraw says.

"To throw us off," Roark says.

McGraw nods. "You can bet on it. While Dudley's not the brightest star in the constellation, he certainly wouldn't incriminate himself, mailing the keys back to himself, would he?" McGraw says.

"We've got a perp that's pretty smart," Roark says.

McGraw turns to Roark. "Did you check the VP at BancFirst in Athens and those names Dudley put on the list he gave you?" McGraw asks.

"I did, and they verified everything Dudley told us," she says.

To Kramer and Gomez, he says, "Dudley must have a friend or two, or a couple of acquaintances. See what you can find out."

"Are you thinking someone he knows wants to implicate him in his wife's disappearance?" Kramer says.

"Either that or someone Ms. Hamilton knows."

Gomez rubs his chin. "Boss, maybe Hamilton did it and wants to throw us off?"

McGraw shakes his head. "Good thinking, but I don't believe he's our guy."

CHAPTER FIVE

That evening, Noah McGraw leaves the station riding his dad's Harley, arriving at the Circle M before sunset and pulling into the crushed-rocked driveway, then heads into the garage and parks it. His sky-blue RAM 3500 pickup isn't here because his mother, Anna Marie, has taken it to the bingo parlor. McGraw removes his helmet and reaches for his hat on the back, walks up the flagstones to the two-story white frame antebellum that sits back close to two-hundred feet from the road. Two German shepherds, Prince and Tucker, know he's coming and bark up a storm as they meet him at the door, jumping up on McGraw with their tails wagging. "I know what you guys want," he says, rubbing their backs. He moves into the kitchen, reaches in the cabinet for a box of treats and slips them one. The red light on the coffee pot is on, and the odor of sautéed veggies mixed with salmon left on the stove for him wafts to his nose. This is the handiwork of his mother. She's the best cook in the world—he ought to know, she taught him—and has made one of his favorite dishes, but at the moment he isn't hungry. *Maybe later*, he thinks. He grabs his favorite coffee mug from the cabinet, fills it, adds cream to the brim, and drinks some before carrying it outside with his canine buddies racing ahead of him, chasing cats, squirrels and rabbits that hang around the barn. The horizon is bright orange and the sky is blue, not too cold. Whitey Berry, his ranch hand from Texas, is an old buddy that lives in the small house on the back of the property, oversees the ranch, the two horses, feeds the strays and sells the hay. They meet by the barn and talk briefly and McGraw does the two things he enjoys most, talking to his horses, Mystery Lady and Texas Rodeo, and walking around the property to mull over what's on his mind.

The ranch house, with its tall windows and enclosed wrap-around porch, is situated on two hundred acres of an old horse farm and a perennial garden with plants and flowers, a horse barn, abandoned chicken coop and acres of timothy grass and alfalfa, sold as hay to the horse people. McGraw loves the smell of the roses in his mother's garden, the odor of the hay, enjoys seeing animals roaming the property and finds it relaxing when riding his horses. All of these things are part of his Texas upbringing.

He walks over to the south gate, puts his foot on the wooden railing, tips the brim of his hat back and leans on the top rail and sips his coffee. This pose reminds him of the Marlboro Man billboards that Roark refers to almost weekly. *I guess I am,* he thinks. McGraw swallows more coffee, sighs and thinks about the perp that has Eva Hamilton. Why did he abduct her? What is his motive? It doesn't appear to be money. No ransom calls. McGraw has the feeling that the perp is someone in her past. He finishes off his coffee and gazes at the horizon.

Often, while out here, completely relaxed, he slips into this dream. *He hears Dixie playing as Lee's Army marches through these streets in sorry appearance—men barefooted, limping, hatless, ragged and dirty—but passing with dignity, smiles and the will to go on, yet they loathe the enemy that heaps misery upon them. Desolation sweeps over the South and the suffering is immense. The clouds of sin and sadness cannot be dispelled by even the great emancipator, Abraham Lincoln, who, with a heavy heart, rides his horse through the field of bodies so thick that not a speck of dirt is seen. Brothers killing brothers, Lincoln must be thinking.*

McGraw's dogs begin barking in the distance, bringing him out of his reverie. He wonders if he would have been among those rebs lying on the ground. He's never told anyone about this vision lest they think him delusional. He sighs, turns and strolls back towards the house.

Life has been good to McGraw since he left the farm in west Texas. The only hurt that remains with him is from the loss of his wife, Lee Ann, to ovarian cancer. Before he met Lee Ann, while in the marines, he lost his dad, Weldon, in a tractor accident. At the time, he thought he couldn't be more devastated, until he lost Lee Ann. His dad was a good man, left Noah money for his education, and a substantial life insurance policy. These, along with Noah selling the homestead, have allowed him and his mother to live a comfortable life in Atlanta. Weldon had no college degree, but was very wise in the eyes of his son. The man taught Noah to always be the best he could be in whatever he did, and to remember that when good people do nothing, evil triumphs. McGraw recalls those words, "evil triumphs," to be paraphrased from Edmond Burke. He rides his father's Harley-Davidson whenever he can, and sometimes in the summer he rides with other biker friends of his dad on long trips in honor of Weldon's memory.

Toughness and meekness were hard for this cowboy to balance in his early years. His mother told him he was a maverick, like the cows he couldn't brand. Anna Marie taught her son how to cook. She said learning recipes would warm his heart. She instilled a respect for God in him from birth, and taught him: "Poverty and comfort separate us from our Lord." She read scripture to him in the evening to balance out his toughness. Proverbs bore its themes into his heart, and today he finds its thirty-one chapters a way to give him wisdom and knowledge and courage in his work.

McGraw, the Eagle Scout and valedictorian of his high school graduating class, chose to go into the marines before college. After serving four years in military police, he went to Harvard, graduated with a psychology degree, and then on to the University of Maryland earning a master's degree in Criminology and Law Enforcement. McGraw scored off the charts on the Civil Service exam while in the police academy, and during two years as an investigating officer for the Maryland Highway Patrol earned a reputation for being highly perceptive and analytical in his investigative skills.

McGraw joined the Atlanta PD at the age of twenty-eight, went through the local police academy and spent two years in patrol, where he demonstrated street smarts and the ability to read people and to get them to talk. These skills the last ten years propelled him into the Investigation Bureau, Narcotics Division where he was promoted through the ranks. The chief recognized McGraw's ability to multi-task and to lead an investigation, which opened the door to the Homicide Division. After two years, he was promoted to lieutenant and the department approved his request to go back to wearing starched white shirts with jeans, boots and his Stetson. He is known affectionately among the detectives as the Marlboro Man and is one of the finest investigators in Atlanta, if not in the east.

CHAPTER SIX

The next morning, Noah McGraw rises at six a.m., sits on the edge of the bed and glances at his wife's picture on the nightstand. Lee Ann is poised behind Noah on his Harley, wearing an embroidered jean jacket, smiling into the camera. McGraw sighs. He slides fingers over her face, and says, "Good morning, sweetheart." *You were the most loving person in the world.*

After breakfast, Noah walks the grounds and stops to say good morning to his horses and talk with Whitey before driving off to the precinct. He enters the squad room around eight, heads to his desk, removes his Stetson and places it on the desk. The forensic file on Eva's 2011 white Lexus is on his desk. He sits and opens it. Ten minutes later, Roark arrives.

"Anything at the M.E.?" he says.

She shakes her head. "Eva's not there."

"You checked all the hospitals?"

"Sure did. Don't you know I'm efficient?"

He smiles. "Good to know."

He turns back, reads the file. Ms. Hamilton's Lexus had no prints. There was a little mud and grass under the vehicle. Eva's folded slip, panties, and bra on the seat were sent to the lab, but they found nothing incriminating. Someone had washed them. McGraw could always tell a lot about how good detectives were by the case files they kept. It was a reflection on how they worked their cases. His team was the best—Roark, his partner, Kramer, and Gomez. Their reports were always complete, their notes easy to read, and their summaries clear and easy to follow.

McGraw rises, picks up his coffee mug and a piece of paper from his desk and walks over to Kramer and Gomez who are at their desks behind Roark.

"I read your incident report," he says. "Good work."

They nod and smile.

"No prints were found in the Hamilton woman's Lexus," McGraw says. It wasn't a question, just a statement of fact.

They nod.

McGraw heads to the coffee stand, fills his cup again, adds cream and walks back to his desk. Passing Roark, he eyes the eight-by-ten photo of her ten-year-old son Dusty, with Mattie and Lloyd Martin, a retired couple that lives next door to them. They take care of Dusty when Roark's not there. In the picture, Dusty is dressed in a baseball cap and is at a stance on home plate with a bat on his shoulder. No father in the picture. Roark had told McGraw about the divorce from her husband when the boy was only two. The successful real estate mogul couldn't take it that his wife was not available at his beck and call. He really wanted a sexy model to take to his parties. She fits the bill for a showcase wife, but she's not the type to model for her husband's clients.

"How's Dusty's batting average these days?"

"You need to come to dinner some Sunday and ask him. He keeps talking about you, and Mattie is in love with you."

"She reminds me of my mother."

"That's good, isn't it?"

"I guess." He goes to his desk, sets the mug next to a pile of papers, and sits. "Now I have two mothers."

Minutes later, the phone on Roark's desk rings. McGraw tries not to listen to what seems to be a personal conversation. He can't help notice how Roark is acting like a teenager, laughing up a storm. "Sure, that'll be fine," she says, and hangs up.

"This wasn't about the case," she says. "It's personal." The glow in her face gives it away.

McGraw continues to stare at her for a few seconds, but says nothing.

"What?" she asks. "What?"

"Let me guess. That was Pretty Boy Stallone with the motorcycle cop sun shades."

She frowns. "His name is not Stallone. It's Kingston. Max Kingston," she says with emphasis on Kingston. "If you have to know, he's taking me to dinner tonight."

McGraw pretends he's not interested, takes a drink of coffee and glances at her big brown eyes staring back at him. He hasn't been with a woman since he lost Lee Ann. He has concern for his partner's welfare, maybe a little more than he cares to admit.

"What?" she says.

"Nothing," he says.

"Why am I getting the feeling you're acting like a big brother I don't have. Is that what you are now? I can take care of myself, thank you."

"Do you need a babysitter this evening?" he says to change the subject, but realizes he just said it without thinking.

"Have you forgotten about the Martins, the folks next door?" she says. "They watch Dusty."

McGraw nods, then shuffles papers, pretending not to be interested.

"What's with you?" she says.

McGraw doesn't like Kingston. He's too syrupy and is the type that thinks he's God's gift to women, and dresses the part. He doesn't know what she sees in the guy.

Roark turns to her computer and punches the keys on her keyboard. Minutes later, she calls out to McGraw.

"I'm getting something on Austin Payne," she says scrolling down his credit report. "Oh, my, his credit is in the tank. He's in debt up to his eyeballs; has one DUI that was dropped. Wonder who he knows?" She scrolls further. "No outstanding warrants for any crimes in Georgia or any other state. He's divorced and has two boys."

"How about Dudley Hamilton?" McGraw says.

"I was waiting until we interviewed him," she says.

He frowns. "Don't wait. He's our prime suspect. And don't forget the ladies at the bank."

"I know. We'd check on the pope if he was involved," she says. "I'll get right on it."

CHAPTER SEVEN

Uniformed officer Dexter Price and his partner Trevor Wilson are going off duty at the Fourth Precinct and have changed into street clothes. On the way to the parking lot a little after four, Dexter says, "We need to get it in gear. My guy will be waiting."

Dexter, a 45-year-old, has been with the Atlanta PD for sixteen years and hasn't moved up through the ranks. He's just an average cop, who doesn't like to do any more than he has to. He gets his kicks out of controlling his partner, who has been with him six months riding in a black-and-white in the uniform division, but on the force for a year. Trevor has finally bought into Dexter's mantra that the Atlanta PD doesn't pay a living wage to cops. He's now brainwashed into believing that they have to find other ways to make money. Dexter has determined that Trevor is now ready for the big time. He's about to take him into his dark world.

They get into Dexter's canary-yellow pickup that has dents in the fenders and a slanted front bumper and pull out of the parking lot. Twenty minutes later, they move slowly into a neighborhood of boarded-up houses with yards minus grass, barking dogs, and cars resting on concrete blocks. Dexter pulls up behind a black Mercedes parked by the curb next to a deserted playground and turns off the engine.

Trevor says, "Dex, what's that guy in the Mercedes doing in this shitty neighborhood?"

"You gotta be kidding. What did I tell you about us cops looking the other way?" He gazes hard at Trevor. "So this guy here can operate in this district." Dex turns back and waves to the person sitting behind the wheel in the Mercedes.

"'Operate' meaning dealing drugs?" Trevor says.

Dexter shakes his head. "No, he sells condoms out of the trunk of his car. What the fuck do you think I mean?" He rolls down his window.

A thin black man, just under six feet tall, dressed in a yellow shirt with open collar, black slacks and a leather jacket, is wearing diamond earrings and enough jewelry around his neck and on his fingers that if Dexter had it in cash, he could live for a year. The dealer moves to Dexter's side, removes his sun shades with long thin fingers, glowing with diamond rings, bends down and peers in at Dexter.

"We cool?" the dealer says.

Dexter says, "Man, we're cool."

"Who's the bro?"

"My partner. He's cool."

He reaches into his coat pocket, pulls out a large brown envelope and hands it to Dexter.

Dexter puts it on the seat and bumps knuckles with the guy.

"You got my back, man," the dealer says.

"As always, man," Dex says.

He stares at Dex for a second or two. "And don't forget to answer my call when I need some info."

"You got it, man," Dex says. "Don't I always?"

He nods with a grin that tells Dex he'd better continue to do so and not double cross him. "Have you seen the man?" he asks, putting his shades back on.

"Not yet, but in a few days," Dexter says.

"Better move fast, man. He's expecting you. I went to bat for ya." The dealer backs away, making the figure of a gun with his right thumb and index finger, gesturing at Dexter saying, "You stay cool, bro."

"You too, man," Dexter says.

The dealer gets into his Mercedes and takes off.

"That was scary, Dex," Trevor says. "Did you see that Glock he had under his jacket?"

"No shit. Do you think he'd pack a water pistol?"

"He's a drug lord, isn't he?" Trevor says.

"Naw, man, he's just a dealer. We're going to meet the drug lord. And one other thing, don't ever say dealer. Just say 'the man' when we talk."

"I wouldn't want to cross him," Trevor says.

"You'd be one dead stiff, if you did."

"What's his name?" Trevor asks.

Dex's hand flies up in Trevor's face. "What'd I just say? First thing you learn in this business, no names, and no titles."

"You mean he doesn't know your name?"

"He knows, but he ain't ever going to say it. We don't do that in this business. The less said, the longer we live."

"What's in the envelope?"

"Whadda you think?" Trevor frowns.

"Open it," Dex says.

Trevor's eyes widen when he pulls out a stack of hundreds and begins counting.

"Dex, there's a hundred of 'em."

"And forty are yours."

"You don't mean—"

"You're my partner, ain't you?"

"For sure, Dex. Thanks. Thanks a lot. This'll pay our bills."

"I know. Your cute little girl Lilly is in the hospital a lot with those bad allergies and asthma attacks," Dex says."

"Yeah, man. The medical bills from the ER alone are eating us alive. Betty and me can't seem to make ends meet."

"Well, now you can. If you keep your trap shut, there'll be more."

"Lilly'll give you a big hug when she sees you," he says, counting his money for the third time.

"She's a darling and you better take good care of her and not squander that dough, or I'll have your ass."

"I will, Dex. I will."

CHAPTER EIGHT

"Lead the way," Austin Payne says to Dex as they clamber out of his egg-white Cadillac and walk towards Santino's retro bar with Trevor behind them. Parked in front is a black stretch Lincoln town car limo with a handsome-looking guy dressed in a tux sitting behind the wheel.

"You think that's the man's chauffeur or his body guard?" Payne asks Dex.

"Yeah, that's Brad Knox, and yes, he's both of those and even more."

"Whadda you mean, 'more'?" Payne asks.

"It's only a rumor, but Brad's thought to be the man's pimp," Dex says.

Payne only nods. He wouldn't put it past someone like Parino.

They climb the stairs and approach a large steel door to Santino's known for its Mafia ambiance and southern Italian menu. The place resembles the speakeasies of the twenties. Dex rings the doorbell. A window opens. "Who you?" the guy asks.

Dex and Trev frown at each other.

"Here to see Johnny Parino," Payne says. "He's expecting us."

The door opens. They step between heavy golden drapes into a dark foyer no bigger than a five-by-five box. It takes a minute for their eyes to adjust. The room is lined with damask-style wallpaper. They follow the big guy in the tux into the dining area. Tables with dark tops and red leather chairs are grouped in the center of the room. A few feet away is a semi-circular bar with a black granite top. A large glass mirror is behind it with rows of liquor bottles. Overhead, crystal chandeliers make this part of the room sparkle. Subdued lighting prevails around the periphery of the room, with rich red leather booths and gray columns. The place is packed with professionals talking above each other.

"Johnny's over der in the back room," says the big escort, leading them down a narrow hall. "Some guys to see the boss," he says to another giant guarding the door.

36

The giant pats Payne down, looking for a rod. Then he does Dex and Trev. When he's satisfied that they aren't carrying, he leads the way into the room. "They're clean, boss."

A large guy in a black suit is sitting behind the only table in room with two goons, also dressed in black suits, standing behind him, nods. "Have a seat," he says. No smile on his face. The place smells of cigar smoke.

Dex nods to Parino as he sits to his right facing him and Trev to his left. Payne takes a seat in the middle, directly opposite Johnny.

"How yuh doin', Dex?" he says with a sober face, not extending a hand.

"Good, Johnny," Dex says. "You doin' okay?"

"Great," he says with a nod, "Always great." He scoffs at Payne and Trev. "Who's these guys?"

Dex turns to Payne. "Johnny, this is my boss from the bank I told you about, Austin Payne, and that is my ugly partner, Trev Wilson." Dex pauses and then says, "This is Johnny Parino, boss." Dexter's drug dealer had introduced him days earlier to this mafioso.

"Trev, I wouldn't let this creep call you ugly," Johnny says. "Maybe you need to teach him a lesson."

The visitors give out a nervous laugh.

Johnny Parino's father abandoned him and his five siblings when he was ten, leaving his mother to struggle on welfare, food stamps, stinking cheese, while working two jobs cleaning other people's shit. He never went past the eighth grade; became street smart and learned to do whatever it took to survive. Cleverness and getting an understanding of the political and social structure of the criminal element helped him over the years to reach the big time. He made the right connections, learned to grease the palms of the right people inside and outside the criminal element, decided narcotics was the enterprise he would pursue to make his fortune. Through the years he branched into prostitution and the sale of weapons. No one ever double-crosses Johnny Parino and lives.

Payne is thinking that Johnny looks like Tony Soprano. He must be close to three hundred pounds, broad shoulders, almost bald, but has a pleasant round face that could easily turn sour if you crossed him.

"What's your pleasure?" Johnny says.

"It's our first time, Mr. Parino," Payne says. "What do you recommend?"

Johnny frowns. "Cut the 'mister' crap. No one calls me that. I'm Johnny to all my friends. You call me that, okay?"

"Sure thing, Johnny," Payne says.

"Good." Johnny motions for one of the big guys to get a waitress. Seconds later, a good-looking gal with a thin, shapely body dressed in a short red dress comes into the room.

Not bad. Payne thinks.

"Hey, Gina baby." She walks over to him. "Whatcha need, Johnny?"

"These are my friends."

She smiles, turns to the guys and nods. "Nice to meet you, gentlemen."

"Let's have my favorite, baby," Johnny says, slapping her on the rear.

"Sure thing, Johnny," Gina says and dashes off.

Payne glances around the room, thinking about how the movies portray mobsters in Italian restaurants, spilling spaghetti sauce down the front of their ties and on white table cloths. No table cloths here. The room is plain, no pictures on the cream-colored walls, and no windows. *There must be a reason there aren't any windows,* Payne thinks.

"You come here often?" Payne says, knowing the answer, but wanting to strike up a conversation with the big man.

"Why not? I own the joint and nine others like it." He shrugs as if to minimize the importance of owning so many. "Not all are Italian restaurants."

Yeah, and a few whore houses thrown in, Payne thinks.

"I saw your sign in the entrance that says cash only."

Johnny frowns and looks off in the distance, thinking. "Yeah, them checks can bounce, credit cards are a pain in the ass, but cash is always cash, and can be trusted," Johnny says.

I guess you know your business, Payne thinks.

Gina brings a bottle of red wine. A blonde dressed like Gina stands beside her holding four glasses upside down, stems between her fingers. Gina pops the cork and is about to pour when Johnny reaches for the bottle, "I'll pour, baby." The blonde hands him one glass at a time. Once filled, she hands each one to Johnny's guests.

"Did Dex tell you about our deal?" Johnny says.

"Sure did," Payne says.

"You a man of your word, Austin?" Johnny says.

Payne nods. "Sure am."

Johnny frowns at him. "You in?"

"I'm in," Payne says with emphasis.

"Good. Even a homeless man can be a man of his word. But I would never trust him. He has no guts." Johnny takes a swallow of his wine. "Drink up, gentlemen." They reach for their glasses and begin drinking their wine, follow Johnny until he sets his glass on the table. They do the same.

"Your word better be solid, Austin. Don't want to make promises you can't keep."

"I don't do anything I can't deliver, Johnny."

"Some clowns can't keep from lying. The second I don't trust 'em is when I lose 'em for good," he says, patting the bulge in his suit coat. "Know what I mean?"

Trev's eyes are as big as saucers and Dex isn't smiling.

"Sure thing, Johnny," Payne says with some anxiety. He didn't need to tell him. Payne knew. Johnny will blow his head off if he screws up.

"Good. Cause I never forgive any *cafone rozzo* who betrays me."

"I understand," Payne says."

"Today's men are neutered by women; they're weak compared to men of my generation. We live by old-school values," Johnny says. "Whadda you think about that, Austin?"

"I like people with old-school values, Johnny."

"Yeah, you can trust 'em."

Johnny lifts his glass and says, "To our partnership."

Trev shoots a furtive glance at Dex. Their glasses clink together above the middle of the table and they say in unison: "Partnership."

Two hours later, Austin, Dex and Trev are coming out of Santino's and walking to Austin's Caddy. Payne opens the back door, throws the suitcase on the seat and Trev slides in. Dex moves into the passenger seat.

"Johnny scared the shit out of me," Trev says, attempting to make himself comfortable next to the suitcase. "Man, I bet there's a lot of dead bodies of guys that crossed Johnny," he says, slapping the suitcase.

"You can bet your life on it," Dex says. "Did you see that rod he was packing?"

"Mr. Payne," Trev calls out. "What is caf... ruz..., or however you say it? I didn't get what Johnny meant."

"*Cafone rozzo*," Payne says. "*Cafone* means ill-mannered and *rozzo* means rough guy. Put them together and an Italian is saying that the guy is a rough pig who'd betray his own mother," Payne says.

"Do you think Johnny can be trusted, Mr. Payne?" Trev says.

Payne is concentrating on the road and says nothing.

Dex glances at him. "Bet I know what you are thinking, boss—"

"—I know, too," Trev says, not letting Dex finish. "You're thinking about all this money Johnny wants you to hide for him. Sure is a lot."

"You're both wrong," he says. "I was thinking: if we screw up on this, we'll all be fish bait at the bottom of Beaver Lake, riddled with bullets and a wheel tied around our necks. That's what I'm thinking."

CHAPTER NINE

Noah McGraw and Holly Roark show up at Dudley's home around nine this morning. Dudley and Eva Hamilton's two-story house could be called a mansion. Not as large as Dudley's parents, but still a gorgeous white house with columns, flat roof, turrets on the four corners, and lots of windows. The driveway courses between rows of circular green boxwoods and curves in front of a four-car garage connected to the house.

McGraw stops the black Impala cruiser at the garage, steps out the driver's side and puts on his hat. Holly gets out on the passenger side. Both stand by the car, surveying the green lawn manicured to perfection. "Déjà vu," McGraw says.

"That's what I was thinking," Roark says. "These Hamiltons have it all."

"Not all."

"Oh, I forgot," she says, smiling.

They're met at the door by Dudley. What, no butler?

"I'm Lieutenant McGraw," he says, holding up his ID, then turns to Holly. "This is Sergeant Roark."

Dudley neither nods nor breaks a smile, but stares at McGraw's hat and boots.

"We'd like to come in and talk," McGraw says.

Dudley doesn't move, blocks the door with his body. He appears to have just gotten up, hasn't shaved, hasn't combed his hair and is in a sweat suit.

"Do you have a warrant?" he says brushing his hair back.

"Don't need one, just to talk," Roark says.

Dudley scowls, turns and leads them into the living room with six-foot windows and a sliding door leading into a rock garden surrounded by three-foot hedges. Four dirt loading trucks could fit in this room with leather furniture, a glass coffee table loaded with carryout boxes exposing remnants of yesterday's meals, along with stacks of old newspapers. Clothes are in a pile in the corner and on a table against the wall are ledgers piled two-feet high.

40

Dudley doesn't ask them to sit nor does he apologize for the clutter of his own making. He appears aggravated and twitchy. The first thing he says is "When can I get my wife's Lexus back?"

He doesn't ask about his wife or if the detectives have any leads or who might be the perpetrator.

"We'll let you know," says McGraw. "For now, it's evidence."

"I just bought it for her a few weeks ago, and I demand that you return it as soon as possible."

McGraw takes it as a statement and doesn't answer him; instead he asks him when he last saw his wife.

"It was the morning she disappeared. I fill in as a bank examiner, and this time I had to be in Athens at BancFirst by seven a.m. I left around five-thirty."

He still shows no emotion over the disappearance of his wife. *What's with this guy?* McGraw thinks.

"Do you know of anyone who might want to harm Ms. Hamilton?" McGraw asks.

"No." He walks towards the window overlooking the garden, and stares out at something. "My wife has a few friends, but for the most part, she is very dependent on me. At times she can be afraid of her own shadow."

Roark frowns. "Did Ms. Hamilton give you any reason to believe someone was harassing her or following her?"

"Not really." He turns to look at her, but appears to be in deep thought. "There was this guy... it was in the bank... he tried to come on to her. Then one day when she told him to get lost, he said something that upset her. After that he never bothered her again."

"What's his name?" McGraw says.

He shakes his head. "She never told me."

And you never thought to ask, McGraw thinks.

"We would like to see Ms. Hamilton's room, if that is okay," Roark says.

"It's not okay. You'll need a warrant."

"How about phone records and charge card statements?" she says.

"How many times do I have to tell you? Get a warrant."

"We'll, we won't need a warrant for phone numbers and names of anyone you had contact with at BancFirst," McGraw says, losing his temper.

Dudley scowls at McGraw. "You don't believe me?"

"Not my job to believe you," McGraw says. "So get them for us, and I mean now."

"Am I a suspect?"

"Husbands are always at the top of the list," McGraw says.

"Give me a minute." He heads into the next room and disappears.

"Do you realize he never once asked about Eva?" Roark says. "He just wants her car."

McGraw nods and goes to a door in the rear of the room, opens it and looks around, then shuts it. Heads to the patio door and goes outside. Seconds later he returns.

"What are you doing?" she asks.

"Getting a feel of the place," he says.

"Looking for a fresh dig in the garden?" she says with a smile.

McGraw doesn't respond.

Dudley returns and hands McGraw a sheet of paper.

"You'll find the names and numbers for the bank president and his VP," Dudley says. "They'll vouch for me."

McGraw glances over it and hands it to Roark. "Does it always take you more than two days to do an audit? I was told you were to be back in town by Friday evening, but you didn't return until last night."

"This one took longer than usual," Dudley says.

"So, you didn't have dinner with anyone?" Roark says.

"No."

"Did you leave the bank at any time?"

"Only for lunch with the VP," he says

McGraw removes a pen from his shirt pocket and hands it to Dudley. "Write down where you had lunch, the time you entered and left, who you talked to while in the restaurant and any calls you made or received on your cell."

Dudley shoots him a scorching glance, grabs the paper out of Roark's hand, goes to a table and writes for a couple of minutes, then hands it back to her.

"Now," McGraw says, "you're sure you never left the bank at any other time during the daytime, except for lunch."

"Detective, I don't like what you're insinuating."

McGraw shrugs. "Answer the question: Did you or did you not leave at any time while working in the bank?"

"I did not," he says with disgust in his voice.

"What about in the evening of the first day?" Roark asks.

"I had dinner alone in my room and worked on their books until midnight."

"Can anyone vouch for you?" she says.

"The night clerk can."

"How'd you get that scratch on your face?" McGraw says.

Dudley sighs. "Shaving, detective, shaving. My wife didn't scratch me, if that's what you're thinking."

"What should I be thinking?"

"Nothing."

"We'll need you to come down to the station," McGraw says. "We'll have someone pick you up at eight in the morning."

"Why? I've told you everything. There's nothing more." He pauses, raising his hands. "I know what you're up to. You guys want to break me so I'll confess to something I didn't do."

"You've been watching too many crime shows on TV," McGraw says.

"It's just that we'll need a full statement from you," Roark says.

42

Dudley moves them toward the door.

"You're barking up the wrong husband. I'm not your man."

"Be ready tomorrow morning," McGraw says. He steps outside.

Dudley slams the door shut.

"He's meaner than a barracuda, and almost certainly did her in," Roark says.

"Let's wait to see where the evidence takes us," McGraw says.

"Oh, aren't you the smart one. You must know me by now, that I was just blowing smoke."

"He's a parasite that feeds off everyone," McGraw adds.

They return to the cruiser and head down the driveway to the street below. McGraw looks around, then drives across the street, pulls to the curb and stops.

"Ready to do some walking?" he says.

"I'll take the south side," she says.

"That leaves the north side for me."

"You Harvard guys really catch on fast."

"See what happens when you don't play those video games? You learn things," he says.

They separate, and an hour later, McGraw returns to the car, but notices Roark talking to a bald-headed chubby guy in his sixties, standing in front of his house. Minutes later, she comes to the car. They slide in and she says, "The little guy you saw me with, his name is Colin Joyce, a retired banker, no less. He is fond of Eva and has been taking her morning paper to the front door. She's invited him in for coffee on several occasions. He states that Dudley's a cold fish; he barely speaks even when Mr. Joyce sits directly across from him at the breakfast table. Only reads the paper."

McGraw says, "Eva's next door neighbor told me about your man Joyce having morning coffee at the Hamiltons, and also she's seen a white van driving pass the Hamilton place whenever Mr. Hamilton goes out of town."

"Did she get a make on it?"

"She didn't see the driver, only that the van was white."

"No one on my side could tell me who would want to harm Eva," Roark says. They thought she was a sweet person."

McGraw adds, "That's what the north side neighbors said."

CHAPTER TEN

Noah McGraw parks his sky-blue 2011 RAM 3500 pickup in front of McAteer's Coffee Shop a little before seven, reaches for his hat on the seat next to him, slides out and walks to the entrance. He side-steps a couple of officers when he enters, and looks for his friend, Tony Zamperini, known as Zee to his friends. Shane McAteer used to be on the force, and after retirement opened this coffee shop. It's popular with many on the force.

Zee's sitting in a booth in the back against a mirrored wall that makes the place look much larger than it is. He waves to get McGraw's attention. At the counter, a handful of cops are eating breakfast. They nod at McGraw and one calls out, "How yuh doin', cowboy lieutenant?"

"Marlboro Man," another whispers with a laugh.

"Better than you deadbeats," he says, and nods to McAteer, whose face is filled with a smile. McGraw orders a tall cup of half-caff hazelnut, adds cream and goes to the back.

"Zee," McGraw says, nodding, removes his hat and places it on the seat next to the wall.

"Don't let the uniforms get to you, champ. They're jealous."

"I know."

Zee was born in Atlanta some sixty-eight years ago to Italian parents. The family name, Zamperini, is at times linked mistakenly to the famous Olympian medalist, war hero, and ocean survivor, Louis Zamperini. But that's as far as it goes. Zee isn't related and he is no athlete, even though he does work out at the police gym a few days a week and maintains a slender physique, which McGraw finds unusual for an Italian. His hair is peppered with gray, and he has a handsome, narrow face. Zee retired a year ago from the Police Department after forty years—thirty of those as a decorated homicide detective.

"I bet you're working the Hamilton case," he says.

McGraw nods. "I'm calling it the Vanishing Bride case." He drinks some of his coffee.

"Been reading about the Hamiltons in the paper," Zee says. He's talking about the Atlanta Journal-Constitution. "It's another one of them high-profile cases that I never liked."

McGraw nods. "Neither do I, and that family is a pain in the ass."

He becomes quiet as his eyes land on a guy in a wheelchair, a former cop who got shot in the spine while on duty. Every cop that leaves home, one day or other, wonders if this is the day. At night, they give thanks to see their families again. *Why do we do it?* he wonders.

"What're you thinking, champ?"

"Poor Billy over there with his friend," he says, tilting his head. "That could have been you or me."

McGraw feels Zee's dark eyes piercing him. "Don't go there, man. You know damn well, it'll get into your head and play tricks on you. Have you forgotten what I taught you?"

McGraw takes a few swallows of his coffee. "I know. I know. That's one of the first things I learned from you."

"Come on; tell me about how the case's going? That Eva Hamilton is sure a pretty thing. Time is running out."

"We're doing all we can, still interviewing those closest to her." He shakes his head. "She must be a really sweet person, to put up with that husband of hers. I believe he's a narcissist. We're interrogating him after I leave here."

"You remember what I taught you about narcissists, right?" Zee says, looking over his cup. "You can tell when you get into the interrogation. If you suspect he is, you gotta handle him different than other jerks," Zee says.

McGraw nods and swallows more of his coffee. "I remember."

"Maybe the lady took off, couldn't stand the bastard," Zee says. "It happens."

"Eva Hamilton is not the type that would leave on her own. She doesn't seem that strong of a person. Actually, I am surprised she left Oklahoma. Someone must have convinced her to come here."

Zee stares at McGraw. "You're on to something?"

He nods. "Something about her troubles me, but I haven't figured it out just yet."

"Maybe she's too clean," Zee says.

"She's not one to break her marriage vows, but there could be someone before she met her husband."

"You'll figure it out, champ," says Zee. "Listen, I gotta go out of town for a few days, a friend of mine is not doing too well, but when I get back I'm going to take you to a fabulous restaurant. Are you game?"

"Absolutely."

"Ever hear of The Pitcher's Mound?"

McGraw shakes his head and finishes off his coffee. "From the name, it must have something to do with baseball, and that's my game."

"It does, and I want you to meet a guy," Zee says.

"Sounds interesting. Anyone I know in baseball?"

45

"You bet. Remember the Braves pitcher, Moose Johnson?"

"Of course," McGraw says with surprise in his voice. "He's the Mississippi boy who won the Cy Young?"

"That's the one. He's got this wonderful steakhouse called The Pitcher's Mound. I'll give you a call when I get back and pick you up. Don't want you getting slammed on that Harley."

"You know I can handle it, Zee," McGraw says. "You forget I'm a marine."

"Hell, you never let me forget it."

They laugh.

CHAPTER ELEVEN

Noah McGraw arrives at his desk a little after eight. Kramer and Gomez are to bring in Dudley Hamilton any minute now. His phone rings. The caller is Leslie Winfrey, who says Eva Hamilton's picture in the Atlanta Journal-Constitution is the person she saw leaving Prestige Square Mall at the same time she did, around eight that Thursday evening. Leslie remembers because Eva was in a white Lexus exactly like the one she drives.

He hangs up and turns to Roark. "Just got a call from Leslie Winfrey. She remembers seeing Eva Hamilton leaving the mall in her Lexus Thursday night the twentieth around eight o'clock."

Roark looks up from her computer. "That certainly establishes the time. Now all we need is for someone to call in and tell us what happened to her," Roark says.

"Don't hold your breath," McGraw says with a grin.

"Just finished checking on the girls at Citizen's," she says staring at her monitor. "They checked out okay. Also, Dudley hasn't been in any trouble and leads a pretty dull life from all I can find. The VP at BancFirst in Athens verified everything Dudley told us about his time there. He's certainly not a ladies' man."

McGraw nods. "He's too dull to have a mistress."

"You think he could have hired someone to abduct her?" she says.

"As of now, I don't see a motive," McGraw says.

"Speak of the devil," she says.

Detectives Kramer and Gomez come through the pit with Dudley Hamilton sandwiched between them. The six-foot, long-legged, narrow faced, thirty-eight-year-old now is looking ten years older. "Let's get this over with," he says. "I'm very busy and got better things to do than waste time with you people."

McGraw grabs a pad and leads him into interview room three. In the corner of the squad room next to Roark's desk is a monitor on which she and

47

Gomez and Kramer are viewing number three.

Inside, McGraw asks, "Can I get you something to drink?"

Dudley shakes his head. "I'm good."

McGraw flips on the recorder on the desk and sits facing him.

"You going to record everything I say?" Dudley says.

"Any problem with it?"

He shrugs. "Guess not."

"You last saw Ms. Hamilton before you left Thursday morning the twentieth around five-thirty, is that correct?"

He nods. "That's right."

"How would you describe your relationship with Ms. Hamilton?"

"Nothing spectacular."

"Why not spectacular?" McGraw says. He writes something on his notepad.

"I meant we had a good marriage, but nothing to sing about. We had our ups and downs."

"You said *had*, using the past tense. Do you believe your wife is dead?"

"How do I know? You're the cops. You tell me."

"Did you love your wife?"

"What kind of question is that?"

"Well, you're rather sophisticated and an intelligent guy and, you know, you come from a very influential family and your wife is a country girl. I just assumed that there being such a gulf between you two, there were..." He pauses. "That perhaps there were some problems."

Dudley frowns, but says, "Eva is a little slow and isn't quite in my class, but we get along okay. She is a good homebody and takes good care of me."

"So you love her even though she isn't as intelligent or from as good a background as you?"

Dudley's eyes tell McGraw he's not used to people telling him how good he is.

"Of course I was willing to put up with her shortcomings. I guess that makes me a pretty good husband, doesn't it?"

"I'd say that was very good of you. Most men wouldn't have."

"Thank you. I try, even though it's hard at times."

"But I guess you do miss your wife?"

He took his time answering. "Listen, detective. Some people react differently. I'm one of those guys who don't show much emotion. I was brought up that way. Just ask that old lady I call my mother."

McGraw took his time to write down a few things of no value, glancing a couple of times at Dudley, who is feeling superior at the moment.

"I imagine a man of your status in the community had a difficult time finding ladies to go out with. I mean those who weren't after your money. That could be why you didn't have many dates."

Dudley looks the other way for a few seconds and turns and gazes deeply into McGraw's eyes. "Detective, it amazes me how well you understand me. Even my own parents don't know me as well as you do." He pauses. "I never had time like most men to associate with women. My folks needed me at the banks. They can be demanding, you know?"

"I understand," McGraw says.

McGraw gets up, shuts off the recorder. "I'll be right back." He stops at the door and turns back. "Sure you don't want something to drink, Mr. Hamilton?"

"Thank you, no."

McGraw then leaves the room and joins his team at the monitor. They looked stunned.

"What in the world happened in there," Roark says.

"Boss," Gomez says. "Hamilton was eating out of your hand."

"Hamilton's an egotist," Kramer says. "The lieutenant was pulling his chain to get a reaction out of him."

"Something I learned from Zee. Hamilton is somewhat of a narcissist, but not as severe as those with the type known as narcissistic personality disorder. It seems that he's incapable of loving. His parents may be part of the reason," McGraw says.

"I doubt if they showed him much affection," Roark says. "We saw how cold the mother's attitude was toward Eva."

McGraw nodded. "You saw what went on in there. He doesn't miss his wife; he only misses her help around the house. Roark and I saw the condition of his home when we went there."

"She has to be an angel to stay with him," Roark says.

"That's for sure," Gomez says. "He only wants her car back."

McGraw nods.

"Well, he sure played right into your hands," Roark says looking at the monitor to interview room three. "Now he's looking at his cell phone, wondering whether he should call his attorney. Should I go in?" she asks McGraw.

"Try another approach with him and let's see what happens," McGraw says.

Roark enters the room and asks Dudley if he'd like coffee or a soft drink.

"What's this: Good-cop-bad-cop bullshit?"

Roark shrugs. "Have it your way," she says as she turns on the recorder and adjusts herself in the bucket seat facing him. "Do you know anyone that might want to harm your wife, Mr. Hamilton?"

"No. How many times do I have to tell you guys?"

"Do you get along with everyone at your bank?"

"I know where you're going with this. There's no one there that would hurt me or my wife."

"What about unhappy customers? Maybe someone who didn't get their loan approved."

"That's crazy; we do tons of loans every year. And we've never had an unhappy customer."

"What about old boyfriends? Maybe there's one out there that didn't like it because Ms. Hamilton married you."

"We never discussed such a thing, but I doubt it. She's shy and weak."

Roark is feeling her free hand forming a fist. "How do you know she never had any lovers if you never discussed them? Maybe there's a secret lover."

"Nonsense, she never had it so good as with me."

Roark's fingernails are digging into the palm of her free hand.

"I am puzzled about something, Mr. Hamilton. I need your help here." Roark looks at her notes. "One of the workers at her bank overheard Eva talking on the phone with someone we think is a man. She says this: "'I can't come over there anymore, I'm married now, but you can come to our place.'" Roark looks up at Dudley, who is staring at the wall with his arms crossed. "Did she ever mention this caller to you?"

"No. I doubt if that worker heard it right. It could have been one of her girlfriends."

"She heard it very clearly, and that's what's puzzling me."

He frowns. "What's that?"

"Eva must have known this guy; otherwise, why would she tell him she couldn't come over there anymore. That's the operative phrase, 'couldn't come over there anymore.' Ms. Hamilton wouldn't have said that to a girlfriend, Mr. Hamilton. It tells me she'd been seeing someone at his place before she married you. And someone you know, too, since she invited him to your home."

He shrugs. "She never discussed any of that with me and I don't know who he could be. Whoever it is, he never came to our house."

"Please try to think."

"I told you, she never went with anyone before we married."

"The girls she roomed with prior to your marriage said she had a few dates."

"Those are the idiots at Citizens bank. They're damn liars."

"Okay, then tell me this. Why do you have your neighbor across the street, Mr. Joyce, follow Eva around when you go out of town? Were you suspicious she was seeing someone?"

He stares into her eyes. "How'd you know about that? Did he tell you?"

"We have ways. Answer my question. Why did you have her followed?"

He sits up straight. "Because she's a wimp, afraid of her own shadow."

"Is that the only reason?"

He scowls. "What do you mean?"

"Perhaps you thought some jealous lover from her past was out to harm her or steal her from you."

"That's bullshit. Where's detective McGraw—?"

She doesn't give him time to finish. "Or perhaps you thought one of your old girlfriends was jealous of Eva and might harm her."

He shakes his head. "I never had anyone before Eva. She's the only one I could tolerate. The others were never good enough for me."

And they didn't like you, either, smartass, she thinks. Roark wonders why Dudley married Eva if he never found one good enough.

"Why was Eva different?" Roark asked. *Easy to control*, she thinks.

He shrugs, stalling for time to consider what he would say next.

"Even with all her faults, she's easy to get along with and waits on me." He sighs. "My father really likes her."

"Did you or Eva get into an argument with anyone recently?"

"No, no, no. I want to talk to McGraw. This is gone far enough. Get him in here."

"He'll be here in a minute. Answer my question."

"How many times do I have to say it? We don't associate much, and there's no one out to get us."

"Someone did. Do you have something to hide?"

"Hell, no. I want to talk to McGraw."

"Do you have a mistress?" Roark says.

"No. I don't stoop to that level."

"Do you know anything about your wife's disappearance?"

"I was seventy miles away."

Roark chooses to pause for a few seconds. Dudley stares at her and squirms in his seat. "You're thinking I hired someone to kill her, aren't you?" He jumps up. "I wouldn't harm my wife," he screams. "I want my lawyer."

McGraw pushes his way between Kramer and Gomez. "I've got to get in there," he says.

He rushes into the room. "Mr. Hamilton. I'm sorry. Detective Roark doesn't understand you. Please sit down."

Dudley eases back into his chair. "She sure doesn't. How many times do I have to tell you cops, I didn't harm my wife? And I didn't hire anyone to do it."

"I know, I know. It's just that we have to ask certain questions for the record. Sorry, if detective Roark was a little harsh."

Hamilton sighs, "Are we done? I'm tired and want to go home."

"Of course." McGraw turns to Roark. "We're done here aren't we, Detective Roark?" he says, winking at her.

"We're done," she says.

"One last thing, Mr. Hamilton," McGraw says. "While I believe in you, we have certain procedures we must follow. So, I was wondering, would you be willing to take a lie detector test?'

He frowns. "Does it hurt?"

"No, no. It's painless and doesn't take much time."

"I guess it will be okay, but let me run it by my attorney first. I'd feel better that way."

"Of course, we want to cooperate with you in any way necessary."

"So I'm free to go?"

"Any time you're ready," McGraw says.

Roark shuts off the recorder and stands.

Outside the interview room and back at his desk, McGraw receives a phone call from Laura Dunbar.

51

"Lieutenant, we've found something," she says.

"What is it?"

"We've found car tracks and brush pulled up where a car must have gone off the road about ten miles north of the mall. Also, I can't be sure, but it appears that another car could have been involved."

"Are you there now?"

"Yes. You can get here by staying on I-75 for ten miles and you'll see our cars on the side of the road. You can't miss us."

"Stay put."

Clare Dunbar, Eva's closest friend, has been supervising a group of volunteers over a twenty-five-mile radius around Prestige Square, an area they divided into four quadrants since Eva disappeared, handing out fliers and posting them in shops and on telephone poles. The volunteers have been searching these areas inch by inch. Dunbar's home decorating shop in the mall is the command center. The Atlanta Journal-Constitution helped with a cover story on the "The Vanishing Bride," which led only to false tips.

McGraw calls for uniforms, then slips on his Stetson and calls out to his team. "Let's go. Dunbar's people have found something ten miles north of the mall."

"What did they find?" Roark says.

"I'll explain on the way."

In the cruiser, McGraw flips on the bar lights and they take off, with Kramer and Gomez following behind them. Twenty minutes later, McGraw pulls up behind the car Clare Dunbar is standing beside. Uniforms have arrived and secured the area. The detectives step out and slip on blue gloves. McGraw turns to Kramer and Gomez, "See what you can learn from the folks up here and keep them up here."

McGraw examines the area close to the road.

"Looks like a vehicle stopped up here rather abruptly," he says. "Lots of loose gravel." He stoops and eyes the flattened area leading down into the woods, like a golfer judging the distance to the hole on the green, which appears to be wide enough for a car. "There was also a second car that lost control and flew deep into the brush."

"More than road rage, McGraw," Roark says. "Someone was run way off down there."

"Did your people trample into the area down there, Ms. Dunbar?" McGraw asks, pointing toward the crumpled brush.

"No, sir, we stopped here at the road, thinking we'd better not go in. It could be a crime scene," Dunbar says.

"Good thinking," he says. "Like for you to come to the station this afternoon to get a complete statement."

"Can do, lieutenant," she says.

"Everyone, let me have your attention," he says. "Please stay where you are for a little while longer until our detectives get your statements. We appreciate your cooperation. Thank you."

He follows outside the tracks deep into the woods. Roark retraces his steps to meet up with him. McGraw is examining the ruts. "These tire tracks will make good impressions," he says.

Roark's cell rings. She answers it. "Forensics is on the way," she says. "That was Alan."

"Good," McGraw says. "Notice that the brush on the left side of these tire tracks has been trampled more than on the right," McGraw says.

"Whoever ran the car off the road must have struggled with the driver on this side of the vehicle," Roark says.

"I agree. And if Ms. Hamilton was the driver, then whoever did this struggled with her after opening her car door." McGraw turns and heads a few yards back towards the highway and stops. Something catches his eye and he moves into the brush. He calls the CSI tech over. "There's something in there," McGraw says. As the tech reaches in with a gloved hand and pulls out a small towel. "Smells like some chemical, lieutenant," the tech says, bagging it.

About 20 feet from the road, McGraw crouches down to survey the ground leading into the woods. "Note these holes," he says, pointing." Could be heel marks. They lead up the way. The perp dragging the vic back to his vehicle."

"So you think the vic was unconscious?" Roark says.

"Some chemical, probable chloroform, used to subdue the vic."

Alan, the forensic chief, along with his team members, dressed in white coveralls, are beginning to process the area.

"Looks like we have abduction, Alan," McGraw says. "This could be where Ms. Hamilton was run off the road. Also, there are pretty good tire tracks back there."

"We're getting after it, lieutenant," Alan says. He moves in, passing Roark, and says, "How you doin,' sergeant?"

She nods. "Doing well, Alan."

On the way back to the cruiser, McGraw meets the forensic tech working the tire tracks close to the road. "The tire markings are quite visible," McGraw says. "You can even make out the name, Michelin, and there's a number."

The tech begins pouring a mixture that looks like pancake batter into the tracks. "Yeah, it should make it easier to identify the vehicle."

"Only problem," McGraw says, "the vehicle may be stolen."

The tech nods. "That happens a lot, lieutenant."

McGraw and Roark reach the top of the road and meet Kramer and Gomez who have finished speaking with the volunteers. McGraw thanks Ms. Dunbar and her volunteers and tells them that they now can go.

"Got anything?" Roark asks Kramer and Gomez.

Kramer shakes his head. "Dead end," he says.

"One person saw a guy driving away as he walked up this way, but didn't know if he stopped to do something in his car," Gomez says. "He couldn't remember the make or model of the car, thought it was white."

"White cars are the most popular, with black second," McGraw says.

"So, it could have been anyone," Roark says.

"The only thing we have now is that towel, which leads me to believe that it was soaked with chloroform. We'll see if forensics turns up anything that can help us."

"Someone could have used it to subdue Eva Hamilton," Roark says.

CHAPTER TWELVE

Clare Dunbar arrives at headquarters around one-thirty and is taken into an interview room, where she is given a bottle of water.

'Thanks for coming," McGraw says after he and Roark enter.

They pull away a chair from the desk and sit facing her.

"We would like to learn all we can about Ms. Hamilton," he says.

"Pleased to help any way I can."

Clare Dunbar is dressed in a blue jacket and skirt, white blouse, unbuttoned at the top. She is workout slender, with long legs, and wears her hair long, cupping around a slender strong face. She has a pleasant smile and radiates an aura of professionalism.

"Thank you. Did Ms. Hamilton seem depressed the last few weeks?" McGraw asks.

She shakes her head. "No, not really," she says.

"How about being out of sorts at any time before her disappearance?" Roark says.

She frowns and shakes her head again. "No. Eva was even planning a party for Dudley the next day, that Friday night, when Dudley was supposed to come home."

"Mr. Hamilton led us to believe they didn't have many friends," he says.

"They were mainly Eva's. Dudley could put on the charm when he wanted to, but he had no friends to speak of."

"I get the impression that Ms. Hamilton didn't live in reality for some reason. Is that your observation?" McGraw says.

"It seemed that way at times. I accepted it as her way to survive in her marriage and didn't think much about it."

"I sense that you are not a fan of Dudley."

Her lips narrow and she stares hard at McGraw. "To be honest, I am not." *I don't like him, either*, he thinks.

"Would you say he was good to Eva?" Roark says.

"I never considered them a good match, but she never complained about him. She wouldn't. Not the type. Eva's kind, compassionate, but Dudley, well, he's the opposite." She fiddles with her hands. "We girls saw through his façade and didn't like him from the beginning." She pauses, appearing in deep thought. "He's overbearing, self-centered, and snobbish, but..." She pauses a second time. "I never saw any marks on Eva, nor did she ever tell me that Dudley hit her."

"Did Ms. Hamilton ever mention a high school or college friend or maybe a steady boyfriend before she married Dudley?" McGraw asks.

"She dated a couple of times, but never brought them around our place when I was living there. Never talked much about her past, except there was a girlfriend that Eva moved in with when she first came to Atlanta. I believe she was with her for a year. That was before moving in with us."

"Do you know her name?" Roark asks.

She nods. "Olivia Jordan. But she moved to New York several years ago. Maybe the other girls in the bank might know more about her."

"What can you tell us about Eva's relationship with the workers at the bank, other than those she roomed with?" McGraw says.

"She was popular with all the employees."

"So there's no one you know who would want to harm her?" Roark asks.

Lines develop in the corners of her eyes. She takes her time answering.

"Yes, Ms. Dunbar?" Roark asks. "You want to say something?"

"Eva's afraid of being alone. And when Dudley goes out of town, she's extra cautious. She told me a man follows her in a white van whenever Dudley's out of town."

"Did she recognize the person following her?" Roark says.

"Only that he was around retirement age, chubby and balding."

Roark raises her eyebrows at McGraw. He smiles, nods, and turns back to Dunbar.

"Anything else you can think of?" he says.

"A couple of things: Laura Cook told me once about a guy who comes into the bank quite often. He tried several times to flirt with Eva. She wouldn't give him the time of the day, and one time he got really mad at her. Someone had to pull him off."

"Know his name?" McGraw says.

She shakes her head. "No... I don't know if Laura ever told me. But the other girls would know."

"Anything else you can think of?"

"The week before Eva disappeared; she called me about another man following her on the way to her car after work. And two days before she disappeared, he was there again. This time, Eva rushed to her car and hopped in and locked all the doors. He tapped on her window and told her the back tire was flat. She raced out of the parking lot and stopped at the first service station she saw. None of the tires was flat."

"Interesting," McGraw says.

"Needless to say, she was traumatized."

"Could the guy have been the same one that followed her in the van?" Roark says.

She shakes her head again. "No. He was younger, taller and muscular."

Could he be the one that harassed her in the bank? McGraw thinks. *Hopefully she reported it to the police.*

"Did she say if she had reported the incident to the police?" McGraw says.

"I don't know." She pauses for a moment, appearing to be bothered about something.

"What is it, Ms. Dunbar?" Roark says.

"I knew Eva often overreacted when Dudley went out of town, but the time that guy followed her to her car she said something very unusual."

"What was that," McGraw says.

"She said, 'You may never see me again.' I thought that was creepy and she was overreacting." Dunbar glances at the floor then looks up. "Oh my god, you don't think her premonition came true, do you?"

McGraw doesn't respond, so Roark takes over. "I think what you've done, organizing volunteers to find Eva, is so wonderful," she says, apparently trying to raise Dunbar's spirits.

"Thank you," Dunbar says. "Many of those people you saw out at that site are Eva's friends. They've been handing out fliers and posting them all over the place. The police helicopters have really been supportive, and we're all doing all we can for Eva."

"Please let us know if anything else turns up," McGraw says.

"You'll be the first to know, lieutenant," she says.

McGraw gets up and thanks her. Roark escorts her out. When Roark returns, McGraw grabs his hat and goes to the door.

"Where to?" she asks.

"Mr. Joyce."

"I figured as much."

Thirty minutes later, Roark pulls the cruiser into the driveway of Colin Joyce's home. McGraw rolls out on the passenger side and waits for her. They make their way to the door. Mr. Joyce opens it and recognizes Roark. He smiles.

"This is my partner, Lieutenant McGraw," she says. "We'd like to ask you a few more questions, if that's all right."

"Please come in," he says. They follow him into his study, which is in the front part of the house, filled with books, a gleaming desk, two cloth chairs, a couch against the wall and a credenza behind the desk bearing family pictures. McGraw and Roark move to the cloth chairs and sit, while Joyce pulls his chair round the desk and sits facing them.

"Can I get you something to drink?"

They thank him, but decline.

Joyce sits with his hands in his lap. He has a pale round face, sad eyes, and hair only on the sides of his head. His feet barely touch the floor and his waist is about a 44, and he is dressed in a clean white shirt and brown trousers.

"How can I help you?" he says.

"Do you own a white van, Mr. Joyce?" McGraw says.

"No, I don't." His pupils begin to dilate and he fidgets in his chair.

"Have you ever rented one?" Roark says.

He takes his time answering, looks at a picture on the wall, and crosses his legs. "I'm trying to think. I do remember renting such a van."

"How long ago was it?" McGraw asks. "You know, sir, we can check the rental places, but we thought we'd give you a chance to explain before taking you to the station."

"To the station? What for? And to explain what? I haven't done anything."

"Why were you following Ms. Hamilton the week she disappeared?" Roark says.

"Do I need an attorney?"

"Depends," McGraw says, "on what you've done."

Joyce stands and moves to the window facing the street. After a few seconds, he says, "I'm sorry. I haven't been up front with you. I did rent the white van to follow Ms. Hamilton. But I didn't harm her or whatever you think I might have done. Mr. Hamilton hires me to keep an eye on her, without her knowing, of course, whenever he's out of town."

"So, you've followed her on more than one occasion?" Roark says.

He nods while he focuses on the UPS truck that passes by. He sighs, turns back and sets his sight on Roark. "Yes, three times."

"Why do you think he hired you?" she says.

"He told me Ms. Hamilton is afraid of her own shadow and gets very paranoid when he's out of town."

"If he hired you as a bodyguard, why didn't he want Ms. Hamilton to know?" McGraw asks. "It seems she would have felt more secure."

He shrugs. "I don't know. Mr. Hamilton is hard to figure out sometimes. He'd give me strict orders not to let her see me." He returns to his chair.

"Seems to me she'd be more frightened if she saw you in the van following her around," Roark says.

"That's what I thought, so I made sure she never saw me."

"We'll she did and so did your neighbors, Mr. Joyce," McGraw says.

Joyce's brow rises and his eyes widen. "They did?"

"Are you telling us you don't know why Mr. Hamilton had you following her? Being afraid doesn't seem to be the whole package," Roark says.

"Did he ever mention that someone might be out to harm her?" McGraw says.

"Maybe Ms. Hamilton got a threatening letter," Roark says.

He raises his hands. "You've got to believe me, detectives, please. I know nothing about Mr. Hamilton's motives. All I did was keep an eye on her and I'd report to Mr. Hamilton on his cell phone from time to time. Like you said, maybe he thought someone was going to hurt her, but I didn't know. He never told me."

"You never thought to ask?" McGraw says.

He glances at the floor. "It was none of my business. He paid well and I kept my mouth shut. Do I need that attorney?"

McGraw shakes his head. "Not at the moment."

They rise and Joyce ushers them to the door.

Outside, Roark says to McGraw, "I wouldn't put it past Dudley being more worried about harm coming to the Lexus than his wife."

McGraw nods. "Good point."

CHAPTER THIRTEEN

Armed with a search warrant, McGraw and Roark drive to Dudley Hamilton's home with Kramer and Gomez in the cruiser behind them. Dudley, with his attorney behind him, meets them at the door. McGraw shoves the paper into his chest. "This is a warrant," he says pushing his way past the two men.

Dudley grunts and hands it to his attorney.

McGraw instructs Kramer and Gomez to search everything on the first floor while he and Roark climb the stairs. Roark takes the bathroom and McGraw walks into the bedroom, looks under the bed, then runs his arms under the mattress from the foot to the head on both sides. He finds a couple of girly magazines on the side of the bed that he thinks is Dudley's. He opens the door to a walk-in closet and examines Eva's clothes, hung carefully on both sides. About two dozen pairs of shoes are arranged neatly on the floor against the walls. Boxes on the top shelf contain photographs, which McGraw takes to the bed and sorts through. He removes one of Eva taken with an older couple that could be her parents and another with girls and boys of high school age. He slips them into his coat pocket. *Could be old boyfriends and girlfriends*, he thinks. He returns the boxes to the closet and goes through the sweaters and blouses on the shelves. Under a stack of sweaters he finds a small notebook. He opens it. Eva had made only a few entries about personal things; particularly, about Dudley.

Roark comes into the room. "Where are you?"

"In the closet," he says, holding a small black notebook open in his hands.

"Whadda you have there?"

"A notebook," he says. "Not too much in it. Eva writes that she's not happy in her marriage, but nothing more. Apparently stopped entries after their relationship improved."

"Probably her way of releasing her frustrations," Roark says. "She certainly didn't like talking about their marriage to her friends, that's for sure."

Roark holds up a bag. "I've bagged Eva's toothbrush and hairbrush and a few strands of hair from Dudley's hairbrush for DNA."

McGraw nods.

Roark goes to the side of the bed and rummages through the two drawers in one night table while McGraw inspects one on the other side. Roark finds body lotion, manicure set, tissue, a mask to cover the eyes, and a few bank magazines. "Not much in here," Roark says, "just girly things. You ready to go down?"

"One more closet,' he says. McGraw opens the door and goes in. Nothing out of the ordinary, just suits lined up against the wall and a dozen or so pairs of shoes on the floor. On the top shelf are hat boxes and a few folded sweaters and shirts.

"Now I'm ready," McGraw says.

Downstairs, Dudley is drinking tea with his attorney. "Everything okay, detectives?" he says.

"We'll need Eva's cell phones records, gas and credit card statements, Mr. Hamilton," Roark says.

Dudley looks at his attorney. Before he could speak, Roark says, "As your attorney can attest, the warrant covers everything."

The attorney nods and Dudley leaves the room. McGraw and Roark talk with Kramer and Gomez, who found nothing. Dudley comes out of his home office with a shoebox and hands it to McGraw without saying a word.

McGraw turns and says to the attorney, "Your client was considering our request for a lie detector test. Has a decision been reached?"

"Mr. Hamilton will cooperate," attorney says.

"Good," he says. "We'll call and set it up."

"We'd like to take a DNA sample. It's in the warrant," Roark says.

The attorney nods his approval.

Roark removes the swab from a glass tube, scrapes the inside of Dudley's mouth several times, and places it back into the tube.

"Thank you for your cooperation. We'll be in touch," McGraw says as they leave.

Outside, Kramer mentions that following Dudley Hamilton around for the last few days was like following an elderly man around. "He's dull as hell and does the same thing over and over. He must have the obsessive compulsive disorder."

Gomez adds. "He's a weakling. He wouldn't have the guts to kill his wife. Having someone else do it would be more his style."

"We've ruled that out for now," McGraw says.

Once inside the cruiser, Roark says to McGraw. "Man, did you see that look Dudley gave me? He's taken to you, McGraw, but he hates me."

McGraw smiles, and touches the brim of his Stetson. "Don't you know that I'm liked by everyone, Roark?"

"So, now you're narcissistic, too?"

They laugh.

2

He reaches in his pocket and hands the photos to her.

"What are these?" she says.

"I think one is a picture of Eva and her parents, and in the other she's with some teenagers, could be high school graduation."

"They're definitely high school age," she says.

"Two guys and two gals," he says.

"Eva's the one in the middle. She hasn't changed much from the latest pictures we have of her," Roark says. "Look at the kid with the cowboy hat. You and he would get along, McGraw. Wonder who these other kids are?"

"Transmit them to the sheriff in Oklahoma," McGraw says. "Let's see what he comes up with."

CHAPTER FOURTEEN

Back at their desks, McGraw receives a call from forensics. The tire tracks at the site north of the mall were from a stolen black Ford pickup that belonged to Mahoney's Construction Company. The truck was found in a ditch close to the company with a few streaks of white paint on the right front fender. Samples taken from the fender match the paint on Eva Hamilton's white Lexus.

"Thank you," McGraw tells Alan. He swivels his chair and tells Roark.

"Just as we thought," she says.

Kramer walks through the squad room escorting Laura Cook, Tammy Ingram and Karen Harvey from Citizens Bank into the conference room, waiting to be placed in separate interview rooms.

"I'll take Laura Cook in one," McGraw says, "and Roark, you interview Tammy Ingram in two. Kramer, where's Gomez?"

"He's got a sick kid. Called in and won't be in for another hour or so."

"Okay, you take Karen Harvey into three. When you guys finish bring them into the squad room and wait for me. Maybe Gomez will come by then."

The detectives nod.

McGraw stops by the monitor before entering number one to study Laura Cook. The rooms are just large enough for three chairs and a table, designed so those being questioned can't get too comfortable. She is in the chair facing the table, her legs crossed, pumping one foot in the air and staring around the room. She takes a bottle of water out of the side pocket of her purse on the floor, takes several swallows and places it back in its slot.

She's well-groomed, has shoulder-length auburn hair, red nails and an attractive body dressed in a red dress cut low in front and much above her knees. Nice looking legs.

McGraw enters the room with a tape recorder, pen and yellow legal pad, takes a seat in the chair facing her. "Thanks for coming," he says. "Appreciate your cooperation."

"Glad to help," she says, smiling and eyeing him more closely than he thought necessary, still kicking her foot forward. *She's got too much lipstick on*, he thinks. He sets the recorder on the table and presses the button. "Do you mind?" he says.

"Not at all," she says, staring at his boots.

He states his name, then Laura's full name, and the time and date of the interview.

"We would like to ascertain if Eva Hamilton ever talked about her high school friends from Perry, Oklahoma?"

Laura shook her head and frowned. "We know nothing about her high school days, lieutenant, except Olivia Jordan, Eva's high school friend from back there. Eva lived with her for a year or more here in Atlanta until Olivia moved to New York. Then Eva came to live with us."

McGraw nodded. "Do you know where Eva and Olivia worked for the time they were together?"

"Olivia worked for April Dawn, a designer of women's clothes. April's place is a high-class women's store, and Olivia didn't mind bragging about her work and was quite proud of what she was learning from April. I guess she felt she learned all she could and took off to New York."

McGraw makes a few notes on his pad.

Laura continues. "Eva had a job with the Red Cross downtown working with children. She liked little ones. That's about all I know."

"Did she have any men friends?"

"She did go out a few times with a guy we thought could have been an old high school flame, but we never saw him and she never talked about him. She wasn't one to go out much and when she did, she never brought her dates around the place, except after she got serious with Dudley. We got our fill of him."

"From your tone, it sounds like you don't like Dudley."

"No."

"How about Ms. Ingram and Ms. Harvey?" he says. "What are their feelings toward him?"

"None of us like him. Dudley's rich and he doesn't mind letting you know about it. He really liked to talk about himself and show off his Rolex and fancy suits," she says with contempt in her voice. She pauses to reach for her bottle of water and takes a drink. "Dudley thinks us girls are stupid. He was mean to Eva, putting her down in front of us. He acts like she isn't good enough for him, but we think she's too damn good for him."

"Do you know if they fought?" McGraw says. "Do you think he would hit her?"

She shakes her head. "Nothing other than being verbally abusive. I don't think he'd ever harm her. To be honest, we didn't know what she saw in the guy, and some of us were tempted not to go to her wedding, but we just couldn't stay away. Eva's too sweet of a person."

"Please review what you told us about Eva's relationships with the other workers when Detective Roark and I met with you at the bank. Don't leave anything out, even if you feel it's insignificant." McGraw wanted to know if Laura and the girls had held anything back in front of their boss, Austin Payne.

Laura takes her time answering. "Eva got along good with everyone." She pauses again, and takes a sip of her water. "Except two men we didn't mention in front of Mr. Payne, because they have dealings with him. They'd come through our lobby a couple times a month to go to the second floor, but would meet with Mr. Payne before heading upstairs."

"What kind of dealings?"

She glances around the room before answering. "We have our suspicions."

"Go on."

"Rumors have floated around from the first day I started working there."

"What kind of rumors?"

"That Mr. Payne and these guys are involved in something, we don't know what it is, and then there's that employment office on the second floor. Rumor has it..." she hesitates, and then says, "that office on the second floor is used as an escort service."

"Men or women?"

"Women," she says. "We don't know for sure, but we believe they're prostitutes."

"Have you seen them?"

"Oh, yes. We seen them walking out with guys all the time. Even the two guys that are friends with Mr. Payne."

"What are their names?"

"The muscular guy is Dexter Price and the shorter, thin guy is Trevor Wilson.

"Are they always with the same women?"

"No."

"Did you ever see Mr. Payne with any of the girls?"

"Oh, I'd rather not say."

"It would be helpful to our investigation."

She unscrews the cap on the water bottle again and takes a drink, then replaces the cap. "Yes, I've seen him."

"So, he doesn't hide it?"

She shakes her head. "We've seen him coming out of a club with one of the women from the second floor."

"What else goes on in the bank?"

"That fellow Dexter, he tried several times to put the make on Eva." Laura turns away, her face flushes. "Oh, I'm sorry. I should have said he flirted with her. Anyway, she wouldn't give him the time of day. Once he got so mad at her for not showing him any attention that Trevor had to pull him away from Eva's desk. I thought he was going to sock her." She sighs. "Now Dexter's flirting with that new gal Austin hired as Eva's replacement. I think they're going out together."

"What's her name?" McGraw asks after he makes a notation.

"Her name is Bonnie Richards. She's a sexy blond who wears tight clothes and high heels, and is drawing lots of attention." She shook her head. "She dresses more like a cocktail waitress than a secretary. We think she's a snitch, tells Austin all that goes on in the office. We watch our p's and q's around her, if you know what I mean. None of us girls like her."

McGraw makes a few more notes. "Anything more you can add?"

She nods and looks around the room as if she's afraid someone will hear her. "Tammy, Karen and I have seen Mr. Payne in Santino's restaurant with Dexter and Trevor and a big Italian that could pass for Tony Soprano. His name is Johnny Parino. We eat there a couple of times a month and we see them about half the time." She pauses. "You ever eat there?"

McGraw shakes his head.

"The place is a hoot. Just like a speakeasy. It's like going back into the twenties."

"Notice anything unusual that they do there?"

"Every time we've seen Austin there, he leaves with a large briefcase. More like a suitcase."

"Does he bring it into the bank?"

"Naw, he takes it into his office late at night."

"How do you know that?"

"We girls go to a club in Prestige Mall on ladies' night for drinks and dancing, and usually don't leave until after eleven. On several occasions, we've seen him taking the suitcase from his car into the bank around that time."

"I see. Did you ever see Johnny Parino at any other place besides the restaurant? I mean, particularly at the bank?"

"Never."

"Anything else about Parino that could help us?"

"I know he has a chauffeur who drives a beautiful, black stretch Lincoln."

"Do you know his name?"

"Brad Knox. He picks up Johnny and takes him places. Parino owns the joint. Us girls think he's Mafia, and know he's Brad's boss. We…" She doesn't finish her sentence.

"Go on, please. You were going to say."

"Well, I was going to say, we kinda feel like old Brad's boss may be involved in prostitution, too."

"Why is that?"

"The other girls and me have seen Brad transporting girls around town. Sometimes there's a big guy riding along with him. He sits in the front."

"Do you know the guy's name?"

"Sorry."

"Did you ever see them in any drug deals going on around the restaurant or anywhere else?"

She shakes her head. "No. Most of the time, Brad and this guy are parked in the limo when we go in Santino's, and they're gone when we come out. We've heard they also use the limo to attract women in the bars."

Speculation, McGraw thinks. He reaches into his pocket and hands Laura his card. "If you think of anything else, or if you see Mr. Payne and his friends together at Santino's, or this Brad fellow and the big guy driving around with women, would you give me a call?"

She reaches for the card. "We kinda quit going to Santino's, lieutenant. We're afraid Austin will see us and who knows what."

McGraw stands. "I understand. I believe that'll do for now." He shuts off the recorder.

She rises and follows him out. They walk down the hall to the squad room where the others are waiting. Gomez has arrived and is drinking coffee from a Braves cup.

McGraw tells the gals he'd appreciate a call from them the next time Dexter and Trevor appear at the bank. The girls nod and say they will.

"Okay, then. That'll be all for now," McGraw says.

Roark motions for the ladies to follow her and she ushers them out the door and down the hall. On the way to the exit, Roark notices Laura Cook is staying behind a little and waits until the other girls leave the building. "Anything I can do for you, Ms. Cook?" Roark asks.

"I was just wondering. Is Detective McGraw married?"

"Why do you ask?"

"I didn't see any wedding band and, well, just wondering about a wife or if he's seeing anyone."

"He's not married now, but he is seeing someone and they're pretty thick." Roark doesn't know why she said that, or perhaps she does.

"Oh," she says, "too bad. I've never been with a cowboy before. He's quite the hunk."

Yes he is. And the cowboy's all mine. When Roark returns to the squad room, she plops in her seat. *McGraw, you're mine.*

"Is something bothering you, sergeant?" McGraw says, standing in front of the evidence board with Kramer and Gomez, who are gazing at her.

"Nothing, everything's fine."

"Let's see what we've learned from the girls," McGraw says. He starts off by telling them everything that he and Laura Cook covered. He then asked each member of his team to cover what they learned from the other girls.

When they finished, McGraw turns to the evidence board next to his desk and writes—Austin Payne, Dexter Price and Trevor Wilson. "This trio," he says, pointing at them, but says nothing more.

"Yeah, Dex and Trev are pals with Payne," Roark says.

Kramer says, "Also, they're seen in the bank and with Payne at Santino's talking to Johnny Parino—"

"—And don't forget that Payne leaves with a suitcase," Gomez says.

"What does all this tell us?" McGraw says.

"These guys are involved in drug money taken out of Santino's in a suitcase,"

Kramer says.

Roark jumps up and walks over to the board. "Money laundering," she says. "Payne is taking the Mafia guy's drug money into his bank and laundering it."

Kramer nods in agreement.

"Good thinking, everyone," McGraw says. "Payne's inserting dirty money into his bank and depositing money into other banks and making bank transfers to offshore accounts. These two guys," he says, pointing to Dex and Trev, "they're the ones making the bank deposits."

"Maybe Ms. Hamilton found out about Payne and his boys and he got rid of her," Gomez says.

"Let's not forget the flowers that Eva received," Roark says. "Payne could have sent them and made those phone calls."

McGraw shakes his head. "Not Payne."

"You thinking Dex and Trev?" she says.

"Dex went into a rage when Eva Hamilton resisted his advances. He apparently can be violent," McGraw says. He turns to Gomez, who is back at his desk.

"What did you guys find on the flowers sent to Eva Hamilton?" he says.

"All the florist could remember was a girl about sixteen came for the flowers and paid cash. I'm running Dexter Price and Trevor Wilson through the computer, boss," Gomez says.

"While you're at it, see if Ms. Hamilton filed a police report on a guy who followed her to her car one evening after work. He claimed she had a flat, but she didn't. It happened in the week of her disappearance."

"He could be our perp," Kramer says.

"Boss, nothing in the NCIC or state, but you won't believe this. Local records show Dexter Price and Trevor Wilson are one of us. They're cops in the Fourth," Gomez says.

Silence blankets the squad room.

"Damn, they're dirty cops," Kramer says.

"When we get the call that they're in the bank, I want you two to follow them and shoot me some pictures."

"Will do, lieutenant," Kramer says.

"Gomez, run Johnny Parino." McGraw says.

"Ms. Hamilton didn't file a police report, boss," Gomez says. "I'm running Parino now."

"Oh, oh, here comes Mr. Hamilton," Kramer says.

"He's here for the lie detector test," McGraw says. "Roark, show him to the room."

McGraw moves to Gomez's desk.

"Parino's got a rap sheet a mile long, boss."

"How about in the last five years?" McGraw says.

"Let's see... he was arrested five years ago for running a prostitution ring. Fined $5000 and released. Four years ago, he was hauled in on drug trafficking. Paid a fine of $4000 and let go. Arrested for arms possession three years ago, charges dropped. No fine. Two years ago, Parino was brought in on a suspected murder charge. Interrogated, but cops had no evidence to tie him to the crime and they let him go." Gomez looks up at McGraw. "I think Parino has someone in his back pocket."

CHAPTER FIFTEEN

McGraw enters the squad room around noon after visiting with Zee and finds on his desk a report on Eva Hamilton along with her phone records. Kramer's note is attached. McGraw begins thumbing through the pages. Minutes later, his phone rings. "McGraw, we need to talk and now," Capt. says.

Roark is passing through the aisle and frowns as she watches her partner walking and pointing toward the Lion's den, the name his team gave the Capt.'s office. She sits at her desk, lifts the phone and places a call to Oklahoma.

"Sheriff, this is Sergeant Holly Roark with the Atlanta PD, Homicide."

"Atlanta? Well, I'm honored, sergeant. What can I do for you?"

"We're investigating the disappearance of Eva Bingham Hamilton and would like your help with some background information on her. We've learned she was born and raised in Perry, Oklahoma."

No immediate response on the other end, but a woman talking in the background is audible. Finally, the sheriff says, "How long has Eva Bingham—she was a Bingham when living here—been missing?"

"Several days now, sir."

"Why is homicide on it?"

Roark is surprised at the question. *This guy is sharp.* "Eva married into the Hamiltons, one of Atlanta's wealthiest banking families."

"Someone called in the big boys on a highfalutin' case, huh?"

"We call 'em high-profile cases, sir."

"Here in Oklahoma, we call 'em like we see 'em." He pauses. It sounds like he's sipping a drink of sorts. "It appears a lot has gone on in Eva's life since she left little old Perry."

"Like to learn all I can about her, sheriff."

"Sinclair, ma'am, that's my name. Tom Sinclair."

"Yes, sir, Sheriff Sinclair.

"By the way," he says. "Atlanta? You wouldn't happen to know detective

70

Noah McGraw, would you? I knew his dad Weldon. He told me Noah's quite the investigator and is supposed to have been in Maryland, and the last I heard he was in Atlanta."

Roark almost falls out of her chair. "I can't believe this, Sheriff Sinclair. Lieutenant McGraw is my partner, but he's not here at the moment."

"Well, you tell him that his daddy and I used to ride across country together on our Harleys. But I'm sure he knows that."

Oh, no, not another one of those biker junkies, she thinks.

"Weldon and I rode with some of my sheriff buddies. We'd hook up in Oklahoma City off I-40, and head out to the east coast every summer. Just tell McGraw that Tom Sinclair says hi."

"Will do, sir."

"Getting back to Eva," Sinclair says. "She was raised in a good family. Both parents are dead. Her father was president of Statewide Bank. Eva was very close to him. Fifteen when he died. All she talked about after his passing was getting out of Dodge. She and her mother never got along, sergeant."

"Did Eva have any serious boyfriends?" Roark asks.

"Sure did. Name's Cody Guthrie. His daddy owned a plumbing shop and did pretty good until Cody got his hands into it after his daddy died. Cody was a good plumber, but a lousy businessman."

"Is he still in Perry?"

"Naw, he took off after his business tanked, couldn't stand the gossip. Around here folks can be pretty hard on you. Word has it that he did a lot of drinking and didn't pay his bills."

"How long ago did he leave Perry?" she says.

"Oh, I'd say a few months, can't really be sure. One day he's here and then he's not."

"Did Eva and Cody get along okay?" she asks.

"They kinda broke up after high school. I guess he wasn't her type."

"What would be her type, Sheriff Sinclair?"

"Oh, let's see. I'd say Cody was closest to the kinda guy she'd like, easy-going and down-to-earth. That's why I was surprised they split. But she wanted more, to try to better herself. I guess she did, according to you."

Roark wonders if Cody would follow Eva to Atlanta. "Is it possible that he went looking for Eva?"

"I'd bet my bottom dollar on that, all right. Don't believe he ever got over her. He never went with anyone after she left."

"Anything else you can tell me about them or her other friends?"

"I can't think of anything right off, except that she only had one other friend. Her name was Olivia Jordan. Last I heard from her grandmother, Olivia was in New York somewhere."

"I see. Perhaps you can help me with one other thing, Sheriff Sinclair. I have a couple of pictures we took from Eva's home. I'd like to transmit them to you to see if you can identify the kids in them? One has four teenagers in it. I imagine they're high school friends of Eva, since she is recognizable in the

71

center of the picture. One boy is wearing a cowboy hat."

"That'd be Cody Guthrie. He never left home without it, and he was her sweetie."

Sweetie? Hmm. She pauses for a moment, wondering what all that shouting is about coming from the Lion's den.

"The other boy is standing at the end, but he's difficult to make out. The picture isn't the best. In the second one, Eva's between two middle-aged people who I'm thinking are her parents."

"Send them on. I'll give you my number." Roark writes it down and thanks the sheriff and hangs up. She immediately goes to the counter against the wall and transmits the photos to Sinclair. On her way to the crime board, she posts the two pictures. McGraw comes out of the Capt.'s office, stops at the coffee stand.

"What was all that shouting about in there?" Roark asks as she returns to her desk.

McGraw shakes his head in disgust. "Capt. was chewing on me for the way I'm handling the investigation. Dudley's mommy called the commish and said I was rude and disrespectful to them. She wanted me off the case." McGraw swallows some of his coffee, sets the cup on his desk and sits.

"What else is new?" Roark says. "That's not the first time, and it won't be the last."

McGraw doesn't respond. Instead, he opens a report that was placed on his desk.

"So, what did he decide?"

"I am to carry on, but to be nicer. I'll have to work on being a nice guy," he says with a wry smile.

"Why am I not surprised he tried to drill you a new one?" she says. "Capt. should know by now that threatening you won't work. He'd never take you off this or any other case. You're too damn good and he knows it. He's doing it mostly for show so he can tell the commish that he read you the riot act."

"Thanks for the vote of confidence. What are you working on?" he says to change the subject.

"I just transmitted the photos we took from Dudley's to the Sheriff in Perry. He says the kid in the cowboy hat is Cody Guthrie, Eva's high school sweetheart, and he could be here in Atlanta."

"Guthrie here?"

"He thinks so."

"Then that'll make your job easier to find him."

She nods and holds up a couple of sheets of paper. "These are my notes from my conversation with the sheriff on Eva Hamilton. But first, I've got something to tell you."

He frowns. "What's that?"

"Do you know the name Tom Sinclair?"

"Is he the sheriff there?"

She nods. "Did he really ride with your dad?"

He nods. "Every summer."

"He said your dad 'went on about you' and that the last Sinclair heard you were with the Maryland State Police and then ended up in Atlanta. I nearly fell out of my chair when he asked if I knew ya."

McGraw smiled. "Dad and he were big buddies. They rode across country, hooked up with other sheriffs Sinclair knew."

"Lieutenant, did you read my report?" Kramer shouts, as he gathers up papers from his desk and hurries to McGraw, with Gomez in his wake.

"Got it," McGraw says holding it up.

Kramer spreads sheets of paper out on McGraw's desk. "I found something in Eva Hamilton's cell phone records. There's a number that appears five times. They were placed a week before she disappeared from a throwaway cell with no GPS system."

McGraw shakes his head. "This is becoming quite the thing these days," he says, "anonymous cell phones."

"Better get used to it, boss," Gomez says, "the bad guys are getting smarter."

McGraw checks the dates of the calls. They match the timeline.

"The caller could be our perp, making these calls to Eva Hamilton after sending her roses."

"That's not all," Kramer says, "you won't believe this, but the vic used her gas credit card hours after she disappeared."

Roark jumps up. "What?" She huddles round the desk with the other detectives.

"Yeah," Kramer says. "Look at the dates and times on these receipts. She made purchases five hours after leaving Prestige parking lot around eight."

McGraw is scrutinizing the calls, sliding his finger down each one and stops. "This one," he says, "shows she charged gas at a 24-hour ExxonMobil station in Charlotte at one a.m. the next morning. You're right. That's five hours after she was last seen."

"Charlotte is 200 miles from here," Roark says.

"It doesn't take five hours to drive 200 miles," Kramer says.

"So what did they do part of the time?" Gomez says.

"We have to factor in the abduction scene," Roark says.

"And she could have been held some place for a period of time to break her," McGraw says.

"That's not all, lieutenant," Kramer says. "She signed another ExxonMobil receipt in Raleigh the next afternoon around 2 p.m. That would be Friday, thirteen hours later. Raleigh is about two and a half hours east of Charlotte."

Roark shakes her head. "That's strange," she says. "Eva signs for gas in a town five hours away after leaving here, then the next afternoon they get gas again at another station only a little over two hours away, which means she is still alive 18 hours after being last seen driving out of Prestige. What the hell did they do all that time?"

"Obviously, they didn't need a full tank to go from Charlotte to Raleigh," McGraw says.

"They're no more charges after that," Gomez says.

"Don't forget, her Lexus was brought back around noon the next day, a Friday," McGraw says, "sixteen hours after she pulls out of the mall."

Roark regards McGraw. "You've got that frown again. What is it?"

"Either Eva Hamilton has a lover who paid Eaton Banks to return her car before they took off to God knows where, or there's a guy who abducted her, left her car for Banks to return, drove Eva to North Carolina, and made credit card charges to make us think she ran off with him. My bet, he's got her hidden someplace."

"Why would the perp hide her? What would be his motive?" she says.

"To keep her for himself," McGraw says. "Sociopaths get a thrill out of keeping their victims under their control and making them succumb to their every wish."

"That means she could still be alive," Roark says."

McGraw reaches for the phone, places calls to his contacts at the Charlotte and Raleigh PDs, tells them about the receipts from the Exxon stations in their towns, and adds, "We'll be coming into your area to talk with the Exxon clerks about the missing woman, Eva Hamilton." He gives them the dates she was in their area, and asks them to pick up the surveillance videos from each gas station for those days.

When he finishes reviewing Eva's phone records and receipts a second time, McGraw looks at his watch, grabs his hat and says to Roark. "Call me on my cell when the detectives from Charlotte and Raleigh call back. I'll be at home."

She nods without looking up.

———— • ————

McGraw arrives at the Circle M a little before sunset, goes into his room, throws his hat on the bed, hangs his jacket on the hook behind the door, removes his shoulder holster and sets it on the top of the chest of drawers. He touches the face of Lee Ann in the gold-frame picture as he does every morning and night and says "I love you," then goes out to the heated wrap-around porch and settles into his favorite chair next to the cushioned couch with a small table on his right. He props his feet on a stool, leans back, and watches the sun ball sink into the horizon.

Light shoots from afar through the heavenly clouds, forming an image of Lee Ann Weaver McGraw, the wife he buried back in Texas close to his dad. When she died, it felt like someone ripped his heart out. She made him promise to remarry if he found someone. *Why would she say something like that?* He only loved her. They were supposed to live together for sixty years and have children and grandchildren and great-grandchildren. That's what they talked about. She wasn't supposed to leave him. His marriage vows were his life. He lived them for Lee Ann. He stood in front of the preacher and said he would take care of her, and he did for one year before she died. They wanted a child. Two months pregnant, she became very sick with the cancer and miscarried. He lost someone he never knew.

McGraw's father wasn't supposed to leave him, either. Noah grew up with great respect for him. Losing two loves weighs heavily on Noah at times, but he feels fortunate to still have his mother, sweet Anna Marie, and he thanks God for her.

Annie Marie comes in and rouses him from his reverie, placing a glass of iced tea on the table, kissing him on the forehead as she sits on the couch next to him and places her hands in her lap, as she does most nights. Her eyes tell him she knows what he's thinking. "Thinking about Lee Ann, son?"

"Yeah, maw," he says, drinking his tea.

"Wish I could do something to ease your pain," she says, rubbing her hands. They sit quietly watching the squirrel climb up the oak tree. Noah knows what she's going to say next. "Isn't it time you move on, Noah? Lee Ann would want that," she says, as she rises and goes into the house.

He nods. "I know, maw. Doc says someday I'll find happiness again."

He finishes his tea. His cell vibrates and he answers it. It's Kramer; he reports that the video cameras in the Exxon stations were dummies.

"Damn."

CHAPTER SIXTEEN

The next morning, Captain Dipple flies out of his office. "McGraw?" he shouts, voice booms throughout the pit. "Got a call from the M.E. Two fishermen found a woman's body at the edge of Beaver Lake north of here." He stops between McGraw and Roark's desk. "You guys get down there and find out if it's our vic. I'm hoping the damn hell it isn't her."

They take off for the door, hitting the steps on the run, heading to the lower level.

Roark is first through the sliding glass doors to the M.E.'s floor. "Can't ever get used to the smell down here," she says. "I know, you always said I would, but I don't believe I ever will."

"Best not to think about anything in this place."

"You're right."

They enter a room filled with steel tables, wall freezers and large sinks against white walls that look sterile. The M.E., Dr. Nora Philips, is standing next to one of the steel tables, in white coveralls, working on a body. Philips is in her late thirties, has hair the color of a walnut, cut close to her pretty doll face, slender body. McGraw thinks she's motivated to stay healthy because she doesn't want to end up on one of her postmortem tables. He doesn't know how she keeps her positive attitude in this line of work.

Philips glances up as the detectives approach the table. A naked female body stitched from the chest down to her pubic area is on the metal table. Philips smiles, nods, and says, "lieutenant." McGraw nods and moves with Roark to the opposite side, facing her.

"What do you have, doc?" he says.

She glances at Roark before answering. "How are you doing sergeant?"

"I'm good," Roark says. "Thanks for asking."

McGraw shudders when Roark uses the adjective, good. "Well," he says in a whisper, which the girls hear. "Never ever say, 'good' when asked how you are doing."

Roark looks at him. "I know," she says, "it just slipped out."

"Is this Harvard guy correcting your grammar again?" Philips says.

"Always," Roark says. "Isn't it a shame that we all didn't go to Harvard."

"Smartass, I'd say. How can you stand working with him?"

"It's not so bad, doc, if you pretend he's not around."

"That's really funny," McGraw says without joining in on the laughter. "Guess I asked for it," he says. "Can we get back to the vic?"

"What you see here is a female between 30 and 40 years of age. I'd say she's been in the water for a couple of weeks." M.E. bends over the vic's head. "Hard to make out the face," she says, "the fish and turtles have done their dirty work on the body. She has blunt force trauma to the back of the head, meaning she was hit with a blunt instrument and dumped in the lake after someone beat her to death. There is no water in the lungs. Don't know where the crime scene was, and it's difficult to say if some of these marks are defensive wounds or all fish and turtle bites."

"Poor thing," Roark says.

Philips looks up. "I concur."

"Can you tell if this person is black or white," McGraw asks.

The ME pulls the overhead lamp down lower, and increases the illumination.

"She's black, McGraw," Philips says.

He shakes his head. "Eva Hamilton is white, so this is not our vic," he says.

Roark frowns, maybe because she hasn't heard the ME call him McGraw before.

Around seven that evening, McGraw's walking to his truck in the parking lot and spots Nora Philips near her car. She waves. "Hard day, lieutenant?" she says.

"No more than usual," he says.

"Maybe you need to relax. Care to walk over to Tony's and have one for the road?"

McGraw thinks about what his mother had said to him the evening before. It may be time to see how it feels to be with another woman, and McGraw heads over to Philips and says, "Lead the way."

CHAPTER SEVENTEEN

Dudley Hamilton is at his desk in one of the family's bank branches, reviewing the loan made to a customer who has just left. The phone rings and the male's voice on the other end is harsh and confrontational. He has Eva and if Dudley wants her back alive, he must deliver one mil in hundreds at a location to be given later.

A mil? Hell no! She isn't worth it, he thinks. *This's gotta be a scammer.*

"How do I know you have my wife, or if she's even alive?" he says. "You could be some crackpot that read about her in the newspapers."

Silence on the other end. Dudley wonders what this guy looks like. Then says, "I'm not paying you one damned cent until I talk to her." He can hear heavy breathing in the phone.

"Oh, I have her, all right." He hangs up.

Dudley wonders if this guy is for real. He can only wait for his next call.

————◆————

"Homicide, this is Detective Gomez."

"This is Dudley Hamilton. I need to talk to Lieutenant McGraw."

"He's out of the office, won't be back for a while. Can I take a message?"

"Is that woman cop there?" Dudley asks.

Roark's desk is two in front of him, and he calls out, "Roark. You want to take this one from the vic's husband? He wanted to talk to the boss, but asked for 'that woman cop' when I told him the boss was out."

"'Whadda you mean 'that woman cop'? Thanks a lot, Gomez."

"This is Sergeant Roark, 'that woman cop.'"

Dudley is oblivious to the sarcasm in her voice, or doesn't care. He begins telling her about the caller and the ransom money.

She knows the perp disguised his voice, but she has to ask. "Did you recognize his voice?"

"No, it sounded muffled. He did call back, however, but only allowed me to listen to her voice. I believe it was taped. When I tried to talk to her, he hung up on me."

Man, what's up with you? Roark thinks. *You never call your wife by her given name.* "Did he say anything about a drop?" Roark asks.

"He's calling back. I can't help thinking this guy is out to scam me."

"You did the right thing calling us. If he calls again, tell him it'll take time to round up that much money, and that you'll call when you get it together. More than likely the guy will tell you he'll be the one to do the calling. I'll be in touch after I talk to the lieutenant."

Roark calls her partner on his cell. "McGraw?"

"Yes."

"Dudley Hamilton received a call from a guy who said he has Eva hostage. Wants one mil in hundreds, but would only let Dudley listen to what he thinks is a tape of her voice."

McGraw is sitting in McAteer's coffee shop with Zee.

"Did you hear what I said, McGraw?"

"Doesn't smell right," he says.

"Whadda you mean?"

"Kidnappers seeking ransom don't wait this long to call."

"Maybe he's a greenhorn."

"Could be a swindler," McGraw says.

"Dudley thinks he's a fraud, too."

"No surprise. Dudley cares more about money than he does Eva."

"Oooh, that's cruel," Roark says to tease McGraw. "But true." She pauses. "On second thought, I believe you're right," she says. "What are we going to do?"

"What did you tell Dudley?"

"I told him to tell the perp he'd have to call him back because it'll take some doing to get that much cash in hundreds."

"Good, anything else?"

"The perp was pretty angry. He thought Dudley could get the money because he owns a bank."

"That shows he's investigated Dudley. He could be our guy and is trying to throw us off the trail by calling for ransom late in the game." He pauses. "I'll be back in a short while."

Thirty minutes later, McGraw is in the squad room talking with Dudley on the phone covering their strategy with Dudley to catch this guy. When finished, McGraw breaks the circuit and punches in a number. He glances over at Roark. "The abductor has given Dudley twenty four hours to get the cash. I'm calling Drew Nelson."

When McGraw finishes talking with FBI Special Agent Nelson, he stands and tells Roark that they have to wait and enter Dudley's under the cover of darkness in case the perp is watching the place.

Around nine, Roark pulls the Impala cruiser with its lights off behind a black SUV on the side road next to Dudley Hamilton's home. McGraw steps out of the passenger side and meets Agent Nelson, dressed in black, coming from the front of the black suburban.

"Howya doin', lieutenant?" he says in a whisper.

"I see you've brought your boys."

He nods. "As always."

Roark rounds the front of the squad car to greet him.

"Hello, sergeant," Nelson says.

"Good to see you again, sir," she says.

He gestures for them to lead the way.

There are no lights on in the house or around the property. Nelson knocks a few times and Dudley opens the door to a dark room. He whispers, "Haven't heard anything."

Nelson and his men enter and close the door. "I am Special Agent Drew Nelson with the FBI. These are my men and they'll need a place for our techs to set up their equipment."

"In my office," Dudley says, leading the group into the spacious room, with a single light over a walnut desk. All windows have their blinds closed. A sofa and two chairs are positioned on an oriental rug in the center of the room; a glass table is between the chairs. The gold-framed pictures on the walls are mostly bank buildings, the ones owned by the Hamiltons. There's a long table against the wall with folders on it.

"Can we use this table?" Nelson says.

"Let me first remove my stuff," Dudley says.

As the technicians begin setting up, McGraw asks Nelson if they'd be able to determine where the perp's last call came from. He's heard about new technology that can search backwards with pin-point accuracy, even when a perp is no longer on the line.

"We'll see as soon as my guys get hooked up. Back-tracking sometimes isn't so easy, even with our new equipment, but my men are the best." Turning to Dudley, he asks what the caller had said in the last call.

"Just like on TV. He said if I wanted to see my wife again, I should get 1 mil in one hundred dollar bills. He was to call me again to give directions to the place where I'm to make the drop. He also said he may let me talk to her when he calls again."

"We'll see if he's a man of his word," Nelson says. "We're about ready so we'll try the back-track now."

One of the techs comes in with canned soft drinks and sets them on the glass table.

Two hours pass, and nothing from the caller.

"Think he's changed his mind?" Roark says.

"Doubt it," Nelson says. "These types love money. However, he could be an amateur, taking his time to make sure he doesn't screw up. We'll be able to tell." One of the techs taps Nelson on the shoulder and they go into a huddle.

After a few minutes, Nelson returns and says, "Looks like your perp is smarter than we've given him credit. He's used a disposable cell without a GPS. We'll have to perform cell phone pinging or triangulation when he calls again."

"What's pinging and tri...?" Roark says without completing her sentence.

"Pinging is turning the perp's cell phone into a honing device. Hopefully, he's not smart enough to remove his battery. Triangulation is another technique and I won't go into it now," Nelson says.

"Do you have to know the number or serial number of the phone?" Roark asks.

"We can get it when he calls," the tech says as he works his equipment.

"What are you thinking, McGraw?" Roark says. "You have that look."

He shakes his head. "This guy is playing us for fools," he says.

Nelson asks McGraw how he came up with that theory.

"The perp isn't after the money," McGraw says as he walks to the tech.

"Isn't that what this is all about? Money?" Roark asks.

McGraw turns around to face the group. "The guy knew all along that it would take more time if he asked for 1 mil in smaller denominations. He's stringing us along because he knows we aren't going to give him the money, and he doesn't care."

Nelson frowns. "I'll admit he doesn't fit the pattern, but what does he want?"

There's a knock on the door. Dudley looks at Nelson, who nods for him to wait until they're out of sight and then he can answer it. Dudley goes to the door, flips on the outside light and opens the door.

A man in a brown uniform is standing with a cardboard envelope in his hand. "Special delivery for a Mr. Dudley Hamilton," the guy says.

"I'm Dudley Hamilton."

"Sign here, sir," he says pointing to the bottom of the slip.

Dudley closes the door, flips off the light and moves back into his office, where the group is on their feet waiting for him.

"There's no name on it, but mine," Dudley says as he enters the room. "Do you think it will blow up?"

Nelson shakes his head. "It's too thin. It may be the directions to the drop. The guy is pretty smart."

Dudley eyes Nelson with suspicion.

"Well, open it," Nelson says.

Dudley rips at it and pulls out a single sheet of paper. "It's directions—"

"Let me see that," Nelson says, grabbing it from him. He reads it out loud.

Go to the McDonalds on Masonic Road around ten. Inside you'll find directions taped under the table in the second booth from the door.

"This guy knows we can't ping him unless we have the number, so he uses UPS. He's not taking any chances," Nelson says. He turns to McGraw. "What does this guy really want if it's not the money?"

"Power," McGraw says. "He knows we'd come here. He's got us bundled and he loves it."

"So, is she's alive?" Roark asks.

McGraw nods. "Yes, for now."

Nelson shakes his head. "We don't know anything about this perp. We have to play along, even though he could be a kook. Don't want him to go off the deep end and kill her," Nelson says.

Dudley's in the corner looking like he saw a ghost. Roark is staring at him like she wants to beat up on him, or maybe she's thinking Dudley may finally be missing Eva after listening to all this discussion. She knows McGraw doesn't think he's capable of missing anyone.

"Are you okay, Mr. Hamilton?" Roark says.

He rubs his face. "I'm just thinking. I need to go back to work."

Roark's anger is raging. She turns away to keep from slapping him, then moves next to McGraw. "You're quiet," she says, "which means you're sensing something again. Let's have it."

"Power isn't the only thing this guy is after."

"Then what is it?"

He rubs his chin. "I wish I knew."

"We're ready," Nelson says. "We got the decoy money with a GPS tracking device in it and Dudley has been briefed on the drop. We will have air support in the area."

CHAPTER EIGHTEEN

Dudley Hamilton is wearing a wire and he pulls his black Infinity into a spot next to the McDonalds entrance, clambers out and walks in close to ten o'clock. He's wearing jeans, a flannel shirt, blue sweater and white sneakers. Inside, two people are at the counter placing orders and the place smells of French fries. A couple in their late teens is in the second booth from the door eating ice cream in cups. The booths in front and behind them are empty. Dudley walks to the counter, orders a medium size coke and ambles through the aisles, passing the teenagers a couple of times. They look at him and smile, but show no sign of leaving.

"There's a couple at the table," Dudley says to Nelson through the hidden transmitter. Nelson is listening in an SUV a block away.

"Get them to leave."

"How do I do that?"

"Think of something, dammit."

Dudley feels like wringing the young couple's necks. *Maybe if he offered them some money. That's it. Everyone likes money. Yeah, that'll work,* he thinks.

He ambles over to them and asks if they'd mind giving up their table. They look at him like he's out of his mind when two empty booths are next to them. Dudley slides a twenty in front of the guy and sits, telling them that he and his wife first met at this table and that she's coming to meet him here. The youngsters look at each other and smile. "That's sweet," the girl says. The guy grabs the twenty and stands. Dudley lets him out and the young couple hurries off.

Dudley sits and drinks his coke and looks around, but doesn't think he's being watched. He slides his hand under the table and makes a sweep of it. The envelope isn't on this side, so, he moves into the opposite seat and feels under the table for the envelope. "Where in the hell is it," he says. Only wads of gum are stuck underneath. "It's not here," he says through the mike to Nelson.

"Whadda you mean it's not there, it's gotta be there."

"I can't speak any plainer. The envelope isn't here."

"Did you actually look under the table?"

Dudley bends down and spots the envelope in a crack close to the wall, barely visible. "I've found it."

Outside, Dudley hurries to his car. He has instructions to hold the envelope on its edges and not to open it. He takes off and ten minutes later pulls into a mall parking lot alongside Nelson's black SUV, steps out and slips into the passenger seat; McGraw and Roark are in the seat behind him. A helicopter is in the area.

"Okay, let's have it," Nelson says, grabbing it with gloved hands. He opens it and pulls out a single sheet of white paper, and begins reading it out loud: *Drive ten minutes north on Wilshire Blvd, till you come to a Shell / Quick Stop station at the four corners, turn left and go five miles to the stop sign. On the right there's a freshly painted billboard sign. Make the drop in the box behind it.*

"I know that area," Nelson says. "It's heavily wooded. He could be watching us without us knowing it. I'll radio the helicopter. Once we pass the sign, me and my guys will circle back and slip into the woods across and wait," he says. "Keep your radios open," he says to McGraw and Roark.

"Got it," McGraw says. They rush to their cars and McGraw pulls in behind Nelson. Fifteen minutes later, McGraw notices Nelson's taillights flickering.

Nelson voice comes through the radio. "We're approaching,"

Moving along at a slow pace, Roark shouts, "There's the billboard. I don't believe it."

"What don't you believe?" McGraw says as he pulls over to the shoulder and looks past Roark at the lighted billboard.

"It's one of those signs from the '70s with a cowboy on a horse, lighting a cigarette with "Marlboro" beneath it in big letters," she says. "This guy knows you, McGraw."

"What's your assessment, Nelson?" McGraw says in the radio.

"Dudley is making the drop as I speak. If the guy doesn't show he's a fraud, but we'll have a bead on him if he shows."

"No, no, Nelson. This's our guy, but he's not going to show."

"How can you be so damn sure?"

"He wants us to think he's abducted Ms. Hamilton for the ransom, but this charade is more about him mocking me."

"So, are you saying he doesn't have her?" Nelson says.

"No, no. He has her all right. He's playing a game, wants me to figure out when he's going to kill her."

"A psychopath," Nelson says. "There's a car coming. Everyone, be alert."

"Is it him?" Roark asks.

"The perp's not going to show," McGraw says. "He's had his fun."

"I'd bet a week's pay he comes," Nelson says. "We should know shortly."

"I can't take your money," McGraw says.

"The vehicle is slowing," Nelson says. "Get ready to write me a check, McGraw."

McGraw knows that most murderers delude themselves into thinking they can do no wrong because their vics are responsible for their own deaths, and it's no crime to kill them. McGraw believes the mind can justify anything. Has the perp killed Ms. Hamilton? Not yet.

The car doesn't stop and disappears into the night.

"Shit," Nelson says. "It's not the one. We'll wait."

Two hours later, Nelson says, "Dammit, McGraw, you son of a bitch. He's not coming."

CHAPTER NINETEEN

Gomez approaches McGraw and Roark as they enter the squad room. "Boss, I think I can get some info on Parino and Payne from this friend who owes me a favor. He's into things and has helped me on other cases, and could shed some light on Parino.

"I'm more interested in Payne and his cop friends, but it might be helpful if we learned more about what's going on between them and Parino. If your friend gives up anything, we'll turn it over to the other bureaus," McGraw says. "Go ahead. Give it a shot."

"Thanks, boss."

After work, Gomez swings his Honda into the parking lot at Velasco's Mexican bar in the Hispanic section in the east end.

"This here is my treat you were telling me about?" Kramer asks Gomez.

"Yeah. I'm treating you to tequila, and to meet the friend I mentioned to you."

"Your informant, you mean," Kramer says.

Gomez doesn't say anything. They get out of the Honda and walk to a red brick building built in the '30s. Inside, the place is painted in warm colors and Mexican music is blasting on the jukebox, and it's almost half full of customers at thirty minutes past five. A Hispanic teenager is working the windows inside with a sponge and a bucket of soapy water; *looks like a high school kid,* Gomez thinks. Kramer follows Gomez up to the bar. The smell of tacos and beans travels from the open kitchen door in the back. A middle-aged woman lurches out, carrying plates of food on a tray above her head; she flies past them with a smile across her face.

"Gomez, my man, How yuh doin'?" the bartender says, shaking his hand. "Thought you've forgot about your friend Marco."

Gomez knows what he means. He'd like some cash more often.

Behind the bar along the counter in front of the mirror are rows of liquor bottles and an ancient cash register.

"Been busy, Marco. You know... I got other people, too."

"I know, I know," he says waving a hand in the air. "Who's your gabacho friend?"

"This is Kramer, my partner. He's okay." Gomez turns to Kramer. "This is my old school buddy, Marco Velasco."

Gomez knows Kramer isn't buying the school buddy cover. Kramer just nods with a frown.

"What are you guys having?" Marco says.

"Tequila," Gomez says.

"With sangrita?" he asks.

"No sangrita. Just tequila," Gomez says, and smiles.

"What's with sangrita?" Kramer says.

"Man, I thought you were worldly."

"Cut the crap, Gomez. I've never drunk tequila."

"Okay, partner. Here's the scoop. You can drink tequila with sangrita or take it with lime and salt. Would you like a side?"

"No, just whatever you're having."

Marco fills two tumblers and sets them in front of the detectives.

Gomez downs his drink in two swallows and sets the glass on the bar for a refill. Kramer takes his time sipping his drink. His throat is burning.

Gomez looks up and down the bar. There's only a guy at the far end eating a burrito. Gomez leans in to Marco and says in a whisper, "I need some information."

Marco's eyes narrow and he whispers back. "I don't know. The walls have ears."

Gomez grabs Marco's apron and pulls him forward. He's so close to Marco he could kiss him on the cheek. "Cut the bullshit, Marco. You forget who you're talking to. How much is it going to take?"

He shakes his head. "Things are not so good."

"I'm not asking again. How much is it going to cost me?"

Marco stares at Gomez like he's thinking hard, turns and goes over to the dark-haired waitress standing at the end of the bar, whispers something, then returns, fills their glasses, takes off his apron, grabs a glass, fills it with beer from the tap and comes round from behind the bar and says, "Let's go to that booth back in the corner." He's the first to slide in. Gomez and Kramer, carrying their drinks, move in facing him.

Gomez is the first to speak. "Tell me what you know about the man who owns Santino's."

Marco shakes his head. "Oh, he's mala persona." He sips his beer. "That's J.P. I don't say his name in here. His boys..."

"Are they shaking you down?" Gomez says.

"Once a month two of his thugs come in here, squeezing me for money. They're doing it to all the places around here. And they're pressuring me to get into drugs. I don't want no part of drugs."

Gomez doesn't believe the crap Marco is putting out. He lives pretty high

87

and would rat on his mother if it got enough cash.

Kramer wants to know if Marco's heard where J.P. (Johnny Parino) stashes his drugs and weapons.

"Man, you're asking the wrong questions." He takes a swig of his beer.

"Come on, Marco. You can't bullshit us. You must be dealing. You know we can close this place."

"Man, you gotta cut me some slack. I got a wife and kids. J.P.'s goons'll kill me if word gets out I talked with you."

"We can make them go away with a little help from you," Gomez says.

Marco's eyes widen. "You can do that?" he says.

"Do what?" Gomez says.

Marco leans in and whispers, "Make J.P. go away?"

"For a long time," Kramer says, "if we get the goods on him."

He swallows more of his drink and wipes the foam from his mouth with the back of his thick hand. "Okay. Okay. But this'll cost you big."

"Let's hear it first before we make a deal," Gomez says.

"Okay. Here's what I got. This customer, no name," he says, looking around as if he suspects Johnny Parino to pop up out of the floor at any moment, "brings a truck once a month filled with drugs from Mexico to Atlanta for the man. After he drops his load in town, he comes in here and vomits his guts out. He's scared to death. The big man doesn't put up with screw-ups. This driver wants out, but he knows too much and no one walks away from J.P. His hoods hacked the last guy to pieces for being a day late. Sometimes the goons follow this driver to my place."

"You need to get your customer to tell us where he drops his load." Gomez says.

"It must be a warehouse somewhere," Kramer says.

"That much I know," Marco says nodding.

"Does J.P. ever come to that warehouse to meet the truck or does he send his boys?" Kramer asks.

"He and his guys are at every shipment, inspect the goods and throws a party, drinking and laughing and making jokes. If any items are missing, the driver comes up missing. J.P. shoots off his mouth about how stupid the cops and government are, and brags how easy it is to get things across the border, if you know the right people."

"Marco, we gotta put the bastard away for a long, long time," Gomez says.

Marco's slow to answer. "It ain't gonna be easy."

"Just find out when the next delivery is. The narcotics people would be happy to know it. A raid would close the man down and put his ass in federal prison for a long time," Gomez says.

He shrugs. "I don't know, Gomez. This driver's afraid of his own shadow."

"Tell him that's the only way he can get out from under J.P. You gotta at least ask him?" Kramer says. "Do you hear me, man?"

"If he spills, it'll cost you big," Marco says. "But I can't guarantee nothin'."

"Have you ever heard the name Austin Payne?" Kramer says.

"Never," he says shaking his head.

"How about Dexter Knight or Trevor Wilson?" Gomez whispers.

Marco moves back in his seat a little and stares at Gomez. "Dexter's a bad cop." He shakes his head. "Don't want nothin' to do with him."

"How about Trevor?" Kramer says.

"Never heard of him."

"How do you know Dex?" Gomez asks.

"He's been in here a couple of times with this black guy who my friend says is always in the warehouse with J.P.'s thugs when the load arrives, and deals for the big man."

"Why do they come in here?" Kramer says. "No offense, but I thought dealers always mingle with the big money people in fancy places."

"The black guy's girlfriend used to work here. She told me he was scaring the shit out of her, so she took off. Sometimes he comes in here asking if I've heard from her."

"You think Dex is dealing for the black dude?" Gomez says.

He shakes his head. "Word is he's selling information and providing protection for him."

CHAPTER TWENTY

Lunch isn't what's on Roark's mind this cloudy noonday. Sitting next to Max Kingston in his silver BMW, she's wondering if she should end this relationship. He's been quite the gentlemen, and she enjoys being with him, but at times he can be controlling and she's beginning to wonder if he's narcissistic. The psychological scars from her divorce are still with her, and, of course, there's Dusty to think about. Men these days are noncommittal and only think about one thing, hitting the sack. If they were like McGraw, she'd jump at the chance to be with him, but hell would freeze over before he'd ever become interested in her. After her ex wanted out of the marriage, Roark promised herself no more relationships for a few years, but she dropped her guard when Mr. Physical Fitness came into her life.

Max pulls the BMW in front of his office building in Prestige Square Mall to take her to Belafonte's Bistro. Max rolls out and goes to the passenger door, opens it and Roark slides out dressed in a white blouse and dark blue suit. He's wearing military sunglasses as usual, gray sport coat, an open-collar light blue shirt and navy blue trousers. Roark wonders if he sleeps with his shades on. He rarely takes them off. It is one thing that interests McGraw, who thinks Max has something to hide. But Roark believes McGraw just says it to discourage her from dating Max.

"I'd like you to meet my secretary, Mary Turner, and see my office before we lunch," Max says. They walk to the door of the glass-front building, step inside and go to a bank of elevators. The elevator opens on three.

They walk down the hall to the door labeled Kingston Investments. Roark envisions meeting a sexy blond behind a desk because of Max's flashiness, a characteristic that is beginning to bother her.

Inside, a middle-aged brunette with smooth skin and a nice figure, dressed in a red dress, is seated at the desk in the center of the waiting room. Two offices are behind her with the doors closed. The brunette smiles and stands as they enter. Max introduces Roark and they head to his office directly behind

Ms. Turner. Inside are two chairs facing the desk and a hall tree against the wall next to the desk, and a washroom with its door open. No windows. Lots of pictures and awards hang on the walls. Roark spends a few minutes looking at them. *Might know he'd be in all of them,* she thinks. "My, you've sure received a lot of awards."

"Don't let that fool you. They're from hard work and long hours."

"Is this Dudley Hamilton with you?" she says, pointing to a glass-covered framed picture.

"Yes, he's one of my best clients."

"I see," she says.

"What does that mean?"

"I mean, you sure hang out with the big people."

"The Hamiltons are strictly business."

He goes to a filing cabinet in the corner, pulls out the top drawer and removes a glossy packet. They leave the office and walk down the stairs. Outside, they stroll to Belafonte's Bistro a half-block away. A sexy redhead comes swaying toward them, dressed in a tight skirt, high heels, and a butt-length fake fur coat. She calls out, "Hi, Max. How yuh doing, honey? You were going to call me."

"Been busy; catch you later."

"An old flame?" Roark asks.

He shakes his head. "Naw, I took her to lunch once to get her business, but she wants to hang on. Not my type."

They enter the bistro and are seated in a booth next to the bar. Max places the packet on the seat next to him. The bartender waves and smiles at them. Max returns the gesture.

"You must come here often?" Roark asks.

"I enjoy the place," he says, removing his shades. "Come here a couple times a week. Thought you'd find the place interesting; they have great stew and corned beef sandwiches."

"It's old-world for sure," she says. "I'm not a stew person for lunch, but the corned beef is right down my alley."

The waitress arrives and places menus in front of them. "Good to see yuh," Max, she says.

"Same here, Annie; we don't need menus, bring us your wonderful corned beef sandwiches, and I'd like a cold ale."

"I'll just have water with lemon, thank you," Roark says to Annie, a woman in her fifties and a little on the heavy side. She reaches for Roark's menu.

Max hands off his menu and turns to Roark. "Your partner McGraw doesn't think much of me, does he?"

She is surprised at the question. McGraw can be rude at times, but she didn't think he was to Max. All she can think to say is, "He's thinking, every time he sees you, you're going to corner him about a retirement plan."

Max laughs. "I get that a lot. I know I can be pushy, but in this business you have to help people make up their minds. Some are afraid they'll lose money, but I feel like I'm helping them." He shrugs. "I guess it's all about how you look at it."

"I wouldn't pay much attention to McGraw. He doesn't mean anything by it; he's very businesslike at times. It takes a while to get to know him."

"You can tell him I'll wait to hear from him, and won't bother him again."

"I'm sure he'll appreciate it."

Max reaches for the packet on the seat next to him and sets it in front of Roark. "I don't want you to think I only asked you to lunch to give you this packet, but I've worked out something for you and would just like for you to review it at your leisure. No pressure. Just want to make sure you will have financial freedom when you leave the force."

Roark can't determine from looking into his eyes if he's only been interested in getting her business, like he did with the gal they passed coming to the bistro, or is interested in her, or both. "Thanks. I'll look it over."

Max smiles. "Good."

The sandwiches arrive and they dig in. Max wipes his mouth and says, "How's your investigation going? I believe the press is calling it the Vanishing Bride case."

"It's moving along," she says, taking a drink of her water.

"You have any suspects?" He must have seen the frown on Roark's face. "Oh, I guess I shouldn't be asking. Sorry."

"That's okay. I just can't discuss any specifics."

"I've always been interested in mysteries and read a lot of them. It's my understanding that the spouse of a victim is always considered the first suspect. Is that correct?"

"That's true, but in many cases they may not be involved in the crime at all. So they may not be the perp."

"Perp for perpetrator?" he says, taking a drink of his ale. "I haven't read about any arrests; do you expect any soon?"

She doesn't answer. "You're frowning again," Max says.

"Why the interest in this case?" Roark asks, reaching for her water.

"To be honest, Dudley Hamilton is one of my best clients. No, I take that back, he's my best client, and we've been friends for years. You saw me with him in that picture on the wall in my office."

"So, you must know Eva?"

"Of course, but not very well. I've been to their place a few times for them to sign papers but we never socialized, except to have lunch with Dudley once in a while."

"I see now why you're interested in Eva's disappearance. Wish I could tell you more."

He pauses, and then says, "I have another reason for asking."

He seems uncomfortable, she thinks. "What is it?"

"Dudley thinks that you and Detective McGraw have been harassing him. He knows I've been seeing you and he wanted me to ask if you guys can lay off. That doesn't sound good, I know, and I hesitate to ask it."

She waits a few seconds before answering. "I'm surprised he thinks that. We only follow police protocol, and he's treated no differently than anyone else."

"Sorry. You're right. Let's just drop it and enjoy our lunch."

CHAPTER TWENTY-ONE

Noah McGraw steps into the foyer of the Pitcher's Mound Restaurant with Zee around seven-thirty this Friday evening. A large, gold-framed painting of a lean black man in a Braves uniform, posed in a pitching stance on the mound, is hanging on the wall. The headwaiter approaches McGraw's old partner.

"Good evening, Detective Zee, your table is ready," he says, and escorts them past a row of tables covered with white linen, to one in the back. The place is packed. McGraw doesn't sit. He slips between the tables and goes to the dozens of neatly framed pictures horizontally lined along two walls. The main attraction is the thin ballplayer, standing shoulder to shoulder with fans, some taken in the ballpark and others in the restaurant. Movie stars and politicians aren't excluded. There is one taken in the restaurant with Moose with Bill Clinton. Most pictures are the same size, except for the one in the center—Moose accepting The Cy Young Award from the Baseball Writers Association of America. He is smiling ear to ear.

"You a sports fan?" says a voice behind McGraw, startling him. McGraw flips around. The forty-something black man seemed to have jumped out of the picture.

"You're Moose," McGraw says, holding out his hand.

"That's what they calls me," he says.

"You scared me for a moment. I thought you jumped out of this picture." They smile and shake hands.

Looking over the pictures, McGraw says, "Cardinals. They're my team."

"Damn good one, too," Moose says.

McGraw points to the picture with Moose accepting the Cy Young Award and says, "The proudest day of your life, right?"

He nods. "Guess you could say that. But I'm much happier now."

McGraw feels himself frowning. "How can you say that? We're talking about the Cy Young."

"Doesn't last, my friend. Helping people, that's what lasts."

"I'm a fan," says, McGraw, "but I'm sure you hear that all the time."

"Still like hearing it," he says. "What's your name?"

"Noah McGraw. Most everyone calls me McGraw. I'm here with ole Zee." Moose turns around and glances over at the big Italian. "Let's go see the man," he says.

"Hey, Moose," Zee says, not getting up, giving Moose a knuckle punch. "I see you've met my old partner."

"Sure have. Seems like a bright young man."

"Oh, he is. But I have to keep an eye on him." They laugh.

"Is he as good a cop as you?"

"I'm better," McGraw says, smiling.

"Thought I'd bring this young whippersnapper to meet you, and after he tastes the food around here, he'll want to come back," Zee says.

"Nothin' better to hear than satisfied folks," Moose says.

"Can you sit for a while?" Zee asks.

He shakes his head. "Got to visit with the folks but I'll be back after you finish your meal."

Moose motions to the waiter. "Take care of my friends."

"Yes, sir. What'll you have, gentlemen?"

"Let's start with a drink," Zee says. He orders scotch on the rocks. "What're you havin' McGraw?"

"A glass of merlot."

The waiter nods and leaves.

"Love this place," Zee says. "Been coming here for a couple of years. Don't know why I never invited you before."

"You're cheap, that's why," McGraw says. They laugh.

"Next time, you pay," Zee says.

"How long has this place been around?" McGraw asks.

"Soon after Moose blew out his shoulder, he retired and opened this place. That was about eight years ago. He was looking for a way to make money to support his soup kitchen on the other side of town. He does it mostly for the kids. He always showed his love for 'em when he was playing for the Braves. Now, he has a smile and something for them when they come through the line at the kitchen. He was married for ten years, but no children. She took off after the divorce with a lot of his money. Nearly broke him."

"I hear that a lot," McGraw says.

"Women today don't want to do all the things like our mamas did," Zee says. "Anyway, his wife was a stupid bitch. He's better off without her."

The waiter returns with Zee's drink and places McGraw's wine in front of him. McGraw takes a swig. "Tell me about Moose's kitchen."

"It's called Home Plate, a brick building that seats around 100."

"Home Plate?" McGraw says. "Why that name?"

Moose overhears the question when he comes from behind McGraw and says, "Man, don't you know that's the most important plate in baseball? I

95

named it that because we do a lot of good for folks at that kitchen—it's very important to them."

"Now I understand," McGraw says.

"You need any help at the kitchen?" Zee asks.

"You kidding me, man? We always need more people. Are you volunteering?"

"Naw, man, it's for my friend here," he says pointing to McGraw.

"Zee's too lazy, but I have two good hands," McGraw says, holding them out, palms up.

"I could use those two hands."

"How about this Saturday?" McGraw says.

"I'll expect you."

"Hey, Moose," Zee says. "McGraw won't brag about his talents, but I will: he's a damned good cook."

"Well, you're full of surprises, aren't you, detective McGraw?" Moose says.

"That's what my partner Roark says. And you can start off by calling me Noah."

"Noah it is. Well, enjoy your meal," Moose says as he turns to leave but looks back at Noah. "I'll be expecting you at Home Plate."

CHAPTER TWENTY-TWO

This late afternoon in early November, a muscular man dressed in jean shirt and pants, his head nearly touching the roof, wearing a Reagan mask and an Atlanta Braves baseball cap, is seated behind the wheel of an older model dented red Ford pickup parked by the side of the road with the motor running. He rubs his hands over the steering wheel and waits with his heart pounding. Lieutenant Noah McGraw travels this route on his Harley, heading home around this time when he volunteers at Moose's soup kitchen. "The son of a bitch is getting too close for comfort," the guy says to himself. "It's time to give the lieutenant a warning. Then his sidekick, Sergeant Roark is next."

———— • ————

McGraw leaves Moose's soup kitchen around five on his motorcycle. The wind is light and it is a good day for riding. Shadows from the trees float over him as he barrels around a curve heading home. As he motors down the road, he spots a battered red pickup in his side mirror, racing up behind him. *Too close for comfort*, McGraw thinks. He can hear the roaring engine of the truck and senses he's about to be run over. He glances around for the next fifty yards for an escape route. *This is it*, he thinks, and swerves to his right, dashing across a clearing, loses control and heads for a large oak tree. He maneuvers the bike on to its side and slides in circles over twenty-five feet of grass and rams into the tree.

When he wakes up, McGraw is blinded by a bright light overhead. He hears Roark's voice. "Good, you're waking up," she says. "Do you know where you are?"

He blinks and now sees her standing over him, stares at her a few seconds without saying a word. He looks around.

"You're in the ER. How do you feel?" she says.

"Find out who has my Harley."

She sighs. "You were nearly killed on that damn thing, and that's all you care about."

"But I wasn't. I need you to locate it for me."

"It's in the precinct garage."

"Good. Do you have my hat?"

"It's with your things on the counter." She shakes her head. "The EMTs said you kept asking for it even while you were out of your mind."

"Let me see it."

Roark goes to the counter and holds it up. "See, it's still okay, but you may have to get it cleaned." He takes it and looks it over. "Okay, put it back."

"Tell me what happened, McGraw," Roark says.

"This guy in a Reagan mask behind the wheel of a battered pickup ran me off the road, deliberately," he says, attempting to sit up just as the nurse and doctor enter the room. The nurse hurries around the end of the bed to him.

"Not so fast, cowboy," she says, pushing down on his shoulders. "Lay back down."

The doctor moves in next to Roark. "Your CAT scan is normal, detective. We had to stitch up a wound on your head and arm." He turns to Roark. "Was he wearing a helmet?"

Roark shrugs. "He usually wears it, doctor, but he can be stubborn about it."

"Detective McGraw, I'd recommend a helmet over a cowboy hat any day," the doctor says. "You may not be so lucky next time."

"Oh, he doesn't believe in luck, doctor. And to expect him not to wear that crown is like asking an alcoholic not to drink."

"There won't be a next time, doctor. Can I get out of here?"

The doctor looks at the nurse. "I'll sign him out. Are you in any pain, detective?"

"None. I just want out."

"I'll be back with the paperwork," the nurse says as she follows the doctor out of the room.

"My, my," Roark says, "you're in such a pissy mood. You should be thankful you're alive."

"I just want to get the guy who did this."

"Did you get a good look at him?"

"How could I? He was wearing a mask."

"Then what's your hurry?"

The nurse enters and McGraw signs the release forms as she covers the things he's not supposed to do for the next twenty-four hours. She looks at Roark: "Will he follow doctor's orders?"

"Don't count on it."

McGraw slides out of bed still in his hospital gown. "Don't move," Roark says, helping him to a chair. "I'll get your clothes for you." She returns. "You look pretty sexy in that gown, McGraw," acting like she's going to lift it up as he attempts to stand. He slaps her hand. "Wait for me in the hall."

Outside, fully dressed, McGraw adjusts his hat and they head to Roark's silvery-grey Chevy Tahoe. He goes round to the passenger side and eases in. She slips behind the wheel. "We'd like for you to come to the house," she says. McGraw doesn't say a word. "Dusty is worried about you and says he hasn't seen you in a while. I'll make you some coffee."

"You don't have to keep an eye on me. I have a mother."

"Please, McGraw."

"Maybe long enough to say hello and let Dusty know I'm okay."

Thirty minutes later, Roark drives into a middle-class neighborhood. The lawns are trimmed, trees are lined up in military formation along the curbs, and the driveways have mid-size to full-size SUVs parked in them. She pulls the Tahoe into the driveway of a red brick house with a red door. This house she got out of her divorce from her ex, the real estate developer. Once they're out of the SUV, her 10-year-old Freckled redhead rushes to McGraw and hugs him around his waist. "You okay, McGraw? I've been worried about you."

McGraw rubs the boy, who reminds him of Tom Sawyer, on the top of his head, McGraw's way of showing affection for the boy. "I've missed you, too, Dusty."

The Martins, Mattie and Lloyd, are working in their rock garden next door. They're good friends with Roark and they take care of Dusty. "Hello, detective," Mattie says, while her husband waves. Mattie is the grandmother type and Dusty loves her, especially her cookies. Lloyd is a good story teller.

McGraw raises his good arm and nods.

"What happened? Your arm and face are banged up," Dusty says.

"He had an accident on his motorcycle," Roark says with displeasure in her voice.

A black Toyota Sequoia pulls in the driveway next door.

"Aw, mom. It's not a motorcycle, it's a Harley." He turns to McGraw. "Isn't that right, McGraw?"

McGraw smiles and they stroll to the house. "Your mother doesn't understand bikers."

Because she's afraid to get on the Harley, McGraw thinks.

"How did it happen?" Dusty asks.

"Some guy in a pickup ran McGraw off the road," Roark says.

"You mean he did it on purpose?" Dusty says.

"I'm afraid so."

"But you'll get him, won't you, McGraw?"

He nods. "You can bet on it. Have you finished that book I gave you?"

"Sure thing," Dusty says. "Loved it and I'm waiting for another."

"What's the title?"

"*To Kill a Mockingbird.*"

"Who's the author?"

"Harper Lee."

"And what did I tell you?"

"That I should always remember the titles of books and their authors."

"Good. Now we'll think about reading *Gone with the Wind*."

"So, you like Southern authors?" Roark asks.

"Isn't Martha Mitchell from here?" he says.

"She was born in Arkansas," Roark says.

"Well, I'm impressed," he says. "Anyway, I find something special about them. Maybe their messages resonate with me more."

"It couldn't be because you're from Texas, could it?"

He smiles. "I reckon."

They laugh.

An hour later, Roark drives McGraw to his ranch at the edge of town. She pulls the Tahoe into the chat driveway. The white frame house sits back from the road about one hundred feet. A blue RAM pickup and a cherry-red jeep are parked on a chat drive leading to McGraw's workshop. They get out and walk up the flagstones. The porch light comes on. Anna Marie, a seventy-four-year-old with salt and pepper hair, narrow face, with a strong jaw and a pleasant smile, wearing cotton house dress, steps out on the porch.

"Yes, mom, it is I."

"Oh, my Lord, you're hurt. Did you hit something with that motorcycle?"

Roark smiles as she follows him up the stairs.

"Just a little accident," he says.

"This is Holly Roark. She's my partner."

"My, you're a pretty one," she says. "Oh, I like your hair, matches your pretty eyes."

"Thank you. That's very sweet of you."

McGraw turns to Roark. "This is my mother, Anna Marie McGraw."

"Pleased to meet you, Ms. McGraw," Roark says.

"Likewise," Anna Marie says, waving her hands, "please come in; don't stand out there." She grabs Roark's arm and leads her in.

"Just finishing the dishes," she says. "Just call me Anna Marie. Come, I have some coffee and peach cobbler on the stove. Please sit."

"You sure you're okay, son?"

"Fine, maw. Stop worrying."

She turns to Roark. "He never tells me anything. Please, tell me what happened."

Roark looks at McGraw seeking his approval to tell his mother the truth. She doesn't want to worry Anna Marie, but Roark knows a mother has to know.

"Someone ran him off the road," Roark says. "But we'll get him."

A hand goes to her mouth. "You could have been killed, Noah," Anna Marie says. "You should be driving your truck instead of that motorcycle. You remember how your father and I used to get into it over that bike."

McGraw doesn't say a word. Instead, he glances around the table while his mother reaches in the cabinets for cups and plates. "Mom, how would you like to do some cooking for a homeless kitchen where I volunteer? Now, it wouldn't be every day, maybe just weekends now and then. They'd love your Irish stew."

"Me too, McGraw," Roark says. "Can I help?"

"I guess so. Why not? The more the merrier,"

Anna Marie says as she sets the table. "How did they learn about—?" She stops and stares at McGraw with her brow together. "You made it for them, didn't you?"

He holds his hands up. "I'm guilty."

"Well, I'll forgive you. I'd love to cook for them." She cuts into the peach cobbler and hands them a plate.

"What's wrong, maw," McGraw says. "You have that worried look."

"Do you know who did this to you?" Anna Marie asks without looking up.

"I believe I do," he says as he takes a bite of his dessert.

Roark looks puzzled. "You do? Who?"

"Dexter Price."

CHAPTER TWENTY-THREE

McGraw eases to the edge of his bed around five-thirty to the smell of coffee, removes the restraint from around his arm and throws it on the chair next to the bed. This Monday morning couldn't have come fast enough for him. He slips into his robe and heads into the kitchen. *Mom is in her caring mood,* he thinks. Usually, he likes to rise early and savor several cups of coffee before she rolls out of bed.

A stack of pancakes is on the counter and bacon is frying in the skillet. The smell of coffee is stronger now and it is making his mouth water. "I was going to let you sleep a little longer. How yuh feelin'," she says.

"Better."

"Have a seat. I've made some pancakes and bacon and your favorite coffee."

"You shouldn't have. I generally have an egg and a few pieces of fruit."

"Well, this time it's different. You're hurt and you need some good food in you."

———◆———

The man who ran McGraw off the road enters his work area around 7:45, before anyone arrives, and closes the door behind him. He walks over to a desk, pulls out a chair and sits. He opens the narrow pencil drawer, reaches into the back and pulls out a toy laughter box and sets it next to the phone. On the lid of the small wooden box is printed, *JOKER.* There's a volume control knob and a button to depress to release the sound. He looks at his watch and places a call to Lieutenant Noah McGraw at 8:05 a.m.

———◆———

McGraw arrives at the station garage around 7:30 to check on his Harley.

The weather is clear but cold. He finds the motorcycle isn't in as bad a shape as he had thought, just some minor repairs that the mechanics say they can handle. He looks to the heavens. *It's okay, Dad,* he says under his breath. Inside the station, McGraw finds Gomez and asks him to run the partial plate of the red 4x4 pickup. Unfortunately, McGraw only caught sight of the first part of the license numbers when he shot off the road on his Harley.

"Will do, boss. You okay?"

"I'm okay. Thanks."

Roark arrives at her desk. "How are you feeling this morning, McGraw?"

"I'm fine."

"I enjoyed meeting your mother last night. You are a lucky man."

He smiles and nods.

Captain Dipple comes out of his office, hurrying toward McGraw.

"Here comes the Lion," Roark says.

"McGraw, how you feelin'? I heard about your accident. You okay?"

"Actually, much better, thanks for asking."

"Good. Good. Now tell me what's happening with the Hamilton case. You got any leads?"

"Not yet, Capt., but getting close."

"McGraw. Now you know... close ain't good enough. The commish is on my ass. Let's pick it up. Okay?" He turns, nods at Roark and heads back to his office.

"Sure thing, Capt.," McGraw shouts after him.

Roark frowns at McGraw. "What's he so angry about?"

McGraw shrugs, which means he doesn't give a damn.

Kramer shouts. "Lieutenant, I've checked the costume shops and no Reagan masks have been sold since last Halloween."

"Maybe he got it from Walmart," Roark says.

"More like he had it for years," McGraw says. His phone rings. He looks at his desk clock, it registers, 8:05. He lifts the receiver. "Homicide, Lieutenant McGraw speaking."

"How yuh doin', lieutenant?" the voice says in a sardonic tone. "Got yourself banged up pretty bad, did ya?" A high-pitched laugh blasts in his ear.

McGraw flips on the speaker phone and motions to his unit to listen up.

"You there, lieutenant? I hear you b-r-e-a-t-h-i-n-g. It does seem a little heavy. Bet your blood pressure is goin' up a little talkin' to me, ain't it?" Again, the laugh, reminiscent of the Joker laugh blasts in the phone. *Has to be some toy device,* McGraw thinks.

"Aw shucks, come on, copper. You ain't pissed, are you? Can't a guy have a little fun with you?"

Copper?

"How'd you like my Reagan mask? The best pres we ever had until he let all those fuckin' Mexicans into this country." The caller was now breathing harder.

Gomez jumps up from his desk, his hands rolled into fists and his eyes ablaze.

"You still there, detective?" the caller asks.

"I'm listening," McGraw says.

"Next time you won't be so lucky."

"There won't be a next time."

"Don't be so sure. Anything is possible, lieutenant." He exhales a deep breath.

"What have you done with Eva Hamilton, you scumbag?" McGraw says, trying to rattle him.

There's a pause.

"What's wrong, scumbag? You think you've outsmarted us?"

Finally the caller says, "Eva who?"

"You're nothing but a dumb-ass, and you're not fooling us. Eva Hamilton didn't want anything to do with you because you're a loser."

Roark gives McGraw thumbs up.

The caller is now breathing harder in the phone.

"How would I know anything about her?" He pauses. "What's wrong? You up against some guy smarter than you, and so you are trying to pin this on someone else. Guess you ain't as smart as you think, huh, lieutenant?"

There's that dreadful Joker laugh again.

"We know you've got her somewhere," McGraw says, "and we're closing in on you."

"You're a lying son of a bitch! I didn't do her."

McGraw is surprised at the caller's use of '*didn't do her.*'

"So, you know she's dead."

"Whoa! I know nothing of the sort."

"You just said you 'didn't do her.'"

"You can't pin anything on me. But you can do me a favor. Tell that pretty partner of yours, what's her name? Oh, yeah, Sergeant Roark, that she better watch her pretty little ass. Cause I like what I see."

He releases the Joker laugh again.

McGraw jumps up. "Listen to me carefully—you no good son of a bitch—if you lay a hand on her, you'll regret the day you were born."

"Easy, copper, watch your blood pressure. Police brutality is not your style."

There's dead silence on the other end, except for heavy breathing. *Maybe he's thinking about what I said*, McGraw thinks. "Your ass is mine, and I'm coming after you," McGraw says.

The phone goes dead.

McGraw sits back down and slowly replaces the receiver. *This is our suspect. I know it,* he thinks. He's far more evil than McGraw had thought.

"You okay, McGraw?" Roark says.

He stares at her big brown eyes. *I'm not okay.* He just now becomes conscious of how much he cares for Roark.

"What's wrong?" she asks.

"Just thinking," McGraw says. "Did you get anything on the guy?"

"He used a non-traceable cell phone," she says. "No GPS."

Gomez shouts from his desk. "The 4x4 is owned by Red River Construction Company, and they reported it stolen four days ago."

———————◆———————

Close to three a.m. there's a loud crash and the sound of peeling wheels screeching away from Roark's home. She grabs her Glock from the nightstand and darts to the door. Flames are spewing from her silvery-grey Chevy Tahoe parked in the driveway. The whole neighborhood is lit up like the fireworks on the Fourth. Ten minutes later, the first responders arrive and work the fire. Not much is left of the SUV—windows blown out, tires burned off the wheels, springs in place of seats, and the paint burned down to the metal.

Strobe lights are flashing in the faces of onlookers wearing coats over nightgowns and pajamas, standing by the curb across the street, gawking, guarded by uniformed officers. Soon after, McGraw races in, tires squealing as he slams on the brakes of his pickup.

He talks with the firemen as the ambulance pulls away. He heads to Roark. "A Molotov," he says, "You okay?"

"I just wish I could of gotten a few rounds off."

"Let's go inside," McGraw says.

Dusty is sitting at the kitchen table holding a cup of hot chocolate up to his lips between two hands. Mattie Martin has finished pouring herself a cup. "Would you like some hot chocolate?" she says. "There's plenty."

"Not for me, thanks," McGraw says.

"Yes, I'll have some to quiet my nerves," Roark says, reaching for the cup.

"Wow, McGraw," Dusty says. "You should have been here. There was a big boom and this big ball of fire." He extends his hands to demonstrate. "I was telling Mrs. Martin not to worry. My friend McGraw will get 'em."

McGraw puts a hand on Dusty's shoulder. "Dusty's my biggest fan," he says.

"Finish your drink and let's get you to bed," Roark says.

"Can't I stay up just a little while?" he says. "Please, mom."

"I'll take you to your room and then I must be off," Mrs. Martin says.

"Thanks, Mattie," Roark says.

"Don't mention it, honey," she says as she escorts Dusty to his room.

"You'll find 'em, won't you, McGraw?" Dusty asks.

"Sure thing, pal, don't worry."

Roark turns to McGraw. "Guess the perp really thinks we're getting close," she says.

CHAPTER TWENTY-FOUR

McGraw rolls into the Pitcher's Mound around eight the evening and locates Zee at their table in the back, sipping his favorite drink, scotch. The waiter rushes over with red wine for McGraw.

Zee's eyes are glassy. "I see you're keeping company with Johnny. How many does that make?"

"Who's counting?"

"I'd say, from the look in your eyes, that's not your first."

"And you'd be right, champ. Now sit your ass down and tell me about your accident. I told you someday it was going to happen. I never liked those bikes."

McGraw knows something's bothering Zee. He only curses when he's had too much to drink, which happens when he is facing a problem in his life.

"There's nothing to tell. Some guy in a Reagan mask, driving a Red Ford pickup ran me off the road. That's all."

"Red pickup? He wanted to make sure you saw him," Zee says.

"I agree."

McGraw parks himself in the chair facing Zee and takes a draw on his wine.

"It was a warning, champ," Zee says.

"You think so?"

"Don't you? He could have run you over and made mincemeat of you on that bike."

McGraw nods. "I only saw the Reagan mask, and was able to determine that he was a big guy. And that's not all. He fire-bombed Roark's car early this morning. I think I know who he might be."

"You're getting close, champ. You'll figure it out."

McGraw takes a swallow of his drink. "You'd also be interested in what we've learned about Ms. Hamilton—"

"Cut the 'Ms.' crap. By now you should know the inside and out of the vic, so that you feel for her. Have you forgotten what I taught you?"

McGraw smiles and looks into Zee's glassy eyes, thinking he's had one too many. "Are you okay?"

"Naw," he says, shaking his head. "Bad damn day. The wife of a dear friend of mine back in New York called me. Her husband dropped dead yesterday of a heart attack."

"Sorry."

He shrugs. "I'm gonna miss the guy. We usually get together every summer to fish. He saved my life once when I was a rookie. I always felt I owed him." He waves his hand in the air. "But let's get off that. Tell me what you've found interesting in the Vanishing Bride case." He takes another drink.

"Eva Hamilton was alive for at least eighteen hours after leaving Prestige Square. Receipts taken from the Hamilton home verify that she signed for gas at two ExxonMobil stations: one in Charlotte early the next morning around one, five hours after leaving the mall, and a second fill-up in Raleigh around 2:00 the next afternoon, 13 hours after the first fill-up in Charlotte."

"What'd her husband say about all that?" Zee asks.

"Nothing much, like he doesn't care. He had no idea who would want to hurt his wife. He's dragging his feet on going through her stuff, and only keeps asking when he is going to get her Lexus back."

"He's the type you like to knock the shit out of," Zee says. "What in the hell did the abductor and Eva do for thirteen hours after the first fill-up in Charlotte?"

"Maybe he drove around trying to figure out what to do with her," McGraw says, "but I'm leaning toward a more suitable theory."

"Let's hear it," Zee says.

"The abductor may have a special reason to go to that area."

"Like a cabin on a lake?"

McGraw nods. "It could be isolated, where they could hole up for a while. For now, I have contacted our friends in the Charlotte and Raleigh PDs to find what they can come up with at the Exxon stations."

Zee glances at the waiter, who's bringing another round of drinks to the table.

"Don't need menus," Zee says to him. "Bring us our usual. Remember, I like my steak with some blood dripping out. My friend here," he says pointing at McGraw, "likes his cremated."

The waiter smiles as he always does when they place their orders and leaves.

"Another piece of the puzzle exists," McGraw says. "We had three women from Citizens Bank—friends of Eva who were her former roommates—come to the station for questioning. Something interesting emerged from our inquiry."

McGraw tells him about the flowers and the telephone calls Eva Hamilton received.

"One of the friends working next to her office overheard one of the conversations Eva had with the caller. She said Eva was impatient with the caller but told him, 'I'm a married woman now. You can come over to our house any time you like, but I can't come over there anymore.'"

"Hmm. I'd bet money on him being your perp," Zee says.

"If she invited him to her place, then that means Dudley knew the guy, too, and wouldn't mind," McGraw says.

Zee nods. "She must of gone with the guy before she married that jerk of hers. Do you think she had an affair with the guy and he never got over her?" Zee says.

"I'm thinking he could be a high school sweetheart who never got over her," McGraw says. "He seems to have gotten more aggressive with her during the telephone calls, which tells me he wants her badly."

"So have you eliminated the husband?"

"Dudley is manipulative, and seems to have verbally abused her, but I don't think he would harm her."

McGraw takes a swallow of his drink.

"He didn't take out any life insurance on Eva. Since they were married only six weeks, he hadn't gotten around to it."

"Money isn't a motive. Why would he get insurance? The guy's family is loaded," Zee says.

"And we haven't uncovered any enemies of theirs, nor have we found any infidelities on Dudley's part."

Zee grumbles. "No surprise there. Who could get romantic with a guy like that?"

They laugh.

"His polygraph was inconclusive, and we've scheduled a second one."

Zee raises his glass. "He could have hired someone."

"His alibis are solid and our investigation hasn't turned up any hit man. The evidence is pointing more to a former lover—"

Zee interrupts. "Look, there's Sergeant Roark with Rocky," Zee says interrupting.

"Where?"

"They're being seated across the way, in the corner."

"What did you just call him?" McGraw says.

"Rocky, why?"

"Interesting," McGraw says. "I called him Stallone from the Rocky era and Roark got mad at me."

"Does he ever take off those sunshades?"

"Must shower in them," McGraw says.

They laugh, again.

"Roark hasn't seen us yet," Zee says.

"What is she doing here?" McGraw asks.

Zee frowns. "You mean she can't come here?" he says with surprise on his face. "Man, what's with you?"

McGraw's cell phone vibrates. As a rule he keeps it on vibrate when in public places; he thinks it's rude to talk on it in front of others, especially when eating. Glancing at the caller ID, McGraw says, "Sorry, Zee. I gotta take this. It's Larry with Charlotte PD." He flips it open "McGraw here. We were just talking about you. I'm with Zee. Oh, I will." He whispers to Zee, "Larry says hi." Zee raises his glass. "What do you have for me?" McGraw lifts his glass, signaling to the waiter he needs a refill. "I don't believe it. You mean they didn't call the cops?" Zee's brow rises with interest. "It's a good thing I wasn't there; I'd have cleaned the place with them." There's a pause, and then laughter. "No, I haven't forgotten I'm a cop. But someone needs to teach those punks a lesson," McGraw says.

Zee raises his glass and whispers, "I'll drink to that."

The waiter brings their steaks and sets the plates in front of them. McGraw's merlot arrives.

"What about the security cameras?" McGraw says. He shakes his head. "Sometimes it doesn't pay to get out of bed. Well, thanks anyway, Larry." McGraw swallows some of his drink.

"Let's have it," Zee says. "I can tell it ain't gonna be good."

"'Ain't'?"

"Oh, horseshit. Let's hear the bad news."

"Larry compared notes with David at the Raleigh PD. The two clerks working at the Exxon stations recognized Eva from the photos after a lot of prodding, but one acted like he didn't know who she was, or didn't want to remember. They remembered seeing her picture in the paper, too, and said she was definitely in their stations, signed the receipts in front of them. They both told officers that Eva was with a guy who was ordering her around. The Charlotte clerk said she kept her head down most of the time."

"And they didn't bother to call the cops?" Zee says.

McGraw shakes his head. "They didn't want to get involved."

"I'd like to kick the crap out of 'em," Zee says. "What about security cameras?"

"They're dummies, just for show. In the Walmart tapes so many people were going in and out at the time that it was difficult to see faces on them, but Larry thought they might be one of the couples pushing a basket with some bags, going out the store. The guy was wearing a stocking cap and looking down the whole time."

"If it wasn't them, maybe only the abductor went in," Zee says. "You know, looking for duct tape, bags, shovels, and stuff. The Walmart receipt should have the items listed."

"Larry didn't say anything about a shovel. I'm sure he would have spotted it sticking out of the basket. I believe they'd go there to get clothes for Eva, since most of what she was wearing at the time of her abduction was returned with the car."

"What about the car they were in? Bet the punks were standing around with buds in their ears listening to music and didn't see it," Zee says.

"The attendant in Charlotte didn't see the car, but the guy in Raleigh saw a black car but couldn't recall what make. He remembers two guys being with her, while the guy in Charlotte saw only one man."

"That's something to consider. One guy with her at the first station and two guys with her at the second one," Zee says.

"Unless the other guy stayed in the car at the first station," McGraw says.

"Very likely," Zee says.

Silence prevails while they cut into their steaks. Moments later, McGraw shakes his head and says, "Nothing makes sense, Zee. I'm thinking our guy staged the whole thing in North Carolina to throw us off the trail."

"So you think she was definitely abducted, and didn't run off with a lover?"

He nods. "I do. If Eva ran off with someone, she wouldn't have blood on her stockings, would she?"

"Maybe they ran off the road and had to get out to push, or something," Zee says, taking another bite of his steak.

"More likely she tried to get away and fell and hurt herself," McGraw says, shaking his head. "Another thing, nothing of hers was missing from the home. Her jewelry, money, clothes and personal items were all there. She would have packed them if she took off with her lover." McGraw takes a bite of his steak and washes it down with some water.

"That's very convincing," Zee says.

"And we learned from the security tapes that the valet driver in Prestige Mall was involved. Someone hired him to drive her Lexus to its parking spot."

"Did the driver see the guy who hired him?" Zee says.

"Only spoke on the phone. Keys and money were in the car, directions given over the phone."

"I would have guessed it was the husband that hired someone to kill her," Zee says, "but, like you, I'm beginning to believe that the suspect instructed the valet driver about returning the car to make it look like she had been abducted and raped."

Zee reaches for his scotch and McGraw downs his wine.

"Champ, you better go to North Carolina and check everything out for yourself. Larry and David are good, but they're no Noah McGraw."

"I have been giving it some thought."

"One other thing; didn't you tell me that Eva Hamilton roomed with a friend from Oklahoma when she first came to Atlanta?"

"Her friend's name is Olivia Jordan, now living in New York City."

"What surfaced on them?"

"We know only that they both were high school friends and lived together in Atlanta."

"Need to find out about those two," Zee says.

McGraw nods and leans in to the table and says, "Call it a hunch, Zee, but Eva Hamilton seems too virtuous, too Goody Two-Shoes, and for me that creates a mystery in this case." He stares off in space. "I'm getting the feeling that the perp is more involved than just being her lover."

"Maybe her roomie wasn't too upright, either. As always, follow your hunches," Zee says. He glances across the room. "Uh- oh, Roark's seen us," Zee says. "She's waving. Wow, she's a pretty thing. How come you and she...."

McGraw acts like he doesn't hear Zee and fixes his sights on Roark, sauntering across the room toward them in a red dress, snugly fitted around her hips, high heels, her shiny brunette hair combed to one side, behind her right ear, and extending down in front of her, covering her right breast. McGraw had never seen her looking so beautiful. He feels a tingling race up his spine.

"Hey, boss," she says, smiling at McGraw and then turns to Zee. "How yuh doin', Captain?"

"Doin' great, sweetheart." He raises his glass to greet her. She bends over and kisses him on the check. "I hear your car got fire-bombed," he says.

She glances at McGraw and turns back to Zee. "Yeah, nothing left of it. I'm in the market for another."

"Glad you're okay," he says. "You look mighty pretty. If I were just a few years younger..."

"Thanks. You're a honey. I've been watching you guys," she says. "Bet you're working the Hamilton case?"

"Yeah," McGraw says.

"Well? What's the verdict? Is she dead or alive?"

"Dead," Zee says.

"I don't know," McGraw says.

"We're past forty-eight," she says. "Chances are slim for finding the poor thing alive. I guess I am in agreement with Captain Zee."

"You got it, honey," Zee says. We've always seen eye to eye."

McGraw is staring at Max the macho man across the room. *Don't think I'll ever like that guy. There's something about him.* He turns back to Roark. "Would you and your movie star friend like to join us, or would you rather be alone?" he asks.

Roark turns to look over at her date, who is talking to the waiter. When she turns back, she scowls at McGraw, and says with smugness, "Yeah, Max does look like a movie star, doesn't he? Let me ask him," she says as she leaves.

"Wow, she's a looker," Zee says, taking a sip of his drink. "What are you looking at," he says.

"At her date."

"Sure it's not something else?" He smiles. "Not a smidgen of jealousy?"

"You're drunk."

"And you must be blind or dead."

"I can see. Here they come," McGraw says.

The waiter follows them with their drinks, sets them on the table and adds two other chairs. "Your order will be out momentarily," he says.

McGraw and Zee stand.

"It's nice of you, Lieutenant McGraw and Captain Zee, to invite us to join you," Max says. They shake hands. "Thanks," he says as he pulls out a chair for Holly.

Such a showoff, McGraw thinks.

"Good to see you again, sir," Max says to Zee as they sit.

"Likewise," Zee says. "What are you having?"

"Oh, we've ordered. I believe the waiter is coming with our entrees now."

Roark is sitting close to McGraw's left and Max is between her and Zee. McGraw can smell her cologne and feel the warmth from her body. His eyes travel to her red lips, down to the top of her exposed cleavage, and gaze at her red fingernails. Her hair with its fresh shampoo scent is a few inches from his nose. He reaches for ice water and gulps it down.

"I understand you gentlemen were discussing a case," Max says. "Hope we haven't interfered."

"Not at all," Zee says.

"Is there anything you can discuss, Captain? I love mysteries."

"We generally don't discuss our cases," McGraw says. Max turns to him and frowns.

"Oh, I'm sorry, I'm out of line," Max says. "One thing I can bet on, though. In your line of work, you run into a lot of people who do stupid things."

"You can say that again," Zee says, before McGraw can get a word out.

Max is all smiles. His eyes are visible through the shades he's wearing. His white shirt is open at the collar and strands of hair are arched down on both sides of his forehead, touching his brow. He takes a couple of draws from his drink. "Yeah, in my business, I meet a lot of folks who haven't used many of their brain cells in years. But my major gripe has to be those fools in the markets that ride scooters through the aisles, blocking other shoppers. Did you ever notice how many of them are so overweight that their flesh hangs over the seat? It's like the old saying: when God asked if they wanted brains, they thought he said trains, and they said they didn't want any." His laugh bellows throughout the restaurant. "Let's drink to that," he says, raising his glass.

Yeah, and you're one of them who said no at the time brains were dished out, McGraw thinks.

CHAPTER TWENTY-FIVE

The next morning Noah McGraw is looking over some of his notes on the Hamilton case when his partner comes in. She throws her purse in the top drawer of her desk and slams it shut. McGraw looks up, but doesn't say anything. From her appearance, she could have used a few more hours of sleep. He reaches for his coffee and takes a few swallows, ruffles the papers on his desk to get her attention. Finally, he says, "You okay, sergeant?"

"Why wouldn't I be?" she says.

"I don't know. You look tired." He was eager to know where they went after leaving Moose's place.

"I had a great evening," she says. "Thanks for inviting us to your table. I know you didn't really want to."

"You're wrong. I enjoyed it very much. You looked very nice, and Max was fairly decent."

"Thanks." She rises, heads to the coffee stand and returns, stirring her cup.

She takes a drink of coffee and moves a stack of papers on her desk to make room for the cup.

McGraw is eager to know more. He's about to ask when she says, "We went out dancing after we left you guys and I'm afraid we stayed out a little too late."

McGraw straightens up in his chair. He suspected as much, but still, after hearing that, he dislikes Pretty Boy even more. Roark is only his partner, so why is he feeling this way? *What's wrong with me?* He thinks. *I'm acting like a teenager.*

"If you had such a good time, why do you look irritable?"

"Stop telling me how I look. You and Zee are the ones that went kinda heavy on the booze, wouldn't you say?"

"No more than usual for me. Zee was depressed over losing a friend. I'm glad to hear Rocky is working out for you."

"Stop pretending, McGraw. You don't care an iota about us."

"Why would you say that?"

"It's your pompous-ass attitude every time his name comes up."

"Do you have to use language like that in here? Anyway, I'm not too pompous. I'm just not taken with him, and I'd bet the feeling is mutual."

Roark's face tightens. "You keep calling him Rocky. His name is Max, not Rocky. And he's a gentleman, more than I can say about you," she says, turning to look at Gomez and Kramer, who are at their desks gawking at her. "What are you guys looking at?"

"You okay, sarge?" Kramer says with a frown.

In a gruff tone she says, "Why is everyone asking me how I am? Once and for all, I'm fine."

Kramer and Gomez look at each other and shrug.

The phone rings. Kramer picks up, calls out to McGraw, "Lieutenant, Laura Cook is on one."

He picks up. "Lieutenant McGraw," he says.

"Detective, this is Laura. You told me to call when Dex and Trev came into the bank. They passed us a few minutes ago on their way into Mr. Payne's suite."

"Thanks for the tip," he says and then shouts to Kramer and Gomez, "Get over to the bank. Dex and Trev are there. Follow them and don't let them out of your sight."

"You got it, boss," Gomez says.

Minutes later, Detective Kramer moves the black Impala cruiser into a spot across the street from Citizens Bank, leaving the motor running. He reaches for his coffee from the slot between him and Gomez. The car's gentle blower wafts the smell of hazelnut to his nostrils. The late-morning sun is behind the clouds and the temperature is dropping. Gomez is finishing off a chocolate donut in the passenger seat and licking his fingers.

"Wonder what those creeps are up to?" Gomez says, wiping the icing from his lips with a napkin.

"They're talking about their next money shipment," Kramer says, taking a quaff of his coffee. "Didn't one of the gals say Payne gets a briefcase when they meet with Parino?"

"Yeah," Gomez says.

Kramer finishes off his coffee. "They're planning something."

After nearly an hour, the two guys come out of the bank. One is taller and bulkier than the other.

"I believe these are our guys," Gomez says, reaching for the camera with a telephoto lens, takes aim and snaps off several frames as the suspects walk to a canary yellow pickup parked a block away and hop in. The taller guy is behind the wheel and the other guy is in the passenger seat. They drive off.

"Hey, wait a minute. I recognize the taller guy." Kramer says, pulling away and racing after them. "He's Dexter Price. He was in the Academy with me, but was thinner back then."

"Then the smaller guy has to be Trevor Wilson," Gomez says.

"Yeah," Kramer says. "Old Price wasn't liked much by the guys in the academy."

Ten minutes later the pickup slows, turns right at the corner, pulls to the curb next to a playground and stops. Kramer slows but doesn't turn; instead he stops the cruiser close enough to the corner where they can still observe the yellow pickup. A Mercedes pulls in front of the pickup and this tall black guy gets out, looks around, and walks over to the driver side.

Gomez readies the camera and begins snapping frames in rapid-fire succession.

The guy talks briefly to Dex and then he passes something through the window, goes back to his luxury car and takes off. The yellow pickup makes a quick U-turn and races past Kramer and Gomez without glancing their way. Kramer takes off after 'em.

"Marco said Dex was on the take, getting info for the black guy and protecting him," Gomez says.

"Yeah, and it looks like it's true," Kramer says.

Gomez removes his cell from his suit coat and calls headquarters. "Boss, Dex and Trev met up with a drug dealer, and we're following them now. Kramer recognized Dex from their time together at the academy." Gomez listens for a few second. "Will do." He turns to Kramer. "Boss says to stay on 'em."

Dex pulls into the parking lot of the Fourth Precinct and parks. He steps out and Trev jumps out of the passenger side and they hurry into the station. Ten minutes later, they come out. Trev goes to an olive green 2005 Honda Civic that badly needs paint, hops in and drives off. Dex slides back into the pickup and takes off out of the parking lot.

"Those bastards," Kramer says. "I hate dirty cops."

"Me too," Gomez says. "They give the rest of us a bad name."

They head back to the station. When they enter the squad room, McGraw is at the evidence board and Roark is working at her desk.

"By the way, Gomez, did you find an incident report on Eva Hamilton's stalker?"

"Nothing boss. She didn't file."

"That's interesting," McGraw says.

Roark frowns. "Why is that interesting?"

"We have to consider her motive, why she didn't report it."

"I know why," Roark says. "She was afraid Dudley would find out. He's always on her case about being afraid of her own shadow."

"Our guys," Kramer says, "got an envelope from a drug dealer, and then returned to the Fourth to get Trev's car and then they left."

"My friend Marco told us Dex is providing information and protecting the black dude," Gomez says. "Here are the pictures I took," Gomez says, heading to the lieutenant's desk.

McGraw reaches for the camera and slides through the pictures. Roark looks up from her computer. She must be wondering what's going on, but he says nothing.

Moments later, McGraw looks up. "Price is definitely a macho guy and Wilson is the opposite." He hands the camera back to Gomez. "Make the prints," he says.

"I'd put my money on Dex leading Trev around," Gomez says as he takes the camera and returns to his desk.

Kramer calls out from his desk. "Lieutenant, I just got off the phone with the desk sarge in the Fourth, who was in the academy with me. There's been several disciplinary actions taken against Price and Wilson for being late, and several complaints of police brutality have been levied against Dexter Price. Also, someone called in with a tip that our guys are involved with drug pushers and the Mafia."

"Anything come out of the Mafia thing?" Roark says.

"The Fourth is still checking it out. It was just one call."

"Checking it out means that'll be the day," Roark says.

"Did the sarge say anything about reporting them to IAD?" McGraw asks.

"Their investigation hasn't gotten that far," Kramer says.

"Nothing I hate more than protecting crooked cops," McGraw says.

"Amen to that," Roark says.

"You can bet there are other cops involved with them, too," Gomez says.

"Keep digging," McGraw says. He rises and heads to the Capt.'s office. Norman Dipple is sitting behind his desk chewing on a sandwich, and looks up when McGraw enters. "Can we talk, Capt.?"

"It's about time," he says, placing his snack on the napkin in front of him. "You got something for me?"

McGraw nods. "Here's what we have. Two cops from the Fourth are taking what we think is a payoff from a drug dealer. We got pictures of them receiving an envelope, and they are working with Eva Hamilton's boss, Austin Payne, in Citizens Bank, laundering drug money for Johnny Parino."

"I know Parino. You got any proof they're laundering?"

"We're working on it, before we turn the evidence over to the IRS agents."

"How are you tying Parino into the Hamilton case?"

"These cops are involved in Ms. Hamilton's disappearance because she allegedly discovered what they were doing with Parino and Payne. One of the officers, Dexter Price, has a bad temper. He became raging mad at Ms. Hamilton when she didn't respond to his advances, and the other officer, Trevor Wilson, had to pull him away. Dex could be our man." McGraw knows the captain will want to know if the bad cops have been reported to IAD (Internal Affairs Division). McGraw's concerned that they could take over his investigation of Dex and Trev.

"What about IAD?" Capt. says. "Have they been informed?"

"Not yet. The sarge at the Fourth told us that they are still investigating, and recently they received anonymous tips that Dex and Trev are involved with the Mafia. I want to keep both of these guys under surveillance as long as I can."

"I need something to get the commish off my ass."

"Tell him there's very little forensics and no body. This case is going to take a little more time."

The Capt. doesn't say anything; instead he rises and goes to the door. He looks out into the squad room, sighs and returns to his seat. "Do what you have to do, but get me something."

McGraw leaves without saying a word and heads back to the pit.

"Hey, McGraw, I've got good news," Roark says.

"I need some good news."

"I've found Cody Guthrie."

"Here in Atlanta, I bet."

"Yeah, can you believe it?"

"Tell me about it."

"Sheriff Sinclair told me Cody's a plumber, so Gomez and I had been calling all the plumbing companies until you sent him out after Dex and Trev. I just hit a lucky streak on my own and found Cody works for Brandon's Plumbing on the west side. He hasn't been to work for a week."

"You get his home address?"

"Got it," she says. "He doesn't live far from work."

"Well, what are we waiting for?" he says. They jump up.

"Don't forget your crown," she says to mock him.

"Never. I wouldn't want to disappoint you."

On the way out, they pass the Capt.'s office and she says, "Lately, the Lion has been on you, McGraw. What's up with that?"

"He's just doing his job," McGraw says.

"Oh, now you're Mr. Nice Guy, huh?"

McGraw cracks a smile. Outside, he opens the driver side of the unmarked black cruiser and hops in. They peel off to the east side. McGraw eases up to the little gray frame house and stops.

"Don't see any movement," Roark says. They scramble out and go to the front door. McGraw pounds several times on the door. No answer. Dogs are barking in the neighbor's backyard. He moves to the front window, cups his hands against the glass and peers in. "Looks like he hasn't been home in a while. Dirty dishes in the kitchen sink."

"Maybe he's a slob like my ex," Roark says.

"Or he took off in a hurry," McGraw says. They head to the back of the house to a gate and fenced backyard. No dog or cats. They move up the steps and knock, again, no sounds. McGraw can't see through the curtain covering the glass. He tries the door, but it doesn't budge.

"Maybe the neighbors can tell us something," he says. They split up and start canvassing the neighborhood, knocking on doors. When they meet back at the car, they compare notes: Cody is a nice guy, stays to himself, doesn't seem to have any interest in the ladies, and doesn't cause any trouble. He hasn't been seen for a few days.

"It's looking more like he and Eva ran off together," Roark says as they slide into the cruiser. "He has to be the one who sent her those roses and made those phone calls."

"Maybe," McGraw says.

"Is there ever a time, McGraw, when you'd let yourself guess at something?" Roark asks. "I bet you're thinking they took off, but won't admit it."

"Let me ask you this. So you think Dudley Hamilton knew Cody Guthrie?" he says.

She hesitates for a moment.

McGraw wonders if Roark remembers Eva's invitation to the caller to come to their home anytime, which suggests that Dudley knew the caller, too.

"I have to admit, that's a good point, McGraw. I guess Dudley didn't know Cody, but did know the guy she was talking to."

"Okay," McGraw says. "Here's the rundown: Eva and Cody were high school sweethearts. Olivia Jordan came to Atlanta and Eva followed her. So maybe Olivia and Eva paved the way for Cody. Remember the sheriff in Perry said the gossip about Cody was brutal. So he left there to get away from it and to be in an area with old friends. We don't know if he came primarily to be with Eva or to just get away from Perry. Since the gals at the bank never saw her dates, we have no way of knowing who Eva Bingham dated before she married Dudley. We can, however, surmise with some certainty that Dudley did not know Cody. Also, it is unlikely that Cody sent her the flowers or made those phone calls to her. There's still a lot we don't know."

"You have to agree that it's highly likely that Cody came here to be close to Eva, and maybe he persuaded her to go off with him. The Perry sheriff would agree with me. He believes Cody never got over Eva."

"You're both romantics. The sheriff would have no way of knowing if Cody would convince her to leave Dudley," McGraw says.

"I know, I know," Roark says with frustration in her voice, "you only favor evidence."

"Evidence will take us in the right direction."

"But sometimes guesswork leads to finding evidence. You gotta start somewhere, McGraw."

"And we're going to start at Brandon's Plumbing when we come back from Charlotte and Raleigh."

She frowns. "I didn't realize we were going there. So you do think they ran off together?"

He doesn't answer her.

CHAPTER TWENTY-SIX

McGraw drives the black cruiser out of the station lot at five a.m. on the dot, gets on I-85 heading north to Charlotte, N.C. A little after eight he takes the off ramp to Charlotte and slows to forty-five miles per hour after passing the welcoming sign into Charlotte.

"Ever been here before?" Roark asks.

"A few times; how about you?"

"I never got out of Cleveland, always too busy. Once I arrived in Atlanta, well, you know how police work can eat away at your time. And I have Dusty to look after."

"Charlotte's a great southern city. It's sort of on a hill surrounded by two rivers, Sugar Creek and Irwin Creek. We need to bring Dusty up here to pan for gold. Some groups still pan in local streams and creeks for fun."

"Trying to hit it rich, are you?" she says laughing.

"Panning is somewhat like going fishing, very relaxing. Here's our turn." McGraw takes the off ramp and ten minutes later pulls into a parking spot on the side of the Exxon station. Roark looks at her watch. "We timed it just right," she says, "Jimmy Wilkes should be there. He sounded like a young kid." They get out of the cruiser and ramble to the front entrance. McGraw holds the glass door open, waiting for two customers carrying drinks in their hands to come out before he enters. He leads the way to the counter. The smell of popcorn is strong. A young redheaded man in his late teens is behind the counter waiting on a customer. When the customer leaves McGraw goes to the counter. "We're here to see Jimmy Wilkes." He pulls out his ID. "I'm Lieutenant McGraw and this is my partner, Sergeant Roark."

"I'm Jimmy."

I believe you talked with the sergeant."

He nods. "Hi ma'am, how yuh doin'?"

"Fine, Jimmy," Roark says. She smiles at his sweet demeanor.

"I'm fixing to go on break. Do you mind going next door to the café? We can talk there, if you don't mind. I don't want my boss to hear what's going on. He's not too friendly, and he wasn't too happy that the cops came by a couple of days ago."

"The café will be fine," McGraw says.

"What did the police want?" Roark says as they walk out of the store.

"They said they got a call from Atlanta, and that the missing lady was in our store and needed to know if I remembered anything about her."

"What did you tell them, Jimmy?" McGraw asks.

They follow Jimmy to the café and head to a table near the window, close to the parking lot. "I told them that I didn't remember much."

"Like some coffee, Jimmy?" McGraw asks.

"How about a large coke from the machine, sir," he says. "Lots of ice, if you don't mind, sir."

"Sure," McGraw says, heading to the counter. Only a few customers are waiting to be served.

Jimmy turns to Roark. "Am I in some kind of trouble?"

"Oh, no. As I mentioned on the phone, we just want to ask a few question about the early morning of the 21st when you were on duty."

He smiles. "You said something about that missing woman the police were here asking about."

"Yes, that's right," she says.

McGraw returns carrying a tray with their drinks, picks up a 32-ounce coke in a large plastic cup and sets it in front of Jimmy. Drops of water are sliding down its sides. He hands a cup of coffee to Roark, then removes one for himself. He drops several napkins on the table, takes off his coat and throws it over the chair.

"How old are you, Jimmy?" McGraw asks as he sips his coffee.

"Seventeen, sir."

"Are you in college?"

"Going to State in January, sir," he says.

"Good, good. Well, Jimmy, as you know, Charlotte is out of our jurisdiction, and that's why I called a friend of mine in the PD here to tell him we might be coming this way. We're hoping you can help us with our investigation of Ms. Eva Hamilton, who disappeared from Atlanta on the night of October 20th and stopped at your station for gas at one in the morning the next day, the 21st. We know this because we have records of all her gas receipts." McGraw reaches for his coat, pulls pictures from the inside pocket, and slides them on the table. "This is the person we're talking about," he says.

He nods. "Yeah, she's the one I saw in the paper. I remember her coming into the station early that morning, and when she got to the counter, she wouldn't look at me. She kept her head down like she was ashamed or somethin' and signed the receipt after I ran her credit card. She paid cash for other items."

"Was there anyone with her?" Roark says.

"A man. I didn't see anyone else."

"Did you get a good look at him?" McGraw says.

"He was a big guy in a brown coat. He stayed most of the time in the next aisle and kept looking at the candy bars while the lady signed for the gas. I can't remember much more than that. I'm sorry."

"We understand," McGraw says. "Could the man who was with her be anyone in these pictures?"

Jimmy bends down closer to look at them. Moments later he shakes his head. "I can't really say."

"Was there anyone else working in the station that night who could have seen Ms. Hamilton?" Roark says.

"No. I was the only one on duty that night."

"Did you notice anything unusual about her besides what you've told us? Anything at all," Roark says.

"Let's see. She was wearing a tan coat, couldn't see what she was wearing under it." He takes a drink of his soda. "But there was something. The stocking on her right leg was torn and hung down. I think there was blood on it and she had dirt on her shoes. I'm sure about that."

"Why didn't Ms. Hamilton pay for the gas at the pump?" McGraw says.

"We have problems with them sometimes. That night they were acting up and I put signs out for the customers to please pay inside."

"Did you notice what kind of car they were driving?" Roark says.

"No ma'am. I had posted the signs before they came, and I couldn't see the car from inside. I never went out while they were here—couldn't leave the register."

"Did Ms. Hamilton and the man talk to each other while inside?" McGraw says.

"He mumbled something to her when he picked up some items and gave them to her then he went to the other aisle. I thought maybe he was telling her these were the items he wanted."

"How about when they came in; did they come in together or did she come in first?"

"Actually, the man came in first. He kinda looked around and then went back out. There was only one other customer in there at that time and she left when the man went out. A few minutes later, Ms. Hamilton came in with him. They went around and got some things off the shelves and then she brought them to the counter. After that he went to the other aisle and had his back to me."

"What did they buy?" Roark asks.

"Just sandwiches and candy."

"You're remembering quite a bit," McGraw says.

He nods. "All your questions are loosening up my memory a little about that night. I kinda believe it also helped that they acted strange, making sure I didn't see their faces." He nods. "Yeah, I think that helped me to remember more."

"At the time, did you ever think about calling the police or maybe getting the license number off the car and calling it in?" McGraw says.

He shakes his head. "Sir, if you knew how many weirdos come in here at that time of night, you'd be shocked. We're kinda used to 'em, and don't pay 'em a whole lot of attention. I only keep an eye on the psychos who come in and stand around with their hands in their pockets. They scare me. They could have a gun or a knife."

I know exactly what you mean, McGraw thinks.

"Did the man with Ms. Hamilton have his hands in his pockets?" Roark says.

"You know what, now that you mention it, I believe he did. I guess I was watching her so much I forgot about that." Jimmy looks at his watch and turns to McGraw. "Sir, are we about done here? I need to get back to work."

McGraw pulls a card out of his shirt pocket. "Here's my card. If you think of anything, anything at all, please call me."

Back in the cruiser, McGraw gets back on I-85 and heads toward Raleigh.

"Don't you find it strange that Eva Hamilton didn't try to make eye contact with Jimmy so he could alert the police?" Roark says.

"I've been thinking on it, too. There's a reason she didn't. We just have to stay on it until we find out."

"Maybe she was afraid the perp would kill her," she says.

"That's the obvious reason, but I don't buy it. Mystery man wouldn't shoot her in front of the boy, which he had the makings to do, nor would he kill her outside somewhere. He wanted her alive for some reason. Anyway, she could have alerted Jimmy since the suspect was in the next aisle and would not be able to see her face."

"You're right," Roark says. "There must be another reason."

Halfway to Raleigh, they stop to have lunch, and an hour later they turn into the Exxon station looking for Billy Ray. Inside, they ask the lady at the counter and she points to the section reserved for the Subway chain. They find him rising from one of the tables, carrying his trash to the receptacle. Billy is a big boy, over six feet and around 240 pounds. Nice features. He wears his hair short and has a light shadow of whiskers. He's muscular, but not fat, no belly. One would guess he played high school football and may be heading somewhere on a football scholarship.

"Are you Billy Ray?" Roark asks.

"Y'all from Atlanta PD, aren't you?" He turns to Roark. "You must be the lady that called me."

"I am. And this is my partner, Lieutenant McGraw."

"Pleased to meet y'all, I hope."

They laugh. "We won't hurt you, Billy," McGraw says.

"Do you have time to talk?" Roark says.

"Sure. Can we go to that table in the back?" he says, pointing. "You folks look too much like cops and I don't want anyone to think I'm in trouble." He frowns. "I'm not, am I?"

"No. We just want to ask you a few questions and it will be fine to sit in the back," McGraw says.

Once seated, McGraw opens with the questions.

"Are you in college?" he says.

"On football scholarship at North Carolina," he says. "They red-shirted me last year, but I'm on varsity now and playing. I'm just home for the weekend, my mother was sick, but she's okay now. She doesn't have anyone else. My dad died when I was fourteen, and I kinda watch over her. I come here to see everyone when I'm home. Maybe you've heard of me. I play right tackle on defense."

"I don't follow football much," Roark says.

"I have," McGraw says, "heard of you," with emphasis. Roark frowns at him. She must be wondering if he's making it all up.

"You scored a safety against State."

Billy Ray's eyes widen like saucers, says, "Man, you're cool. That's right. That was me."

"Great game," McGraw says.

After that, Billy is so elated he's eager to answers any question with a smile on his face like he's really important. Roark follows along, interjecting questions at times. After ten minutes, McGraw says, "Just a few more questions."

"Sure, I'm not going anyplace."

"That second man you saw in the car; how were you able to see him? Did you go outside?"

"No. They pulled the car up to the pump which I can see from the counter. It's the only one visible from inside."

"Could you make out what the second guy looked like?" Roark says.

"Not too good. He was in the back seat. I couldn't see his face. He had on a cowboy hat."

McGraw looks at Roark. Her eyes widen.

"Was it like mine?" McGraw says.

"Yeah, like yours, sides curled up and a crease in the crown, but it was black, not white."

"You know about cowboy hats?" McGraw says.

"Yeah, my pawpaw came from Texas and he always wore one. But he's gone now."

"Sorry about your pawpaw," McGraw says. "I'm from Texas, too."

"Sure enough? Man that's cool. I like folks from Texas. Pawpaw and I used to go there in the summers to one of our family member's place. Did a lot of fishing."

Roark was smiling.

"Did you notice what Ms. Hamilton was wearing?"

"Let me think." He glances up at the ceiling. Seconds later he says, "A tan coat, but I couldn't see what she wore underneath. She had it buttoned up."

"How about her shoes?" Roark says.

"Nothing unusual about them. Black, I believe."

"How about her stockings?" McGraw says.

"They looked fine. Actually, she looked kinda nice. Pretty lady from what I could see."

"You said she didn't try to make eye contact but didn't look distressed," Roark says.

"That's right."

"And the man with her wandered around in the store while Ms. Hamilton paid for the gas," she says.

"I seem to remember he picked up a couple of sandwiches and gave them to her."

"Did they get anything else?" McGraw says.

He shakes his head. "Only the gas and sandwiches."

"So the man didn't appear to threaten Ms. Hamilton in any way?" McGraw says.

"No sir."

"Can you describe him?" Roark says.

"He was big, like those wrestlers on TV."

"Was he bald?" she asks.

He shrugs. "He had on a cap."

McGraw pulls out pictures from the inside of his coat pocket. "Do you see either of them in any of these photos," he says, sliding them across the table.

Billy takes his time. "That's the lady in this one," he says, handing it to McGraw. "I don't see the guy in any of them."

"Why do you think they didn't pay at the pump?" Roark asks.

"To get the sandwiches is my guess," Billy says. "A lot of folks do that. Not everyone pays at the pump."

"So there was no need to call the police?" McGraw says.

"No sir, they acted like most of the people that come in here, lieutenant."

McGraw rises and sticks out his hand and says, "Well, Billy thanks for your help. We appreciate your cooperation."

"Sure, man. I'm glad to help y'all."

When they step outside, Roark asks McGraw if he really watched that football game between North Carolina and State. "Sort of," he says. "It came up when I searched him on the Internet like I did Jimmy Wilkes. Billy's an NFL-type player. He'll go far."

"Well, surprise, surprise," she says.

McGraw slips in the cruiser behind the wheel. Roark slides in on the passenger side and shuts the door. "What surprises me is that Billy saw two men with Eva Hamilton and Jimmy only saw one," he says. "Other than that, both accounts are in agreement, except Eva may have purchased new underclothes and stockings in Charlotte before coming to Raleigh."

"And the suspect sent the original ones, washed and folded, with her Lexus to make us think she may have been molested," Roark says. "The folding of the vic's underclothes may be his MO."

"Two things are clear," McGraw says. "The guy with Eva was big as a wrestler, and the second guy was wearing a cowboy hat," he says, making the turn onto I-85 south.

"I can see the wheels turning in your head, McGraw," Roark says. "You're thinking about the guy in the back seat with the cowboy hat."

"He could be Cody, but why was he with them?" he says.

"If he was Cody, then that means he and Eva didn't run off together," she says.

Roark reclines her seat. "I think I'll get a little shut-eye. Didn't get much sleep last night, thanks to you."

"Before you doze off, I want you to do something for me."

"What is that?"

"When you get a chance, dig into the time Eva and Olivia lived together. Find out all you can about who they associated with at work and after, and who they dated. Zee thinks something is there, and I'm beginning to think the same thing."

Roark moves forward with interest. "Such as?"

"Don't know. That's why I want you to dig deep. Especially find all you can on Olivia. Get Gomez and Kramer to help when they're free. The girls seem too clean for my money. The perp could have something on them."

"Will do," Roark says as she tilts her body backwards in the seat.

McGraw sets the cruise control at sixty-five and wiggles himself into a comfortable position. A few miles down the interstate, he begins to wonder: *Why was Cody with Eva and how did they hook up with the perp? Cody wasn't with her when she left Prestige Mall. Why didn't Eva Hamilton pass a note or make eye contact with one of the clerks—she had two chances—or signal the clerks she was in trouble? It seems that Eva was acting in a role the perp wanted. What did he have on her? Did she have a secret life?*

125

CHAPTER TWENTY-SEVEN

The next morning, McGraw leads the way to the customer service counter in Brandon's Plumbing. Brandon's is in a large rectangle building, offering services in three sections: one for customers to purchase plumbing supplies like at a Lowe's, one for contractors to make their selections, and another section for customer service and paying bills.

He and Roark show their IDs and introduce themselves, and McGraw asks for the manager, who turns out to be a six-foot-four burly, red-headed guy with a bushy red beard. He's wearing jeans and a red and green plaid shirt with long sleeves. "How can I help you, detectives?" he says. "My name is Jim, Jim Harlowe."

"We're looking for Cody Guthrie," Roark says.

"So are we," Harlowe says. "We haven't seen him since the 15th. Is he in trouble?"

"Just want to talk to him," Roark says.

"What can you tell us about him?" McGraw says.

"Well, he's a danged good worker. Knows plumbing like the back of his hand. I'm told he worked for his dad somewhere in Oklahoma. Stays to himself mostly. I wish he'd show up, because we have lots of work."

"We'll need the names of your people who hung out with Mr. Guthrie," Roark says.

Harlowe frowns like he's in deep thought. "Give me a sec," he says, walking away and stopping at one of the stalls to talk to a worker who has just come from the back of the store. When Harlowe returns, he says, "Like I said, Cody sorta keeps to himself here at work, and I don't know of anyone he's friendly with. Kevin, the guy you saw me talking to, says Cody does go with the guys to Jerry's Roost after work for a few beers."

"Jerry's Roost?" McGraw says.

"Yeah, it's not far from here. It's actually in walking distance. Go back out our drive, turn right and go about a mile. It's on the right. You'll see the big

126

beer bottle sign above the door with Jerry's picture on the label.

They thank Marlowe and head out to the cruiser.

"This isn't the best of neighborhoods," Roark says as McGraw drives out of the parking lot and down Jackson Street.

"This isn't what you'd call a high-rent district," he says.

"There it is," she says, "on the right. You can park next to the building."

McGraw looks at his watch when they enter. It's four-thirty and the place has only four customers. The smell of smoke and stale beer is strong. Two guys in Falcons sweatshirts are at the bar, drinking beer from mugs, smoking cigars, and watching sports on the three large TVs. A couple is sitting at one of the tables eating fish sandwiches and fries and drinking beer. George Strait is singing "Baby's Gotten Good at Goodbye" on the jukebox.

"Too early for the working crowd," McGraw says.

Roark nods.

The guy behind the bar looks like the picture on the beer label outside. He is wearing a baseball cap with SL letters in red—St. Louis Cardinals—has several days' growth on his face and is wearing a white shirt with the sleeves rolled up. He's about half the size of McGraw and weighs around 120 pounds soaking wet.

"What can I do for yuh, cowboy?" he says.

In the mirror behind the bar, McGraw sees the two guys at the bar smiling and staring at his hat. He and Roark pull out their IDs and McGraw introduces his partner and himself. "We're looking for Jerry," McGraw says.

"What do you want with him?" the bartender asks, his dark eyes narrow.

"You Jerry?"

"Yeah. What can I do for you coppers?"

Coppers? McGraw ponders. *Only in Atlanta.*

"We understand that Cody Guthrie comes in here a lot," McGraw says.

"Whadda you want him for?"

"Just want to talk to him, that's all, about someone he once knew," Roark says.

"He comes in here a lot after work, with the guys from Brandon's. They don't cause no trouble."

"That's right," the two guys at the bar say, nodding.

Turning to them, McGraw says, "You guys know him?"

They nod again. "Sure do," the taller one says. "He's not a bad guy. Hope you won't rope him when you see him." He burst out laughing and slaps the bar.

McGraw turns to Jerry. "When did you see Cody last?"

Jerry frowns. "Lemme see. It's been some time. I don't really know."

"Does he hang out with anyone special?" Roark says.

"Naw, kinda likes to go around and talk to folks. He's very homey. That's the Okie in him."

"So he's well-liked?" Roark asks.

Jerry frowns again. "Hmmm. Well, he did get into a big ruckus with a guy

127

one night, but they sorta made up, I guess, 'cause they left together."

"Was the guy a regular?" McGraw says.

"No. Never saw him before. He was a big guy," Jerry says. "Like one of those guys you see on TV who's working out in a gym."

The shorter guy sitting at the bar says, "I was here that night, Jerry. The big guy seemed like a friend of Cody's."

"Can you give us more of a description?" Roark asks, writing in her notebook.

"He was over six foot and, like Jerry said, he had a body like someone that pumped iron. Black hair, eyes that looked like he was mad all the time, and dark whiskers, hadn't shaved in a few days." He sipped his beer.

"Did Cody call his friend by name?"

They shook their heads.

"Well, can any one of you remember what their argument was about?" Roark asks.

"Could have been over our guv," Jerry says, drying a glass.

"The governor, what about him?" Roark asks.

Jerry looks over at the two guys at his bar. "While Cody was getting pushed around by this friend, it came over the TV that our guv, a married man with three children, was involved with some bimbo—"

"—That was old news, man," the tall guy at the bar interrupts. "Some sleazy reporter was trying to make a name for himself and went after our guv again."

"Well, most of my customers are Irish and we love the guv and we forgave him long ago. We think this floozy wanted his money."

"Was Cody arguing with his friend before the news report, or after?" McGraw says.

Jerry turns to the little guy at the bar, and says, "Billy, do you remember? I was busy tending bar at the other end."

"It was before," Billy says, "'cause everyone got real quiet when the news report hit the screen."

"Then what happened?" McGraw says.

Jerry shrugs and looks at Billy.

"Cody was calling our guv names because of the affair," Billy says. "Cody'll let you know right off that he's a Christian and he said our guv committed adultery and is going to hell. The guys in here didn't like what he was saying about our man. They started shouting cuss words at Cody and shoving him. Things was getting out of hand."

"What happened next?" Roark asks.

"Lucky his friend pulled him out," Billy says. "Cody might of been worked over pretty bad by the guys."

"Did Cody and his friend leave through the front?" McGraw asks.

"Naw. I saw his friend pull him out the side door, over there," Jerry says, pointing to McGraw's right. He walks over to the door and looks outside. It's an alleyway that ends at the building behind Jerry's.

When McGraw returns, he asks if any of the customers use the alley.

"Naw," Jerry says. "Mostly used for deliveries and trash pickup."

"Do you remember the actual date this happened?" Roark asks.

Jerry shakes his head. "I can't, ma'am."

"How about you guys?" Roark says to them as she walks around McGraw.

McGraw has been watching the tall guy who has been leering at Roark since they came into the joint. Tall guy says to Roark, "Now that depends. I might remember something if you're nice to me, maybe buy me a drink and then we can go to my place."

Billy is getting jumpy. He whispers to his friend, "Shut the hell up, she's a cop."

"I'd take your friend's advice," Roark says, "unless you want to spend a few days in jail."

"I ain't afraid of no bitch even if she's a cop," he says with a twisted smile.

McGraw walks over to him. "You don't talk to women that way, especially my partner. You apologize. Now!"

"Bullshit!" He stands and takes a swing at McGraw, who shoots up an arm to ward off the punch. McGraw grabs him and flips him around and pushes him against the bar. Roark cuffs him.

"Police brutality, you're hurting my wrists," he screams as they take him out and put him in the back of the cruiser.

CHAPTER TWENTY-EIGHT

Back at the station, McGraw has Kramer and Gomez process the drunk he and Roark brought in, and then instructs them to meet with forensics at Jerry's Roost to check out the alley and treat it as a potential crime scene. Then he heads to the coffee stand. Captain Dipple comes out of his office. McGraw sees him out of the corner of his eye, turns his back to him and returns to his desk without filling his coffee cup.

"McGraw, are you avoiding me?" Capt. says. "I want to know what the hell is going on in the Hamilton case."

"Not now, Capt." McGraw grabs his hat and says to Roark, "Let's get out of here."

"Where to?" she says.

"To pick up a search warrant," he says. "Maybe we'll find something in Cody's house that'll lead us to the guy he had an argument with in Jerry's."

With the warrant, Roark slides behind the wheel of an unmarked black Impala and drives off with McGraw in the passenger's seat. Roark glides the car to the curb in front of a gray frame house. The detectives step out and they walk to the porch. Roark bangs on the door. The rapping sound brings out barking dogs and a next door neighbor peeping out through the curtains.

"Mr. Guthrie, this is the police. Please open up, we want to talk to you," Roark shouts. A few seconds later, she says, again, "Mr. Guthrie, police." No answer.

Roark steps aside and McGraw examines the door. No dead bolt lock. He shoves a credit card between the lock and frame, and pushes through with his shoulder. They end up in the living room, with a couch and recliner on bare hardwood floor, and a three-shelf stand supporting a DVD player and a land-line phone next to a recliner. The detectives begin their walk-through. To the left is a small dining area with only a table and three chairs. A hallway leads to the back, ending into a bathroom and in the middle of the hall is a bedroom. Off the living room is the kitchen with overhead cabinets, a table and two chairs, and a stove. Dirty dishes are in the sink and the table is covered with newspaper clippings about Eva Bingham Hamilton. McGraw collects them as evidence. Cody's interest seems more than just romance.

McGraw moves back into the living room. A pair of slippers is under the table, a dirty work jacket is on the couch, and magazines are scattered on the floor in front of it.

"Got something," Roark shouts.

He heads back to the bedroom.

"I've found another pic with Eva and the teenagers, just like the one we took from Dudley's," she says. "Since Cody has one too, it has to be their high school graduation."

McGraw flips on the light.

"What do you have in your hands, McGraw?"

"Evidence for when we meet up with Cody. These are newspaper clippings of Eva Hamilton he cut out of the local paper. Cody's interest may be more than just romance."

"Maybe not; Sinclair said Cody never got over her. He may have a broken heart."

McGraw shrugs. "Let me see that picture you're holding," he says to Roark. He holds it up to the light. "These kids are definitely high school age. Cody's definitely next to her. He's very thin." McGraw pulls the picture in closer to get a better look. "Eva looks the same," he says. "We gotta get a make on the other two kids." McGraw takes it out of the frame and hands it to Roark. He stops and looks around. Clothes are strewn over the floor. *Whadda mess*, he thinks.

Roark says, holding up two plastic forensic bags, "I collected his toothbrush and hairbrush."

"Good. Let's get out of here. I'll drive."

"What? You don't like my driving?"

"I just feel like driving." He slides in behind the wheel and drives back to the station. Once inside, McGraw removes his hat and places it on his desk, as they examine the photo more closely.

"I know it's a long shot, but maybe the other guy in this photo is the one that met Cody in Jerry's Roost?" Roark says, examining it.

"Worth checking out," he says. "Obviously, Cody knows him, but again, the guy could be anyone."

"Cody knows him or he wouldn't have left with him," she says. "I wonder what they were arguing about."

"It could have been over Eva," McGraw says.

"That could mean the other guy may have come from Perry, too," she says.

McGraw nods. "Something could have happened to Cody and Eva after they got back from North Carolina," McGraw says.

"So you think they came back to Atlanta?" Roark says.

He nods. "It's highly probable."

CHAPTER TWENTY-NINE

The next morning Roark gets a call from Sheriff Sinclair. "I have some information for you, sergeant," he says. "It took me some doin' to get people to remember those youngsters in the pic you sent me. It's been a long time and they really had to study it."

"I know, sheriff. We really appreciate your help."

"They are definitely Perry High School students. The photo was taken in '91 at their graduation. I can identify three of the eighteen-year-olds, but the fourth one, I'm not sure."

"Let's have it," Roark says.

"Eva's the one in the middle as you most likely guessed, and her girlfriend, Olivia Jordan, is to her left, and Cody is on her right and that last boy on Cody's right... I think is Sonny Burke."

"Sonny Burke?" she says. "What can you tell me about him?"

"He wasn't very popular, kind of a loner. Most of the students didn't like him, and that's why I have doubts he's the one in the picture."

"Why did they not like him?"

"The youngster's family wasn't the best."

"We found the same photo in Cody's home," Roark says. "So there's a good chance that each of the teenagers in the picture has a copy."

"That sounds reasonable, since it was their graduation."

"Then wouldn't you say at least Eva, Olivia and Cody liked the guy since he's in the picture? They're all smiling? Why would he be in the picture if this Sonny wasn't liked?"

She could hear the sheriff snorting. "Well, I don't know how to make it any plainer. I knew Sonny, but we can assume it is him, if you wish. The problem I'm having is that the picture isn't very clear. Is the one you have any better?"

"I'm afraid not. It's a little fuzzy, too. I believe the tree in the photo is casting a shadow over the young man that could be Sonny."

132

Sinclair is silent for a few seconds. "I believe you're right. Maybe that's why I can't make him out too good."

"Anything specific you can tell me about him?" she asks.

"Sonny's father left when the boy was in grade school. And... and his mother, well, she was the town... I mean, she took to all men, if you know what I mean."

"I do. And I bet that was hard on little Sonny?"

"It was. Folks gossiped a lot about the Burkes. Sonny kinda withdrew into himself and wouldn't have anything to do with no one, wouldn't talk to no one, had no friends to speak of. To his credit, he was a damn good football player. Ole Miss was high on him, but he damaged his shoulder in a game and that was that. He didn't stay around here long after graduation. We lost track of him. Word has it that he wanted to be an actor, so maybe he went to New York or Hollywood. Only thing, though, Sonny's distant cousin here said he heard that Sonny went to Mississippi to live with a relative. I guess that's why he was considering Ole Miss."

"Could you find out where that family member lives in Mississippi?"

"I already asked around, and his cousin, the one here, said he didn't know. It's like Sonny dropped off the face of the earth, sergeant."

"I'll do a name search in Mississippi. Maybe I'll hit it lucky," she says.

"That's your best bet," he says.

"Okay then, Sheriff Sinclair. Thanks. You've been a big help."

"Glad to help, ma'am."

Roark places the receiver in its base, turns to her computer and enters Sonny Burke into the databases. Moments later, nothing on the mystery man after high school is recorded. He has no criminal record, no service record, isn't wanted by the FBI, and doesn't appear in the child molester database. Mississippi has a Sonny Burke, but he is black and ninety years old.

Roark heads to the crime board and looks at the photo. "Where are you, mystery man?"

McGraw finishes a call from forensics and glances over at Roark, who's still at the evidence board. He rises from his desk and goes to her. "What are you working on?"

"Been talkin' with Sheriff Sinclair, he thinks this guy in the photo," she says pointing, "could be Sonny Burke, but isn't sure because Burke's hard to make out. I've run him, but it's like he vanished after graduating in '91. But I'll do some more checking."

Kramer calls out from his desk. "Call for you, lieutenant."

McGraw goes to his desk and picks up.

"That was forensics," McGraw says to Roark, returning to the board. "They found nothing more at Jerry's Roost than what Kramer and Gomez reported. Duct tape, cigarette butts, and trash around the dumpster."

"Just what we expected, but it was worth a try. Maybe the duct tape will give us a clue down the road," she says.

McGraw heads to the coffee stand and fills his cup.

Roark reaches for her phone and calls Sheriff Sinclair back again. "Sorry to bother you, again, sir. I forgot to ask about Olivia Jordan. She seems to be another mystery."

The sheriff takes his time answering. "I would never mention it to anyone else, but since you're doing an investigation, I can give my opinion. You have to realize, Olivia had never been arrested or anything like that, but in my opinion, I didn't think it was a good idea for Eva to go to Atlanta to be with her."

"Why?"

"Olivia had a lot of boyfriends."

"Some high school girls are very popular," Roark says.

"While there's nothing wrong with being popular," he says, with hesitation in his voice, "she was promiscuous. The high school coach had to chase Olivia and a boy out from under the bleachers at the ball diamond. They were in a compromising position, if you know what I mean, and there were rumors about her going away on weekends with a couple boys, but nothing that could be proved."

"You said she never got into trouble. Apparently, she didn't get pregnant."

"That's true," he says.

"Do you know if she ever went out with Burke?"

"I doubt it, but wouldn't put it past her," he says.

"Thanks again, sheriff." Roark turns to her computer. After forty minutes, she looks over at the lieutenant. "McGraw," she says, "got off the phone earlier with Sinclair. He said Olivia was very promiscuous. She had a few escapades in high school and he didn't like the idea that Eva came to Atlanta to be with Olivia. He was good friends with her father."

"Didn't the ladies at the bank say Eva came to live with them after a year with Olivia?"

"They sure did."

His brow rises. "We need to find out what Olivia and Eva did in that year together."

CHAPTER THIRTY

McGraw pulls the sky-blue RAM pickup into a spot behind Home Plate around eight o'clock. Anna Marie and Roark pile out of the truck.

"Hurry up," Anna Marie says.

They enter through the back door and are met by Moose and his crew. After introductions, Johnny grabs Annie Marie's arm. "We're going to make your Irish stew. The troops have been clamoring for it."

"Oh my, how wonderful," she says.

McGraw watches Ms. Elli take Roark to the dining area and explain what they do on the serving line. "You'll be helping me, sweetie," she says. "Breakfast is over, so we'll take the food off the line and take it into the kitchen. Then we'll come out and wipe this steam table down with special water. How does that sound?"

"I can do that," Roark says.

In the kitchen, Moose says, "Noah, are you going to work, or stand around all day?"

"I thought I'd manage the place, since you aren't doing such a good job."

They laugh. "Okay, what's the drill?" Noah says.

"Look at the menu posted on the board over there by the fridge," he says, pointing, "and prepare something that no one else has checked off. Irish stew is the main dish, but some of my people do the same old thing and are kinda stuck in a rut. But I expect big things from you, being a chef and all."

"I'll check to see what's being done for lunch and come up with something different."

"Now you're talking."

Lunch is served at eleven. They have two-and-a-half hours. Noah scans the menu on the board. All items have been marked off. *My salad concoction and mom's bread recipe has to be it*, he thinks.

While mixing the salad ingredients in a large bowl, he glances over at his mother, who is taking charge of the stew, and Johnny is all smiles. At the serving

135

line, Roark is following Ms. Elli around, placing plates and eating utensils on line. *She's really enjoying this*, he thinks. Nearly two hours later, Noah is gazing at the loaves of bread in the oven and determines it's time for them to come out.

"Okay, folks," Moose shouts through the place. "We got thirty minutes to get everything on line." *Just in time*, Noah thinks.

———◆———

"That's the last pan," Ms. Elli says to Roark as she lets it slide into a slot in the steam table. Dozens of people are waiting outside.

"You're sure pretty, honey." Ms. Elli says. "Those big brown eyes you got could get you in trouble," she says, bursting out in laughter. "Are you sweet on that cowboy?"

"He doesn't know I exist."

"Him must be blind."

"Should I open the door?" Roark says.

She shakes her head. "Oh, no, Mr. Moose don't like folks to come in till we're ready to serve."

"I feel sorry for them. It's so cold out there. They're freezing. Couldn't they just come in and have some warm coffee while they wait?"

"You have a soft heart, honey, but we'd better wait." She pauses. "I need to get some ladles from the kitchen, be right back. You keep an eye on things," Ms. Elli says.

"Okay."

The dining area can seat close to 100 people at ten long tables. The front of the building is glass. The busy street and sidewalks can be seen from anywhere inside. No drapes or blinds are on the windows. *Maybe Moose wanted it that way so people could see what's going on inside*, Roark thinks.

The entrance opens out onto the sidewalk facing the street. The traffic is heavy, seems everyone and his brother is out. Several grocery carts filled with odds and ends are parked close to the glass front. Several homeless men are standing at the telephone pole near the curb, talking. Roark is wondering if they have to be coaxed in. According to the lettering on the door, Home Plate is open for breakfast from 6 a.m. to 9 a.m. and lunch from 12 noon to 3 p.m. No dinner is served. Noah told her Moose has his evenings reserved for his Pitcher's Mound steakhouse.

Ms. Elli is rummaging through the drawers for spoons when she hears commotion coming from the dining area. She grabs the utensils in both hands and rushes to the serving line, and is stunned to find the dining room packed with homeless people sitting at the tables while Roark is passing out coffee. Ms. Elli's anger subsides when she sees the smiles on their faces and how cheerful they are talking to Holly Roark. A number of them are calling out Roark's name, thanking her.

"What's going on here?" Moose says. "Who let them in? How many times—"

"Wait a minute," Ms. Elli says interrupting him. "Don't get your dander up. Look around. This is the happiest I've ever seen 'em."

Moose doesn't respond; instead, he moves to the end of the line. He turns to Ms. Elli and says, "I don't believe it."

Noah and Anna Marie walk in behind Moose. "What's happened?" Noah says. He glances around and realizes what Roark's done. "Moose, I'm sorry. I'll have a talk with her."

Moose blocks him with his arm. "No. Let her alone," he says. "Your partner has taught me something. Get out there and help her." Ms. Ellie and Anna Marie rush to fill cups and distribute coffee alongside Roark, who is all smiles.

"I thought I was doing something by feeding these people. They need more than food. And your partner is providing it."

"That's a side of her I haven't seen," Noah says, eyes fixed on Roark.

Fifteen minutes later, Moose announces to the crowd that lunch is ready. Home Plate workers are behind the steam table in readiness. Anna Marie begins dishing out her Irish stew in bowls. "Sure like your stew, ma'am," one guy says. "Thank you," she says, turning to her son, and winks. Noah hands out corn bread, Ms. Ellie is heaping on the mashed potatoes and gravy, and the others are scooping out a vegetable mix, and finally dessert and drinks. After an hour there's a lull, and only a few stragglers are left at the line.

"What's that man doing out there, looking in at us?" Anna Marie says. "Why don't he come in?"

"That's Fred," Ms. Elli says. "He won't come in."

"Why?"

"No one knows. Mr. Moose tries and tries to get him to come in, but he won't budge from that cart. In a little while, Mr. Moose will take him a box of eats."

"I'm going to go talk to him," Anna Marie says.

Ms. Elli frowns. It takes her a minute to realize what's happening.

"What's my mother doing now?" Noah asks.

"I believe we're going to witness a miracle," Roark says.

Outside, Anna Marie is holding Fred's hand and it appears he's smiling. Everyone at the steam table is watching.

Just then, Anna Marie, holding on to Fred's hand, leads him inside. She sits him at the table closest to the door, and then comes to the serving line to fill a plate for him.

"My land," Ms. Elli says. "Moose has been trying for months to get him to come in. "How'd you do it?"

"What's going on out here?" Moose says, coming into the area from the back. "Don't tell me that's Fred sitting over there."

"Sure is," Ms. Elli says. "Can you believe it?"

"What did you say to him, Anna Marie?" Moose asks.

"I told him we love him and he's like family, and we're all sad that he won't come in and be with the family. He said I remind him of his mother." She begins fixing him a plate of food.

137

"Well, I'll be damned," Moose says. "I've been trying for months to get Fred to come in."

Anna Marie takes the plate to him, and Roark follows with dessert and drink.

Ms. Elli turns to Noah. "You have a jewel of a mother, detective Noah."

"I've known it for years."

CHAPTER THIRTY-ONE

Bonnie Richards arrives to work in Citizen's Bank forty minutes early to review her report for Mr. Michael Faraday, the bank president. The doors don't open until nine. She enters, walks to her left through the hall that leads to her suite. At her desk, she pulls out the lower drawer, throws in her purse and shoves the drawer back in, but it won't close all the way. She's never had this problem before. In her chair, she yanks the drawer out again and shoves it in harder, but it still won't close. What's going on? She yanks on the drawer so hard it shoots out and hits the floor with a bang, throwing her purse and its contents all over the floor behind her. "Dammit." She looks around. Her boss, Austin Payne hasn't arrived as yet, too early. Bonnie gathers up her things, returns them to the purse and places it on the desk. She slides off her chair to her knees and peers inside the opening. Something's in the back, but difficult to make out. She reaches in and pulls out a white five-by-six spiral notebook about an inch thick. She rises to her chair, kicks the drawer shut with her foot and sits. She lays the notebook on her desk, opens it and reads the first page. "My land, this's Eva's diary."

"Good morning, Ms. Richards," Austin Payne says, but as usual, never looks her way. He turns the key to his office door ten yards behind her, enters and slams the door shut. "Grumpy ass," she says under her breath, "so sour and secretive." Bonnie grabs the notebook and heads to the ladies wash room, finds an empty stall, goes in and locks the door, closes the lid on the stool, and sits.

Twenty minutes later she returns to her desk, puts the book back inside her purse and opens the confidential file containing her report to the president. Moments later her phone rings and the president's secretary informs her that Mr. Faraday is ready to meet with her. She jumps up and rushes to the elevator bank.

———————◆———————

Dexter and Trevor hurry into Citizen's Bank around nine-thirty on their way to the Chief Financial Officer's office down the hall to their left. They pass a series of offices, a conference room and a large room where Eva Hamilton's friends are at their desks working. A few feet away is the entrance to Austin Payne's carpeted suite, with a desk in the middle of the room that Bonnie Richards occupies—the one that belonged to Eva Hamilton—and several cloth chairs arranged around the room with tables and lamps. Payne's office is directly behind Bonnie's area. As they move in, Dexter notices Bonnie's purse on her desk. He stops and looks to see if Austin's door is closed.

"C'mon, we're late," Trevor says.

Dexter raises his hand. "Just a minute," and walks over to the purse. He opens it and finds a white notebook. He pulls it out and glances at the first page. "Man, do you know what this is?"

Trevor shakes his head.

"This is Eva Hamilton's diary."

"Put it back! We don't want no part of it," Trevor says.

"The hell we don't. Old man Payne will want to see this," he says. "Maybe he'll give us some money for it."

"Put it back, Dex! You can tell Payne about it."

"Who you tellin' what to do?" Dexter says, slipping the diary into his suit coat pocket. "I decide on things, not you." He removes the red wallet from Bonnie's purse and unfolds it.

"What the hell are you doing now?"

"Whadda I tell you. Shut your trap. Bonnie's a highfalutin babe. She must have cash in here."

"Austin will cream us if he finds out."

"Who's gonna tell him? It ain't gonna be you or me. Do you see anyone else in this room?"

Dexter takes out five one-hundred-dollar bills and five twenties, "Man, we've made a killing." He stuffs the bills into his pants pocket, places the empty wallet back inside her purse and snaps it shut.

"Bonnie's gonna know you took the diary and the money."

"How in the hell is she gonna know that?"

"Some of the gals next door might of seen us coming down the hall."

"I don't give a shit."

They head to Payne's office and Dexter taps on the door.

"Come in," the voice calls out.

Dexter opens the door and they step inside, taking seats facing Payne, who looks over his glasses resting further down on his nose, making him look like he's in his eighties. Behind him is a large window with a view into a rock garden planted with circular boxwoods and an oak tree in the center. A framed picture of Payne's two boys is on the credenza behind him. Next to the window is a hall tree with an umbrella hanging on one of several hooks.

Dexter reaches into his coat pocket and says, "Austin, you won't believe what we've found."

Payne frowns. "I'm afraid to ask."

Dexter rises, places Eva's diary on Payne's desk and sits back down.

Payne shoves his glasses up on his nose, opens the diary and begins reading. Dexter glances at Trevor, whose blood has drained from his face.

Payne says, "Son of a bitch. Where'd you get this?"

"It was on Bonnie Richards's desk and I thought you'd like to know about it." He doesn't want to tell him he took it from Bonnie's purse.

Payne resumes reading without looking up. The dirty cops sit in silence.

"Son of a bitch," Payne says a second time.

"What's in there?" Dexter asks.

Payne raises a hand. "Shut up!"

Moments later, he says, "We're all in here. Eva Hamilton wrote that she believed you guys were dealing in drugs and prostitution, and I'm doing something with drug money. Also, she mentioned that you are police officers and we all have a connection to the Mafia."

"Whadda we gonna do?" Trevor says, shaking his head. "This is bad. The captain will castrate us, Dex."

"Austin, what if they don't have that book? You can burn it and no one would know," Dexter says.

"You imbecile," Payne says. "You're forgetting about Bonnie Richards and god knows who else she's told." He rubs his face, sighs, turns a one-eighty in his high-back chair and stares out the window without saying a word. His body is casting a shadow over the cops.

Dexter shrugs at Trevor.

Payne turns back and faces them. "This is what you're going to do." He rises and begins pacing the room, stops in front of the cops, handing the notebook to Dexter. "You'll return this diary and make Ms. Richards disappear."

"I don't know if I get what you mean, Austin," Dexter says, reaching for the diary.

"You damn well know what I mean."

"'Disappear', Mr. Payne?" Trevor asks, shaking.

"I don't know, Austin," Dexter says. "We ain't into murder."

"Murder?" cries Trevor, almost falling out of his chair. "I don't want no part of murder."

"Well, then, your asses can rot in prison. You know what they do to dirty cops in prison."

Trevor is sweating profusely and is having difficult time breathing.

"How much?" Dexter says.

Trevor's eyes are about to explode out of his head. "No, Dex. No. We can't...." He doesn't finish his sentence.

"Fifty grand is what I'm thinking," Payne says.

"That's a good figure," Dexter says. "How do you want it to happen?"

Payne returns to his seat. "I don't want to know, just do it!"

Dexter is the first to stand, and Trevor's knees are shaking.

"And do it soon," Payne says.

Trevor rushes out of the door. "I can't go through with this, Dex. Count me out."

"You're out if I say you're out."

Dexter goes to Bonnie Richards's desk. She still hasn't returned and her purse is where they left it. Dexter opens it, stuffs the diary into it, and they leave. When they step out into the sun, Trevor says, "Come on, Dex. There's no way we can do this."

"Shut up! I'm trying to think."

They hop into Dexter's Ford truck. He drives for miles around the city without saying a word. Trevor is fidgeting with the window. "Stop your squirming. I can't think. You're acting like a shithead."

About ten miles later, Dexter says, "Here's what we're gonna do. You remember how Eva Hamilton got roses before she disappeared?"

Trevor is looking out the side window and Dexter can barely see his head nod. "Yeah, so what?"

"Well, dickhead, we're gonna send her a dozen tomorrow. That way when she comes up missing, the guys at the precinct will think the perp that abducted Eva Hamilton did it to Bonnie, too."

"I don't know, Dex, I'm scared."

"When are you going to grow up? Do you want to go to jail?"

"No, but murder! I don't want no part of it."

"You got a better idea?"

Trevor shakes his head.

———— ✦ ————

Bonnie returns to her desk from her meeting with Faraday and throws the file on her desk. Something unusual about her purse draws her attention. She remembers snapping the purse shut before leaving, but now it's open and Eva's diary is sticking out. Bonnie pulls it out, and finds that her wallet is out of place. She opens it. All her cash is gone. *Who in the hell stole my $600?* She looks around the room and at Austin's door. No way would he have done it.

CHAPTER THIRTY-TWO

"Gomez," Kramer calls out from his desk. "There's a call for you. Sounds like your friend from the Mexican bar."

Gomez picks up. Velasco relays a message from Johnny Parino's truck driver that in two days he will be bringing up a load of booze and drugs from Mexico and wants assurance that he'll get immunity from everyone, including the Feds; otherwise, there's no deal.

"Detective McGraw isn't here at the moment," Gomez says. "Tell the driver he has our assurance."

"He wants it in writing, "Velasco says, "and he needs an answer today. Man, I'm afraid he's gonna chicken out. He's scared as hell."

Gomez rubs his chin. "I'll call you back in a few minutes." He gets up and rushes to the Capt.'s office. Dipple has just turned off the lights and is about to go out the door. "What can I do for you, Gomez?"

"The guy from the Mexican bar called. He is relaying a message from Johnny Parino's driver about the delivery we all met about."

"Yeah, I remember the guy."

"Well, he wants assurance from us and the Feds that there won't be any jail time and he will get protection from Parino's boys," Gomez says. "Otherwise, there's no deal."

"McGraw's in charge and has everything arranged with the authorities. Call him on his cell, for God's sake." He slams the door shut and rushes past Gomez.

"I thought I needed your input first, sir," he shouts. That's the reason he didn't call McGraw. He hurries back to his desk and reaches his cell phone.

McGraw walks in behind Gomez, removes his hat, sets it to one side of his desk and sits.

"Gee, boss, am I glad you're here. I was about to call you. Got a call from Velasco. Parino's driver is ready to give him up and I didn't know how to handle it."

"No problem. We're ready," McGraw says. He has brought the bureau in and now Special Agent Nelson is the lead investigator. "Nelson is coordinating the raid on the warehouse with State Police, and our narcotics bureau.

"But the driver wants immunity first."

McGraw pulls out his cell and calls Agent Nelson. When he finishes, he turns to Gomez and says, "Tell your friend that the FBI will meet with them in thirty minutes and the driver will get all the assurance he needs."

"Good enough, boss," Gomez says.

———— ✦ ————

The phone on Roark's desk rings. She lifts the receiver. The caller says it's urgent and she must speak only to Lieutenant McGraw. Roark calls out to McGraw, who is at the crime board. "There's an urgent call for you, McGraw."

He hurries over to his desk. "Who is it?"

Roark shrugs. "Some gal, she seems frightened. Says it's important and won't talk to anyone but you."

He lifts the receiver. "This is Lieutenant McGraw." He sits. "Please, calm down and run that by me again. Yes, I understand. Come to the station. You'll be fine."

"Who was that?" Roark asks.

"Bonnie Richards."

"You mean the gal that took Eva's place?"

He nods.

"She really sounded scared," Roark says.

"She's on her way," he says. "It would be best if you meet her coming in."

"Sure thing," Roark says as she leaves the squad room.

Thirty minutes later, McGraw looks up when he hears women's voices. Roark is bringing this blonde into the area. He can't believe his eyes. It's Marilyn Monroe.

"You must be Lieutenant McGraw," the blonde says in a soft voice, offering up a hand. "I'm Bonnie Richards."

"You've met my partner, Sergeant Roark," he says. She glances back at Roark, but says nothing.

"Did you see anyone following you?" he asks.

She shakes her head.

"Let's go into the conference room," McGraw says, picking up a notepad and then leading the way. Inside they sit at the long table, McGraw at the head and the women take chairs on each side of him, Roark to his left, and Bonnie to his right. McGraw places the notepad on the table and removes a pen from his pocket.

Bonnie's wearing a white blouse and a red skirt that accents her slim figure. McGraw notices Bonnie's sober face, filled with lines like those she might have when first getting out of bed in the morning, and she's frowning. *Not a happy camper,* he thinks.

144

"Now, what is it that has you so upset, Ms. Richards?" he says gazing into her gloomy eyes.

"Someone is going to kill me," she says.

"What led you to that conclusion?" he says.

This afternoon, I received a vase of beautiful red roses with a note that someone wrote, *Secret Admirer*. I know that Eva received roses before she vanished."

McGraw and Roark exchange glances.

"I may be next, and felt the urgency to report this to you."

"Who do you think wants to harm you?" Roark says.

"I did a stupid thing a few days ago. I arrived at the bank before it opened to the public to review my notes for a scheduled meeting with Mr. Faraday, the bank president. I had Eva's diary in my purse sitting on the desk—"

"—Wait a minute," McGraw says, standing up. "You mean you have Eva's diary?"

"Yes, sir." She reaches for her purse on the chair next to her and pulls from it a white notebook. McGraw reaches for it.

"Where did you get this?" McGraw says.

"I found it lodged in the back of one of Eva's desk drawers."

McGraw sits, opens the notebook and begins reading.

Bonnie continues by telling them that she usually places her purse in the lower drawer and locks it, but this day, she was so rattled getting ready for her meeting with the president, that when his secretary called, Bonnie grabbed her notes and rushed to the elevator, leaving her purse on top of the desk. When she returned and saw the purse out on the desk, her heart began racing because she remembered her purse was snapped shut when she left, but now it was open. She quickly went through the contents and found that $600 was taken from the wallet and someone had looked at Eva's diary.

"How did you know the diary was read?" Roark asks.

"The bookmark was replaced between two different pages. And there's a smudge on one of the pages that wasn't there."

McGraw looks up from the journal and asks, "Do you have any idea who took the money and read this diary?"

"The girls in the adjacent office told me they saw Dexter Price and Trevor Wilson come through to my suite that morning."

"So you think Price, Wilson and Payne know about Eva's diary?" McGraw asks.

"I'm sure they took it to Mr. Payne," Bonnie says. "He may even have read it." She pauses. "Dexter is the likely person who took my money and the diary."

"Why not Trevor?" Roark asks.

"Because Dexter is the bad one. Trevor wouldn't hurt a fly."

"Go on," McGraw says, paging through the diary.

"Interestingly, the next day I found an envelope on my desk with six one-hundred-dollar bills in it. I believe Mr. Payne replaced the money after I told him about it the night before."

"Is Bonnie Richards your real name?" McGraw says.

"Richards is real, but Bonnie isn't. I made it up for the job. Elizabeth is my given name."

"What specifically is your role at the bank?" he says.

Bonnie glances around the room before answering, like what she's going to say next is top secret. "I'm working undercover for Mr. Faraday." She hesitates for a moment, apparently waiting for a response, but none is offered and she continues. "No one knows I'm a plant outside of Mr. Faraday, not even the girls in the bank. They told you they thought I was a snitch, running to Austin every chance I got. That's what one of them told me. But now, they realize I'm not, and our relationship has really improved. We even go to lunch together."

"Could Eva have been a plant, too?" Roark says.

Bonnie shakes her head. "I doubt it. She was just an innocent person witnessing things, and kept notes on what she thought was dishonest."

McGraw looks up and says, "She writes that her husband told her to stay out of bank politics, and apparently that's why she kept this diary."

"You think Eva might have told someone about her diary and it got back to Payne and the boys and they took her out?" Bonnie asks.

"Very possible, but at this time it's uncertain," he says, not wanting to reveal to her his suspicions about Dexter Price.

"I know Eva never met with Mr. Faraday. He didn't really know her," Richards says.

McGraw closes the diary and looks into Richards's eyes. "Because of what's in this diary, I see now why Mr. Faraday feels he needs you. Please go over what interests the president mostly."

She nods. "Faraday suspects that Mr. Payne is involved in drug money laundering, and that he's supervising prostitution on the second floor, just what Eva wrote in her diary. He believes as I do that Dexter Price and Trevor Wilson are Payne's partners in his ventures. Dexter is Mr. Payne's brother-in-law, you know."

"Yes, we know," he says, as if he's not interested. "Have you seen them with Mr. Payne?" McGraw asks.

She nods. "Oh, yes, they meet in Payne's office at least once a week."

"So you think they're the ones who sent you the roses?" Roark asks.

"I do," she says. "After reading Eva's diary, they would have concluded I know too much. I doubt if they know I'm a plant; otherwise, they would have taken me out long ago."

"They've determined you have told or will be telling us and workers in the bank," Roark says.

"Tell us more about Payne," McGraw says.

"For starters, I know that he is strapped for cash. His wife, Dexter's sister, divorced him and took a big chunk of his money during the settlement, but gave him the home and custody of two boys who are in college, and they're draining him financially."

"Can't help feeling sorry for the guy," Roark says.

"You may want to hold off on that, sergeant," Bonnie says. "He's no angel. His situation makes him ripe for criminal activity and he's definitely dirty." She pauses looking at McGraw who is taking notes. "Payne's raking in the cash from drug money."

"What proof do you have?" McGraw asks.

"Laura Cook told me that she and the other girls have seen him on several occasions with Dexter and Trevor having lunch in Santino's restaurant and Payne leaves with a suitcase. Have you heard of Johnny Parino?"

"We know all about him and suspect the suitcase is filled with drug money," Roark says.

She nods. "That's right."

"Have you ever seen Mr. Payne with it in the bank?" McGraw says.

"No, but the girls have seen him bring it in late at night."

"What roles do you think Dexter and Trevor play in this?" Roark says.

"Trevor slipped up once and told me they make bank deposits for Payne throughout the city, but we girls knew that because we've seen them. I dated Dexter to pump him for information for Mr. Faraday."

Roark glances at McGraw.

"Dexter's not very bright," Richards says, "but thinks he's a ladies' man. He'll flirt with any skirt he sees. The girls at the bank don't like him and avoid him. He's known to fly off the handle easily. I was told when Eva didn't give him the time of day, he went into a rage and Trevor had to pull him away. They thought Dexter was going to club her. He's a heavy drinker. The booze gives him more courage to brag on himself, and he starts talking, and talking. Once, I asked him how he could afford expensive restaurants, clothes and a diamond Rolex on a cop's salary. He told me cops have ways. Once he slipped up and told me there's a lot of money in drugs and prostitution."

"How much investigating have Mr. Faraday's people done?" McGraw asks.

"Faraday's accountants are through reviewing Payne's accounts, checking with other banks for deposits and searching off-shore deposits. They've been in touch with law enforcement. He told me they have tons of evidence, and have turned everything over to the Feds. The last meeting we had, Mr. Faraday got a call from an agent Nelson with the FBI. Apparently, he is coordinating everything between agencies."

"That's correct," McGraw says. "He called us and shared all of it with us."

"I see," she says. "Looks like Payne and his boys could spend the rest of their lives in prison."

"That's the plan," Roark says. She looks at McGraw and then to Ms. Richards. "What about the prostitution? How does that work?"

"Mr. Payne is in charge of renting out all the offices on the second floor. One large office is occupied by an escort service, providing women."

"Have you seen the girls?" Roark asks.

She nods. "Dexter and Trevor use the service and I've seen them going through our lobby with them when I'm at the elevator."

Bonnie gets up, walks to the door and back to her chair and sits.

"Dexter Price may be the one who's planning to kill me, lieutenant."

"When you received the flowers, did you receive any phone calls from anyone?" McGraw says.

"No."

"The flowers were sent to put the fear of God in you, Ms. Richards, and to make you and us think the person who abducted Eva is the same person who sent you the flowers," he says,

"Did anyone at the bank see who delivered the flowers?" Roark asks.

She shakes her head. "The other girls and I had just come back from lunch and the flowers were on my desk. I asked other bank employees, but no one saw the delivery."

"You can bet whoever bought them paid cash and isn't the person who delivered them," Roark says.

"It sure put the fear in me," Richards says. "The girls and Mr. Faraday are the ones who told me to call you, lieutenant. I'm afraid for my safety."

McGraw rises and so do the ladies.

"I'll notify patrol in your area to keep a closer watch on your house," he says. "You have my cell number and can call me at any time. If things get serious, we can move you to a safe place."

He reaches for Eva's diary and tells Bonnie that they'll have to keep it for evidence.

"Good, 'cause I don't want it," she says, following them out of the conference room.

"An officer will follow you home," McGraw says, "and Sergeant Roark will escort you to meet the officer."

CHAPTER THIRTY-THREE

Dexter Price and Trevor Wilson are watching the home of Bonnie Richards from across the street in a 2011 black Cadillac they stole from a drug dealer that is moving in on their guy's territory.

The sun set an hour ago, and the drizzling rain has stopped. Dexter is in the driver's seat, drinking his fifth can of Samuel Adams, while Trevor stares out the passenger's window, drinking coffee from a Styrofoam cup. Dex reaches over and turns off the windshield wipers with his free hand, looking at the dashboard clock. It's a little past seven. The light from the street lamp two houses away in the cul-de-sac barely illuminates the houses north of it, leaving the Richards's home in the dark. A patrol car had passed them earlier as they were entering the neighborhood.

"We gotta be careful," Trev says. "They got patrol keeping an eye on her place."

Dex nods, and says, "Gotta give you credit, Trev, coming up with the idea of stealing Alfredo Ortiz's car. He'll crap in his pants when the cops come after his ass after they run this Caddy and find her body in it. Ortiz ain't getting away with causing our guy problems, trying to move in on Parino's boys. We told our guy we'd protect him. That's why he's paying us."

"Yeah, remember what Parino said. He don't like no rivals," Trev says. "Maybe that'll put us in good with Parino."

"Man, you crazy. We ain't gonna get between them. If Ortiz finds out, we're toast."

Dex downs the rest of his beer, reaches for the last one in the carton.

"Don't you think you've had enough?" Trevor asks. "You've gone through five already. You need to be able to think straight."

"Now you're becoming my ex? Get off my back, man."

Everyone's on my back, Dex thinks, as he removes the cap from the can. He especially hates that no-good brother-in-law of his, Austin Payne. He's been a thorn in his side ever since Dex's sister left him. He takes several draws on his

149

beer, glances in the rear-view mirror and sees the face of a troubled man. *You're a piece of work*, he thinks about himself. *Yeah, even the captain thinks I'm a bad cop. Maybe so, but what would anyone else do if they were in my shoes? The PD barely pays us a living wage. I thought about doing something else, but what? Maybe I should feel lucky being raised in a screwed-up family. My father was a drunk, who beat the shit out of my old lady and that stupid woman took it. What decent woman would take that?*

He continues staring in the mirror. *Look at you; you're no better than your old man, beating up on women when you're drunk. The acorn doesn't fall far from the tree. Isn't that what they say?* He takes a pull on his beer again. *I now have this weakness. I love money. You're nothing without it. I'm drawn to it. It's going to bring me down, but to tell the truth, I don't give a shit. Now I'm into killing. My life is over.*

"What's wrong with you, Dex? Have you changed your mind?"

"Shit, no. Sit tight."

"Let's call it off, Dex. Come on, we don't need to do this for Payne. Let him do it. Why should we do his shit?"

Dex finishes his beer, squeezes the can and throws it on the floor.

"Stop you're damn whining."

Minutes tick off. "Something's not right," Dex says.

"Whadda you mean?" Trev says.

"It's too quiet. There's no one on the street. When have you seen a neighborhood where no one has their lights on?"

"Okay, then, this may be as good a time as any to make our move."

"You're never gonna be a good cop. You're too naïve, Trev. Don't you know that when things seem too good to be true, there's trouble?"

"This couldn't be a setup. No one knows about this except Payne," Trev says.

Moments later, the porch light at the Richards home comes on and the door opens. A middle-aged woman is silhouetted in the doorway from the light in the room; she's talking to Bonnie. The older woman turns and glances at Dex and Trev.

They slide down in their seats. "I see what you mean," Trev says. "Think she spotted us?"

"Shut up and watch."

Seconds later, the lady with large hips comes down the steps with a covered dish in her hands, waddles across the lawn like a turkey, slippers flopping, and enters the house on the south side.

Bonnie shuts the door and switches off the porch light. A light comes on in the living room, and she can be seen through the curtains in the large window, moving past. She's alone.

"It's time to go," Dexter Price says. He eases out of the driver's side and closes the door without slamming it, moves around the front of the car. Trevor Wilson is waiting by the front fender. The dirty cops, dressed in black sweats, creep across the street like panthers on the prowl, scanning the neighborhood as they make their way to Bonnie's house. Dex moves along the sidewalk and up the driveway like a large cat and waits for Trev at the door. They slip into latex gloves, hair nets and shoe covers. Dex turns the knob with ease, as if he's expecting it needs oil. He pushes the door a few inches inward with his hands and they slip in.

An hour later, Trev slips out of the house onto the porch, and immediately drops to the floor and whispers, "Holy Mary, mother of God." A police car is coming down the street. Trev's heart is beating out of his chest. He waits. Beads of sweat are popping out on his brow.

Dex opens the door a crack and whispers. "What the hell are you doing?"

"Cop car."

"Shit. Stay down."

Trev edges his head out around the post. The cruiser moves past after stopping at the Caddy they came in, turns around in the cul-de-sac and heads back, moving about ten miles per hour. "Don't shine your light on this house, please, for God's sake," Trev whispers to himself.

"Has he gone yet?" Dex asks.

Trevor raises his head, and sighs. "Yeah, he's gone."

"Then get going."

Trev glances around the neighborhood before moving down the steps, his heart hammering as he inches across the lawn. A light comes on in the house across the street; the one they parked in front of. Trevor falls and hugs the ground. He's having hard time breathing.

"Hope that cruiser doesn't come back," he says to himself.

The light goes out. Thank God these neighbors aren't very nosy. He reaches the car and slips inside, pulls the door in but doesn't lock it, starts the engine and looks around—nothing unusual, no cars, no one walking their dog. Trevor maneuvers the Caddy with its lights off up the driveway and parks next to Bonnie's black Buick, flips the trunk switch, slips out but doesn't close the door and opens the trunk wider.

Trev darts to the house. Inside, Dex is waiting by the wrapped body on the floor. "Grab the other end," he says.

They lift Bonnie's body, carry it out to the stolen car, toss it into the trunk like a sack of cement and Dex closes the lid without putting too much pressure on it, to minimize the noise. They remove their shoe covers and latex gloves. The plan is to drive Bonnie to Ortiz's warehouse in the south end and set this Caddy on fire after they stop by Dex's place to clean the Caddy and get his pickup with the accelerant. Sixty minutes after leaving Bonnie's house, Dex pulls the Caddy behind the warehouse and Trev pulls the yellow pickup in behind him, but facing the opposite direction for a quick getaway. They hop out of the vehicles and Dex rushes over to his truck, puts on heavy rubber gloves and lifts out the accelerant and torch. It takes Dex ten minutes to douse the car inside and out. Trev serves as watchman.

"Get in my truck, Trev, and start her. I'm ready to set this baby on fire."

CHAPTER THIRTY-FOUR

McGraw is sitting with Zee in The Pitcher's Mound. The place is packed for a week night. He chooses Wild Turkey honey bourbon and takes small sips, gazes around the room, watching Moose talking with guests at their tables. Zee is enjoying his Johnny Walker red.

"Something's bothering you, Champ," Zee says, taking a pull on his scotch, "you haven't said a word in the last ten minutes."

"Well, let's see: The Capt. has been on my back because the commissioner doesn't like the way I've handled the Vanishing Bride case, my partner's SUV was fire-bombed; Eva's replacement at Citizens bank has received a death threat from the two dirty cops working with her boss in the bank, who is laundering drug money. All three are persons of interest. Dudley is no longer a suspect; he passed his second polygraph. And I am no closer to finding our suspect than I was days ago. Roark is investigating Olivia and Eva's time together. Let's see, did I miss anything?"

"Sounds like you need me, like the old days." He finishes off his scotch and says, "Okay, now let's review everything from the beginning."

McGraw first takes a draw on his honey bourbon and sets the empty on the table. The waiter hurries over with more drinks. In the next ten minutes, McGraw reviews the evidence.

Zee adds. "In our previous discussions, we decided Eva Hamilton definitely knew the caller."

McGraw feels himself nodding. "That's right, and one of her friends at work overheard the conversation." He takes a swallow of his drink. "We decided she must have dated the guy before Dudley, but Dudley had to have known the caller, too; otherwise, why would she have invited him to come over to their place?" He sighs. "No one knows who sent the flowers. Our investigation at the florist didn't help. Now we have something new to add to the case. Eva's replacement, Bonnie Richards, received roses, too, but only once and there was no phone call."

"Sounds like a copycat deal," Zee says.

"I agree. Someone is trying to throw us off with the Richards's roses. Whoever sent them to her didn't know Eva received the phone calls. I find it informative that Bonnie Richards didn't get a phone call, which tells me the senders are two different perps."

"I agree," Zee says. "Now who's high on your list of suspects?"

"Bonnie Richards deliberately dated a dirty cop named Dexter Price, and she told us plenty about him. We've been looking at him. Dexter harassed Bonnie in the bank like he did Eva, but Richards played into his hands to pump him for info. She's a plant in the bank hired by the president. Dexter has a very bad temper and he can be provoked into a rage that I believe could lead to murder. Dexter and his partner are involved in money laundering in the bank with Austin Payne, and are on the payroll of Parino. My theory is: Dexter was angry with Eva Hamilton for shunning him and he had to think she was about to turn him in. I believe he never got over her and abducted her."

"Do you believe he has her hidden some place?" Zee says.

"I do."

"What about Payne? Is he tied in in some way?"

"He's a suspect."

"Champ, if all your evidence points to this Dexter guy, you are on the right track."

CHAPTER THIRTY-FIVE

Roark is at the crime board posting info on Olivia. Roark's learned that she worked for April Dawn, a designer of expensive women's clothes before going to New York. Seems she's doing well there. Eva had a job with the Red Cross as a clerk in human resources. She worked there for nearly a year. The phone on Roark's desk pings.

Roark hurries to it and answers the call. Austin Payne is on the line asking for Lieutenant McGraw. "The lieutenant is out of the office at the moment; can I help you?"

"Ms. Richards has not shown up for work and I'm having a déjà vu moment."

Oh my God. Roark looks up at the wall clock. It's eleven-thirty.

"Did you call her cell and her home landline phone?"

"Yes, but no answer from either one. Maybe I'm paranoid since..." His voice trails off, and Roark is surprised he's having a hard time saying Eva's name. He didn't impress her as one who showed much emotion.

"Maybe she told the other girls that she'd be late today. Did you ask them?"

"I've asked everyone. We're a little jumpy since Ms. Hamilton's disappearance."

"We'll check into it, Mr. Payne," she says. "I'll get back with you."

"Thank you," he says.

McGraw comes from meeting with the Capt. as Roark hangs up the phone. "Guess who called?" she says.

"You know I don't do guessing games."

"Austin Payne. Bonnie Richards didn't show up to work this morning. I've checked and she's got folks in Minnesota. Maybe she went to see them and didn't tell anyone," she says.

"Could be," he says. "You have Richards's cell phone number, right?" he says.

"She gave it to me when she was here. I was about to call it, but Payne couldn't reach her on it." Roark opens her cell and punches in the number and

154

holds the phone to her ear for six rings. "I'm not getting any answer, McGraw."

"Do we have her parents' number?" McGraw says.

Roark turns to her computer and taps on the keys. "I'll have it in a sec."

McGraw calls patrol to head out to Bonnie's to check the place.

"Got the number," Roark says and makes the call to Richards's parents.

Minutes later she hangs up the phone.

"What did you find out?" McGraw asks. He can tell from her expression that Bonnie's not there. He had suspected as much.

"They talked to Bonnie last night around seven, but she was about to go out and do some shopping. They want to come, but I told them maybe it was nothing and we'd be in touch soon. I don't think they bought it."

McGraw grabs his hat. "Would you? Let's go," he says. He turns to Kramer and Gomez. "You two, let's go."

The two cruisers pull out of the precinct parking lot with their light bars flashing. McGraw and Roark are in the lead Impala. Minutes later, they arrive in a middle-class neighborhood with brick homes, pull into Bonnie Richards's driveway and stop in front of the garage next to a black Buick. Kramer and Gomez pull up behind them.

The house is red brick with porch and bay window. Garage doors are to the side and the sidewalk curves to the entrance from the driveway.

McGraw and Roark rush to the front door while Gomez and Kramer dash between the houses to the back.

A uniform pulls up in front.

"Don't see anyone inside," Roark says as she glances in the window.

"The appearance of a home invasion," he says. "The door is ajar and there's a light on in the living room." They draw their weapons and McGraw pushes it open. Roark slips in behind him. They enter the living room with their weapons held in outstretched arms, easing around every corner until the place is declared "all clear" by Roark.

Kramer and Gomez enter through the back door. "Nothing unusual outside, boss," Gomez says. The detectives pull on blue latex gloves and do their walk- through. Minutes later, Gomez reports blood in a crack in the bathroom sink and someone's done a cleaning job.

There's evidence of a struggle in the kitchen. Items are scattered all over the counter, cookies are on the floor, and on the free-standing butcher's block in the center of the room are a carton of milk and a half-glass of milk. Kramer calls attention to a large stain on the kitchen floor. "Looks like someone tried to clean it up. Something bad has happened here," he says.

McGraw tells Kramer and Gomez to comb the neighborhood. "Maybe someone saw or heard something. Also, tell the uniform to cordon off the place." He turns to Roark. "Call forensics?"

"Done that; they're on their way."

He moves into the kitchen and stops at the kitchen sink.

"What's got your attention?" Roark says

"Two hairs are on the edge of the counter and a broken fingernail is on the floor," he says.

The forensic team arrives in coveralls, hats and masks. One member begins shooting pictures in all the rooms. The lead says hello to McGraw.

McGraw says, "Appears we may have another female vic, Alan."

"We'll get on it, lieutenant," he says.

Gomez and Kramer return. Gomez reports that the lady across the street said she saw a black car parked at the curb in front of her house around seven or seven-thirty last night, and later she thought she heard a noise, looked out, but didn't see anything and went back to her favorite TV program. She couldn't tell the make or model of the car.

"Did she see anyone get out of the car?" McGraw says. "Or when the car left?"

"Naw," he says.

"And the next door neighbor to the north said he heard a noise a little later than the lady across the street," Kramer says. "He peered out and saw a car in the driveway here. It was dark and he thought it was either Ms. Richards's or a visitor. He couldn't tell the make or model, or anything."

"Did he see anyone?" McGraw asks in frustration.

"He didn't."

Gomez says, "The lady to the south was with Ms. Richards for about fifteen minutes, took her some pie and left around seven. There was a car parked across the street. She didn't see anyone in it."

"What about calling the police?" Roark says. "Did they ever think of that?"

"They didn't see anything that caused them alarm. I believe they didn't want to get involved, a common thing these days."

Alan, the forensic chief, comes into the kitchen. "We found streaks of blood in the cracks of the bathroom sink. Appears someone had washed something in there. Got hairs off the brush and we bagged the tooth brush. All blood samples have been collected. Nothing was found in the garage. The place has been brushed for prints. We're ready to do the kitchen," Alan says.

"There are two hairs here next to the sink and a fingernail on the floor," McGraw says.

"We'll take care of it, lieutenant," he says, stooping down to retrieve the fingernail.

"Appreciate your help, Alan," McGraw says.

"Sure thing, lieutenant."

McGraw turns to his unit, "Let's meet back at the squad room and regroup." Thirty minutes later, McGraw enters the pit and goes to the evidence board. His stomach churns as he eyes Bonnie's picture. *Here we go again,* he thinks. He turns to Roark, "Run Bonnie's profile through NCIC, and Kramer, you send out a teletype to all agencies to be on the lookout for Bonnie Richards."

"Will do," she says. "You've still got your hat on, Noah."

He doesn't respond, instead, he turns to Gomez.

"Gomez?"

"Yeah, boss."

"I want you to find out if any vics in the state could be our Bonnie," he says heading to the coffee stand.

"Will do."

McGraw pours a cup, adds cream and heads back to the evidence board, drinking his coffee, pushes his hat back on his head, and stares at the board. He notices the info on Olivia Jordan.

"Hey, boss," Gomez says.

McGraw turns to look over at him. Gomez is on the phone.

"You won't believe this. Uniforms reported that the fire boys just put out a burning Caddy behind a warehouse in the south end. There's a charred body in the trunk."

"Everyone, grab your stuff. Gomez, tell them we're on our way, and don't move anything. We'll be there in five minutes."

CHAPTER THIRTY-SIX

McGraw is in the lead as his team races to the warehouse with their sirens blasting and strobes flashing. A fire truck is pulling out from the lot of the warehouse as McGraw speeds in and stops behind a patrol car. Everyone is out of the cruisers in seconds and rushes over to the car with its paint burned off, rubber tires gone, rims touching the concrete, and nothing visible inside the vehicle except springs that once were in the seats.

A uniformed officer meets McGraw.

"What do we have?" McGraw asks as his team begins their inspection of the car.

"I was able to make out the plate and run it, lieutenant. It's a 2011 Cadillac CTS-V, registered to Alfredo Ortiz."

"Hey, I know that name," Gomez says. "He's big-time drug dealer."

"Word on the street is he's moving in on Parino's territory," Kramer says.

"Interesting," McGraw says. "There may be some connection here."

"Parino?" Roark asks.

"Or his stooges," McGraw says.

The uniform says, "This warehouse is also owned by him."

"What's the condition of the body?" McGraw asks.

The trunk is up and Roark is looking in.

"I didn't look too close," officer says. "It's pretty bad."

"Pretty bad is right," Roark says, "Have forensics and the M.E. been notified?"

"Yes, sergeant."

McGraw leans over the bumper next to Roark, looking in at the corpse. He turns to Roark, and says shaking his head. "I hope this isn't Bonnie."

"Me, too," she says.

"Who's the sick bastard that did this?" Kramer asks.

Dr. Philips, the M.E., walks over. "You guys are keeping me busy," she says. "Is this one of your vics?"

"We think so," Roark says.

"The forensic team has arrived, boss," Gomez says.

Alan and his techs survey the damage to the vehicle. "This may be a difficult one, lieutenant, but we'll take it in and do our best."

"I know," he says.

Philips begins her examination of the corpse. Seconds later, she says, "Most of the body is charred. This will be a challenge."

McGraw asks her if she could rush the ID of the body.

"I'll start right away, but I would like for you to meet me back at the morgue."

"Is there a reason?" McGraw says.

"I may need some info, if this is your vic."

She motions for her people to remove the body from the car.

———— ◆ ————

Back at the station, McGraw has a message from Bonnie Richard's parents. He's hoping the poor soul downstairs isn't their daughter, but he feels it is. *I'll wait to call them until we're sure.* He walks down to the morgue and finds Philips standing next to the charred body on the dissection table, dressed in a green gown and gloved. She glances over at McGraw and nods. "Lieutenant."

"Just got a message from Bonnie Richards's parents," he says. "Worst part of my job."

"You can say that again," she says. "Showing the dead to their loved ones is something I dread. And this poor thing, they don't want to see."

He moves in next to the M.E. , shaking his head. "We'll get whoever did this."

"Who do you think this person is, lieutenant?" she asks.

"Is that why you asked me to meet with you?"

She nods. "I'm going to need some help with this one. There isn't much to go on. The tips of her fingers have been burned away. Access to the teeth is going to be very difficult because the tissue is very rigid. Charred jaws are very fragile."

"Bonnie Richards is who I think this is," he says.

"What can you tell me about her?"

"She is or was a sexy blond somewhere around five-five, maybe 120 pounds."

"The height is close," she says.

"You say the vic has no fingers?" he says.

"That's right. And to ID her teeth, I need to resection the jaws and that will take some time." She pauses. "You're frowning. Do you have something to add?"

He nods. "There is one other thing. When we interviewed Bonnie Richards, Roark and I had thought she was rather endowed for a woman her size, if you know what I mean."

"You were looking, huh?" she says with a big smile. "It would certainly

159

help us ID the vic much faster, if Ms. Richards has implants." She reaches for a scalpel among the instruments on the tray next to the table. "Let's see." Philips continues talking while dissecting the breast area. "In 2009 a former swimsuit model in LA had had her teeth knocked out and fingers cut off. The only way they identified her was from her breast implant serial number," Philips says. After a few minutes she reaches for forceps, and seconds later she has something. "We're in luck, lieutenant. The numbers are still visible. We can ID her with a phone call," she says, placing the implant in a pan on the tray with the instruments.

"What luck, is right," he says."

Philips removes her gloves and carries the pan to her desk against the wall. "It'll take about thirty minutes to an hour," she says.

"I'll head back and wait for your call," he says, walking towards the door.

Forty minutes later, McGraw receives a call from Dr. Philips.

"Is it she?" he asks.

"They're registered to Elizabeth Richards."

"I forgot to mention that Elizabeth is her given name, she went by Bonnie at the bank."

"Well, together we've ID'd your vic."

"Thank you, Dr. Philips.

McGraw calls out to his unit, telling them about the identity of the charred victim.

"Oh, I was hoping it wasn't Bonnie," Roark says.

"It's time to bring in Dex and Trev. I need to speak with the Capt."

He hurries to the chief's office, knocks and enters. He's on the phone, raises a hand with two fingers held up, meaning give him two minutes. He places the phone in its cradle and looks at McGraw.

"What's up, McGraw?"

"Capt., I believe it's time to bring in the two dirty cops."

"Got somethin' that'll stick on 'em?"

"They killed Bonnie Richards. The M.E. has identified the body as Ms. Richards. Forensics has found Dexter Price's DNA at the scene. It's time to bring these guys in. I'll call IAD. Can you call the Fourth and arrange for them to come?"

"Will do," Capt. says.

160

CHAPTER THIRTY-SEVEN

McGraw is in the corner of the squad room with his staff watching Dexter Price and Trevor Wilson on separate monitors. The lieutenant is concentrating on Dex, who is in Interview Room One in a macho posture, smoking a cigarette and drinking from a soft drink can. He takes several puffs and inhales the smoke. Seconds later, smoke streams out of his nostrils when he exhales. His body language is exhibiting contempt. There's something about the big guy that attracts McGraw's attention. He has to be the guy in the red pickup that ran him off the road.

Trev is in two, sitting in the corner by the table, rocking his body, head facing down.

"Trev's as nervous as a kitten in a room full of rocking chairs," Kramer says.

They laugh.

"Wouldn't care to be in his shoes," Gomez says. "Dex's gonna hang him out to dry."

McGraw grabs a notepad. "We'll see," he says, walking to Interview Room One. Inside, Dexter Price straightens in his chair. He's just finished his cigarette and presses the butt into the hole at the top of a soft drink can, anger in his eyes. He glowers at McGraw.

"Is this the way you treat a fellow officer? I want to know why you're holding me and keeping me waiting like a common criminal."

McGraw presses the button on the recorder.

"You know the routine," McGraw says. "This conversation will be recorded. I just want to ask you a few questions. Relax. Are you Dexter Price?"

"Yeah, of course." He reaches in his pocket for an open pack of Marlboro cigarettes.

"I'd rather you not," McGraw says.

"Come on, lieutenant. You don't believe that bullshit about second-hand smoke, do you?"

"How do you know Mr. Payne?"

161

"He's my brother-in-law." Can I get another Coke?"

"When we're done."

"You've been seen in Citizens Bank on several occasions. Do you bank there or do you have some business with your brother-in-law?"

"Austin helps me with my money. I have trouble saving it. What's this all about?"

"You and Trevor Wilson have been seen with Mr. Payne having lunch with Johnny Parino at Santino's."

"So?"

"You know who he is?"

"Who in the hell doesn't?"

"Are you and Trevor involved with Parino in drugs and prostitution?"

"No. Hell, no. We go with Austin just because he doesn't like to be alone with Johnny."

"What do they talk about?"

"Just stuff."

"What kind of stuff?"

"Bookkeeping stuff. He does the guy's books."

"What's in the suitcase Mr. Payne takes away from Santino's?"

His brow rises. "I don't know nothing about that," he says. His pupils dilate. McGraw knows he's lying. "Listen, lieutenant, I don't get involved with that stuff. Johnny Parino is no one to mess with. What my brother-in-law does for him I don't want to know."

"We think you and Trevor Wilson are involved in money laundering with Mr. Payne."

Dex shows no sign of giving anything up. "I told you, what Austin does is none of our business and we ain't involved."

"Did you know Ms. Eva Hamilton?"

"Of course; she worked at the bank."

"We have witnesses that saw you getting a little rough with her and Trevor had to pull you away from her desk."

"Oh, that. It was just a misunderstanding."

"Was it about dating Ms. Hamilton?"

"No."

"It seems you have trouble with women," McGraw says, attempting to push his buttons.

He frowns. "What the hell do you mean by that, lieutenant?" he says brushing his hair back. "The ladies like me. Some of them think I'm some movie star."

"I guess Ms. Hamilton didn't think so. She rebuked you."

"You don't know what you're talking about. She thought she was better than everyone else, one of those highfalutin' Hamiltons." He shrugs. "Anyway, she wasn't much. I'm glad I never went out with the bitch."

"Do you know anything about her disappearance?"

He shakes his head. "No, why should I? What the hell are you driving at? Just because we had a little argument doesn't mean I'd do anything to her." He jumps up. "Lieutenant, I don't like what you're up to here. You seem desperate to pin something on someone and it ain't going to be me. I didn't touch the woman."

"Sit down." Dex eases into his chair and stares at the floor.

"Let's see. You say you don't deal in drugs?"

"Are you forgetting I'm a cop?"

"We have witnesses who will attest that they saw you and Trevor taking a bribe from a drug dealer who drives a black Mercedes."

"They're mistaken. It's someone who looks like us. Someone's trying to pull one over on you, lieutenant."

"We have pictures."

"I don't care, they must be fake."

"You know what happens to cops that take bribes from drug dealers? Who else is involved with you?"

Dex jumps up. "You ain't pinnin' nothin' on me."

"Sit down. I'm not going to tell you again. We don't need any drama from you. Answer my questions."

McGraw pauses until Dex gets hold of himself. "What can you tell me about Bonnie Richards?"

Dex's eyes widen. "She took Eva's place at the bank."

"How well do you know her?"

"Not too good."

"I understand that you and she dated."

"Oh, that. That didn't last long. She wasn't my type."

"What is your type, Dexter?"

"I like 'em like the women in the olden days. They respected their men."

"Didn't Bonnie respect you?"

"Hell, no. She was like that Hamilton woman, thinking she's better than me. They're ain't no woman better than me."

"Do you know Alfredo Ortiz?"

Again, Dex's eyes widen. He's slow to respond. "Only thing I know is what a friend in narcotics told me. Ortiz's a drug dealer and he's trying to expand his territory."

"You have any dealings with him?"

"Hell, no."

McGraw closes the recorder.

"Stand up."

"What? What's going on?"

"I talked with IAD and you're on suspension. Give me your badge and gun."

"Lieutenant. You can't take my badge, man. This's all I got."

"You should have thought of that before you got involved with the wrong people. Hand me your badge and gun, now!"

Dex pulls off his badge and hands it to McGraw, and yanks his gun from its holster and hands it to him.

"You're free to go," McGraw says. "You'll be hearing from IAD.

McGraw picks up his notepad and opens the door, leads the way out into the hall. Dexter heads down the hall, not looking at the detectives who are eyeing him as he passes.

McGraw hands Dex's badge and gun to Roark and goes into Interview Room Two. Inside, Trev jumps up. McGraw tells him to have a seat, and he pulls out the only other chair from the table, sits, and places the notepad on the table in front of him and turns on the recorder.

"Why am I here, Lieutenant? You know I'm a police officer."

"I know. Just need to ask you some questions. Your name is Trevor Wilson, correct? This is for the recorder."

"Yes, I'm Officer Trevor Wilson."

"Tell me about your dealings with Mr. Payne, Officer Wilson."

"All I can tell ya, lieutenant is, that he's Dex's brother-in-law and we go to see him now and then. Dex has some financial dealings with him and I tag along." Trev fidgets with his belt buckle. "I never pay much attention to what they discuss; all those figures bore me."

"What are you afraid of?"

"Afraid? What do you mean? I'm not afraid."

"You seem rather nervous for someone that doesn't have anything to worry about." McGraw pauses to let that sink in.

"You afraid of Johnny Parino?"

Trevor's eyes are as wide as saucers. "Johnny Parino? How... how do you know about him?"

"You and Dexter were seen meeting with Mr. Payne in Santino's, having lunch with him."

He holds up his hands. "Now, wait a minute, lieutenant. I have no business with Mr. Payne or that Johnny Parino. I've been with Payne in Santino's, yes, because he wants Dex and me to be with him. He doesn't like to be by himself with Parino. He's a mean dude."

"Why does Payne meet with him?"

"I don't know."

"C'mon, you had lunch with them on several occasions and you're sitting right there with them, and you're telling me you don't know what they talked about?"

"It was all business stuff. Mr. Payne is like a CPA. I think he's taking care of Parino's books. They talk figures. I ain't good with figures."

"What's in the suitcase that Payne takes out of Santino's?"

He shakes his head. "Man, I don't know and don't want to know."

"Do you suspect that Payne could be doing something with the money?"

"I guess, but I don't know." He shakes his head. "Look, lieutenant, I don't want no part of Payne or Johnny Parino. You cross Johnny and you'll end up dead."

McGraw thinks about pressuring Trevor further.

"You've been seen making deposits in other banks. Payne is money laundering and you're an accomplice."

"I know nothing about money laundering. I work with Payne and he had me doing things like making deposits."

"Earlier you said you had nothing to do with Payne. Would you be willing to take a polygraph?"

Trev turns pale. "Why, lieutenant? Don't you believe me?"

"Don't you want to be cleared of any wrong-doing?"

"What wrong-doing? I ain't done nothin', lieutenant. How many times do I have to tell you? Please, can I go now?"

"You say you haven't done anything wrong, but you and Dexter have been seen taking a bribe from a drug dealer."

Trev's hands shake. "There's some mistake."

"We have witnesses. Who else is involved with you and Price? Alfredo Ortiz?"

"Oh, no. He's another bad one. He's getting into a war with Parino. That's all I know."

He jumps up.

"Sit down. I'm not through. Do you know Eva Hamilton?"

"Sure. She used to be Mr. Payne's secretary."

"What was the confrontation between Ms. Hamilton and Dexter Wilson about?"

"Dex always tries to act macho around the women and Ms. Hamilton didn't go for his flirting and he flipped."

"You had to pull him away or he was going to clobber her."

"Sometimes he goes off the handle, but he's harmless."

"Are you sure?" McGraw says, but doesn't allow him to answer and proceeds. "Do you have any idea what happened to Ms. Hamilton?"

"How would I know anything about that?"

"Dex said you know a lot about Ms. Hamilton, that you kinda like her."

"What's Dex trying to say, that I had something to do with her coming up missing? No way. Yes, I liked her. I thought she was a nice lady and I didn't like the way Dex treated her. And that's the truth."

McGraw thinks about how he's going to get a message back to Dexter through Trevor.

"Then Dex must have done something to Ms. Hamilton without you knowing about it."

Trev shrugs. "I don't know."

"What can you tell me about Bonnie Richards?"

"Bonnie Richards?" Trev's hands begin shaking again and he's turning pale.

McGraw knows he's stalling to think how he's going to answer.

"What can I tell you? I only know she took Eva Hamilton's place at the bank. Honest, that's all I know."

"You sure there isn't more to your relationship with Ms. Richards?"

"No, lieutenant. I don't know what you mean."

McGraw rises and comes around the desk. "Stand up."

"What? I don't understand."

"Stand up, now!"

Trev jumps up.

"I've talked with IAD and you're on suspension. Put your badge and gun on the desk."

"Lieutenant, I ain't done nothin'. You gotta believe me."

"Put your badge and gun on the desk, now!"

Trev moves to the desk and reaches for his badge. His hands are shaking so much that he has a hard time getting it off his shirt. Finally, he removes it and sets it on the desk, then pulls his gun from the holster and drops it on the floor. "Sorry." He reaches for it and places it on the desk.

McGraw shuts off the recorder and picks up his pad. "You will be hearing from IAD. You are free to go."

Trevor flies out of the room and races to the exit.

"They're both lying," Roark says as McGraw returns to the monitor.

"You letting them go, lieutenant?" Kramer says.

"Yeah, boss," Gomez says. "Why you letting those dirty cops go?"

"You guys don't know?" Roark says.

They frown. "Know what?" Kramer says.

"McGraw knows what he's doing. He thinks Dex's our perp," she says.

"He does?" Gomez says with his brow coming together.

"They're not going anyplace," McGraw says. "IAD won't be acting for a few days. I want Dexter Wilson to leads us to Eva Hamilton."

"She can't be alive, boss," Gomez says.

"Let's see. Keep an eye on them."

———◆———

Outside the precinct, Dex is sitting behind the wheel of his canary-yellow pickup, with the motor running, waiting for Trev to come out. Trev darts down the steps of the station, rushes to the passenger's side door, opens it and slips in, out of breath.

"We're out of here," Dex says. Can you believe that shit?" he says. "That dick- head lieutenant took my badge and gun."

"Mine too, Dex. Whadda we gonna do? They know everything. They know about the drug dealer, what Payne is doing with Johnny Parino, Ortiz and Bonnie Richards."

"Nothin'. We sit tight."

"But Internal Affairs, Dex. That's serious stuff.

"IAD will try to scare the shit out of us with so-called evidence they don't have. It's an old interrogation trick."

"I don't know. We're suspended. They'll be coming after us. Dex, I'm scared."

"Give it a rest. You worry too much. Unless the guys at the station rat on us, we're safe with our drug guy. The detectives have to catch us in the act of taking the money, and they know it. We just gotta lay low for a while. The lieutenant will have his guys dogging us."

"What about Austin?" Trev says.

"They can't tie us to anything my brother-in-law's doing. He's the one doing the laundering, not us. All we do is making the deposits; there's no law against that."

"You think so?" Trev says.

Dex nods. "Of course, now stop worrying."

"But the lieutenant thinks you did something to Eva Hamilton. He told me you are involved."

He waves a hand to dismiss it. "Those bitches in the bank must of told him about me arguing with her. They blew it all out of proportion like maybe I killed her or something."

"You didn't, did you Dex?"

Dex's eyes are ablaze. "Are you going off your rocker? I never laid a hand on her."

"I'm scared, Dex. McGraw asked about Bonnie. What will they do to us?"

"'I'm scared, I'm scared.' Man, you sound like a schoolgirl. Are you going to cave in on me? They'll blame Bonnie's death on Ortiz, not us. We're covered. If you fold, they'll put your ass away and throw away the key. Just shut your trap and stay around the house until this blows over."

CHAPTER THIRTY-EIGHT

Trevor Wilson is awakened by several rings on his cell on the nightstand next to the bed on his side. The three days of rain belting the windows has finally stopped. He looks at his watch.

"Hello," he says, still not totally awake.

"Is this Trevor Wilson?"

"Yes, who's this?"

"I'm Dexter Price's aunt Deanna, on his father's side. I didn't know who to call, hope you don't mind."

Trev's wife turns over in bed. "Who is it, Trev?"

"Dex. Go back to sleep." He jumps up and goes into the bathroom.

Dex never talked about an aunt. "How can I help, ma'am?"

"I haven't heard from Dexter in a few days. We were to have lunch yesterday, but when I went to the house, he wasn't there."

"Maybe he went fishing," Trevor says.

"I don't think so. He always tells me when he's gonna be away for more than a day. We've become very close since I came back from South Carolina six months ago. Well, last night I went back to his house. I have a key, and this time I went inside. The place looked like he hasn't cleaned it in a while. Dirty dishes in the sink and clothes and newspapers scattered all over the living room. I'm worried." She sighs.

"Did you find a note? Maybe he left one and you missed it?"

"No. I searched the house pretty good. I'm really scared, Mr. Trevor. I saw a receipt on the kitchen table for whiskey, Jim Beam. I didn't find the bottle. He usually drinks beer. There was an empty six-pack on the table."

"I'm sure he's okay. He's been a little down lately. I bet he just took off to get away and be by himself for a while."

"Oh, I don't know. He doesn't seem to have many friends, but he does talk a lot about you. 'My partner, Trevor,' is what he says. That's why I called you. I tried to locate his sister but don't really know where she is these days."

168

"No one does. Do you want me to come over?"

"It'd do no good."

"Has Dex done this before, gone away, I mean?" he asks.

"No, never, not without telling me first," she pauses again. "There's..." She doesn't finish her sentence.

"What? What is it?"

"I found a writing tablet on the kitchen table. Dexter was doodling while drinking his beer. The writing was poor, that's why I think he was doing it while drinking."

"What did he write?"

"Just two words, over and over, on three or four sheets of paper."

"What was the words?"

"Willet's farm. That's all, just Willet's farm."

"Oh my god," Trevor whispers to himself.

"Do you know anything about Willet's farm?"

Trev knows it's a place where the high-schoolers go to make love, but isn't going to tell her. Dexter's aunt becomes quiet. Trevor can hear her deep breathing. *This poor lady really cares about Dex.*

"No, I don't," Trev says.

"The last time I was here, he was cleaning his gun. Now it's gone, too," she says in a low voice, almost in a whisper, like she's afraid to mention it. "He's going to kill himself. I know it. There, I've said it."

Trev knows it, too, but has to give the lady some hope.

"I know Dex, he wouldn't do that."

"Oh, I don't know. I've seen another side to him since I've been back. He isn't himself." She inhales a deep breath. "Should I call the police?"

"I am the police. Let me have your phone number and I'll call you back," he says. "Give me time to check around, maybe an hour or two." He flips off his cell and writes her phone number in the palm of his left hand. Trevor dresses in a flash and dashes out of the house, zipping up his jeans, hops in his blue Honda Civic and drives off to Willet's farm. There's overcast, but it's not too cold. Forty minutes later, he turns into the farm, fishtails down the muddy road, spattering mud over the hood and across the windshield. Halfway in, the Honda sinks in a deep rut. "Damn," he screams. "Don't need this now." Trevor guns it forward and backwards until the car spins out and shoots forward, sliding to a stop twenty yards to the left of Dexter's pickup. Trevor doesn't get out. His heart is beating so fast he feels like he's going to pass out. He's terrified of what he'll find. He grabs the door handle, pushes his shoulder hard against it, and falls out into the mud, "Son of a bitch!" He struggles to get to his feet, holding on to the fender. He doesn't see Dex in the truck. Maybe Dex's fishing in the pond, he thinks, but knows better. Standing beside Dex's pickup, Trevor eases around the back to the passenger side, he's afraid to open the door on Dex's side. He grabs the handle, takes a deep breath, and yanks the door open.

He screams. "No, Dex, no!"

CHAPTER THIRTY-NINE

The detectives pull into Willet's farm to investigate a suicide called in by a patrol officer. Uniforms have sealed off the area with yellow tape, and the detectives duck under it and end up behind a blue Honda Civic twenty feet from the M.E., who is working on the vic behind the steering wheel of a yellow pickup with its doors open. The rain has stopped and the sun is a welcome sight.

McGraw and Roark are met by Kramer and Gomez.

"What do we have?"

"A suicide," Kramer says. "The M.E.'s with the corpse now."

"You and Gomez work the area see what you can come up with."

"Sure thing, boss," Gomez says.

He and Roark walk over to Dr. Philips.

"Not a pretty sight," she says.

McGraw looks in. The male corpse is lying back in the driver's seat with half his head blown off. A silver .45 magnum is on the floor. Blood is splattered over the driver's side window and sprayed across the dashboard.

"Who called it in?" McGraw says.

"Uniform said a cop named Trevor Wilson."

"Trevor Wilson?" he says with astonishment in his voice.

"You must be kidding," Roark says.

She shrugs. "He's over there in the Civic. He's in shock."

Kramer and Gomez are over there.

"We know who the vic is," McGraw says with dread.

"Dexter Price," Philips says. She frowns. "You know these guys?"

"They're persons of interest in the Eva Hamilton disappearance and the Bonnie Richards murder," Roark says.

"Well, Price's done your work for you, lieutenant. Here's his suicide note," she says, handing it over to him. "He confesses to murdering her and much more, but nothing about the Hamilton woman."

McGraw reads it without looking up.

170

"I guess this and the forensic report on Bonnie Richards's home definitely ties him to her murder," Roark says, as she reaches for it with a gloved hand, reads it and hands it back to him. "I don't believe this. Dex's taking all the blame. He says Trev didn't have anything to do with Bonnie Richards's murder."

"We'll see," McGraw says. He slips the letter into an evidence bag, gives it back to Roark, and heads over to the Honda.

"It may be Dex's way of trying to make things right," Roark says as she joins him.

McGraw doesn't respond. He keeps walking. The driver's side door is open and Kramer and Gomez are standing next to Trevor, who's inside the vehicle.

"He's out of it, boss," Gomez says, as they come towards him.

Roark steps around to the passenger side. McGraw looks in and finds Trevor with his head in his hands, resting against the steering wheel.

"We must talk," McGraw says. "Please step out."

Trev is slow to respond.

"Did you hear me, Officer Wilson? Step out of the vehicle. Now!"

Trevor is shaking, rolls out, falling to his knees. "I had nothing to do with this."

Kramer pulls him to his feet.

McGraw glances into the vehicle but doesn't see anything unusual. Roark opens the passenger side door and examines the inside.

"Did you touch Dex's body?"

Trevor's eyes widen. "No, I didn't. I only opened the passenger door and after I seen what he done to himself, I ran back here and called 9-1-1. I've been here the whole time, not able to move, like I was paralyzed or something."

"A dead man can't hurt you," McGraw says.

"Sir, don't you know it's a sin to do what Dex did?"

McGraw glances over at Roark, who raises her brows. *He's concerned about God, now?* McGraw thinks.

"Dexter left a suicide note," McGraw says.

He rubs his face. "I know nothing about that."

"What was your involvement in the death of Bonnie Richards?" Roark says.

"Dex killed her, but I helped clean up." He shakes his head. "I'm sorry, Lord, I'm sorry for what I've done."

McGraw gives him a little time to collect himself, then says, "Go on, what next?"

"We rolled Bonnie's body up in the rug and placed her in the trunk of a car we stole from Ortiz, a drug dealer, then drove it behind his warehouse in the south side and Dex set it on fire."

"Is that all?" McGraw says.

"I don't know what you mean," Trev says.

"There is something else. Explain what you guys did to Eva Hamilton?" McGraw says.

Trev frowns. "Man, I don't know what you mean. We didn't do anything

171

to her. You can't pin that one on me."

"I think he's telling the truth," Roark says.

McGraw asks, "Do you think Dex did Eva?

He shakes his head. "No man. He would have told me."

"Well, you know what this means," McGraw says."

He nods. "I'm going to jail."

"And for a long time," McGraw says.

"As you know, you're an accessory," Roark says.

"Anyone you want to call?" McGraw says.

"I called my wife and told her she better get to the station."

"Good." McGraw turns to Kramer. "Read him his rights and take him. We'll deal with him later."

"Yes, sir," Kramer says, cuffing Trev's wrists behind his back while Mirandizing him and placing him in the back of a cruiser.

He tells Gomez to have forensics tow Dex's truck, then he turns to Roark.

"Do you buy Trev's statement?"

"Did you not see his body reaction when you asked about Eva? Completely different from when I asked about Bonnie," she says. "Just like when you had him at the station."

"Good observation. I did notice that both times," he says. "That's why I felt they did Bonnie Richards." He sighs as they walk over to the M.E., who is waiting to take the body. "There went my theory with Dex as our man," he says. "I really thought he abducted Eva and had her somewhere."

"Can we take him?" the M.E. asks.

"You can have him," McGraw says.

She waves to her assistant to remove the body. "I've been meaning to ask, lieutenant. Would you be interested in having a drink later?"

"Thanks, but too busy," he says.

Her smile is subtle. She nods, "Another time, then."

On their way back to the station, Roark is driving the cruiser and McGraw is in the passenger seat, looking out the window. He hasn't said a word since they left the suicide scene.

"You okay, McGraw?" she says. He doesn't respond. "McGraw, I asked, are you okay?"

"Afraid not."

"Why?"

"I screwed up," he says looking down, his hat covering his eyes. "I was certain Dex was our man, and fingered him on evidence that wasn't solid. I failed you and the others." He looks up, pushing his hat back.

"Listen. Based on what we had, you were right to think he was our guy," she says. "We had evidence that Dex and Eva clashed in the bank. She wrote about him in her journal, which made him a prime suspect in her abduction."

He shakes his head. "No. I should have known better. What's that you always throw at me: 'You're too damn smart for your own good.' That's it. What you really mean is: 'you're too cocky for your own good.'"

"Aw, McGraw, I was just pulling your chain."

He turns to her. "No more screw-ups on my part. We are going to shake out the evidence and get the son of a bitch who has Eva Hamilton."

They're quiet the next few miles. Roark glances over at him with a small smile, as if she wants to say something, but is hesitant.

"What?" he says.

"Nothing really, just something I overheard."

"Go ahead. I know you are dying to tell me."

"I couldn't help overhearing Nora ask you something."

He feels himself frowning when he turns to look at her. "And what's that?"

"She invited you to have a drink with her and you blew her off."

"Oh, that. We had a drink once and I guess she thinks I'm interested in her, but that's not how it works."

"How does it work?" she says.

"Relationships build over time, only when both people are interested in each other."

"Did you ever stop to think that's what she wants, a relationship?"

"I'm not interested in her." He turns to look out the side window and mumbles, "Anyway, she's too bossy."

"Like me?"

McGraw turns back to her. "Never thought of you as bossy; maybe persistent, but not bossy."

Roark smiles. "I guess I can be a little persistent."

"How about you?" he says. "Would you like to go for a drink at Tony's when we get back to the station?"

Her brow rises. "You're inviting me out?"

"I don't see anyone else in this car."

"Gosh. Nothing I'd like better."

"But what about Pretty Boy—oh, excuse me—Max. What would he think? He may not be happy about it."

"Oh, I think I'm getting over him. He's too pretty for me."

They look at each other and burst out laughing.

"But you seemed to have gotten along so well."

She shakes her head. "He's stuck on himself, and he's really not my type."

They laugh a second time.

"Glad you're laughing again, McGraw." She hesitates, and then says, "Can I ask you something else?"

"Okay."

"Why don't you ever call me by my first name? We've been partners a long time. Don't you think you could call me Holly?"

"Never gave it much thought, Holly. You can call me Noah."

"Now that's what I like to hear, Noah."

They laugh again.

———————— ♦ ————————

Noah and Holly walk four blocks from the station to Tony's bar, a one-story brick building with a canopy extending over the sidewalk, a large front window next to the entrance lettered with the name of the bar in a semi-circle above a frosted glass of beer with lines of foam streaming down its sides. The entrance faces a brick street. The sun has just set, but enough glow remains that the street lights haven't come on.

The owner's name is John Stryker, not Tony. Legend has it that Tony's was originally owned by a man named Tony Valentino. He bought the place in 1898. There have been several owners since then.

Noah and Holly dodge a couple of cops they know as they step inside. The place is packed with a mixture of cops and civilians, and standing room only this evening, with little room to navigate. Noah spots four people leaving a table in the back and hurries between the bodies to capture the table seconds before another couple is about to reach it. He orders wine for himself and a Heineken for Holly.

"Does the smell of fried fish make you hungry?" she says.

"I'll pass."

"Think I'll have some," she says, and places and order.

"Bet you didn't notice the attorney, Samuel Bennett, at the bar with a shapely brunette?" he says.

She squints and stretches to look over the heads at the next table. "I see them now. They're leaving."

Noah jumps up. "I'll be back in a second." He heads to the window and watches Bennett and his date slip into a black stretch limo and waits until it pulls away. Holly is holding a slab of fried catfish with her fingers when he returns.

"What's so important?" she says, wiping her face with a paper napkin.

"Did you see the limo parked across the street when we came in?"

"I just caught a glimpse of it. Thought for a second how strange it was for it to be in this area, but hey, someone may be slumming," she says.

"That attorney and his date left in it."

"You're kidding?" She shrugs. "I read where he's no longer married, so I guess it's okay. Last I heard, his two teenage daughters live with his ex. So he's free as a bird. She takes another bite of her fish. "Hmm. Why are we discussing Bennett?"

"You're right. Let's drop it." He takes a drink of his wine.

Holly slaps her hand on top of his, her tiger eyes staring a hole in him. "Noah, don't do that to me."

He finds her pleading attractive and has an urge to embrace her, but he lets it pass. The attorney is his concern for some reason which at this time he doesn't understand. Only that he never liked him. He's dirty.

"Do what?" he says.

"You're thinking something, and I'm going to get it out of you, so, spill it. Come back to earth."

He quickly thinks of something else to say. "I was just thinking that this is the first time we've had a drink together as partners, excluding the visits to your home."

"Ever since you told me about how you were coping with your wife's passing, I thought you weren't interested in anyone until I heard Nora ask you out."

"It has been a few years and I was going through some emotional issues, but my dear mother has helped me to understand my feelings more."

"She's a darling person," Holly says.

CHAPTER FORTY

The next morning around six-thirty, Roark pulls her white Jeep Grand Cherokee, the replacement for her firebombed SUV, into the driveway of the Circle M Ranch and parks behind McGraw's sky-blue RAM pickup. The sun is thirty minutes away from appearing in the east. She loves the early morning sunrise. It is the start of a new day, and reminds her that life is okay and that not all people are bad. She removes the two Starbuck coffees from the holder, rolls out of the SUV with one in each hand, bumping the door shut with her hip, and walks up the flagstones to the door and knocks. There's more spring in her step since she and McGraw had a drink together last evening. She has no hold on him, but she is now in touch with her feelings for him. It's time to let him know how she feels, but that isn't going to be easy.

Anna Marie comes to the door in a house dress with a flour-covered apron, wiping her hands on a cloth towel. "Hello, sweetie, come on in." She shuts the door behind Holly. "Just in time; the biscuits are in the oven and breakfast is almost ready. Noah will be back in a minute."

"I've brought coffee."

"Oh, how thoughtful. Noah's in the barn with his horses. He gets up at dawn every morning, says something about the gleaming light of wisdom, or whatever comes to him." She laughs. "He will never go to work without first talking to his babies. I swear that man thinks more of those horses than anyone else. He says they would be jealous of any woman in his life. But don't let that stop you, honey."

Roark wonders if horses do think. If so, they can think what they want, but that could change if she has anything say about it. "You're sweet Anna Marie. I think I'll just go out to see what he's up to."

"Okay, honey, tell him breakfast's about ready."

"Will do," she says, leaving with the coffee. About to go into the barn, Holly bumps into McGraw, who is coming out. "Oops," she says, her shoulders jerking up, almost dropping the Styrofoam cups.

"Sorry. Let me help you," he says.

"This one's for you," she says, "half-caff with cream."

He removes the lid and takes a drink. "You remembered. Thank you."

"I've never seen your horses. Mind if I look in?"

"Be my guest." He leads her into the barn, where a handsome tall thin man in a ten-gallon off-white hat is in a stall wiping down one of the horses. He's wearing a jean shirt and pants and a wide belt buckle with a bucking horse on it. "What's the horse's name?" Roark asks, taking a couple of swallows of her coffee. She doesn't know if it's a he or she.

"Mystery Lady, ma'am," he says.

"She's a beaut," Holly says.

"This is my ranch hand and friend, Whitey Berry," McGraw says.

"Is McGraw as hard on you as he is me?" she says to Whitey.

"Naw, ma'am. We go way back."

"And he's a good hand," McGraw says.

"Can I rub her down a little?" Roark asks.

"Sure thing," Whitey says.

Holly moves in next to him and runs a hand over the horse's smooth coat. *You may be seeing more of me, Mystery Lady*, she thinks. *So get used to me.* "She seems to take to me."

McGraw smiles and says, "Who wouldn't take to you, Holly?"

Hmm. I like the way Noah calls me Holly. "Nice to meet you, Whitey," she says.

He tips his felt hat and says, "Ma'am."

She likes his narrow-toed, snake-skin boots, similar to the pair McGraw wears at times. Whitey appears to be around McGraw's age. *They must be cut from the same cloth*, she thinks.

She walks over to the stall across the way and stares at the stallion. "This is one nice horse, too. What's his name?"

"Texas Rodeo."

"That's an odd name. How'd you come by it?"

"When I was in my teens back in west Texas, I worked for a wealthy rancher who owned a horse named Texas Rodeo. I rode him in several rodeos in calf roping and the horse took a liking to me. Years later, when the horse was put out to pasture, I decided to take his name as a matter of respect to the owner, who did a lot for me."

"I see." She finishes her coffee.

"Here, let me have your cup, miss," Whitey says. "You finished, boss?"

"Not quite, but you can take mine, too. Maw won't like it if I don't have some of hers."

"Thank you," Holly says to Whitey.

"We'd better get to the house or Mother will be upset with us. She doesn't like her food to get cold. Are you coming, Whitey?"

"I'll be along shortly. Gotta make a run to the back forty and check the fence for supplies."

Inside, McGraw and Holly sit at a well-dressed table with a checkered table cloth, place settings and white cloth napkins. Anna Marie has kept the eggs, pancakes and bacon warm on the stove. "I was wondering if y'all were ever comin'. You know I don't like to serve cold food."

McGraw looks at Holly and they smile.

"Can I help?" Holly says.

"Oh, no, it's all ready. You just enjoy," she says as she begins placing the meal on the table.

"Everything smells so good, Mrs. McGraw," Holly says.

"Oh honey. Don't be callin' me that. Makes me feel old." She laughs. "Please. Call me Anna Marie. Everyone does. Now, eat up."

After about ten minutes, Holly tells McGraw that she's called April Dawns, the designer, to meet with them and to learn all she can about Olivia, and to get names, address, and phone numbers.

"Good. I saw the info on the board and was going to ask you about the designer. We need to move quickly on her. I now believe she holds the secret to why Eva didn't alert the clerks in North Carolina, and much more, like what did she and Eva do for the year they lived together."

"Maybe they just lived a normal life, but we'll see," Roark says.

Fifteen minutes later, there's a knock at the door. "Who could that be?" Anna Marie says, rising. "No maw. Sit down. I'll get it. It's Whitey." McGraw sees a silhouette behind the curtain over the window.

He opens the door. Whitey's standing there with the blood drained from his face.

"Noah, you gotta come."

"What's wrong?"

He shakes his head. "You gotta see this."

Roark jumps up. "What'd he say? What's wrong?"

"I'll be back," McGraw says.

"Wait a minute. I'm going with you. We're partners, remember?" Holly says.

The sun is a bright ball of fire and the air is crisp this November day.

Whitey had driven the red jeep up to the sidewalk and parked it by the steps. They hop in from both sides and he races off to the back acreage. He flies through a grove of trees, shoots out into an expanse of greenery and slows thirty yards from the fence, where sits a black 55-gallon oil drum. McGraw turns to Whitey. "You looked in it, didn't you?"

He shakes his head in disgust. "It's horrible. You gotta see it for yourself," he says, stopping the jeep a few feet from the barrel. Holly wraps a hand up around her nose and mouth. "What's that smell? Is that from the drum?"

"You bet, ma'am," Whitey says. "But that's not all, there's someone in it."

"What?" she shouts, "A body?"

Whitey nods. "A man, I think."

"You haven't said a word, Noah. What are you thinking?" she says.

McGraw still doesn't respond. They hop out. He's the first one to reach it, inches the lid up enough to peer inside and then flips it over on the grass.

Inside is a naked body that looks like a man.

"Oh my god," Holly shouts.

"We need to get the M.E. and forensics out here right away," McGraw says. "I don't have my cell with me. Do you, Holly?"

"It's back at the car."

He turns to Whitey. But before McGraw could speak, Whitey says, "I'll run her, boss." They hop in the jeep at the same time and Whitey peels off, shooting grass and dirt back at McGraw.

McGraw places a handkerchief over his nose and mouth and leans in, inching his way around the barrel, studying the corpse. Something about the decomposed face catches his attention. There's duct tape wrapped around the mouth and forehead, the eyelids are visible. He moves in and reads the words, *Marlboro Man*. He studies it, then stoops to retrieve the lid and replaces it on the drum to keep the body covered, to show respect. He walks to the fence, looking for tracks. They're out there.

McGraw leans back against the fence, pushes his Stetson up and stares at the black drum someone dumped on his property. This is the work of our guy, he thinks, a brazen display of arrogance. He is taunting me with the Marlboro thing. Sherlock Holmes had his Professor Moriarty, and now McGraw thinks, *I, too, have my archenemy*. McGraw knows he will be hearing from him soon— that guy who called his office with that crazy laugh just as he did after McGraw's mishap on the Harley, and the time when the guy threatened Holly's life. *He's the one, and now he's becoming more menacing*, McGraw thinks.

———◆———

The next morning, McGraw stands at the evidence board while his team huddles around him. He writes *Body in the Drum* with a red marker. "The M.E. hasn't identified the body yet," he says, turning to them. "At the site she said the vic is a male in his thirties, weighing about 160, brown hair, probable around five eleven."

"Any idea who he is, lieutenant?" Kramer asks.

McGraw turns back to the board and stares at the photos.

"Who up here would you say is the one in the barrel?"

The detectives glance at each other, puzzled.

"Well?" he asks.

"Only two young males up there, so I'd say it could be Eva's high school sweetheart Cody, since we know he's here," Roark says.

McGraw taps the names written on the board with his index finger and says, "Cody Guthrie."

Kramer frowns. "But didn't we say Eva Hamilton ran off with Guthrie—?"

Gomez interrupts. "If the body in the drum is Guthrie, then obviously they didn't run off together."

"That's right," McGraw says, "and if he is the one, then we must find that other guy in that high school photo who the sheriff isn't sure is Burke, because

Eva Hamilton could still be alive. I know it's a long shot, but we have to move on Burke now."

"What about the husband? Have we ruled him out completely?" Roark asks.

"Yes," McGraw says. He turns to Kramer and Gomez. "You guys found duct tape in the back of Jerry's Roost, right?"

They nodded.

"And the body in the drum had duct tape wrapped around its face, McGraw says. "Then Cody could be the one in the barrel. We should learn soon if there's a match from the DNA on file from the items we bagged at his home."

"Don't forget the guy who argued with Cody at Jerry's Roost." Kramer says. "He could be our man."

"He could be Burke," Roark says.

The phone on McGraw's desk rings. He lifts the receiver. "Lieutenant McGraw."

Shrieking laughter bombards McGraw's ear. He motions to his staff to get to their phones.

"How you doin', lieutenant?" the voice says, following with that screeching laugh again. "Have you missed me? You've been pretty busy. Thought I'd leave you a present to get your attention again. How do you like it?"

"What's with the Joker's laugh? You're trying to tell me something, maybe you're my archenemy?"

"Lieutenant, you ain't thinking you're Batman, are you?" The Joker laugh hits McGraw's ears again. "You ain't no Batman," the caller says.

"And you ain't no Joker."

"If it's an archenemy you want, you got one, Marlboro Man," he says.

"What's with the Marlboro Man?"

"Ain't that what you like your flunkies to call you?"

"I know who you are, and we're coming after you," McGraw says.

"You don't know shit."

"You're losing it. We're on to you, Sonny Boy."

The phone goes dead.

"You got 'im scared, boss," Gomez says. "He's definitely Burke."

Roark frowns. "He's definitely our guy," she says.

McGraw feels himself nodding, and slips into deep thought.

Kramer says, "The guy's crazy as hell, lieutenant. He must be a psychopath."

"Kramer, you and Gomez check with the crime scene guys and find out what they've come up with out at my place."

McGraw picks up a file on his desk and tells Holly, "I'll be back in a bit. In the meantime, run Burke in all the databases. I know the last one didn't yield much, but be creative."

"I don't know what else I can do, McGraw, but I'll think of something."

He heads down to the morgue without responding.

In the morgue, Nora Philips is bending over a table examining the body. She looks up. "What we have here is a healthy male in his late thirties. Guess he didn't live long enough to mistreat his body."

"Are these bruises on his head and arms?"

She nods. "I'm afraid so. He put up a good fight, but was bludgeoned to death with a blunt instrument."

"Got anything yet on the DNA that matches Cody Guthrie?"

"You think this is Mr. Guthrie?"

"I do."

She goes over to her desk and retrieves a sheet of paper. "Just got the report on the sample I sent." He reaches for it, and before he can read it, she says, "It's a match. He's Cody Guthrie."

"Thank you."

"Did you see the writing on the duct tape?" she asks.

"We did."

"What's with the Marlboro Man?"

"Some of the guys in the squad joking called me that when I first came to Atlanta because of the way I dress, and it stuck. I put a stop to it, yet it pops up now and then."

"Is the killer taunting you?"

"Unfortunately, he is."

She smiles. "Well, I do see the resemblance between you and the Marlboro guy."

"Please. Not you, too?"

They laugh.

"One other thing, lieutenant," Philips says. "I'm sorry about the other day, about the drink and all. I was out of order."

"Don't give it a second thought. I'm sorry I seemed unfriendly, but we should keep it professional."

"I understand."

McGraw rushes to the squad area and stops at his desk, picks up a picture of the Joker he cut out of an old movie magazine, goes to the crime board and places it between Cody Guthrie's picture and Eva Hamilton's. As his team huddles around him, McGraw tells them that the M.E. has identified the body as that of Cody Guthrie. He points to the photo of the Joker, and says, "This has to be Sonny Burke, the other high school friend of Eva and Cody. My take on this is he's a psychopath that has never gotten over Eva. And I would bet a month's pay that we will find that he followed Eva here."

Roark says, "But why did Sonny kill Cody? He could have just taken her off some place after abducting her."

"Psychopaths don't think that way," McGraw says. "Jealousy and rage blind them. He wanted Cody out of her life completely." McGraw pauses to touch the photo of Eva Hamilton. "He has taken her some place. He wants her all to himself."

"But you're not thinking she's still alive?" Gomez says.

"It's been too long, lieutenant," Kramer says.

McGraw takes a few steps back from the evidence board, musing on the faces in the pictures. He sighs. "The Joker is keeping Eva as his trophy."

"So, is it now safe to assume that Sonny Burke abducted Ms. Hamilton and killed Guthrie?" Gomez says.

"Yes, but we must also be aware that Ms. Hamilton could end up in a 55-gallon drum if she refuses to respond to Burke's advances the way he thinks she should. He is the devil incarnate," McGraw says.

Then he turns to Holly. "You have anything new on Burke?"

She shakes her head. "He has no military or police record, nor anything in the NCIC database. It's like he vanished."

McGraw sees Kramer frowning. "What's on your mind, Kramer?" McGraw says.

"Maybe Burke took someone's identity before leaving Perry," Kramer says. "Like someone that died there at that time."

"Good thinking," Holly says. "That could be it, McGraw."

"If only we knew what alias he took, we'd have our guy," Gomez says.

McGraw says nothing; instead, he goes to the coffee stand, pours a cup and returns to the evidence board, swallowing coffee and staring at the pictures.

"What are you thinking, boss?" Gomez says.

He turns to his partner. "Roark, did Sheriff Sinclair definitely say it wasn't Burke in that high school picture?"

She shakes her head. "Actually, he said he wasn't sure, but he didn't think Burke was that friendly with them."

"Well, I disagree. This guy has to be Burke," McGraw says, hitting the photo with his index finger. "Call the sheriff back and ask him to run down the names of persons that died in Perry, Oklahoma in, what was it, '91?"

"Yes," she says.

"As Kramer suggests, Burke could have taken one of their names and social. We must find him ASAP," McGraw says, "if we expect to find Eva Hamilton alive."

Holly Roark's desk phone rings and she picks up. "Sergeant Roark," she says.

"Sergeant, this is Sinclair. Since our conversation a few weeks ago, I've been bothered about Sonny. No one here knows anything about him. That's not like Perry. So I did more checking on him."

She is shocked. *McGraw must be psychic*, she thinks.

"You must be reading our minds. We were just talking about you, sir. What did you find?"

"It's what I didn't find. Sonny hasn't used his social security since his high school graduation, and it's like he dropped off the face of the earth after that. In cases like this, the suspects usually change their names."

"We've just concluded a staff meeting and have come to the same conclusion. If only we knew where he was last seen after leaving Perry, it'd be a starting place," she says.

"I wish I could help. One other thing you need to consider. Sonny's a good actor, and he may have changed his appearance. One needs to be on their guard in his presence. He is pretty strong and he's known to go off easy if someone upsets him. Around here, we knew he had a short fuse."

"Lieutenant McGraw wanted to know if you'd do him a favor?"

"Sure. What is it?"

"He thinks Burke took the name and social of someone from Perry who died in 1991."

"Hey, that does make sense. It shouldn't take long; there can't be that many. I'll get right on it."

"Sheriff," she pauses, "we're working the clock to save Ms. Hamilton."

"I'm on it," he says.

"Thanks."

Holly looks at the wall clock. It's nearly two. She grabs her purse and darts to the exit.

CHAPTER FORTY-ONE

Roark arrives in the Buckhead area, the Beverly Hills of the east, and one of the most renowned and fashionable neighborhoods in Atlanta, around two forty-five. She drives her SUV into a parking spot in front of the gleaming, black marble store front above which is an ornate sign in black and gold letters: *April Dawn's Women's Designer Clothes and Luxury Women's Clothing.* Roark slides out of the car and takes a few moments to glance at the eye-catching women's clothes draped on mannequins behind a glass-enclosed store front. *I bet they cost an arm and a leg, maybe two arms,* she thinks. Once, when she was a teenager, her mother's brother, the rich uncle who owned a sweater factory in Chicago, took Roark to several of his designers in New York and introduced her to them. They were very resourceful people who earned big bucks.

Inside April Dawn's, Roark glances around the place, which is deeper than it is wide; there's a strong smell of fabric. The place is bright and the walls are decorated with pictures of high-class clothing. A red dress on a mannequin catches Roark's eye. She looks it over and pulls out the price tag: Boat-neck blouse with skirt, $950. Next to it is an Odex shawl-collar blazer for $2290 on sale. She shudders and quickly walks to the first sales person she sees. A shapely, attractive woman in her early forties, dressed in a black dress to die for, with hair that certainly has been styled by a professional, greets her.

"May I help you ma'am?" the lady says.

"I'm looking for Brooke Tubbs."

"I am Brooke. You must be Detective Sergeant Roark."

Roark nods and sticks out her hand, "Pleased to meet you. Is there any place we can talk?"

"Of course," Brooke says. She motions for Roark to follow her, and is escorted to a corner office that appears to be a makeshift meeting place close to the fitting rooms. They move in, but Brooke doesn't shut the door. The office is more like a closet. Holly takes the only chair dressed in white linen and faces a small antique

184

desk. Brooke sits behind it on a petite chair with a curved wire back, more like a child's play chair, but higher, facing Roark.

"Our offices are on the second floor. Dawn and I meet in here during our busy times to be available. Dawn is in New York, and I must stay on the floor. Hope you understand."

"This is fine." Roark pulls a notebook and pen from her purse before she sets it on the floor. "As I mentioned on the phone, we are interested in Olivia Jordan because she was a dear friend and roommate of Ms. Eva Hamilton, who, as you might have read, has vanished."

"Oh, I knew Eva Hamilton, too. She used to come in here, but only while Olivia worked with us. I hope Olivia isn't in any kind of trouble."

"No. Nothing like that, we just need her help in our investigation. How long did she work for you?"

"Close to six years. She began with us when she started college. If my memory serves me correctly, Olivia came to Atlanta several years before Eva. She was Eva Bingham when I knew her."

Roark nods. "Can you provide me with Olivia's New York telephone number?"

Brooke nods and says, "I'll get it for you before you leave."

"That'll be fine. Was Olivia a good employee?"

"Oh, yes. She was great with the customers, had a way of making our ladies feel very important. Olivia was a fast learner and took to the business quickly."

Brooke turns to the wall and points to a glass-covered picture. Roark moves in closer to see the figures in the picture.

"This is Olivia," Brooke says, pointing to the sexy blonde standing left of her. "There I am, of course, and April is here on my right," she says, pointing to a pretty African-American in her late thirties. "We were at a showing in New York when this was taken."

Roark writes in her notebook. She hears voices and turns to the door. A sales person is talking to a customer and is laying a sales pitch on the lady. Holly wonders if the customers fall for it, or if they just like to hear all the sales pitches.

She turns back to Brooke. "Olivia is quite the looker," Roark says.

"Olivia knew how to dress, which is paramount in this business," Brooke says. "And also she watched her weight."

"In her high school graduation picture, Olivia is a brunette."

"She was very particular about her hair and appearance," Brooke says.

"Why did she leave Dawn's?"

"Like I said, she was a quick learner, and she had her sights set on New York to learn more and to make it big as a designer like our Dawn. One day she got an offer and she left."

"Do you have the address where Olivia and Eva lived?"

"Yes, I can give that to you along with the telephone number."

"That would be greatly appreciated. Did Olivia do much dating that you knew of?"

She nods and it seems she wants to say more, but doesn't.

"Did she date more than one guy?"

Brooke looks out the open door. "Olivia was very popular."

"Is that a yes?"

She nods again. "She had many men, and got quite a few calls here towards the last, which Dawn had to put a stop to."

"Was there one particular guy she dated?"

"Yes, a handsome young man with a dark complexion. He would pick Olivia up after work in a black limo, but never got out nor did he ever come into the store. He would wait at the curb and Olivia would open the passenger door and get in."

Brooke must have recognized the surprise in Roark's voice. "A limo?"

She smiles "I know it's hard to believe, but a stretched one at that. The other girls were really envious of Olivia."

"Did you ever meet him at any of your parties, or see them together anywhere?"

"No. I only saw him a few times at our entrance around closing time."

"Would you be able to recognize him from a photo?"

"I'm sorry. I'm afraid not."

One of the sales ladies enters and asks Brooke for her help with a customer. Brooke excuses herself and leaves. Roark takes the time to review her notes and make a couple of entries. She sighs. *I've heard about a black stretched limo somewhere*, she thinks. *Now I remember. In front of Tony's when Noah and I went for a drink. The attorney and his date got into it. Didn't Noah say there were two men in front?*

Brooke Tubbs returns with a sheet of paper and hands it to Roark. "I've written Olivia's New York home and work phone numbers, and the address here in Atlanta where she and Eva roomed before leaving us."

Roark reaches for the paper and stands up.

"One last thing, Ms. Tubbs. When Olivia's date came to pick her up, was there ever anyone else with him?"

She shakes her head. "Just him."

"Okay. I appreciate your cooperation, and I may need to call you again, if you don't mind."

Brooke smiles. "Any time, detective; I hope you find the person who took Eva Hamilton."

———◆———

It takes Roark close to thirty minutes to go across town to the Atlanta branch of the American Red Cross. The white one-story building is on a large lot by itself. After parking, she hurries to the entrance, hoping they didn't close at four thirty. She pulls on the door and it's unlocked. *Thank God*, she thinks. She enters and heads to the information desk.

"I'm here to see Mr. Irwin Nash," she says, flashing her ID. "Please tell him Detective Sergeant Roark from Atlanta PD is here to see him. He's expecting me."

The frown on the receptionist's face is a dead giveaway. Roark knows she's dying to ask if Mr. Nash is in any kind of trouble with the law, but instead she jumps up and hurries to the office down the hall to the left. Seconds later, the receptionist appears with a tall, stately gentleman dressed in a white shirt, tie, and black slacks. He reminds Roark of the butlers in the movies of the fifties.

"Detective Roark, I'm Irwin Nash. Please come to my office." She follows him down the hall and into a spacious room. It is filled with bookcases full of books, a leather couch against the wall, and two chairs facing his mahogany desk. He directs her to one of the chairs and he goes round the desk to sit in a leather chair. *This is a rather swanky setup for the Red Cross*, Roark thinks.

He holds the palms of his hands together against his chest in a prayer pose and says. "On the phone you said you wanted some information on one of our former employees, Ms. Eva Hamilton. She was Ms. Bingham when she worked with us, detective."

Roark nods. "I want to thank you for seeing me on such short notice, sir."

"Glad to help. I read in the Journal-Constitution where Eva had married into the Hamilton banking family, and did very well for herself."

"Not too well; she's missing."

He turns to Roark with his hands on the desk and stares directly at her. His eyes have widened and his skin has turned pale.

"You're not suggesting that I or anyone here is involved in any way—?"

"Oh, no," Roark says, interrupting him. "I just need some information, that's all."

"Please," he waves to her as if he's giving her permission to proceed. "How can I help you?" he asks.

"What kind of employee was Ms. Hamilton?"

"Eva. We call all our employees by their first name; makes them feel like family, you know."

Roark feels she is nodding and wishes for him to get on with it.

"She was friendly and cooperative, did her job well and everyone liked her."

"Was there anyone here that she befriended more than others?"

He frowns as if he's thinking.

"No, I can't say there's one she favored more than the others. Actually, she sorta kept to herself and, to my knowledge, never socialized with anyone."

"I would like the names of all your employees who worked with her. I may have to talk with them."

He frowns, but says, "I understand. I can get those for you." He rises, opens the door, goes to the front desk, and returns in a few minutes.

"My secretary is printing the names of the four acquaintances of Eva," he says, leaving the door open, and taking a seat.

Before Roark can speak, the lady from the front desk brings a sheet of paper and hands it to Roark, who thanks her. The secretary shuts the door behind her as she leaves.

Roark continues. "Did you notice any changes in Eva's demeanor at any time prior to her leaving?"

He takes his time responding, as if in deep thought, again.

"Yes, now that you mention it, I did. A couple of months before she left us, Eva became very quiet and jumpy, almost sorta like she was afraid of something."

"Did she ever mention anyone following her or any other fear she might have had to the employees?"

"No, like I said, she sorta kept to herself. Now that I think over the time she was with us, I guess Eva was sorta private."

'*Sorta?*' *What's with this guy always saying 'sorta,'* Roark thinks.

"What was the reason she left? Did you let her go?"

He shakes his head. "Oh, no, she left on her own and on good terms. The reason she gave us was her roommate was leaving for New York and Eva had found an apartment with ladies that worked at a bank. They sorta influenced her to go to work there. It's my understanding that Eva's father was a bank president back in Oklahoma, and she sorta wanted to follow in his footsteps."

Roark looks at her watch. It's five o'clock. "What time do the girls get off, Mr. Nash?"

"Five thirty. They get an hour for lunch and they have to work thirty minutes past five."

"Would it be possible for me to interview the girls on this sheet at one time in some room? It would only take about fifteen minutes."

His brow comes together and he looks at his watch.

"I think we can make that happen. That way you won't be disturbing us by interviewing each one separately."

"That's what I was thinking, sir."

"Come with me."

CHAPTER FORTY-TWO

Back at the precinct, Roark pulls out her notebook and the sheet Brooke Tubbs gave her with Olivia's phone numbers and plops her purse in the top drawer of her desk. *It's seven o'clock in New York,* she thinks, *maybe Olivia's home by now.* She dials the number. After six rings, Roark says, "C'mon, c'mon, pick up, Olivia." There's a click and the sound of keys falling on a table.

"Hello."

"Is this Olivia?"

Olivia is out of breath. "Yes, who's this?"

"My name is Detective Roark. I'm with the Atlanta PD. Do you have a few minutes to talk?"

"Atlanta PD, you say?"

"Yes."

"Give me a second. I just got in. Need to put a few things down."

Seconds later, Olivia returns to the phone. "How can I help you, detective? Is this about Eva?"

Roark says, "You must have learned about Eva's disappearance?"

"Yes, one of the girls who used to work at the bank emailed me. Through Eva, I came to know Clare Dunbar; they were very close. I did keep in contact with her and she was kind enough to email me about Eva's disappearance. I had hoped you would call."

"You did? Why is that?"

"I thought if there was any way I could help, I'd be glad to for Eva's sake. We were the best of friends."

Why didn't you call us? Roark thinks. "We are interviewing everyone who was close to Eva. I'd like to ask you a few questions, if you don't mind."

"Not at all."

"Do you know anyone who would want to hurt Eva?"

"No. That's the puzzling thing. Eva wouldn't hurt a fly and she had no enemies."

"What about her husband, Dudley Hamilton? Did you know him?"

"No, she dated him after I left. Eva and I were only together for a year before I came to New York. But we continued to stay in contact with each other, and she never complained to me about him, or anyone else, as far as that goes."

"Did you stay in contact with anyone else?"

"Only Clare Dunbar."

"Did Eva date many men while you and she lived together?"

"There was one she dated off and on, but I never knew his name."

"So she didn't date many men?"

Olivia is slow to answer. "What are you driving at, detective? Eva was not the mixer type."

A little testy, are you? Not a good sign. "How about you? I understand you had a boyfriend."

"I used to date, and had several boyfriends."

"But there was one you dated more often, the one who picked you up in a limo."

Olivia becomes quiet. She must be wondering how Roark found out, and how she is going to answer the question.

"What's his name?" Holly says.

"Detective, that was in the past. I did date the guy, but he started running with a rough crowd and I didn't really want to get involved."

"Please, I need his name."

"Brad Knox."

Roark makes a note. "How did you two meet?"

"In a bar. He came up to me and we started talking. He was very nice, and asked me out. We dated for a while."

"He's the one that drove a limo?"

"Yes."

"He used to pick you up after work in it. Correct?"

"Yes."

"What limo company did he work for?"

"Do I have to answer that?"

"I'm afraid so. Now, give me the name of the company."

"No company. My guy worked for Johnny Parino."

"Johnny Parino? You're kidding me. You do know what line of business Parino's in, correct?"

"He's a Mafia boss. When I learned about it, I broke off with Brad. And that's one of the reasons I left Atlanta."

"What was the other?"

"To advance my career, and that's the truth."

"Did you ever meet Parino?"

"No, I never did."

"There's a picture of four of you teenagers taken during your high school graduation. We've learned the two men are Cody Guthrie and Sonny Burke. What can you tell me about Burke?"

Olivia becomes quiet again.

"Did you hear the question?"

"Yes, I'm sorry. I was thinking that I haven't seen Sonny since our high school graduation. We weren't very close. To be honest, I never liked him. He had this thing for Eva. She tried to avoid him, but he was very persistent. I believe one of the reasons she came to live with me in Atlanta was to get away from him and her mother."

"We were hoping you could tell us where Burke might be. We need to ask him a few questions."

"Do you think he's involved in some way?"

She hasn't asked me if we think Burke is in Atlanta. Maybe she knows more than she's telling me.

"We need to interview Burke now. Can you help me?"

"I wish I could tell you more, detective, but I don't know what to say."

"Olivia, you're not being up front with me. I find it strange that you didn't ask me if I thought Burke was in Atlanta, which tells me you know he's here."

"Detective, I seem to remember someone told me Burke was in Atlanta, but I don't remember who, and I didn't mention it because I don't really know for sure."

You're lying. "I'd like to have your email address," Roark says.

"Yes, of course. If you are ready, I can give it to you."

"I'm ready," Roark says and records it. "I'll send you some info that may help you to remember, so if you think of anything you can email me at the precinct, or call me at the numbers included in my email."

"Thank you. I'll be happy to if something comes to me."

Roark hangs up and stares at her computer screen. There's something about Olivia's voice. *She knows a lot more than she's telling me.*

Roark works the keyboard, entering the name of Olivia Jordan. Fifteen minutes later, Roark finds much of which she already knows from a previous search, but this time she hits the department's database. Minutes later, she comes across something that catches her eye. Roark looks up. Everyone in the squad room has left for the day.

She grabs the phone and calls McGraw's cell. When he answers, she tells him she thought a sealed file in the police database can never be opened.

"You're right. Why?"

"Guess what. Oh, you don't like guessing games. Well, here's one for you. There's a file on Olivia Jordan sealed by Judge Murray, and I'd love to know what's in it. She may have gotten herself in trouble with the law and someone in high places quashed it."

"What are you driving at?"

"Sheriff Sinclair said Olivia was quite promiscuous in high school and she had a shady reputation."

"Are you saying you think she may have been prostituting herself?"

"That's exactly what I'm saying. I called her and she told me one of the reasons she left Atlanta was because of her past. I didn't ask for her former address here because I didn't want her to think we're investigating her for prostitution."

"Well, tomorrow morning, call the place Olivia worked and get the address and we'll interview the neighbors."

"I'm ahead of you, bossman. I've already interviewed the manager at April Dawn's and the American Red Cross, and have phone numbers and addresses and a lot more."

"Holly, did I ever tell you were great?"

"Not enough, Noah," she says.

They laugh.

She hangs up and before she can gather her things and leave, her phone rings. She answers, "Detective Roark."

The Perry sheriff is on the line. "Glad I caught you, detective. Yesterday you said you needed the names of the deceased in 1991. There was only one, a ninety-four-year-old woman by the name of Suzy Jackson." He pauses. "Sorry. I had hoped it was a man's name that you could work with."

"Damn," she says under her breath. "Thanks anyway, sheriff."

CHAPTER FORTY-THREE

The next morning, before McGraw and Roark head out in an unmarked squad car to northeast Atlanta to the house in which Eva and Olivia lived together, Holly adds Sonny Burke's name on the board next to the other three in the graduation photo.

Once on their way, with Kramer and Gomez close behind them, Holly tells Noah what she learned about Olivia's boyfriend, Brad Knox, and his involvement with Johnny Parino and the black stretch limo.

"Johnny Parino?" McGraw says with surprise in his voice. "There's more to this than just lovers," he says.

"Do you think Brad was the driver of the black limo we saw in front of Tony's bar?" Roark asks.

"Could be, but what I am most interested in is what Bennett, the attorney, was doing with them."

"I know you don't want to think this, McGraw, but maybe the girl was a prostitute."

McGraw nods. "Okay, so what do we know?" he asks. "We have a guy driving a limo for Parino, who we know operates a prostitution ring, and the driver is likely pimping for him. So what is his relationship with Olivia? Could it be Olivia was prostituting for Brad Knox and they weren't really lovers?"

"It's shaking out that way, Noah," Holly says.

"We saw Bennett getting into that limo with a gal who might be a prostitute," McGraw says. "He apparently doesn't care if he's seen in Tony's with her? Using the service, he could have had a rendezvous with Olivia for all we know. You did say there was a file on her that was sealed?"

"I did. You're thinking he may have gotten caught with her and he called in a favor?" Roark asks.

McGraw nods. "That's what I'm thinking."

He pulls up next to the curb in front of a one-story white frame house with a large concrete porch and wide front yard. The house is empty and a realty sign is in the yard.

"What do you expect to find here?" Holly says.

"Don't know yet, but for starters the neighbors are our best bet for now."

They step out of the cruiser and Kramer and Gomez pull in behind them. McGraw says to Holly. "There's a phone number on the realty sign. Call it and get the owner out here right away."

Kramer and Gomez meet up with McGraw. "Interview the neighbors. Find out all you can about Eva and Olivia. I'm especially interested if they brought men to this house and how often they saw the girls with them, and which one had the most. You know the drill."

"Will do, lieutenant," Kramer says.

Twenty minutes later, the realtor and owner arrive. After introductions, the realtor opens the door. The place is bare.

"How long has the place been vacant?" McGraw says.

"About six months," the owner says.

"Who lived in here last?" Roark says.

"A minister and his wife moved in after Ms. Jordan and Ms. Bingham left us. The minister got transferred to Pennsylvania."

"Did you find anything out of the ordinary when the girls moved out?" McGraw asks.

Both men shake their heads and agree that nothing unusual was left in the house.

"They left the place in good shape, and cleaned it up nicely," the realtor says, "especially the master bedroom. This is only a two-bedroom house."

Holly shoots a furtive glance at McGraw. "Why that bedroom in particular?" McGraw says.

The owner says, "Don't know, but they seemed to have spent a lot of time in there."

"Can we see it?"

"Sure," the realtor says. They move to the back of the house, where a broom closet separates the two bedrooms. "This is it," he says as they enter the larger room to the left of the closet.

It is clean and has only one picture, a framed painting of Dorian Gray hanging on the inside wall.

"That picture by itself seems strange," Holly says.

"We were going to remove it, but the minister's wife liked it so much we left it," the realtor says.

"Seems strange she didn't take it with her," Noah says.

"I thought the same thing," the owner says. "But if you've ever dealt with renters you know that you can expect anything. We thought if she liked it, maybe another renter would, too. So we left it up."

Moving to the window, McGraw feels himself nodding. "Is there a basement or attic in the house?"

"There's a small attic above the other bedroom, but no basement. You can get to the attic from the hallway. You'll need the pole in the broom closet. It has a hook that slips into the slot in the little ceiling door. A ladder comes down," the owner says.

Holly begins her walk-through.

The realtor whispers something to the owner, then turns to McGraw. "Lieutenant, we have an appointment with a client on another piece of property, if you don't need us...."

"No, feel free to go, gentlemen."

"Take your time. I'll be back in an hour or so to lock up," he says.

"That'll be more than enough time," McGraw says.

He walks through the rooms and meets Holly in the living room near the door.

"See anything that stands out?" he says.

"Clean as a whistle. They made sure we wouldn't find anything, if that was their goal," Roark says.

Kramer and Gomez move into the room.

Gomez says, "We learned the gals had lots of male visitors, but the men never arrived on their own. They said the blonde usually came with them in a black limo driven by the same man. And a few times they saw another man with the driver in the passenger seat, but not all the time."

"The blonde would be Olivia," Holly says.

"They never saw the brunette bring any man to the house in the limo, only the blonde. The girls never caused any problems and the neighbors never heard loud music, or arguments," Kramer says. "An older gentleman across the street had me step outside so his wife couldn't hear us talking, told me he was of the opinion that the girls were prostitutes."

"Could anyone describe the guys in the limo?" McGraw asks.

He shakes his head. "They couldn't see them too good. The driver was smaller than the other guy, who they said was pretty big," Gomez says.

"Follow me," McGraw says. He opens the broom closet and reaches in for the pole with a hook on its end. A bucket with a mop in it is on the floor, and a broom with dust pan is leaning in the corner. Some cleaning supplies are on the shelves. He hands the pole to Kramer. "Take this and check out the attic. You can get up in it from a ceiling ladder at the end of the hall, in front of the smaller bedroom."

Kramer frowns, reaches for it and hands it off to Gomez. They head to the back of the house.

"Did you see those four marks on the bedroom floor?" he says to Holly.

"Yeah, that must be where the bed was."

McGraw goes to the picture and turns around so his back is against the wall and his head is at the same level as Dorian Gray's. Standing in front of the picture, McGraw extends his hand in front of him towards the marks on the floor.

"The side of the bed would have been in line with Dorian Gray's eyes," he says. He turns around and removes the picture from the wall.

Holly hurries over and rubs her fingers over a spot the size of a fifty-cent piece.

"Someone's patched a hole here and painted over it," she says. "You can see the difference in the shades of paint color."

McGraw moves out into the hall, opens the broom closet, goes inside, and begins inspecting the walls. Holly moves in behind him. He pounds on the walls with his fist. She does the same.

"The back wall seems hollow," he says, and he begins removing shelves. They slide out easily, and he hands them to Roark. He inspects the corners and pushes on the wall with his shoulder. The wall flips open on hinges into a square room with no windows, which only contains a small, wooden three-drawer dresser. There's barely enough room for two people to move around.

"Notice the marks on the floor close to the wall," he says bending down to examine them. "These were made from a tripod."

"Wow! Are you thinking what I'm thinking, Noah?"

"McGraw looks up at the wall closest to the bedroom, rises and goes to it, removes a pen from his pocket and inserts it into the hole. *A camera lens could have been inserted into it*, he thinks.

He turns to Holly. "They forgot to patch this hole. A camera could be set at an angle like I've done with this pen, to capture a view of someone in bed in the next room. He goes to the little dresser, opens the top drawer, finds a roll of film and a couple of colored pictures and hands them off to Holly. The other two drawers are empty.

She gives one of the pictures to McGraw as she examines the second one. They exchange pictures. In each, men are lying in bed on their sides facing the camera, their faces and upper bodies exposed. A blonde is in one and a brunette in the other. They are sitting on the edge of the bed with breasts bare, sheets covering the lower part of their bodies, one leg hanging over the side touching the floor. The blonde is looking down at the man with her hand in an area that isn't visible, and in the other picture the photographer caught the brunette groping the smiling man while looking toward the camera. The pictures aren't too clear, probably the reason the photographer left them.

"Let's go into the bedroom. We need more light," McGraw says. He closes the fake door and replaces the shelves. In the bedroom, standing by the windows, they examine the pictures more closely.

"The women are Eva and Olivia," he says. "Look closely at the men and tell me who you think one of them might be?"

Holly takes her time staring hard at the picture. She looks up at McGraw and whispers, "The guy with Olivia is that attorney, Bennett."

McGraw reaches for the pictures and puts them in the pocket of his jean-jacket. "We have our proof."

Kramer and Gomez walk into the room. Gomez looks sweaty and rumpled.

"Boss, there's nothing up in that attic but spider webs. I crawled through the whole place."

"I see the picture's off the wall. What did you find?" Kramer says.

Holly glances at McGraw. He moves to the wall and points to the patched area "Someone was taking pictures of the girls in here from a small room behind this wall. The camera was positioned in such a way that its lens was able to see through Dorian Gray's eyes. The picture was hung at a height that no one would find suspicious. We found a roll of film in a small cabinet in the room, which may still be good and could have some pictures on it."

"So, the girls were prostituting themselves," Kramer says.

"And you can bet your bottom dollar someone was blackmailing the men in the pictures," Gomez says.

"That's what we're going to find out," Holly says.

"Let's go over what we know so far," McGraw says. "The neighbors said that the blonde girl, whom we have determined is Olivia Jordan, brought men to this place in the black limo with the same driver, who we know is Brad Knox, but at times there also was a big guy with him. Who is the other guy and how is he involved?"

"The driver has to be the pimp," Roark says. "When I met with Olivia's boss at April Dawn's, she told me Olivia's boyfriend picked her up in a black stretch limo. When I confronted Olivia during our phone conversation, she gave him up as Brad Knox and he was pimping for...." Roark pauses and stares into the eyes of Kramer and Gomez. "You guys are going to be shocked. Knox is pimping for Johnny Parino."

"Parino?" Gomez shouts.

"That scum bag," Kramer says. He turns to Gomez. "That's the limo we saw parked in front of Santino's, Parino's restaurant."

"Olivia didn't admit to prostituting. She just said when she found out what Brad Knox was doing she broke if off with him and took off for New York."

"Of course, she's lying," McGraw says. "Let's get to the station."

The realtor entered the house as they were heading to the living room. "Are you detectives about done? I'd like to lock up."

"We're leaving," McGraw says. "Thank you."

CHAPTER FORTY-FOUR

On the way to the precinct, the clouds are starting to let loose afternoon sprinkles as Noah pulls the cruiser into the lot and parks behind the building. He and Holly take off running to the entrance before the downpour begins.

Once inside, she takes the roll of film to forensics and he is met by Capt. Dipple. After a brief discussion, Noah heads into the squad room. When his team members are back at their desks, he calls them to the evidence board, and writes the names of Olivia Jordan, Brad Knox, and "Big Guy" in quotes, on the board.

He turns to Kramer and Gomez.

"Agent Nelson just informed the Capt. that Parino and his men have been arrested, which means that Knox will be on his own. He'll need cash to live. Pimps never let their gals go. He must be out there transporting them as we speak. He wouldn't be happy if his girls peeled on him, so, he must still be controlling them."

"That's right," Holly says, "Knox, being a pimp, doesn't want to lose one of his girls to another pimp. There has to be one of Knox's prostitutes out there who would like to turn him."

"You guys know where to look," McGraw says. "Go after him and bring him in." He points to the board, and says, "Also, keep an eye out for his companion, the Big Guy."

"We will, boss," Gomez says. He and Kramer head out.

McGraw turns to Roark, who is standing next to him.

"Run Brad Knox through our system and NCIC and get all you can on him. Something might lead us to that companion of his. Also, call Olivia and pump her hard. She knows who this mystery man...." McGraw stops before completing his sentence, and glances back at the board.

"Something's caught your eye, Noah? What is it?"

He takes his time answering. "We keep hearing 'Big Guy,' 'Big Guy.' Didn't we hear that description from the clerks in Charlotte and Raleigh, and now Olivia's neighbors?"

She nods. "Yeah, he keeps popping up."

"Well, if he was involved with pimping Olivia, and if he was the same guy who took Eva to North Carolina, it means he has something on her, and that is the reason she didn't alert the clerks." He turns to Holly. "And what do you think that something is?"

"It can only be one thing: pictures of Eva in bed with the men. Big Guy must have threatened her with going to the news media with them, and, fearing what it would do to the Hamiltons and to her reputation back in Oklahoma, Eva keeps quiet and does what Big Guy wants."

"Did I ever tell you, you're good?"

She smiles.

"Run Brad Knox and go after Olivia. I still think Big Guy is Sonny Burke."

She salutes. "Will do, sir," she teases.

Holly goes to her desk, enters Brad Knox's name into the computer and waits. He has two arrests for pimping prostitutes, but was fined and released. *He sure got off easy,* Roark thinks. She recognizes the name Judge Murray. *He's the judge who sealed Olivia Jordan's file.*

She looks in her notebook for Olivia Jordan's cell phone and dials it. She is hoping Olivia can talk, since she must still be at work. After four rings, Olivia answers. Roark identifies herself and asks if Olivia can talk, it's quite important. Olivia is having a late lunch in her office, and says they were very busy and she didn't have time to take lunch outside.

"Let me shut my door and we can talk. I only have a few minutes."

Roark hears what she thinks is Olivia putting her phone down and then a slamming noise.

"I'm back," she says.

Roark opens her notebook on her desk and reaches for a pen.

"You didn't tell me the last time we talked that you and Brad were involved in more than romance. We have evidence that you and Eva were prostituting while living together here in Atlanta." Roark pauses to get a response out of her. When she only hears hard breathing in the phone, she continues.

"We have witnesses that have seen you bringing men to the house in the black limo and Brad as the driver. What do you have to say for yourself?"

"What I told you was partly true. Brad and I started out as lovers, but then I realized it was just an act. He was running an escort service and he wanted me in on it."

"You mean transporting prostitutes."

"Yes. At first he had me help with his other gals like I was his office manager, but after things were going good, he began manipulating me—he's very good at it—into doing more for him, and I fell for it because of his charm and the money, which was great, and at the time I was blindly in love with the guy. After one time escorting big-money people and getting big tips as well, I got hooked. Then I found out he was taking pictures of me with my clients and was blackmailing them. He had a camera set up in the next room and I never knew until later. He turned into a very bad creep."

"Was he blackmailing the attorney, Samuel Bennett?"

"I was in the back of the limo with Bennett when the cops pulled us over. They took us downtown and booked us, but let Bennett go. Brad found out later that the cops had been watching Brad for some time, so he said. While we were being held, Brad talked with Bennett and made it known to him that he had pictures."

"Do you think it was the attorney who used his influence on the judge to seal your file?"

"Brad told me it was."

"Do you remember the judge's name?"

"Murray, I believe."

"How did Eva get involved?"

"Eva never wanted to get into the business. I tried to keep her out of it, but Brad pressured me to get her to work for him. Knowing I made big bucks, she finally agreed. She was desperate. Eva didn't make very much at the Red Cross, so I got Brad to agree to let me handle her. Eva didn't help him transport the men to the house. He allowed me to assign my clients to her when I got too many calls to handle. Eva never escorted, and she wasn't in the business for long, only twice, and then gave it up. I hated that I dragged her into it."

Roark makes a couple of entries in her notebook.

"As you said, and as Brooke Tubbs told me, one of your goals was to go to New York to learn the business of designing clothes. Brooke gave me the impression you left them earlier than planned."

"That's true. I always had plans to come here. But I left sooner than I intended to because I wanted to get away from Brad."

"We have witnesses who have seen another guy they describe as just a 'big man' sitting in the passenger seat of the limo with Brad, transporting you and your clients to the house. Who is that man?"

Roark can hear heavy breathing in the phone. It takes Olivia a few moments to speak.

"Sonny Burke."

"Sonny Burke?" *McGraw was right.* "Remember telling me someone told you Burke may be in Atlanta, but you couldn't remember who that was and that you didn't really know where he was."

"I know. I'm sorry. But part of what I told you is true. I hadn't seen him until he and Brad became friends a couple of years ago when Brad met Sonny in a bar."

Roark makes additional entries into the notebook.

"They started to pal around together a lot, and date other women. Many women were drawn to that stretch limo. The guys use it as a sex wagon to attract women."

"Where can I find Burke?"

"I don't know. And that's the truth. He quit riding along when he found out Eva was involved. I believe he didn't want her to see him. He always hit on her in school."

"Do you think he came to Atlanta when he found out Eva was here?"

"It wouldn't surprise me. The way he talked about her, I could tell he never got over her."

"When did you last see him?"

"The day he quit riding with us. That was the last time. He never liked me in school and that hadn't changed. He avoided talking to me when we were escorting. Sometimes he scared me the way he eyed me, but he never did anything. He would only talk to Brad."

"Why would he ride along with Brad when you were escorting your date to the house?"

"You can't see the driver or passenger through the smoked window from the back. You'd have to knock on the glass, and Brad would lower it. The customers would never know Sonny was up there. The times he was with Brad, I'm sure they went out looking for women after they dropped me off with my date."

"What else can you tell me about Burke?"

"Not much. Do you think he abducted Eva?" Olivia asks.

"I do, but we must locate him soon if we want to find her alive."

No response from Olivia. Roark hears voices. "I gotta go," Olivia says. "But one other thing: I heard through the grapevine while working the escort service that Sonny used to get pretty rough with the women they picked up. I don't know if it was a sex thing or what."

"What do you mean by grapevine?"

"I really have to go," she says. "My boss is waiting."

"Just tell me how you know he got rough with those women."

"The girls that work the streets have ways of communicating who the bad guys are, and they won't date them. They avoided Sonny like the bubonic plague. I heard he beat up one of the girls so bad that she was in the hospital for weeks. Word on the street is he may have killed a couple of women."

"Do you have any names? Can you verify that?"

"No it's just rumored."

"Did Brad and Burke just pick up prostitutes that Brad knew?"

"They did a few, but mostly they went for women in the bars."

"So the word out on the street is that Knox and Burke are bad dudes?"

"Not Brad, just Sonny." She pauses. "I need to go."

"Okay. But as I said before, if you think of anything else about Burke, please call me immediately."

"I will," Olivia says and the phone goes dead.

Roark slams her hand on the desk. Damn. I didn't get a chance to ask her to describe Burke.

———— ◆ ————

McGraw leaves the Capt.'s office and heads to the squad room, bringing a soft drink to Roark, who is at her desk and has just hung up the phone.

"Thanks for the drink."

"What have you gotten for me?" he asks.

"Anything I should know about what went on in the Lion's Den?" she says.

"Nothing new. Did Olivia reveal anything new on Knox?"

"Knox got off easy. He was arrested twice with only fines. The judge was Murray, the one who sealed Olivia's case file. Samuel Bennett was hauled in with them, and he used his influence with the judge." She takes a couple of swallows of her drink. "You were right. The big guy is Sonny Burke. Olivia told me plenty. Knox and Sonny are pals and they used to pick up prostitutes, but now mostly women in the bars, using the limo to attract them. It is known on the street that Burke is a bad dude. He beats up girls and does a job on them. It is rumored that one of the girls was beaten so bad she spent weeks in the hospital. He may have even killed a couple of them."

McGraw raises a hand to tell Holly to give him a minute before she continues. He picks up the phone and calls the M.E. He asks her if she's heard among her colleagues about women coming into their morgues beaten and raped in the last two months. Some could be prostitutes. Dr. Philips hasn't heard nor has she had such a body come into her morgue. After thanking her, McGraw breaks the circuit and calls a detective friend in another precinct and asks him the same question. The detective told McGraw he did get called out to the edge of town a few weeks ago to work the homicide scene of a prostitute found badly beaten. Then he got a call from another woman who escaped from a guy in a limo who tried to beat her during sex. All she would say was that the guy was big. When the detective asked for her name, she hung up on him. Her call couldn't be traced.

McGraw hangs up the phone, turns to Roark and repeats what his detective friend just told him. "But he hasn't found the perp as yet," McGraw says.

Kramer's voice is heard coming into the squad room. He and Gomez are escorting a thin man in his early forties, around five-eleven, wearing an expensive blue suit, white shirt and red tie and two-hundred-dollar black shoes. He has a swarthy complexion and short dark hair, looks a little like George Clooney. McGraw can see how Olivia would get tangled up with this guy.

Gomez says, "We've got Brad Knox for you, boss."

Holly turns around.

"This is Sergeant Roark," Kramer says.

Knox smiles, while his eyes leer at her.

"Where did you find him?" she asks, "in the sewer?"

"My, my, don't be judgmental, sergeant," Knox says in a condescending tone.

Roark doesn't answer; instead she looks over at Noah.

Kramer says, "We found him out on the street in his limo watching his girls."

"This is Lieutenant McGraw," Kramer says to Knox.

Knox glances at McGraw and bursts out laughing.

Pointing, he says, "A cowboy detective? What is the world coming to?"

Kramer looks at Gomez and they look at Holly.

"You have anything against cowboys?" McGraw says.

"No, sir, I watch them cowboy movies all the time. You ever been in one of 'em?" he asks, bursting out in laughter. Then he stops and stares at McGraw, frowns and points again, shaking an index finger at him, and says, "I know who you are," he says. "You're that Marlboro cop everyone talks about."

McGraw doesn't answer. He can see Kramer and Gomez holding back smiles.

"You gonna lasso me, cowboy?" Knox laughs so hard he bends over.

"Take him into one," McGraw says.

Kramer leads Knox to Interview Room One.

Minutes later, McGraw and Roark enter.

"I don't know why I'm here. I was just driving by some ladies, minding my own business, when your goons pulled me over."

"Have a seat, Mr. Knox," McGraw says. He and Roark take the two seats facing him.

"So, you're Parino's pimp boy?" McGraw says, adjusting himself in the chair.

"Sure is," Roark says.

"I ain't no pimp," he says, faking indignation. "And who in the hell is Parino?"

"Like you didn't know," McGraw says. "Maybe you know Sonny Burke?"

"Never heard of him."

Roark says. "We have witnesses that saw you both driving your girls with their clients in the back of your stretch limo to a house on the east side."

"They're lying."

"Do you know Olivia Jordan?" McGraw says.

Knox's eyes widen. "Why you asking about that broad? She means nothing to me."

He says one thing, but his eyes say something else. *He's lying*, McGraw thinks. "We know otherwise, and Ms. Jordan told us plenty about you and Burke. Now where can we find him?"

"We're waiting," Roark says.

"Okay, okay. Yeah, I know Sonny. But I don't know where he is or where he lives, honest. He only comes to Santino's where I park my limo. He never ever told me where he works or where he lives, or anything like that. We just hang out. He's the kind of dude you don't screw with or ask him a lot of questions."

"We know that you and Burke beat up a prostitute so badly it put her in the hospital for weeks, and one of you battered another woman while having sex with her."

He raises his hands, palms outward. "Hey, you ain't gonna pin that on me. I don't hit babes. That's Burke. Sometimes he can get pretty mean."

"Do you know Judge Murray?"

Knox stares at the floor.

"I refuse to answer that."

"Maybe you'd like to spend some time in the holding cell," McGraw says.

His head jerks up. "On what charge, cowboy? I ain't done nothin'. You dickheads can't keep me on trumped-up charges."

"We can charge you with attempted blackmail, pimping, and maybe go as far as an accomplice in the murder of a prostitute," McGraw says. He was laying it on thick, but Knox would never know. Kramer and Gomez enter and are about to take Knox when McGraw says, "Wait up." They step back to the door.

"Maybe we can give you a break, if you help us," McGraw says. He's not interested in holding Knox; it's Burke he wants. "I may have to hold you for just a couple of days, but I think I can drop all charges."

Knox is silent. He appears to be digesting what McGraw has said.

A smile comes across his face. "Wadda you want to know?"

"How would you describe Burke?" McGraw says. He knows Roark forgot to ask Jordan to describe him.

Knox sighs. "He's pretty tall, over six feet, broad shoulders, and has big hands. He's dresses sharp."

"As sharp as you do?" Roark says.

"No one dresses as good as me, honey."

"Does Burke have any tattoos or scars?" Gomez says.

"No."

"How does he talk?" Kramer says. "Does he have any accents like maybe he's from some other part of the country?"

"When he's been drinking he does have some kind of drawl, but I don't know how to explain it. He mentioned Oklahoma once, maybe it was an Okie accent."

McGraw's eyes connect with Roark's when 'Okie' is mentioned.

"What kind of women does he go after?" McGraw says.

"He likes all women, but mostly brunettes with nice butts. He's a butt man. I like blondes with big tits."

Roark is fuming and appears ready to attack Knox. McGraw's eyes widen and his stare at her is hard, a sign he often uses to tell her to cool it.

"Is there anything unusual about Burke, anything at all?" McGraw says.

Knox frowns and seems in deep thought. "Man, I don't know why I didn't think of it before. The guy wears police shades and he never takes them off."

"Would you say he looks like Sylvester Stallone, the guy who played Rocky in the movies?" McGraw says.

Knox raises a hand and points a finger at McGraw again, like he's discovered gold. "Yeah, man, that's it! Rocky."

McGraw glances over at Holly, who is staring at him with glassy eyes. He wants to tell her that this may not be Max, but she knows better. McGraw's now feeling a little guilty for the way he joked about him. "When did you last see Burke?"

"Two days ago. He said he had to go out of town because someone in his family was dying or died." Knox shakes his head. "I didn't buy it. He just wanted to get away for a while because of that gal he beat on."

"Did he say where he was going?" Kramer says.

"I can't remember him saying anything about where he'd go."

"Did he ever mention Mississippi?" Roark says.

"He once told me he had a cousin there and he nearly played football for Ole Miss. I don't believe he ever said where his cousin lived in Mississippi."

"How about Oxford," Roark says. "Could he have talked about Oxford, Mississippi?"

"Naw, I'd remember that."

"But do you think that's where he would go if he did go somewhere?" Gomez asks.

He shrugs. "I'm no mind reader. I can't say for sure, but maybe he'd go back where he came from. Don't we all want to do that at times?" He shrugs, again. "He only mentioned it once, so it could be Oklahoma."

"Okay," McGraw says to Kramer and Gomez, "put him in holding."

"You mean after two days, you'll drop all charges?"

"That's what I mean."

They leave the room.

McGraw eyes Roark as they head back to the squad room. "I'm not releasing this guy so he can contact Burke. We got enough to hold him for a couple of days."

She nods.

"I know what you are thinking," McGraw says. "Max is Burke."

"And so are you," she says. "Max is over six feet, has big hands, dresses well and never takes his shades off. Isn't that what Knox said? And he thinks he's from Oklahoma and nearly played football for the Ole Miss Rebels. That's Max."

He nods.

"I have an idea," she says. "A few weeks ago he called me and I didn't return his call. Let me try and reach him. He shouldn't suspect anything."

"Great."

She walks to her desk and lifts the phone and places a call to Max's office. His secretary answers. Roark learns that he wasn't in, and was getting ready to leave town and would be gone for a few days.

"Did he say where he was going?" Roark says.

"No, he didn't. Can I take a message, Detective Roark?"

"You might tell him I'll call back in a couple of days—"

McGraw interrupts. "Ask for his home landline phone."

She asks and then writes it on a slip of paper.

"Well, we now know he's going or may have gone out of town," McGraw says. "Call his home and check what he has on his voice recorder."

Roark picks up the phone and dials the number.

"Hello," the female voice says. "This is Kristi Sue."

Roark raises her hand to get McGraw's attention.

"What?" he says.

He can read her lips. "A woman," Roark whispers.

"Is Mr. Kingston in please, I'm one of his clients and couldn't reach him at the office?"

"Can I take a message?" the female voice says. "He's left town and won't return for several days. I am his wife."

Roark almost drops the phone.

"I heard someone in his family in Mississippi has died, and I wanted to send some flowers. Mr. Kingston has been very good to me and my husband," Roark says.

"Oh, there must be some mistake. There's no one in his family that died there," she says.

"Well, that's a relief. I'm sure glad to hear that. I'll just call back later. Thank you."

"As you wish," she says. "Oh, I never got your name."

Roark hangs up, and looks at McGraw. He can see the surprised look on her face.

"He has a wife," Roark says.

"I guess that's no surprise from what we're learning about him." McGraw pauses. He has to get this off his chest. "Holly, I am sorry how things have turned out. I apologize for the way I joked about Max. I realize now how cruel that was of me, and maybe I was a little jealous."

A big smile fills her face. "Jealous?"

He nods. It just slipped out and he has no way to retract it.

"That's sweet, but don't worry, I'm over Max. You were right all along. You saw something in him that I didn't. His charisma blinded me, but I don't like it that he used me to try and extract information. I'm a cop and I'm trained to know better."

"Cops are human, too, Holly. We have emotions like everyone else."

"But I let mine get the best of me."

She gets up and goes to the wall board. "Max Kingston isn't one of the names Sheriff Sinclair gave me," she says, moving to her computer. "Let's see what background I can get on a Max Kingston."

McGraw heads for the coffee stand and waits until another detective leaves before filling his Atlanta Falcon's cup. A detective near the coffee stand tells McGraw there's a call for him on one. When he returns to his desk, he sets his cup down and lifts the phone and takes the message, and glances at Roark. She is staring at the monitor.

"No arrests, not even a speeding ticket. Can't find anything on him prior to two-thousand," she says. "His website is all about investing and preparing for retirement. I'm sure he's hiding something."

"Just got a call from forensics," McGraw says. "The roll of film is blank."

"That's why the photographer left it," she says. "How about getting a search warrant to search Max's Office? We may find something that points the finger at him."

"What's the probable cause?" he says.

"I think the abduction of Eva Hamilton and the murder of Cody Guthrie is cause enough."

"I imagine Max has destroyed all the evidence by now. That's the first place he would think we would come. We'll skip the warrant and talk with the secretary."

"Let's do it," she says with enthusiasm.

On the way out, McGraw tells Kramer and Gomez to come with them and to keep an eye on Kingston's office for the next couple of days.

McGraw says to Roark, "Now that we know he has a wife we can talk to her. We'll see what surfaces."

"I can't wait to see what type of woman she is," Roark says.

CHAPTER FORTY-FIVE

McGraw pulls into Prestige Mall, drives past several shop fronts from the street, and guides the cruiser perpendicular to the curb in front of the commercial building. Roark is first to climb out. He rolls out, tilting his hat forward to shade his eyes from the bright sunlight reflecting off the hood. She ambles through the revolving door, and he pauses to slip into a section behind her. Inside, they head to the elevator and Roark punches the up button.

"Max's office is on the third floor," she says, pointing to the directory between the banks of elevators. I've been here before, as you may have guessed."

"I'll take the stairs," he says, darting to them.

"It's here, Noah. It's here," she says, again, but he's disappeared up the steps.

When the elevator doors open on the third floor, McGraw is waiting for Roark to step out. She jerks back with surprise. "Why didn't you come in with me?" she says.

"I need the exercise. I never ride elevators."

"Oh, Noah, I bet you're afraid," she says, teasingly. "Don't tell me you're afraid of elevators?"

That's for me to know and for you to figure out. He turns and walks down the hall. She hurries to catch up.

They enter Kingston Investments and find a middle-aged woman working at her desk in the middle of what appears to be the waiting room. Two offices are behind her with their doors closed. The attractive brunette looks up, rises, and asks if she can help them. She is wearing a two-piece gray suit, white blouse with a high collar, and has smooth skin and a nice figure.

"I am Lieutenant McGraw with the Atlanta PD and I believe you've met my partner, Sergeant Roark."

"I'm Mary Turner, Mr. Kingston's secretary." She nods at Roark. "Yes, I know Detective Roark. How are you, sergeant?"

"Very well, thank you."

"If you've come to see Mr. Kingston, I'm sorry, but he's gone out of town. He's supposed to call me and give me information on how he can be reached and when he'll return."

"We're here just to ask you a few questions about Mr. Kingston, if you don't mind?" McGraw says.

She frowns. "Can I ask what this is about? Is he in some kind of trouble?"

"Oh, no," Roark says. "We're trying to determine if someone is threatening him and that's why he left town."

McGraw glances at Roark. *Really great gambit*, he thinks.

Mary seems more assured now and smiles. "I'm pleased to do anything to help Mr. Kingston."

McGraw gestures toward four chairs in the corner of the room with a glass table in front of them. "Would you mind joining us over there," he says.

"Certainly," she says. "Would you like something to drink?"

"Nothing for me," McGraw says.

"Nor for me," Roark says.

They move to the chairs and take their seats.

"Ms. Turner, how long have you worked for Mr. Kingston," McGraw asks.

"Let's see, it will be four years in February."

"During all that time, have you noticed anything unusual about Mr. Kingston and his dealings with his clients?"

She shakes her head. "No. He gets along well with them, lieutenant."

Roark says, "So he hasn't been out of sorts recently?"

She shakes her head, but then stops as if she is thinking something.

"Mr. Kingston is funny and jovial most of the time. But lately he seems more irritable. He really treats me well. I do hope he's okay." She pauses. "There was a time...." She stops short. "Oh, I hope I'm not telling anything that would hurt him."

"I'm sure you are very loyal, Ms. Turner, and you wouldn't say anything to hurt Mr. Kingston," McGraw says. "Please go on, we're only trying to establish why he left town."

"What I was going to say is, one morning he was in his office very early and I came in to catch up on some work."

She pauses again.

"And..." Roark says, urging her along.

"And I heard this weirdest noise coming from his office. Of course, he had his door closed, and I could be mistaken about what I heard, but it sounded like he had one of those toys that make funny noises."

McGraw glances at Roark.

"What did it sound like?" Roark says.

Mary glances at the floor and then looks up.

"What was the sound, Mary, please?" Roark says, losing her patience.

"It sounded like the Joker's laugh in those Batman movies. You know that screeching sound that runs chills up your spine. I thought it quite unusual for him."

209

"Interesting," McGraw says. "Did you think he was trying to torment someone?"

"I thought he was playing a joke on some client. But then I wondered if he was...."

"Losing it?" Roark says.

"Oh, I don't know, sergeant," Mary says, looking worried.

"I'm sure he was just playing a joke on someone. Maybe on one of his children," McGraw says. "Could you give us Mr. Kingston's cell phone number? We can contact him to see if he's okay."

She shakes her head. "Oh, he never gives it out, lieutenant. I don't even have it. I'm sorry."

"I have a question," Roark says. "How long has Mr. Kingston been married?"

"Must be over ten years now," she says. "He has two boys, six and nine, and a two-year-old girl."

"How do they get along?" Roark says.

She hesitates. "I guess it's no secret. They have had problems for a few years. I know they're separated. Mr. Kingston loves those kids, but he and Kristi Sue don't seem to be compatible. I feel sorry for her; she's a very sweet lady. Maybe the separation is weighing on him. Do you think?" Mary pauses, a third time. "I'm afraid I've said too much."

"I'm sure he's fine, Mary. Mr. Kingston probably went away for a while to relax," McGraw says.

She smiles. "Oh, yes, that has to be it, lieutenant. I feel so much better thinking that."

"Is it possible Mr. Kingston could have gone to Oklahoma? We understand he grew up there," McGraw says.

"I really don't know. He's never gotten anything here from anyone in Oklahoma." She places a finger against her lips and frowns as if she's thinking. "The only other thing addressed to him outside of his business materials is literature and sport supplies from the University of Mississippi."

"I see," McGraw says as he rises.

"We'll need his home address?" Roark says.

"Certainly," she says.

Mary goes to her desk, writes on a pad, tears off a sheet and hands it to Roark, who has moved to her desk.

"Thank you."

Back in the cruiser, McGraw says, "Maybe Ms. Kingston can give us Max's cell phone number. We can have it pinged through his carrier to get his location."

"Hopefully, he hasn't removed the battery," Roark says.

CHAPTER FORTY-SIX

Max Kingston's home is located in an upscale neighborhood with sprawling manicured lawns, brick walls three feet high separating one property from the next, towering trees, and flower beds against the walls, filled with an assortment of colors and obviously maintained by a landscaper. The homes are huge, all brick or stone, two stories with pitched roofs and 6000 square feet or more.

McGraw drives up the long driveway about fifty yards and stops the cruiser in front of the Kingston's home behind a white Cadillac SUV parked in front of a three-car garage. He is surprised that the man with a smooth tongue has such a castle, but can't help being suspicious. Maybe it's because he doesn't like Max.

"I guess it should be no surprise that Max would have such a showplace," Roark says.

McGraw doesn't respond, wondering instead what they're going to find in the likes of Kristi Sue. He adjusts his Stetson and steps out. Holly comes around the back, joins him in front of the cruiser and they walk the stretch of sidewalk that curves to the entrance. Six large windows in front expose furniture that you don't normally see in a furniture store. *Probably custom made*, Noah thinks.

He removes his ID from his jacket pocket and his partner has hers ready as he rings the doorbell.

A smiling blonde with a narrow face, about five-five and a nice build opens the door and greets them with a "How can I help y'all?"

Noah is expecting a butler.

"I am Lieutenant McGraw with the Atlanta PD and this is my partner, Sergeant Roark. May we come in?"

"Can I ask what this is about, lieutenant?"

"We just have a few questions, it shouldn't take too long."

"Is this about my husband?"

He nods. "It is."

"Please, come in. My name is Kristi Sue." She steps aside while they enter and closes the door behind them. "We can go into the living room, which is to our right." She leads the way.

The circled foyer is bright, filled with sun streaming through the five-foot windows across the way that frame a rock rose garden outside the building.

"Thank you," McGraw says.

Inside the living room, he wonders if he should sit, the couch looks so immaculate and expensive and white. He is relieved when she gestures for them to sit. When Noah walks past a round table, he notices a book on top titled *My Husband, the Psychopath*. Kristi Sue grabs it up, turns it over and sets it on another table against the wall, then goes to a cloth chair decorated with large flowers. She sits and crosses her sun-tanned legs.

Not bad, McGraw thinks. Roark scowls at him.

"I need to tell you, detectives, that my husband and I are getting a divorce soon and we aren't on the best of terms. I haven't seen him in a while, but we talk." She hops up. "Where are my manners? I didn't offer you anything to drink."

McGraw waves it off. "Thank you. We're fine." He takes notice of her sweet southern accent.

She smiles and sits back down.

"Do you know where we might reach Mr. Kingston?" Roark says.

"Max. He goes by Max."

Roark shoots a furtive glance at her partner.

"He cleared out several weeks ago. I know he has an apartment somewhere, and it wouldn't surprise me if he's shacking up with some of his women."

McGraw glances over at his partner, wondering if she is thinking about her relationship with Max.

"We'd sure like to talk to him. Do you know where his apartment is?" McGraw asks.

She shrugs and shakes her head. "Sorry. I don't. Is he in some kind of trouble?"

"He may be. That's why we need to talk to him. He may be running away from us."

"I see. Wish I could help you, but he's good at keeping things from me."

"We suspect he may have gone to his home town in Oklahoma," Roark says, or to visit someone in Mississippi?"

She frowns. "I don't know, but it's interesting you mentioned that. Some client of his called the other day and thought Max had a relative dying in Mississippi. I don't know where she got that. He no longer has family there."

McGraw glances over at the book he saw earlier. "Would you mind telling us about your relationship with your husband?" he says.

She frowns, turns for a few moments to look at the flower garden outside the window before answering. "Max can be very charming; especially when we are with other people, but when we are alone that's a very different side of him. He's very controlling."

"Did he ever harm you, Ms. Kingston?" Roark says.

"Oh, please call me Kristi Sue, sergeant. We southern girls have two names, but I guess you know that, living here in Atlanta." She sighs. "To answer your question, yes. Max hits me. I've gotten black eyes and bruised shoulders. It happens whenever I confront him about his infidelity. It sends him into such a rage; he'd scream that I should never, ever question him. But he stays out late at night and I never know where he is, or what he's doing. What else would I be thinking?"

Kristi Sue looks down at the floor. "He loves to play mind games, and tries to turn the tables on me to make me feel guilty, but it doesn't work anymore. Whenever he is verbally abusive or if he smacks me, he'll tell me afterwards he's sorry, he couldn't help himself, but I see through it. I just got tired of it and told him to get the hell out. He cleared out his things and stormed out telling me he didn't need me, he had other women that appreciated him. I guess he manipulates them, too, like he does me."

McGraw realizes Kristi Sue is dealing with a psychopath who is a narcissist. He learned in his psych classes that narcissists are not necessarily psychopaths, but that the reverse is true. He wonders if she's in control of their assets; otherwise, why would she tell Max to get lost? He looks around the place and wonders how she can afford it.

"Do you have a business, Kristi Sue?" McGraw says.

She shakes her head. "I used to work for my father, but not after Max and I married."

"It appears that Max's business is doing very well," McGraw says, looking over the room. "You have a wonderful home and beautiful lot. What is it, four acres?"

She laughs. "Five. You think Max paid for all this?" she says, gesturing. "His business couldn't buy a home one-tenth this size. I come from a wealthy family. My father is in investment banking and does very well. As you might know, investment banks do not take deposits like commercial and retail banks do. Anyway, Max can turn on the charisma and talk himself out of prison, that's how smooth he can be when he wants to. Daddy fell for it, brought him in and taught him the business. That's how we met."

She gets up and walks to the window. "Daddy gave me this house as a wedding present. My husband eventually went out on his own after learning the investment business from my daddy and opened Kingston Investments. He's done fairly well for himself, but his business isn't able to do more than pay a small part of the expenses on this place. He tried several times to manipulate my money, but daddy caught him at it and no longer has anything to do with Max."

She returns to her seat. "And neither do I."

"So, there's nothing of his in his bedroom?" McGraw says.

She shakes her head. "Nothing."

"Does Max have an office here?" he asks.

She nods, and rises. "Would you like to see it?"

Roark jumps up. "We would," she says, before McGraw can reply.

Kristi Sue leads the way out of the room and down another hall off the foyer.

"Max never wanted me in his office. Sometimes I'd sneak in there to see what he was up to, but he has everything locked up tighter than a drum."

Drum? It's odd that she would use that word. It reminds me of poor Cody Guthrie's body in the one found on my property, McGraw thinks.

Kristi Sue opens the door into this spacious room, with tall windows like those in the rest of the house. A gleaming executive desk with a leather chair behind it is in the center of the room. A leather chair faces the desk. A "Hotty Toddy" Ole Miss banner hangs from the ceiling.

"He still hasn't come back to clean out his desk and files," she says as she enters the room, leaving the door open.

"I see the Ole Miss banner hanging from the ceiling," McGraw says. "He's quite a fan."

"Oh, yes. He loves Ole Miss more than he does me. He never could get it out of his system that he couldn't play for the Rebels when he got hurt in high school. Even though I'm a Georgia girl now, that's the only thing Max and I agree on, the Rebels. My Daddy is a graduate of Ole Miss, and I was born in Oxford while Daddy was in school there. Maybe that's another reason Daddy liked Max at first."

"Max appears to be a neat person," Roark says as she walks around to the back of the desk while McGraw moves along the bookcases filled with leather books and some first editions.

"He's a neat freak and doesn't throw anything away. You should have seen his room before he cleared it out. His suits hung perfectly, his shirts stacked just one way, his shoes lined up on the floor like soldiers. It drove me crazy at first, until he told me to stay out and to never touch anything of his. That suited me fine."

"Was Max a book collector, too?" McGraw asks, rubbing the leather spine of Dante's *The Divine Comedy*.

Kristi Sue smiles while shaking her head.

"He had nothing to do with these books," she says, moving in next to him. This is all my doing. I designed everything in here. I purchased the books, the desk and the furniture and chose the paint. Max didn't care about anything or do anything to help me. When I reminded him it was, after all, his office, he shrugged and told me to handle it; he was too busy."

The lieutenant moves behind the desk next to his partner. On top, there's an ink blotter in the middle of the desk, an Ole Miss clock at the front edge facing them, and a Colonel Rebel coffee mug on the blotter by the telephone; nothing more.

This guy is really sold on Ole Miss, McGraw thinks. He read in one of the national magazines that football games in Oxford attract thousands of fans to the town and the Grove is a sight to see. He knows about Oxford's Square Books, has read Willie Morris and is a fan of John Grisham and Ace Atkins.

"Does your husband have a safe?" he asks, "Or any special place for important papers?"

"One of these drawers is locked," Roark says.

"No safe, just that drawer," Kristi Sue says. "I could never get in it."

"How is it he hasn't cleared his things out of his office?" Roark says.

McGraw is thinking: *for a man that seems overprotective of his things, he doesn't seem too concerned about his valuables.*

"Max called me a couple of days ago," she says. "He seemed rattled. Asked for money, and said he had to get away for a while. If you ask me, I think whatever was troubling him took precedence over his things here, and he wanted to leave in a hurry."

"How do you communicate with him?" Roark asks.

"By cell, but he won't answer if he sees my name in the caller ID. He only calls me when he wants something."

"Can you give us his cell number?" Noah asks

"Certainly, I'll write it down for you." She moves to the desk, writes it on a pad and hands it to McGraw. "But I don't think he'll answer it, lieutenant."

That's not why I want it, he thinks.

"Do you know where he keeps the key to his desk?" Holly says.

"Max keeps it on him at all times." She pauses. "Detectives, if you don't need me, I need to check on my daughter. Would that be okay? I won't be long."

"Certainly," McGraw says, "we're going to be here for about an hour. We need to get a telephone warrant to open this drawer."

"I'll put on a pot of coffee," she says as she leaves.

McGraw removes his cell from his jacket and calls Kramer, tells him to get a telephone warrant from Judge Henderson to get inside Max Kingston's locked desk drawer, and to have Gomez get with the IT guys to ping Kinston's cell number he recites over the phone.

Thirty minutes later, Kramer calls back. "Lieutenant, Henderson issued the warrant. You're a go. I'll bring it to you."

McGraw reaches for his pen knife in his pocket. "Let's try this," he says, and twists the point of the blade inside the keyhole with his right hand and at the same time wiggles the drawer with his left. The drawer slides out an inch and he yanks it out and sets it on top of the desk. Inside is a metal box the size of a cigar box, envelopes, paper clips, stapler, pens with refills, and notepads. He reaches for the metal box. It is unlocked. He opens it while Roark rummages through the rest of the drawer.

Kristi Sue brings in cups, a pot of coffee, cream and sugar, and some cookies on a tray and sets it at the edge of the desk. "Enjoy," she says and leaves.

"Thanks so much," Roark says as she fills two cups, adds cream, and hands one to her partner. "Cookie?" she says, holding it up.

"You know I don't eat sweets," he says, swallowing some of his coffee.

"Oh, I forgot, your mother once told you when you were young, that you were the sweetest thing that ever lived. And that's why. Well, Noah, I got news for you. Your mother lied."

They laugh.

After drinking the rest of his coffee, he lifts a thick, five-by-seven manila envelope, closed at the top by a metal clip, from the drawer, bends the clip, opens the flap and removes dozens of photos of young women in bed with men. He recognizes the background. Olivia and Eva are in them, but Olivia is in the majority of them.

"Look at these," McGraw says, handing them off to Roark.

She shuffles through them.

"This is additional proof that Max was using these to control Eva and Olivia," she says. "No wonder Olivia took off for New York."

McGraw returns to the metal box, finds a couple of credit cards, a passport, a few rare coins, and a receipt. The receipt is from a self-storage unit. *Why would Max keep it locked in a drawer?* He looks at the dates. The unit was rented for a month. He feels himself frowning. These dates ring a bell. They cover a time since Eva's disappearance. He lifts the phone on Max's desk and dials the number on the receipt.

"Sam's Self-Storage," the man says.

"This is Detective McGraw, Atlanta PD. I am interested in knowing if Max Kingston is still renting unit 1207."

"Mr. Kingston is leaving us and has removed some of his things. Just a minute," he says, apparently setting the phone down, and sliding his chair across the floor. When he returns, the guy says, "I just checked Mr. Kingston's file. He rented 1207 for one month. Like I said, he only has a few days before we open it."

The lieutenant knows Max won't be returning to empty the unit.

"We will be right over."

"Yes sir," the man says, and hangs up.

McGraw calls Kramer again to tell him to get a second warrant from Judge Henderson on Sam's Self-Storage unit 1207, rented by Max Kingston.

"I'll get right on it, lieutenant, and will deliver it to you." Kramer pauses. Gomez can be heard in the background. "Gomez wants me to tell you that the IT guys couldn't get anything on Kingston's cell when they pinged it. They think he's removed the battery."

"Max's no dummy."

"That's for sure, lieutenant," Kramer says.

On their way out, McGraw reminds Kristi Sue that they really need to talk to Max."

"I'll be happy to tell him if he ever calls me again."

Sam's Self Storage office is in a one-story brick building with full-view windows. The counter and workers can be seen from the street. Behind the building are series of metal storage units facing each other, extending for a block and enclosed with a six-foot metal fence and a keypad pole close to the gated entrance outside and inside.

The detectives clamber out of the cruiser and move to the glass door. Inside, a short pudgy man in his thirties, wearing a gray uniform with the name Sam's Self-

Storage embroidered above the left pocket, stands up behind the counter. His bushy red hair could use a stylist. Both Noah and Holly have their IDs out.

"You're the cop who called. Guess you want to see 1207 that belongs to Mr. Kingston," the man says, reaching for a key on a board behind him and handing it to him.

"That's right," McGraw says.

"I can raise the gate and you can drive through, unless you would like me to go with you."

"We can handle it. We're waiting for a phone call for court authorization to enter the unit."

"I didn't know you needed that," he says.

"What's your name?"

"Eric," he says, moving down the counter to his left and doing something that raises the gate to the entrance.

The detectives slip into the cruiser and McGraw's cell vibrates. "You got your warrant, lieutenant," Kramer says. "I'm only a block away." Sixty seconds later, he pulls in, hops out and hands the warrant to Roark, then takes off.

They drive through the entrance with its gate up. The storage units are arranged in rows, and he stops in front of unit 1207 in the row to his left. Roark is first to jump out, while he rolls out and they approach the unit.

"Holy Moly," he says. *I know that smell, it lives with me.*

A strong pungent odor assaults their nostrils. They recognize it immediately, the odor from decaying flesh. *I might as well call the M.E. and forensics.*

"I'll get the Vicks out of the glove compartment," Roark says.

He inserts the key, unlocks the unit and raises the door. She returns with the Vicks and they smear some under their noses and a little in each nostril. They slip on gloves and enter the unit. It's a nine-by-ten with vertical metal struts in the walls about twenty-four inches apart. Between the struts is some type of pressed wood that separates the unit from the others around it. The only thing in the unit is a 55-gallon barrel in the back.

The detectives should be used to the smell of death in their line of work, but McGraw would be the first to admit that most detectives never are. It stays with them and leaves a slight scar. Most things cops can handle, but not the death of children, mutilated bodies or the smell of corpses. McGraw is certain he knows who is in the barrel. He didn't want it to turn out this way. He had hopes that this time it would be different, but down deep he's known better. If nothing else, experience has taught him that abductees not found in forty-eight hours will more than likely be found dead. From the looks of the place, Max must have brought Cody Guthrie's body here also. Drops of blood are in the cracks and it looks like Max tried to wash them away, but couldn't get it all. Since nothing vanishes without a trace, he thinks forensics might get lucky when they work the place. DNA could be destroyed if Max used some heavy-duty chemicals. *We might get lucky and find some of Cody's blood in here.*

He lifts the lid but doesn't remove it. A body is stuffed into the barrel. It looks dismembered, but the M.E. will examine it more closely. From its shape, it could be a woman with hair the color of chestnuts. Her skin is greenish-blue and the face is hard to recognize. He would guess she's been dead close to forty-eight hours. He drops the lid in place.

"Is it Eva?"

"I don't really know. It is hard to see the face. I am guessing it's she."

"Poor Eva. I was hoping it—"

He interrupts. "Me, too."

"Maybe this cold weather has slowed the decomposition a little," she says.

They move around the storage unit, examining every inch.

"Max tried hard to clean this place, but he didn't know with today's technology the techs could find something," she says.

While they wait outside for the M.E. and the forensic team, McGraw looks around the place, eyeing the security cameras at the end of the units.

The M.E. wagon pulls up. Dr. Philips climbs out, dressed in white coveralls with a painter's mask hanging down around her neck. Her assistant jumps out of the passenger side, opens the back door and removes a black leather case.

"Whadda we have, lieutenant?" Philips asks.

"Another body in a drum," he says. "The vic may be our female."

"Hope I don't need a gas mask," she says.

The M.E. can tell from Noah's expression that he thinks it is Eva Hamilton.

"The Hamilton woman?" she asks.

"I'm afraid so, only by intuition."

She shakes her head. "Let's hope this weather has helped us some. Is she in one piece?"

"I don't believe so," he says.

Dr. Philips goes into the unit with her assistant beside her, carrying the case. He sets it down next to the drum and opens it. The detectives watch from outside.

Forensic techs shoot pictures before the M.E. takes over. They examine the floor. "Lots in the cracks," one of the techs says.

Thirty minutes later, Philips comes out, pulling down her mask.

"Afraid this one isn't intact, and it's female. She's been dead about 48. I'll have more for you once I get her in. Are you ready to release her?"

"She's yours," McGraw says.

Philips motions and her techs roll the barrel out to the wagon and load it.

Seeing them roll that barrel out to the M.E.'s wagon prompts him to think about the summer job he had once working for Hunter Packing Company, rolling barrels filled with beef out of the weighing room into the chopping room, where they made sausage and lunch meat.

"I know what you're thinking, lieutenant," Philips says.

Bet you don't. I'm thinking that this proves how much Max hates women. He dismembers Eva, but not Cody.

"You want to know how soon I can have something for you. Maybe tomorrow afternoon," she says. "But the DNA will take longer."

"Appreciate it," he says.

The detectives go to the Impala and slip in. Before starting the car, McGraw peers out the windshield for a moment, staring at the unit.

"What?"

"Earlier, when I found the receipt for this place in Max's home, I thought that without it we might never have found Eva. But I hadn't considered a couple of things: How far the odor from a decomposed body travels, so that eventually someone would have gotten a whiff and told Eric; if not, he would have discovered the body when he opened the unit. Either way, Eva would have been found."

"That's for sure," she says.

McGraw drives over to the manager's office and they enter. Eric is sitting behind the counter.

"Eric," he says. "I don't see any security cameras in this area."

"They're only at the corner of the units, sir. The ones closest to us cover this area."

"How long do you keep the tapes before you erase them?"

"You're in luck. With construction in the back, we've been busy and done nothing with them for a month."

"Great. We will need to look at the ones for the last four weeks from the camera at the end of this row."

"That would be number three," Eric says.

"Can you get those for us?" Roark says.

"Yes ma'am. Right away." He rises and heads to the back room.

Minutes later, Eric comes out with the tapes.

"One other thing," McGraw says. "So number three covers anyone coming in and out of this area?"

"Absolutely," he says.

CHAPTER FORTY-SEVEN

After a long night of watching the tapes from the self-storage company, McGraw is sitting in the corner of the briefing room the next morning at the station with his team, revisiting the tapes. He is the first to speak.

"Watch closely," he says. "At this point you'll see Kingston driving up in a pickup with a barrel in the back. There he is, stopping to punch in the security code. Now he's going through the gate. In a moment he'll swing around the first row of units and disappear from view. There," McGraw points, "he's going out of reach of the camera."

"All we see is a hooded guy driving a truck, boss," Gomez says. "How do we know it's Kingston?"

"I interviewed the manager earlier this morning over the phone," McGraw says, "he mentioned that he saw Kingston's face when he drove through with a barrel in the back of the pickup, and only remembers it because he joked with one of his employees that Kingston was bringing in a dead body. But wait, you'll see him come out in a minute with his truck empty."

Roark points at the monitor and says, "Here he comes. There, you can get a glimpse of his face as he comes through the open gate. Stop it right there, Kramer," she says.

"That's him, all right," Gomez says. "I wish we could have grabbed the SOB at his office. Cuffing the Big Guy would have made my day."

Kramer adds, "A waitress in the café close to Kingston's building knew him and said he told her he was going out of town for a few days."

"Interesting that he mentioned he was going away," Roark says. "It seems he wanted it known."

"Did he tell her when he was leaving or where he was going?" McGraw says.

Gomez shakes his head. "All he said was he was going. He didn't say where specifically, or when he was coming back."

"Roark may be right," Kramer says. "That may be what he wants us to think. He may still be around."

"It could be a ploy to cause us to turn out attention out-of-state, to give him a few days before he really leaves," McGraw says, heading to the front of the room, picking up a marker and writes "Atlanta," then turns to face his team.

"Okay, let's think about this. If you are Kingston, knowing the cops are closing in on you, would you stay in Atlanta or would you take off somewhere?"

"We never were able to locate his apartment, boss," Gomez says.

"He's smart," Roark says. "Max knows we'd find him easier here than out of state. No, I think he's left even though he might want us to think he's still here."

McGraw turns and draws a line through Atlanta. "I think we can rule this out."

"What about Perry, Oklahoma?" Kramer asks.

McGraw writes "Perry, OK" on the board.

"Do you really think he'd go there, boss?" Gomez asks.

"Wouldn't that be too obvious?" Roark says. "If I were in his shoes, I'd figure the cops would surely be looking for me in my home town."

"And he'd want us to think that," Kramer says.

"But didn't we learn he has no one left in Perry?" Gomez asks. "What reason would he have for going there?"

"As Kramer says, to make us think he's going there to throw us off his trail," McGraw says. "Max being a psychopath, he's impulsive and reckless and thinks he's smarter than anyone else. I look for him to mess up down the line. For argument's sake, we won't rule it out just yet."

"Sounds logical," Roark says. "Better to list places he'd go."

"Okay, what do we know about Max Kingston?" McGraw says.

"Mostly, his love/hate for women," Kramer says. McGraw writes it on the board.

"That fits into his psychology. Why is that important, Kramer?"

He shrugs. "To go where the ladies are?"

Roark's brow contracts as she's thinking. "He has been with women here in Atlanta," she says. "We don't have evidence of him being involved with anyone outside the city." She pauses for a second. "I can only think of one thing that's more important to Max than women."

"And what is that?" McGraw says. He smiles, knowing what she's about to say.

"Football," Roark says.

"And why is that important?"

"We saw all that Ole Miss stuff on his desk in his home office, and that banner above his desk with "Hotty Toddy" printed on it. He loves the Rebels according to his wife."

McGraw writes it on the board and circles it. "Ole Miss Rebels."

"So he likes Ole Miss Football," Kramer says. "I like the Georgia Bulldogs; so what?"

"Don't tell me you're thinking he's going to Oxford?" Gomez says.

221

McGraw nods and turns to Roark, "We'll need their home game schedule."

"But wouldn't Max be taking a big gamble, going to the campus on game day?" Kramer says. "There will be officers and undercover cops all over the place."

Roark says, "I think I know why that wouldn't matter to Max. He was recruited by Ole Miss when he was in high school, but an injury ended it for him. He has loved the Rebels ever since. I believe he is actually craving to see a game, and now that he's on the run, what better time is there. Besides, there's a lot to do there in town the night before the game and at the Grove on game day. I've read magazines articles and seen pictures of the Ole Miss Grove. It's rated among the top two campuses to visit during football season. Once, when I saw it on TV, I wished I was there. You should have seen it. It was packed with fans and Ole Miss tailgating tents with hanging chandeliers, white tablecloths, and Southern cooking. Not what you'd expect in a football setting. Football fans were inside the colored tents sitting and watching football games on flat screen TVs, eating fried chicken and drinking what looked like booze out of plastic cups."

"Don't' forget, he's thinking the crowd makes good cover," McGraw says, writing the word "crowd" on the board. "Max isn't afraid of the police," he says turning back to face his detectives. "This yearning he has to see a Rebel game probably minimizes any fear he would have of cops. He cares only about the football game. After Roark and I saw all that Ole Miss paraphernalia in his home office, I had to wonder if he had ever been to one of their games. I talked with his wife. She said he never has, talks about it every fall, but never does anything about it. He is a loyal supporter of the Rebels."

"Okay," Kramer says, standing. "The way I see it, he could go to Oklahoma and then Mississippi."

"For now, let's concentrate on both states," McGraw says, and he turns to Kramer and Gomez. "Let's get the word out to the ladies in town that we think Kingston is in Oklahoma. If he hasn't left yet, he may hear it and screw up in Mississippi."

As they step out into the hall to reach the squad area, McGraw tells Roark to send a BOLO (be-on-the-lookout) on Max Kingston, a.k.a Sonny Burke, specifying that he is dangerous and may be heading to Perry, Oklahoma or Oxford, Mississippi.

CHAPTER FORTY-EIGHT

The next morning, McGraw arrives at the station before the other detectives, close to eight, makes coffee in the squad room and sits at his desk sipping his coffee, feeling frustrated over his conversation with the Ole Miss Police Chief the day before. Disappointingly, Johnny Walker wouldn't extend McGraw and Roark the courtesy of interacting with his deputies in the search for Max Kingston on the Ole Miss campus. Rarely is McGraw not in charge when working a case. Walker wasn't sold on the idea that Kingston would come to Oxford, and there was nothing in his voice that revealed he was threatened by a killer coming to his campus. He informed McGraw that he hires a hundred auxiliary police for every home game and the officers are briefed on every situation, so consequently he wouldn't need any help from the Atlanta detectives.

McGraw drinks some of his coffee and looks around the room. His phone rings. He picks up. "McGraw," he says.

"This is Nora, lieutenant. Your vic in the drum is Eva Hamilton. The DNA results on the blood samples taken from the storage are hers and Cody Guthrie's."

"You're the best. Thanks."

No sooner does he hang up, than his phone rings again. "McGraw," he says.

"Lieutenant, this is Kristi Sue Kingston. This may not be important, but you seemed very interested in Max's love for Ole Miss when you were here the other day asking me questions about the Rebels. I thought you should know something."

"What's that?"

"Well, when Max came and took all his Ole Miss stuff from the closet, he left without saying a word. I didn't think much about it, since that was all he had left here. Last night, I opened my computer and checked my emails. There was a confirmation listing the charge for an Ole Miss/LSU ticket to my credit card, made by the Ole Miss Athletic Ticket Office. It appears this time he's definitely going to the game, detective."

"That's a big help." He pauses, thinking about if Max calls her again. *Will she mention the charge to her credit card?*

"Oh, by the way, would you mind doing me a favor, Kristi Sue?" he says.

"If I can, lieutenant, I'd be happy to."

"If Max calls again, please don't tell him you know about him going to Oxford, or that you told us. I'd appreciate you telling him that the last time we talked; we were asking a lot of questions about Oklahoma. Would you do that for me?"

"Certainly, I'd be happy to."

"Again, thank you."

McGraw sets the phone in its cradle and checks the schedule for the Ole Miss/LSU game that Roark placed on his desk. He looks up when he hears his team enter the squad room. "Listen up, everyone. I just got a call from the M.E. Cody Guthrie's DNA was found in the storage unit along with Eva Hamilton's."

"That clinches Max murdering both of them," Roark says.

McGraw jumps up. "Also, I got word from Kingston's wife that Max purchased a ticket from the Ole Miss Athletic Ticket Office for the Ole Miss/LSU game this Saturday." He heads to the Lion's den with a little spring in his step. It's now time to have Capt. call the U.S. Marshals Service for assistance from their Fugitive Unit. When a fugitive is on the loose, it rests with the agency in the town in which the crime originated to make the request.

Twenty minutes later, McGraw returns to his desk, lifts the phone and calls Sheriff Tom Sinclair.

"Sheriff's office," the woman says on the other end.

"This is Detective McGraw, Atlanta PD Homicide. Can I talk with Sheriff Sinclair?"

"One moment," she says. "Oh, he's on the phone, detective. Care to hold?"

"Yes, thanks."

While waiting, McGraw wonders how far Max has gotten. According to Kristi Sue, he could have hit the road over twenty-four hours ago. They should hear something from Mississippi soon.

"Hello, Noah," the sheriff says. "I was wondering when you'd be calling me. What can I do for you?"

"Been too long, Tom. I've got this case that's giving me—"

The sheriff interrupts. "You mean Sonny Burke?"

"That's right. I've got a female body stuffed in a barrel stored in a storage unit owned by him. The vic is Eva Hamilton." He doesn't want to tell him Eva was dismembered.

The sheriff doesn't say anything for a few seconds.

"Sorry to hear that. I've known Eva since she was born. Her father and I...." His voice cracks. "We were great friends; did a lot of fishing together."

"Sorry. The M.E. just gave me the news." McGraw pauses, thinking about

224

how he has failed Eva, not finding her in time. But he's still her advocate. "Burke is on the run," he says.

"I know, we got your BOLO. You really think he's coming here?"

McGraw doesn't answer right away. He doesn't think so for now, but maybe Max would go there one last time. Roark is right. Why would he? McGraw is convinced he's now at Ole Miss.

"Don't think so, but don't want to leave any stone unturned. He might want one last look at his home town."

"Think he expects to end his life?"

"Never know about these psychopaths," McGraw says to the sheriff. "As you know, they come in a range of flavors."

"That's for sure. Well, if he comes here, we'll get him. My men have been briefed." He pauses for a moment. "In the BOLO you suggest he might be traveling here or Mississippi. Why? His cousin there died some time ago."

"Sonny is a big fan of Ole Miss football. The way I figure it, he's heading to Oxford to see the game this Saturday the 19th between the Rebels and the LSU Tigers."

"Good theory," sheriff says, "Sonny was recruited by Ole Miss his senior year, but got hurt in a game and that ended it for him."

"I have a favor to ask, Tom."

"Shoot."

"Would you happen to know the sheriff of Lafayette County, Mississippi?"

"That would be J.R. "Buddy" West. He rode with your dad and me. As you may remember, we had cops from four states—Texas, Oklahoma, Mississippi and Arkansas—riding with us."

"I talked with the campus police chief for permission to join in the capture of Sonny, but he doesn't want us around. We'd like to be there when they capture him," McGraw says.

"You're thinking they're going to get him alive?" the sheriff says.

"We'd like that," McGraw says. "Sonny thinks we cops are stupid and I'm expecting him to let his guard down. Then we move in on him. What do you think?"

"You'll have to be quick, but don't hurry to get him."

This sheriff's sharp, McGraw thinks. *He's quoting, John Wooden, the greatest basketball coach ever.*

The sheriff continues, "He's not the type that could stand to be caged. I've always thought of him as a wild animal." There's a pause. "So, you want me to ask Buddy to put in a good word for you with the UPD chief."

"Something like that, or let us ride along with him. I don't know if the sheriff will be involved, but maybe he would listen to you. I would appreciate anything you can do for us."

"You know, Noah, you could call Buddy yourself. Your dad and him got along good. He'd be glad to hear from you."

McGraw is thinking maybe Tom is right, that it would be better if he introduced himself to Buddy West. McGraw doesn't need a middle man to do his work for him.

"Okay, Tom, I'll give him a call. Thanks."

After hanging up, McGraw opens his computer and googles the sheriff of Lafayette County, Mississippi, writes down his phone number and makes the call.

"Sheriff's office," the man says on the other end.

"This is Lieutenant Noah McGraw, Atlanta PD Homicide."

No response. McGraw can hear the man breathing into the phone.

"Don't tell me it's Weldon McGraw's son?" the man says with optimism in his voice.

"Yes, sir."

"Drop the sir stuff. This is Buddy West. I knew your dad Weldon from our riding days."

"That's what Tom Sinclair told me," McGraw says, realizing he has dropped a name that might help him get his foot in the door. "I remember your name now, but never met you."

"Old Tom, how's he doin'?"

"Doing well. Just talked to him; he sends his best."

"We had a great group of guys that traveled across country together. It's good to hear that Weldon's son is one of us. Bet your call is about Sonny Burke."

"You got our BOLO?"

"Sure did. How can I help?"

"First, we know Burke is heading to Oxford to attend Saturday's game between Ole Miss and LSU. Secondly, my partner and I have been working the case for weeks and want to be there for his capture."

"It doesn't make much sense that he'd come here," Buddy says. "His chances of getting caught during game day are pretty good, and Burke must know that. The UPD hires a bunch of officers to be on campus on game day. The chief even hires some of my deputies and my brother's guys at the Oxford PD as auxiliaries to patrol the campus. My brother, Tommie Lee, is chief of Oxford PD."

"Sheriff, Sonny Burke thinks the cops don't have sense enough to come out of the doughnut shops. My money is on Burke not expecting to be taken alive. He's killed before and murdered two of our vics and stuffed them into 55-gallon drums. He cut one, a female, into pieces before stuffing her. The reason we are certain Burke is heading to Ole Miss is that he loves Rebel football and has purchased a ticket. Besides, he was recruited by the Rebs when he was in high school in Perry, Oklahoma. Got hurt his senior year and that ended his career, but he has followed the Rebs all his life. His wife said he loved Ole Miss more that he loved her, and he always watches the Rebs on TV. His dream has always been to attend a game. He loved seeing the crowd in the Grove on TV, and she said he was yelling at the television doing the Hotty Toddy thing."

McGraw pauses. "One more thing, Burke has grandiose self-perception, thinking he's smarter and more powerful than he actually is. He is extremely dangerous, even though he appears to function normally and is very cunning."

When McGraw finishes, he becomes aware of the silence on the other end, hearing only breathing through the phone. Buddy must be thinking about the messy scene that could develop on the campus or in the stadium if Burke erupts like a volcano when faced with capture. McGraw knows, as does the sheriff, that they're going to have their hands full. Their highest priority is to prevent pandemonium from breaking out on the campus.

"That changes everything," Sheriff West says almost in a whisper. "The UPD and the Feds must work together to get him before things turn sour in the Grove or in the stadium. Did you talk with the UPD chief? His name is Johnny Walker, like the booze."

"I did. He told me they would let me know when they captured Burke, and that we weren't needed. He reminded me about the Atlanta PD's responsibility in requesting help from the U.S. Marshal Service to work with them in the capture of Burke, which our Capt. has done."

"I see," Buddy says.

"We feel we let our vic, Eva Hamilton, down by not finding her before her demise. We've been face to face with this guy. He was our Capt.'s investment advisor. Now he's snubbed his nose at us and thinks he's gotten the best of us. Nothing would please me more than to get my hands on him, Buddy. It's kind of personal now."

McGraw is trusting that the sheriff is quiet because he's thinking this through, about how helpful it would be to have McGraw and Roark with them, since no one else knows Burke like they do.

"And you want me to help you do that?"

"Could you put in a word for us with the UPD chief and the feds when they get there, or if not, maybe my partner Roark and I can ride along with you?"

"Let me think about it. I'll talk it over with my brother, and get back with you. It won't be long, Noah. Maybe we'll get lucky and Burke won't come here."

McGraw knows the sheriff doesn't believe that for a minute. Even if Buddy refuses McGraw's request, he has made up his mind that he and Holly are going to Oxford.

"Thanks," McGraw says, "I will be waiting for your call."

He walks over to the Capt. Dipple's office for the second time today, knocks on the door and enters.

CHAPTER FORTY-NINE

Seated at his desk in the squad room early the next morning, McGraw rises and stretches. Holly's desk is a few feet away. She looks up, watches him for a second, and then swivels her chair towards the crime board against the wall. Kramer and Gomez are at their desks behind her, now looking up at the lieutenant, too. No one says a word while McGraw stares at Max Kingston's photo he had placed on the board. He knows they're wondering if he talked with the Capt. about Holly Roark's former boyfriend, and what they're going to do to catch the bastard.

Holly is first to break the silence. "How did it go with the Capt. yesterday, McGraw?"

"He told me he had called our contact at the Marshal's Service to alert the Fugitive Task Force. They will take charge of the investigation at Ole Miss and should have called the Capt. by now about the deputy in charge."

Roark frowns.

"But we don't know if we're going," she says.

"The Capt. said it was okay with him, but had to run it past the Commish."

Kramer and Gomez rise from their desks and stand next to Roark. Now that he has their attention, McGraw tells them Roark and he will be going to Oxford with or without the approval of law enforcement in Mississippi.

"I guess Gomez and I won't be going to Oxford, then," Kramer says.

"I'd like to see that Grove on game day," Gomez says.

"Sorry, we need to do this one, but don't lose heart. You guys are going to Perry, Oklahoma as a decoy."

Kramer and Gomez frown and just nod. Kramer says, "Maybe we can get in a Thunder game in OKC—"

Roark interrupts. "How's the Capt. taking it about Max being Burke?"

"Not too well. The thought that he was friends with a butcher has him in a delicate frame of mind. He mentioned that whenever he thinks about the killer being right under his nose, it makes him sick at his stomach."

228

YOU'LL NEVER SEE ME AGAIN

"It makes us sick, too, boss," Gomez says.

McGraw sighs. "Let's not bring up Max's name in front of the Capt. unless he does."

They nod in agreement.

McGraw turns back to the board and looks at Max's picture again. "We're coming after you, Burke." He returns to his desk. "We should be hearing from Mississippi soon."

"It won't be easy for the cops there to apprehend Max," Roark says. "They don't know how cunning he is. You know how he fooled me."

McGraw feels himself frowning. "I told you to forget it. You're a good cop."

"The fact is, he's a chameleon and the cops there better be on their toes," she says.

"I was tempted to tell Sheriff West you dated Max and could smell him a block away, but that would lessen our chances of working with them."

She nods. "Yeah, they'd think my emotions would get in the way and I wouldn't be able to take him down, but they don't know how I'd love to put a couple rounds in him."

"We don't want to hurry our pursuit and take risks," McGraw says.

She sighs. "Oh, don't worry. I've learned from the best."

"Just saying," he says.

"But you're right about one thing; I can sense his presence once I focus in on him, that much is for sure."

McGraw goes to the coffee stand and pours a cup. Kramer walks over to him.

"Don't look now, lieutenant," he says in a whisper, "but the Capt. is heading this way."

McGraw fills his cup and carries it over to his desk.

"Any word yet from Mississippi, McGraw?" he asks, entering the squad area.

"Not yet, Capt. What did the Commish say?"

"It's a go."

"Great."

"So you still think Kingston's going to Oxford?" Capt. asks.

"I'm betting he's already slipped into Oxford without being noticed, and has changed his appearance, dressed in Ole Miss game-day gear, cap and all. From all the stuff we saw in his home office, he'll know how to fit in with the fans. Today is Friday and the fans are beginning to stream into Oxford. It's a big game."

"So Oklahoma is out?" Capt. asks.

"Definitely," McGraw says. "But we're not taking any chances. I'm sending Kramer and Gomez to Perry. I'm banking on Max thinking we're looking for him there, so he'll get careless. The sheriff there has been very cooperative from the get-go. He's making it known around town and on his web site that there's a BOLO on Sonny Burke, and that the Atlanta police are coming to Perry. That's in case Max has some contact there or if he checks their local newspaper or web site on the Internet."

"Smart move," he says.

"Besides disguising himself, Max is probably driving with a fake driver's license and an out-of-state rental," Roark says.

"Driver's licenses aren't that hard to fake these days with all the tech stuff available," Gomez says. "You—you can bet on one thing."

"What's that, Kramer says?"

"He won't be wearing those shades."

The pit fills with their laughter.

"Yeah, the bastard never went anywhere without those military sun glasses," Capt. says. "I should have known he had something to hide."

"Those shades won't do him any good if highway patrol pulls him over; they'll run him and that'll be the end of him," Kramer says.

"He's too smart to let that happen," McGraw says. "He'll play it safe."

"You think you'll get him alive?" Capt. asks.

McGraw voices his analysis of Max as a charismatic nut job that has to be in control, engages in criminal behavior, and achieves satisfaction from inflicting pain without remorse or empathy for his victims.

"In addition, he suffers from a deep insecurity," McGraw says, noticing that he still has everyone's attention. "I learned from the Perry sheriff that Max's mother beat him and verbally abused him when he was young. Consequently, he has a deep hate for women. I believe Max beat his women after having sex with them. I learned recently from a detective I worked with years ago that he has had such a case, where the woman's description of the perp fits that of Kingston. You can bet Max will have a companion accompanying him to Oxford, to provide cover."

McGraw pauses, seeing that the Capt. is about to speak.

"Max could be thinking suicide by cop," he adds.

"If we corner him, he may feel like a trapped animal, and God knows what he'll do if he erupts," McGraw says. "That's why all agencies must work together."

The Capt. rubs his hand over his mouth with the thumb and index finger squeezing his nose and stares at McGraw, as if he is contemplating the seriousness of the lieutenant's analysis.

The Capt. shakes his head. "Well, you certainly have it all figured out."

McGraw isn't looking for a compliment, just justice for Max's victims.

Capt. says, "You will be working with Deputy Marshal Paul Polanski when you get to Oxford. He's in charge of the Fugitive Apprehension Team there."

McGraw nods, realizing a big smile has filled his face. "Thanks, Capt. Best news we've gotten today."

"Good luck in Oxford. Keep me informed." He walks back to his office.

The phone rings in the squad room. Gomez reaches for it on Roark's desk. "Lieutenant, there's a Sheriff West on the phone for ya."

McGraw feels adrenaline coursing through his veins.

"This is it," he says.

He lifts the phone from his desk.

"What's your decision, Buddy?"

"I talked it over with my brother. When can you come?"

He looks at his watch. "We can fly into Memphis this afternoon and pick up a rental."

"No need for the rental. We'll come to Memphis, but once you get to the baggage carousel, you'll have to call a number I'll give you when you call me back with your arrival time. Ever since 9/11, no cars are allowed to park curbside. We'll be waiting in a lot close by. Once we get your call, we'll head that way and flash our bar lights when we get close to where you're waiting curbside outside the luggage area."

"Great. I'll get back with you." He pauses. "Sheriff... thanks."

CHAPTER FIFTY

McGraw and Roark get lucky and make it on the first flight to Memphis. The plane's captain, routinely informed that two armed law enforcement officers would be on board, got both detectives choice seats in first class. The pilots and crew are delighted to have armed officers up close to the cabin.

Hurrying through the Memphis airport supporting shoulder bags, McGraw and Roark head for the down escalator to the baggage area.

"I see you are getting lots of looks from the ladies, cowboy," she says as they descend the escalator.

"You're just jealous."

She winks at him and they laugh.

Stepping off the escalator, they head to the baggage carousel. McGraw pulls out his cell and calls Sheriff West.

"They'll be here in ten minutes," McGraw says to Roark.

They grab their luggage, head out the exit and set their luggage at the curb. Rows of cars are flowing slowly past in three lanes, and horns are blaring at an SUV blocking two rows of cars in the middle to collect passengers. Minutes later, McGraw spots the flashing blue lights coming towards them.

"That's our ride," he says to his partner.

The sheriff's cruiser pulls in behind a car that pulls out. A tall, thin man in his forties, wearing a brown uniform and cap, hops out, glances at McGraw and says, holding out a hand, "Lieutenant McGraw? I recognize you from the cowboy hat that you said you'd be wearing." He turns to Roark, "And you must be Sergeant Roark."

McGraw answers with a yes while she nods.

"I am Tommie Lee West, Oxford Police Chief. Let me have your bags. Hope y'all had a good trip."

"Uneventful," McGraw says.

Tommie Lee throws their bags into the trunk and opens the back door for Roark. McGraw slips in on the other side. A large, muscular, round-faced man in

232

his fifties in the passenger seat, wearing the same uniform as Tommie Lee, turns and extends a hand.

"I'm Sheriff Buddy Lee West, but y'all can call me Buddy."

The Mississippi brothers' accents are noticeable, and Buddy reminds Noah of the old TV star Jackie Gleason.

"Everyone calls me McGraw" he says, and this is my partner Sergeant Roark."

"You can call me Roark," she says.

He nods and smiles. "Thank you."

The Oxford Police Chief slips in behind the wheel and pulls away.

"Anything happen since we've talked last?" McGraw says.

Tommie Lee is eyeing Roark in the rear view mirror. *Better keep your eyes on the road or you'll answer to me,* McGraw thinks, staring at him.

Buddy says, "Nothing about Max Kingston, a.k.a. Sonny Burke, but the U.S. Marshals have arrived and taken up a command post inside the Lyceum Building, which faces the Circle close to the Grove where thousands of fans will be gathering on game day tomorrow. We'll show it all to you so you can get the layout. I understand that y'all will be working with Deputy Marshal Polanski."

"That's right," McGraw says.

He shakes his head. "You guys must have connections," he says.

"We do," Roark says, glancing at McGraw with a wink.

"What kind of command has the deputy marshal set up in the center?" McGraw asks.

Buddy responds. "Polanski has a Unified Command System in the Lyceum Building. This is normal for all game days on campus; however, it is much more complex with this nightmare you guys have brought to our town."

Roark is quick to answer. "You mean the nightmare Max Kingston has brought to your town, not us," she says.

"I guess you're right," Buddy says. "Well, we had our meeting with UPD Chief Walker; he reluctantly agreed to share operational command with my department, Tommie Lee's and with Deputy Polanski. He wasn't real happy, but he had no choice since the Marshal Service is in charge. Polanski's an okay guy. You'll like him."

Tommie Lee adds: "Polanski has a regional tactical team off campus, which includes cops from many regional departments. These guys are funded by Homeland Security and are well trained. Hope we don't need them, but they are on stand-by throughout this weekend.

McGraw is impressed and says. "Sound great. What about snipers?"

Buddy nods. "They have two-man teams with a spotter. The plan is to have them posted out of sight on roof tops around the stadium tomorrow, and tonight around the Square where most of the fans will be celebrating. They'll provide eyes from an elevated position in case things go sour."

"Let's hope that doesn't happen," Roark says.

"Amen to that," Tommie Lee agrees.

"It sounds like everything has been taken into account. You can count on Max doing something crazy if he gets boxed in," McGraw says.

"Everyone will be ready," Buddy says.

"Chief Walker didn't want Roark and me here. I guess we'll get the cold shoulder treatment."

"Let's say he's difficult at times, and doesn't play well with others," Buddy says. "Lately, he's been very anxious since you called him about your fugitive."

"A control freak, you mean," Tommie Lee says, eyeing his brother.

Buddy nods. "Walker has worked things out with Polanski and has his people and auxiliary officers briefed and posted. Some are in the Vaught-Hemmingway Stadium, while others are all over the campus. Tommie Lee and I have the Square and the town covered."

"Walker could care less about our fugitive," McGraw says. "He's edgy because it'll be his neck if Max goes ballistic and shoots up the stadium, killing spectators. Walker knows psychopaths are unpredictable. If they feel the heat and have nothing to lose, they'll go ape."

McGraw turns to face the road.

"I suspect Polanski is working on Walker to take you guys in," Buddy says. "We'll find out in our meeting with them in a little while."

"That's good news," Roark says.

"That would make our lives much easier if we could all work together," McGraw says.

"Sure would," Tommie Lee says, nodding.

"I've seen game day shots of the Grove and your Town Square on TV," Holly says. "The fans really do live it up in those venues, don't they?"

Buddy nods. "There's a saying here: 'we may not win all our games, but we never lose a party.'"

They laugh.

"Our Town Square has some of the best shops, restaurants and bars," Tommie Lee says, "and a courthouse in the center, Oxford being the county seat for Lafayette County."

He pronounces Lafayette with the accent on the second syllable.

On the way into Mississippi on I-55 south, Tommie Lee talks about the most popular bars, diners, and shops the fans and students enjoy. He becomes animated when describing the Friday night crowds that gather during home game weekends. "They pack the streets and bars, with music blaring until closing time, which is close to 1:00 a.m. Saturday morning. Then partyers hit the streets and find other locations where something is happening."

He continues describing the scene downtown and how they patrol the area with foot patrol and cops on horseback. As the Oxford Police Chief, Tommie Lee seems proud that he is responsible for keeping the peace and patrolling the town.

"The place will rock tonight," he says. "You'll see."

Buddy glances over at his brother as if to wonder if he is ever going to shut up. He turns back around to face the detectives and says, "During home games everything in this town is booked months earlier and some town folks rent out their homes to fans for the weekend and then leave town. We checked every place for you to stay and nothing is available for you folks. We really want y'all close to the campus."

McGraw is wondering if he's going to tell them they have to sleep in tents.

"I have a farm outside of Oxford, this side of New Albany about 15 miles. I thought you two could stay with me. That is, if you don't mind sleeping in my barn."

McGraw notices Tommie Lee eyeing them in the rear view mirror with a thin smile. Surely he can see Roark's eyes are three times their size. She doesn't know that the sheriff is playing around.

McGraw laughs. "He's pulling your leg."

"Sorry, ma'am," Buddy says, "thought I'd get a laugh out of ya."

"All I could think of were pigs, chickens and hay bales," she says.

Tommie Lee joins in on the laughter and says, "My brother has a sick sense of humor."

He drives off the ramp to the right.

"We're fixing to come upon Batesville. Oxford is only 25 miles from here," he says, exiting I-55 and heading east on Highway 6 while he continues talking.

"Don't listen to Buddy. We have a nice place for you to stay. This past week my tennis buddy Dewey Garner and me had our little match, and I happened to mention the hard time we were having getting rooms close to the campus for you guys. I didn't think any more about it, but yesterday he called me and said he had talked it over with his wife Barbara, and they'd like you guys to come and stay in their home. They have two rooms upstairs with a private bath. There's an Oklahoma author and his wife that stay upstairs when in town, but I'm told they've gone home until next year."

"That's very sweet of the Garners," Holly says, "but that would be too much of an imposition."

"Naw, it wouldn't. They're good people and they'd be happy to have y'all," Buddy says; "besides, there's nowhere else except my barn."

Silence is palpable as Holly gazes at McGraw, followed by laughter.

"I guess that settles it," McGraw says.

"It's perfect, close to the campus and the Square," Buddy says.

"Old Dewey is a nice ole boy, and an Ole Miss professor."

"Well make sure to do something nice for the Garners," Holly says.

"Do either of you keep a list of the homes rented out during game day?" McGraw asks.

"You expect your fugitive to be in a rented home?" Tommie Lee says.

McGraw finds himself nodding. "I do."

"No, we don't ever keep such a list," he says. "But we do patrol the city pretty good."

Buddy chimes in. "Usually, the folks that rent out their homes do it on the Internet or through a real estate agent."

"Our guy's too smart to do either." McGraw says. "He knows you guys would be checking them."

McGraw turns to look out his side window again, watching the trees fly by, all the while wondering if the different law enforcement agencies' egos will clash when Max is spotted. The Feds are in charge, but the jurisdiction really belongs to the University Police Department. The Marshal Service is generally easier to work with than other federal agencies, but even with the best of intentions and communications, things could get messy if everyone isn't on the same page. If they screw up, Max could slip in and out of the crowd. *We'll have to draw him out into the open to grab him. This isn't going to be easy if law enforcement gets into territorial disputes*, he thinks.

"Buddy, how do you think all this is going to play out with the feds in charge of coordinating this weekend?" McGraw asks. "We don't want any mishaps."

"We've never had the marshals with us during a game, but Polanski really knows his stuff. I think all will be okay."

"Since Chief Walker isn't too happy about us being here, how will we fit in?" Roark asks.

"That depends on Polanski," Buddy says. "The way I see it, we can transport you any place you'd like to go at any time, but we'll have to wait to see what he says before developing our strategy."

"That's more than we could ask," McGraw says.

Buddy looks at his watch and then turns to his brother. "We have a little time before our meeting. Let's run them by the Square so they can get the layout of the town for tonight, then we can head to the campus to meet with Walker and Polanski."

CHAPTER FIFTY-ONE

"Here's our turn," Tommie Lee says, pulling onto Jackson Avenue west. "This'll take us around the campus directly into town," he adds, as he comes to the stoplight. "West Jackson is our busiest street; especially, when you add in 20, 000 students to our population of 20,000."

Buddy says, "If your fugitive attempts an escape, he'll probably come out this way because it's the easiest and fastest."

"His name is Max Kingston," McGraw says.

"Whatever," Buddy says. "I'm just saying..."

They drive past the west side entrance to the Ole Miss campus, then entrances to Rebel Drive and the Sorority Row, which angle up toward the center of the campus. After a mile, Tommie Lee comes to a stoplight in Oxford and turns right. A short block later, he turns left on Van Buren and travels east, arriving in an open area. Buddy says, "This is our Square with the Lafayette County Courthouse in the center and our Confederate Monument in front of it."

"I'm familiar with your Square and Square Books," McGraw says.

"Me, too," Roark says, "especially authors like Willie Morris and Grisham. I always liked the name Willie."

Moving along, Tommie Lee completes the circle around the Courthouse.

"The Square will be packed with fans tonight; so much so, you won't be able to turn around. You'll see it all tonight," he says.

Max probably will be coming here tonight, McGraw thinks, *since he's with a companion.*

Tommie Lee passes the side of the Square Books on South Lamar, and turns right at the stoplight. A mile down on University Avenue, he passes the Gertrude Ford Center and proceeds over the bridge.

"The road to our right circles around the Grove, which you can see is kinda busy now, since many fans came in yesterday," Tommie Lee says. "Now you can get a better view of our Grove on your right."

"Sure is pretty," Roark says. "Just like on TV."

"The Grove covers ten acres and is filled with magnolias, elms and oaks," Buddy says. "Every Saturday home game it comes alive with students, alumni and fans who act like one big family."

"I've read where it is called the Holy Grail of tailgating sites," Roark says.

"That's because there are hundreds of red, white and blue tents in there and hundreds of Ole Miss Rebel tailgaters come, women in dresses and high heels, and the guys in khaki slacks, white shirts, bow ties, Sperry top-siders, and blue blazers," Tommie Lee says. "We live it up."

"What are all those people doing sitting on the ground in the Grove this time of day?" Holly asks.

"They're called sitters," Tommie Lee says. "Many have been out there since seven-thirty this morning. They're hired to stake claims for the tailgaters who will come around nine tonight to erect their tents. But they'll have to be out by midnight. At sun rise tomorrow, they'll be back to set up tables and expensive kitchenware. The fancy food they bring is already made because they can't grill in the Grove and many tailgaters use local catering services to bring in barbecue pork and chicken."

I have doubts Max would chance coming here, McGraw thinks. *The place will be swarming with deputies.*

"Up ahead is University Circle, which loops around an island, called 'The Circle,'" Buddy says. "It's coming in view to our left with the flag pole in the center surround by a number of trees."

"Do they put up tents in there, too?" Roark asks.

Tommie Lee laughs. "Everywhere there's open space." He pulls the cruiser to the curb in front of a Greek revival brick building with six white columns.

"This is the Lyceum building where Marshal Polanski has set up his command center," Buddy says. "It houses the Chancellor and other University officials. It was the first building on the Ole Miss Campus, and was used as a Confederate hospital during the Civil War. The front columns still have bullet holes from the time shots were fired at U.S. Marshals in 1962, during the enrollment of James Meredith into Ole Miss."

"Look over yonder. Two deputy marshals are standing by the columns looking out over The Circle," Tommie Lee says.

They're dressed in blue windbreakers, khaki pants, and caps with the Marshal badge—a five-point star in a circle—on the front.

Hard to miss, McGraw thinks. "Deputies, no doubt," he says.

Buddy nods. "You can spot them a mile away. We can get out here and I'll take you in while my brother parks."

They pile out and McGraw adjusts his Stetson, following Holly and Buddy up the steps. The sheriff grabs the brass handle on one of the tall white doors and yanks it open. They step into an ambiance warm from light reflected off pink-colored walls. The tile floor is shiny and the smell of wax is in the air. Two guys are standing outside a conference room down at the end of the hall to the left. The door to the room is open, but no one is inside. Boxes are stacked on a long conference table and some are arranged on the floor. One of the men is wearing a police uniform with Ole Miss insignia, but no cap.

Must be Walker, McGraw thinks. The other man, dressed like the two deputies on the front steps, has to be Deputy Marshal Polanski.

McGraw locks eyes with Walker, who doesn't seem too happy to see him. He is tall and slender, nice looking, strong chin and a little gray at his temples, and he isn't smiling.

Buddy is the first to speak. "Chief Walker, this is Lieutenant McGraw and Sergeant Roark, Atlanta PD Homicide."

Walker's eyes glance over at Roark and he smiles, extends a hand to her and then to McGraw. "Detective McGraw, we've spoken on the phone."

"Yes, sir. Hope we can talk," McGraw says.

Walker doesn't respond, but turns to the man next to him and says, "This is Deputy Marshal Paul Polanski with the U.S. Marshals Fugitive Task Force."

Polanski is a Polish name, McGraw thinks, and it reminds him of Roman Polanski, the guy that got himself in a world of trouble. This guy is a lot younger, has a round bald head with a high forehead. Stands around five-eight, looks like a former marine, and is certainly macho.

"Call me Polanski," he says with a smile. "We were just talking about you detectives. Shall we go into our command post?"

"Yes, let's do," Walker says. "There's a larger conference room on the second floor if you need it."

"This'll do fine," Polanski says. "Anyway, we're settled in here."

McGraw doesn't remove his hat. He chooses a chair away from the stacks of boxes marked on the end with the Fugitive Task Force seal. Roark chooses a chair to his right, while Buddy sits next to her. Walker and Polanski sit across from them. No refreshments are offered to the Atlanta detectives.

Walker is the first to speak. "As Deputy Polanski said, we were talking and came to an agreement that I hope you can live with," he says.

"And what is that, Chief Walker?" McGraw asks.

"Polanski has agreed to allow you and Detective Roark to work alongside him and his deputies. He and I will be in constant contact."

He pauses, apparently giving McGraw and Holly time to think whether they can accept his conditions. Polanski's eyes are smiling, urging McGraw to accept the deal, while Walker's eyes are expressing that this is the way it's going to be, take it or leave it.

Before answering, McGraw turns to Buddy, who raises his brows signaling that he'd better take it because it's as good as he's gonna give.

Tommie Lee enters and nods to Walker and the Marshal.

"Is working with Paul and his deputies agreeable to you, detectives McGraw and Roark?" Walker says.

"That sounds fair, sir," McGraw says. Roark nods her approval.

"Good," he says, and stands, with a hand stretched out. Everyone rises. After shaking hands, Walker says, "I'll leave you all for now." He turns to the marshal. "We'll talk later."

After Walker leaves, Polanski asks everyone to sit.

"To bring you up to snuff, Chief Walker and I toured the campus after our brief meeting this morning. The Marshal's Service will be in charge this weekend. I have men in the Grove, around the campus and at the Vaught-Hemmingway Stadium along with the Chief's deputies."

He pauses and looks at McGraw.

"McGraw, you and Roark have been on this case for weeks. There's one thing my supervisor and I can't figure out. What's your fugitive's MO, his signature? Why would he come to this campus during a football game? Surely he knows we'll be all over his ass. It doesn't make sense to us."

"Good question," McGraw says.

He tells Polanski about how the Rebels recruited Max, and his unfortunate injury in football at Perry High which dashed his hopes of ever playing for the Rebels. But that didn't stop his loyalty to them and he's been an avid fan and supporter ever since.

"Is this the first home game he's ever attended?" Polanski says.

"It is," Roark says. "But he has followed them religiously, according to his wife. You should have seen his home office. It was full of Ole Miss stuff."

"I'm just wondering why he chose to come now."

"Kingston lives a double life," Roark says. "The main reason he rarely left Atlanta is that his business took a lot of his time. He got mixed up in a Mafia prostitution ring, and his ego thrived on the women."

McGraw added. "I'm guessing, but like many fans, I think he was satisfied just donating a lot of money to Ole Miss and watching the Rebels on TV. Regarding his MO, Max Kingston is a psychopath with narcissistic tendencies and has become what I call a malignant narcissist, meaning he's now extreme in his behavior. The challenge of facing law enforcement thrills him. It's almost orgasmic for him to imagine himself pitted against us. He feels he's outsmarted us; the stupid Atlanta cops who are waiting for him in Perry, Oklahoma, his birthplace. We purposely sent two of our detectives to Perry as a decoy. The local sheriff has put out the word in town and on their website that we are concentrating our efforts there."

"I see," Polanski says, staring at them. "Is there anything else I should know that would be helpful?"

"Yes," McGraw says. "Roark and I talked on the plane coming here and I've been doing a lot of thinking since we arrived. I'd like for her to stop me if she has anything as I lay out what Kingston might do."

Polanski straightens up, moves in closer and rests his elbows on the table in front of him. "Go on."

"Our thinking is this: Max won't be traveling alone, because of his past involvement with a lot of women, even though he had a wife. Many of his mistresses were prostitutes. We believe he has brought one with him and they will be together the whole time. Also, he knows that if the law is looking for him, they'll be watching the motels and hotels, so he's booked a private home from one of the Oxford residents, making it harder for us to find him—"

Tommie Lee interrupts. "The home rentals will be difficult to run down."

McGraw adds, "We have to remember Max is no ordinary criminal. He's smart. He's likely staying close to the campus, where he can walk to the game in the crowd. That way he will have crowd cover and won't be bothered with parking, which will be hard to find in a situation like this."

McGraw turns to the Oxford Police chief. "It might be helpful to have your deputies patrol the homes close to the campus, Tommie Lee."

He nods, "That we can do."

"Also, I don't believe Max will go to the Grove tomorrow," McGraw says.

Polanski frowns. "You don't? What makes you think that?"

"I wouldn't delete the possibility entirely from our strategy, but in my opinion, the emphasis should be on the stadium. He hasn't come all this way to not attend the game, and perhaps has already toured the grounds and memorized its layout. He would never put himself in danger by going to the Grove."

"So you think our man will lie low and wait to go to the game tomorrow night?" Polanski says.

Roark says. "He may be forced to go to the bars tonight in the Town Square. His companion will get restless if Max tries to keep her sequestered in the home too long. He's come prepared with booze and food, but you can bet she'll want to get out and enjoy the excitement. These women can smell a good time."

"Maybe he'll let her go by herself," Buddy says.

McGraw feels himself shaking his head. "Max would never trust her. Remember, she's a lady of the street. She could get talkative after a few drinks."

"Our deputies will pay special attention around the Square tonight," Tommie Lee says.

"We'll all be there," says Polanski.

A deputy calls in on his radio. "Deputy Marshal Polanski, we have our man."

He picks up the radio, frowning. "What do you mean?"

"We've got Max Kingston a.k.a. Sonny Burke."

The deputy marshal frowns and looks at the other officers around the table. "You got to be kidding me? Are you sure?"

"Yes sir. We confronted him in the Grove." We're bringing him in now."

Everyone jumps up.

"This is much too easy," McGraw says.

There's a knock and the door swings open. At first glance, the man handcuffed between two deputies could pass for Max's brother. He's struggling to break loose from their grip on his arms, and is yelling, "My name is Howard Pettijohn. I'm from Wiggins, Mississippi, not Atlanta. I don't know any Max Kingston or whatever his name is. I'm here for the Rebel/LSU football game."

Pettijohn is a big man, over six feet, long arms and legs, and could play for the Atlanta Falcons. It's a wonder the two deputies are able to restrain him. After looking at him more closely, it's obvious he's older than their fugitive.

"Did you check his ID?" Polanski says.

One of the deputies says, "He didn't have it on him."

"He said he lost it," the other deputy says.

"Did you come with anyone, Mr. Pettijohn?" Polanski asks.

"I told these jerks, I'm with my son and grandson."

"You wouldn't have a relative by the name of Sonny Burke or Max Kingston would you? We think he has a cousin here in Mississippi," McGraw asks.

"Hell no! That's what I told these guys. What's going on? I'm only here for the game."

"He's not our man," Roark says.

"Are you sure?" Polanski says. "He looks like the pictures you sent out."

"He's not!" she says emphatically. "He's older. Kingston's children are still in school."

"Where is your son now?" Polanski asks.

"He went to the car to get our sandwiches and drinks. I was sitting on the grass waiting for him to come back, and these guys grabbed me, scared the shit out of me, telling me I'm under arrest for murder."

"I'm sure we can clear this up, Mr. Pettijohn," he says. He turns to his deputies. "Uncuff him. Please have a seat, sir."

Two deputies lead a man in his late thirties and a boy about twelve into the room. "What's happened, dad?" the man says.

"Is this your father?" Polanski says to the man.

"Yeah, sure. What's he done?"

"Nothing, just a little misunderstanding. He said he lost his ID."

"Aww, he left it on the dining room table in his home." He turns to his dad. "You didn't lose it, Pop. I saw it on the table. I thought you picked it up."

He shrugs. "Well, I thought I did."

"Are we free to go?" the son says.

Polanski is writing something on a card with a cord attached.

"This is a temporary I.D. from the U.S. Marshal's Service," he says. "Wear it around your neck at all times, Mr. Pettijohn, while you are on campus, and no one will bother you."

Pettijohn slips it over his head.

"Are we free to go now, sir?" the son asks.

"Certainly, we're sorry for the mix-up."

The son nods. His father gets up and as they walk toward the door he mumbles, "A person isn't safe anywhere anymore."

Polanski eyes McGraw and the others and shakes his head. "We could have gotten into deep shit if my deputies had spotted this guy in the stadium and roughed him up. I want you Atlanta detectives with me on this one."

"No problem," McGraw says, "what's our plan?"

242

"We need to get a fix on the Grove and the stadium. I can show you around unless Tommie Lee and Buddy have already done so," he says.

Buddy says, "We gave them a brief tour, but they haven't seen the stadium yet, and we need to take them to the Garners' residence where they will be staying. So, if you don't mind, I'd be happy to take them around, unless you have some other plan."

Polanski nods. "That's okay, but no need to. Tomorrow, we'll tour the Grove and the stadium to get a feel for what we want to do. The game tomorrow is at night, so we have plenty of time. The five of us can meet later tonight on the Square and have dinner. Can't get in anywhere without reservations, I'm told. After that, we can canvas the Square."

"It would be better if we ate away from the crowd so we can talk," Buddy says. "There's a place north of the Square called Volta Taverna, not fine dining, but excellent food. It is in an old gas station, kinda interesting. I can make reservations; we'll need them."

"That sounds perfect," Polanski says.

He reaches into a box next to him for the hand-held radios, pulls two out and gives them to the Atlanta detectives. "You'll need these," he says. "I assume you have your weapons on you."

They automatically touch their jackets, where the .40 mm Glocks are holstered in shoulder slings.

"Then that's it," Polanski says.

McGraw follows Buddy out into the tiled hall. They approach an aristocratic-looking man in his fifties, ruddy face and high forehead, wearing glasses, a gray suit, red tie, and white shirt, standing in the doorway of his office. A gold metal plate on the door is inscribed with the name "Gregg W. Forsythe, Chancellor." He smiles and nods at the officers. "Welcome to Ole Miss, Detectives McGraw and Roark," he says.

McGraw stops in his tracks. He knows his eyes are as big as saucers and so are his partner's. McGraw tilts his hat and says, "Very kind of you, Chancellor."

"Thank you, sir," Roark says.

The chancellor glances at the West brothers. "You are taking good care of our visitors, I hope?"

"Yes, sir, Chancellor Forsythe," Buddy says. And Tommie Lee nods and adds, "We're treating them to good ole Mississippi hospitality, sir."

"Very well, then," he says, and turns to the Atlanta detectives, "If we can do anything for you, please let my office know. Enjoy your stay." He steps back into his office.

Outside, McGraw and Holly follow the brothers to the cruiser, stunned that the chancellor knew their names.

"How in the heck did the Chancellor know our names?" Roark asks.

"He knows everything that goes on at this university. Anyway, Walker met with him today before we arrived," Buddy says.

"That was very gentlemanly of him; especially when he took time to listen for the conference room door to open so he could greet us," McGraw says.

"I thought that was sweet," Roark says.

Many fans are strolling on the campus now and The Circle is full of excited fans. The Oxford Police Chief slips behind the wheel. When everyone is settled in, he pulls away from the curb and drives around the Circle, passing the Engineering building, the Pharmacy building, and the Thad Cochran National Center for Drug Research. On their left is the Grove again, with its magnificent trees.

"There's a lot more sitters out there," Roark says.

After crossing the bridge, he turns right and travels a little more than three football fields down the Taylor road gradient, then turns left on Old Taylor Road and guns it up the incline. McGraw feels like they're driving through a mini-forest with attractive trees and heavy vegetation; at certain openings, beautiful homes come in view.

"Up ahead a little on the left is Rowan Oak, William Faulkner's estate," Tommie Lee says. He turns right on Cleveland Boulevard, then another right on Smallwood Drive. "We'll pass Faulkner's place on our way to town later." He stops in front of the Garners' home and pops the trunk. Outside, he lifts up the half-opened trunk and reaches in for a cardboard box, while McGraw and Holly grab their luggage.

"I gathered up some Ole Miss sportswear," Tommie Lee says. "Buddy and I thought it might be better if y'all was dressed like fans since your fugitive knows ya. I hope they fit."

"Good thinking," McGraw says.

CHAPTER FIFTY-TWO

Max Kingston stands at the front window of the home he has rented on University Avenue for the weekend and spreads the curtains. Fans dressed in Ole Miss caps, sweatshirts and jackets are strolling past, heading toward the campus, while more are walking in the opposite direction toward town. He turns when he hears his companion, Lulu, come into the room.

A slim brunette with a smooth complexion and shapely rear, wearing only a red bra, red lace-frilled panties and high heels, comes into the room carrying a glass of vodka. She sits at the dining room table.

"What are you looking at, baby?" she says with legs crossed, kicking one foot in the air in cadence with the tick-tock of the Hamlin grandfather clock in the corner. She goes by the name of Lulu White, taken from a famous Madame in New Orleans.

Kingston doesn't respond.

She picks up a cigarette from an open pack on the table, lights it, swallows a long puff that fills her lungs and in seconds, fine lines of smoke erupting from her innards, exiting through her nose and mouth as she talks.

"Max. Did you hear what I said?"

"I heard you," he says in a gruff voice. "You're not supposed to be smoking in here. Put it out. You burn a hole in that rug and it'll eat up my deposit and much more."

She crushes it into the tray. "What else is there to do besides drinking and smoking and showing you a good time? I don't want to be stuck in this place all night. They said on TV the fans will whoop it up in the Town Square tonight. We gotta be part of that. You said you'd show me a good time if I came."

"We'll see."

She rises and sashays over to Max, high heels clicking on the hardwood floor. Lulu rubs her breast against his shoulder and her hips against him.

"Come on, baby. Let's go to the back and I'll show you a good time and

245

then you take Lulu out and have some fun. Whadda you say? You promised."

She grabs him by the arm and they head to the back.

Close to nine o'clock, Max and Lulu are dressing in Ole Miss sportswear. After nearly an hour they come out of the house under cover of darkness, and fall in with the eclectic throng of fans walking up University Avenue towards town. Suddenly someone across the street shouts: "Are you ready?" Then those on their side of the street joined in as did Max, yelling:

"Hell yeah! Damn right!
Hotty Toddy. Gosh Almighty
Who in the Hell are we? Hey!
Flim Flam Bim Bam,
Ole Miss by Damn!"

Lulu turns to Kingston. "This is fun, honey. Is that your school song?"

"Naw, don't you know anything? It's the Ole Miss cheer. It's the way we fans greet one another."

"I like these folks. We're gonna have us some fun tonight," she says with her fake New Orleans drawl.

Ten minutes later they reach south Lamar and veer to the left. The street lights are on and the Courthouse in the Downtown Square is well-lighted and can be seen in all its glamour. The fans are shoulder-to-shoulder now, moving at a rate governed by those up ahead. Some veer off across the street and others step into Proud Larry's just south of the Square. Before Max knows it, Lulu has pulled him inside, live music blaring and fans packing in like sardines.

"Get me a drink," she says. "I like this band."

After an hour, Max and Lulu step out and continue along the sidewalk, navigating to the middle of the crowd. Many cops are on foot and one rides past on horseback. When Max and Lulu stop at the corner in front of Square Books, he is stunned at the crowd of fans flowing into the town square from all the side streets. Still stuck in the middle of the crowd, Max and Lulu are pushed along into the street close to the Confederate monument. Standing in a sea of people is making him feel a little claustrophobic. Max never overcame his fear from the many times his mother locked him in that closet when he was ten years old.

"We gotta get to the curb," Max says, grabbing Lulu's hand and pushing his large frame through the crowd like an NFL lineman, until he arrives in front of Regions Bank. He leans back against the building in the shadows, inhaling deep breaths until the dizziness and nausea leave him.

"You okay, baby?" Lulu says.

"I think I drank too much back there. I'll be all right in a minute," he says. Many cops are now on foot patrol, but Max's not concerned about them. He's been outsmarting them for years. He even tricked the Atlanta detectives, McGraw and Roark. These hayseeds here would be no match for him.

An officer pulls his horse to the curb and surveys the crowd. He looks over at Lulu and then at Max.

"There sure are a lot of cops around," Lulu says.

"That one at the curb is eyeing you," Max says.

She puts on a sexy smile for the officer, the kind she uses to seduce her clients.

"Where you goin'? Stay put," Max says to her. "Don't forget about the warrants out on you. Play it cool."

"I know, baby, I know. These cops don't have anything on me, just the guys back home in Atlanta. But I take good care of 'em and they don't bother me no more."

"Yeah I know how you take care of 'em."

"Oh, hush, baby. We're here to have a good time. Don't worry about these guys."

She pushes her way through the crowd over to the curb. "How you doin', baby?" Lulu says to the officer.

"Okay, ma'am. And you?"

"Oh, I'm fine."

"What's your name?" she says.

"Officer Brian, ma'am," he says. "I hope you're havin' a good time."

"Oh, I am, honey. I plan to have an even greater time."

"Well, this is the place. You stay safe," he says, pulling on the reins and guiding his mount to his left through the crowd, and over to the Confederate Statue. Max and Lulu blend in with the movement of the throng past City Grocery and end up in front of Old Venice.

"This may be a good place to get a drink." Max looks up. "There's a balcony up there," he says, still looking up, "where we can see what's going on."

He grabs her arm, but she breaks loose, darts into the middle of the street, and hooks up with several couples that have begun dancing. The crowd spreads and forms a circle around the dancers, edging them on with screams of Hotty Toddy. Max moves back from the fans streaming in front of him and watches as Lulu hams it up. He wonders how she can shake her body in so many ways wearing those spiked heels and tight jeans. Several cops walk past the dancers, keeping an eye on them. Fifteen minutes later, the dancers have had enough and Lulu looks around for Max. He goes to the curb and pulls her out of the way of the crushing crowd.

"Have you had enough?"

"I gotta get a drink. Let's go in," she says tucking her blouse into her jeans.

Max leads the way to the door next to Old Venice and pulls her up the stairs to the Burgundy Room. There's standing room only, and the noise level is deafening. They squirm their way through the crowd and find a small patio door to the balcony. They step out. The place only has six tables. Max spots three college guys at a table by the railing with bottles of beer in front of them. He goes over and flashes a C-note in their faces and asks if this would convince them to give up their table. They jump up. The tallest guy snatches the hundred-dollar bill and says, "Thank you, sir. You've made our weekend." They scramble between tables and are gone in a flash.

Max and Lulu swing two chairs around so they can face the action in the streets. "This is great," Lulu says, watching the crowd below. "You can see everything that's goin' on. Just like Bourbon Street."

Max looks for a waitress, but doesn't see one. Lulu turns to him and frowns. "Where's our drinks?"

"No waitress," he says.

She jumps up, "I'll be back in a minute."

Minutes later she arrives with two scotches on the rocks with a splash of water and sets one in front of him.

"How'd you get waited on so fast?" he asks.

"I have my ways, baby." She swallows some of her drink. "This is my second one, it's pretty good scotch," she says. "I guess I got worked up out there."

"Go easy on that. I can't carry you back."

"Don't worry, sweetie."

Max looks out over the crowd. He thinks about McGraw and Holly looking for him in Oklahoma as he swallows some scotch. When he last spoke with Kristi Sue he learned that the Atlanta PD was interested in his Oklahoma contacts, and wanted to know if he was going to Perry. That means the sheriff there will be involved too. He's a tough old bastard and he never liked Max because of his mother. He'll tell the detectives that Max's really Sonny Burke, a name he dropped when he left Perry. If they don't find him there, then McGraw and Holly will eventually figure out he's here.

"What are you thinking about, baby?" Lulu says.

"The game tomorrow. I'm hoping my Rebels crush LSU. The Tigers are pretty damn good. I've waited years to come to a game and I want my Rebels to win big."

"Your Rebels will do their best, that's all you can ask," she says, finishing off her drink.

"I don't know. They're not as good as they used to be."

"Aw, baby, you worry too much. You can see them in the Grove tomorrow before the game and cheer them on. The school paper said the Rebels will pass through a couple of hours before the game. Let's have another round," she says, getting up, and rushing out.

When she gets back with two more drinks, they move their chairs closer to the railing and sit in silence, taking in the view. The yelling now has reached a new level, and an ocean of fans as far as the eye can see has filled the Square.

Fifteen minutes have gone by and suddenly Max lurches forward against the railing, keeping his head low.

"What?" she says.

"It can't be!" he says.

"Whadda you mean? What are you saying?"

"I think I saw that woman detective from Atlanta."

248

Lulu doesn't know he dated Holly Roark, and he could spot her easily.

"Where? Maybe you're mistaken," she says.

"I'm pretty sure it is her."

"You're scaring me, baby. I don't want none of them to take me back."

"I thought you weren't afraid of them Atlanta cops."

She shrugs. "There might be one or two who ain't my friends," she says. "They watch my place and want to close me down and throw me in jail."

"Sit tight," he says laughing. "I was just pulling your leg."

"You son of a bitch," she says.

CHAPTER FIFTY-THREE

McGraw is the first to step out of Volta Taverna north of the Square, with Holly and Marshal Polanski directly behind him. The street lights are not as bright as around the Square, not as many cars going past, and the foot traffic lighter.

"That was an enjoyable meal," Roark says.

"Surprisingly delicious," McGraw says.

"I enjoyed the uniqueness of the place, a converted service station," Polanski says.

"Sorry that the West brothers had to leave us," McGraw says.

"The message I got from Tommie Lee specified that everything was under control," Marshal Polanski says. "They'll be waiting for us somewhere around the monument."

Now, within a block of the Square, cars are bumper to bumper, inching along. Fans have clogged the sidewalks. Police are on every corner and many are on foot.

"Looks like Tommie Lee has set up a perimeter," McGraw says.

"That was in our plan," the deputy marshal says.

Several cars blast their horns as the fans stick their heads out the windows yelling the Hotty Toddy chant at the uniformed officers, who wave back.

"What is Hotty Toddy?" Holly asks.

Polanski shrugs and McGraw says, "Other than that being their cheer, no one knows how it came about, except for a couple of theories, but no one knows for sure."

"How do you know this?" Roark asks.

He smiles. "How else? I looked it up."

When they reach the monument, they find the West brothers talking with an officer on horseback. Tommie Lee turns and spots them and waves.

"This is Brian, one of my deputies," he says. After the introductions, he asks Brian to repeat what he just told him.

The officer dismounts. "I can't be sure, but I think our man is here. I believe I saw him in front of the bank when I was on my mount by the curb."

"When was that?" McGraw asks.

"A little over an hour ago. He was with a woman."

"Apparently, the street lights were bright enough for you to get a make on the couple," Holly says

He nods.

"When she came over and spoke to me, the guy moved back against the building. Only thing I can be sure of, she was about five-five, wasn't a blonde and she had on a lot of makeup. She wore an Ole Miss blue and red cap and had her hair out the back in a ponytail, just like you have, ma'am."

"Why did you let them out of your sight, Brian?" Polanski says.

"The guy was wearing a Hotty Toddy cap under a blue hoodie and his face didn't register with me right away—"

Roark interrupts. "And he was probably a little hard to see clearly in the shadows, marshal."

Brian continues. "Thirty minutes later, that picture of the guy that the chief passed out at our briefing this morning flashed into my mind, and I felt like there was some resemblance. I'm not sure and could be wrong."

"What did you do then?" McGraw asks.

The deputy takes his time answering, apparently a little intimidated with five law enforcement officers standing around him, and he's making sure he gets it right in front of his boss.

"The last I saw of 'em," Brian says, "they moved with the crowd into Courthouse Square. By the time I got back through the fans nearly an hour later, I couldn't find 'em."

"They could have ducked into one of the bars," Polanski says.

Tommie Lee nods. "But with our perimeter set up, they won't get out."

"Officers are on alert, and have their radios," Buddy says. "We'll get 'em."

"And don't forget the snipers," Polanski says. "Is Courthouse Square this street name?" Polanski asks Tommie Lee.

He nods. "Yeah, but you're only standing in one side of it. The entire street that circles the courthouse is named that. And we're in the west side of it."

"Those are restaurant bars across the way," Polanski says with some doubt in his voice, pointing in the direction of City Grocery. "And those over there," he says with a sweeping finger in the direction of Ajax's and Rooster's.

"Yes," Tommie Lee says.

"What are we waiting for?" McGraw says. "How about you guys hitting the bars while Holly and I circle the Square and some of the side streets?"

"Our deputies are in the side streets," Tommie Lee reminds the group. "No need to go too far off the square."

"Sounds good to me," Polanski says. "If anyone spots them, radio me; otherwise, we can all meet back here at this monument at one a.m."

CHAPTER FIFTY-FOUR

Max Kingston and Lulu White are still on the balcony of the Burgundy Room, drinking scotch and scanning the area. He glances at his wrist watch; it's fifteen minutes to midnight. Cops are now in the middle of every block and on each corner.

"Shit!" he whispers.

"What'd you say?"

"Nothing, just drink your scotch."

He told this bitch they shouldn't have come. Now they're penned in. Max sighs and takes a swallow of his drink. His body stiffens; *he must be seeing things.*

"Where'd she go?"

"Who, baby?"

"That lady Atlanta detective," he says.

"Aw, stop playing games. That's not funny."

If that's Holly, then McGraw's with her somewhere. They're attached at the hip. Max never liked McGraw from the time Captain Dipple introduced him to the detective, because of McGraw's insight into things. Max, a fraud all his life, doesn't know any other way but to put on the charm to get his way with people. McGraw saw right through him. Or maybe he didn't like McGraw because Holly was in love with him and that made Max jealous. He was the one that always got the woman, and if they resisted, he made certain they never got away. Most women couldn't resist his charisma, except Holly. But at least he fooled her. Other women who caught on to him... well, they met up with consequences, and deserved whatever they got. They should have known better than to resist him. They were the weaker sex and they didn't mean diddly-squat to him. Neither did his mother, the bitch. But Holly, well, she was different. He liked her. She thought more like a man, but her being a cop and all, he had to struggle from revealing his true self to her while they were dating. But now she and her partner know everything about him. He knew there'd be a day when they'd face each other, and that time has come.

252

She's nothing but a bitch now, and I'd like to take care of her like I did Eva.

Max leans forward against the balustrade, zeroing in on two snipers on the roof of the courthouse. Two men wearing the same kind of jackets are coming with two uniformed officers past the bank and heading their way. Max spots McGraw and Roark on the west side of the square, rushing toward them. *Someone must have spotted us in here and radioed the others.*

He jumps up. "We gotta get out of here. Cops are in front of the bookstore, coming this way. They'll be coming in here."

Lulu jumps up, knocking over her drink.

"Are you sure?"

"You folks leaving?" a couple asks.

They push past them without saying a word and Max pulls her down the stairs, ending up outside next to Old Venice. The crowd on the sidewalk is so thick they're swept away, having trouble maneuvering along. Max looks for an escape route. A few people next to him are disappearing into what looks like a passageway. He follows along, pulling Lulu behind him. There's a wooden plaque at the entrance with the name: *Faulkner Alley*. Max sees light at the other end. *This is our way out,* he thinks. He shoulders his way through the crowd, still clamping hold of Lulu's hand. Half-way through the corridor, he deliberately rams an LSU fan with his shoulder, bouncing him against the brick wall.

"Watch where in the hell you're going," the LSU fan shouts, hitting the ground. Max laughs to himself. *Gotcha.*

They burst out into a lighted area with a parking lot to the right, packed with vehicles, and directly ahead, an open area. He's enjoying the adrenaline that's flowing through his body to meet this challenge.

Lulu screams, hopping along on one foot, clutching the heel of the shoe with her leg bent up against her butt. "I'm about to lose my shoe."

He drags her to the right between two rows of cars.

"Why in the hell did you wear high heels in the first place? Take the damn things off."

She slips off her shoes and runs behind him in her stocking feet. In the middle of the parking lot, Max drops to his knees, pulling her down next to the back fender of a white Mercedes.

"What's happening? Why are we squatting?"

"Two cops on horseback just shot by on that street up ahead. There goes a police car. Stay low."

"Why are you smiling? Are you enjoying this, you creep?"

Two cops come running from the street through the open lot next to the parking area, darting into Faulkner Alley.

"These cops are stupid. Did you see them run past us? They couldn't catch a fly."

"You're crazy. Cops are everywhere. We're gonna get caught," Lulu says, whimpering.

"Cut the shit and keep quiet." Minutes later, Max says, "Okay, it's all clear."

As they dart off, they slip behind a tree across the street. At Max's left, uniformed police are stationed at the four corners. He remembers now that's where Lamar and University intersect. Rebel fans are screaming obscenities at Tiger fans as they stream away from the cops, heading in the direction that must lead to the campus. *This has to be University Avenue*, he thinks.

"Let's go," Max says, and then he stops. "Hold up!" He pulls her back behind the tree.

"What now?" she says.

An Oxford police car with its strobes flashing, inches its way through the crowd walking in the streets.

"You blind? See that cop car?"

"Man, you're enjoying this, aren't you?"

He doesn't respond.

Once the black-and-white goes past, he and Lulu dart across the street and slide in among the Rebel fans. They move to the inside, away from the curb so the fans can shield them. No one pays attention to these intruders. They're too busy singing and calling for the Rebels to kick LSU's ass. Some have had more than enough to drink.

"This is the right way," Max says to Lulu in a whisper. "I remember those buildings on the corner. We're only a block from our place."

He grabs Lulu's arm and pulls her close to him as the returning police car, with its bar lights still flashing, approaches at a snail's pace. The car stops dead in the middle of the street about ten yards up ahead. An officer hops out looking in their direction. They keep walking with the crowd. Max's heart is pumping so much adrenaline into his body he feels he could beat a horse in a half-mile race. *C'mon copper try and catch me.* The urge to flight is strong, but Lulu would slow him down and if he left her, she'd crack like an egg during interrogation. Lulu has no loyalty to anyone but Lulu. So he decides to keep his eyes straight and to act like a true fan.

He screams, "Are you ready?"

The crowd responds in the way he was hoping. They erupt into a chorus of "Hell Yes! Damn right!" The drunks become so energized one falls down, which prompts the officer to come over to assist him back to the black-and-white, allowing Max and Lulu to race on and dart into the yard of their rental house.

He laughs to himself. *I've outsmarted you hayseeds.*

———— ✦ ————

McGraw and Roark have just completed another circle around the Square, looking for Max and his companion, and end up at the Confederate Monument. One of the officers radios that the fugitives were spotted in front of Old Venice, but they eluded law enforcement.

McGraw is amazed at the tsunami of partyers coming out of the bars with cups in their hands. The streets are filled to such a capacity that there's barely room to navigate.

"The bars are closing," Tommie Lee says.

McGraw remembers him saying they close at 1:00 a.m. He glances at his watch. It's twelve-fifty-five.

"But that doesn't mean they'll stop partying," Buddy says.

"They'll find places to go and party until dawn," Tommie Lee says. "And others will stick it out here for a few hours."

"Well, they sure know how to live it up, that's for sure," Marshal Polanski says. He continues, "Now to determine what we know at this time."

"We know for sure our suspects are here," Tommie Lee says. "My men spotted them running through Faulkner Alley."

Polanski nods. "That's correct, but unfortunately they evaded us." He glances at his watch. "It's after one a.m., and it's now Saturday. We'll have another chance at them either at the Grove this afternoon or at the game tonight. If McGraw is correct, then our fugitive will be at the game for sure. Anyone have anything else to add?"

No one voices anything.

"Then I think we'll call it a night, or I guess I should say morning, and head back. We'll meet again at the Lyceum around nine," Polanski says. "That should give us around eight hours. I know you must be as worn out as am I."

CHAPTER FIFTY-FIVE

Lulu is sitting at the kitchen table drinking coffee this Saturday morning, game day. Max Kingston comes in through the back door. The clock shows eleven.

"Hi, baby, where'd you go so early?"

Max removes his hoodie and cap without saying a word and goes over to the counter, reaches for the coffee pot and pours a cup, keeping his back to her.

"Baby, what's wrong? I asked you where you went. You woke me up when you banged the door going out."

"Are you my mother now? You think I give a shit if I woke you up?"

"Aw, baby, Lulu was only concerned." She lights up a cigarette and draws in several puffs.

"I can take care of myself," he says.

"I was scared. I thought maybe them cops gotcha. What was I going to do if them took you away, baby?"

He shakes his head, feeling like bashing her face in. *You bitch.* "You'd survive. And what did I tell you about smoking in here?"

"Aw shit, you ain't no fun," she says, smashing the cig on a saucer being used as an ash tray. "I shouldn't have come."

He turns around to face her. *You're lucky that you're still able to walk,* he thinks.

She frowns. "What have you done to your hair and face?" she says. "Your eyes look different."

Early this morning Max dug into the supplies of his transformation kit that he brought with him and performed what he hoped would save him from the law. He likes the results.

"What do you think?" he says.

"I like it," she says. "You look a lot younger and sexier with blond hair and blue eyes."

"Colored contacts," he says.

She rises, comes across the room and stops a few feet from him to stare at

256

his face.

"I like the tan, too," she says. "You look like one of those beach boys in California."

"Good, maybe I can pass for one."

"You turn me on, baby. Why don't we go to the back and Lulu will give you the New Orleans treatment."

"And what's that?"

"Oh, the whole works, baby. You'll see."

"Later. We gotta make plans."

Max wasn't going to tell her that he had met this guy Ron who was walking his dog Elli, and Max kinda hit it off with him. He offered to show Max around the campus, once he put his dog behind the fence. Ron, a retired pharmacy professor, has lived in Oxford over forty years. Kingston told him he was in investments and had his own company in Atlanta. Ron led him through the Grove to the Student Union, using the walkway that runs through the middle and ends up across from the Union, where they had coffee before continuing their tour of the campus. Everything seemed to be going Max's way. They decided to meet in front of Ron's place two hours before the game tonight, as Max suggested, and go to the Union to get some eats, which he'd pay for in appreciation for all Ron had done for him. Max's motivation for going to the Union is to make sure they don't arrive at the stadium too early. The cops will be expecting Lulu to be with him, but he never planned to take her along. Ron will take her place and be his cover.

Outside the Union after coffee, Ron and Max went to the stadium, strolling past cops standing around their black-and-whites talking, not paying any attention to them. Max felt comfortable in Ron's company and didn't worry about being recognized, since the police were looking for a man and woman team like Bonnie and Clyde. They walked the campus filled with fans constructing tents all over the place. Some fans were bringing food and coolers to the tents.

Since Vaught-Hemingway stadium didn't open until two hours before the game, they could only tour outside it. Max spotted a building with its back facing the stadium entrance. They walked around to the front. The name above the door was Kennon Observatory. He mentioned to Ron how much he liked stargazing and wondered if they could go in and look around. Ron told him that some buildings would be open before the game for use of the restrooms, but were locked during the game. He didn't know about the observatory. Fortunately, it, too, was open. Inside, Max walked around and cased the joint while Ron was attracted to something across the way. Max removed the Glock 42 from his front waistband and placed it behind a series of books on a shelf in the wall. The Glock is a good fit for his big hand, and he knows how to use it.

"Why are you so quiet? Is something bothering you?" Lulu asks, bringing him out of his musing.

"Nothin's bothering me."

257

"Well, we gotta get ready if we're going to the Grove—"

"Are you nuts? Cops are all over the place and they'll be expecting us together. Besides, Rebel fans are not like other fans. They dress up. Women come in dresses and high heels, the works."

Max is prepared for how he has to dress to fit in. He learned men came to the Grove and the game wearing slacks, white shirts and bow ties, jackets or sport coats, and even Sperry Top-Sider shoes.

"Well, I'm not sitting around here all day until the game tonight. I'll go bonkers. I'm going even if I have to go by myself."

"You do and the cops will grab your ass. Remember last night? You just had to show yourself in front of that cop at the curb. By now they've got a make on you after you danced in the middle of the street. You're gonna have to dress differently tonight or you're not going to the game." He says that, knowing he isn't going to take her.

"I'm going to the Grove and you ain't stopping me!"

CHAPTER FIFTY-SIX

McGraw and Roark are in the command center drinking coffee and studying a map of the stadium on the wall. Empty boxes of donuts are still in the middle of the table, left over from this morning's nine o'clock meeting with the deputy marshals and Chief Walker to strategize tonight's game. Once McGraw learned that sometimes golf carts were used at home games and around the campus, he requested the use of one to circle the stadium.

Walker stated that his legion of deputies will have been stationed throughout the stadium when it opens, two hours before the game. McGraw presented his theory that Max Kingston would not come to the stadium early, but would wait until the crowd was heavy before making his approach. Max is no dummy and he knows it will be much easier for law enforcement to pick him out of a thinner crowd if he comes too early. Polanski's agreement with McGraw seemed to annoy the chief.

Immediately after the morning's meeting, the group canvassed the campus and concentrated their efforts on exploring the area around the Vaught-Hemingway stadium. Chief Walker took them inside. McGraw, Roark, and Polanski will be dressed as Rebel fans and will be positioned at different entrances, each with a deputy. Once the game begins, they'll remain in the stadium for the first two quarters. At halftime, McGraw and Roark will begin their cart ride around the stadium. McGraw saw no need to do so earlier because he theorized that Kingston would stay for most of the game. If he were spotted leaving in either the third or fourth quarter, they would initiate a radio call. Roark tells McGraw that she wants to be the one taking down Max. McGraw agrees, unless things get out of hand.

Tommie Lee has deputies in unmarked cars canvassing University Avenue for Max and his female companion walking to either the Grove or the stadium.

Meanwhile, Marshal Polanski is sitting at his makeshift desk writing in a notebook, waiting for Tommie Lee and Buddy to come. McGraw thinks the Marshal's notebook will end up as the final report to his commanding officer detailing what has befallen at Ole Miss. Polanski rises, closes the book, puts the pen in his shirt pocket, and looks up. The wall clock shows three p.m.

"Shall we take the tour of the Grove?" he says. "The West brothers should arrive out front in a few minutes."

Roark nods. "That's why I came," she says, laughing. "Don't want to go home without getting a feel of the place."

Polanski cracks a smile, but just barely. "Well, then, let's see if what they say about this place is really true."

Buddy and Tommie Lee meet up with the other officers as they step out of the building into a blast of sounds coming from screaming tailgaters, loud music, and sports announcers on the TVs. McGraw is amazed at the number of fans now on campus. Chief Walker told them that for the big games with teams like LSU, Alabama, and Auburn, the fans begin arriving on Thursday afternoon. The Circle directly in front of them is filled now with wall-to-wall tents and hundreds of fans. Tents have even been erected in front of the buildings around the Circle.

Tommie Lee and Buddy lead the group, dressed in Rebel gear, along the familiar route traveled earlier in the morning. They arrive across from the Student Union at the Walk of Champions Arch at the north edge of the Grove.

"This is where the Rebels make their entrance in about thirty minutes," Buddy says as they proceed through the arch. "This walkway divides The Grove into two sections."

"Oh my gosh, look at the sea of red and blue tents," Roark says, "This is a gorgeous site."

"Everything you expected?" her partner asks.

"Look," she continues, pointing to her left, "there's actually a crystal chandelier in that tent. Can you believe that?"

"This is where Buddy and I leave you," Tommie Lee says.

"Let's hope we get Kingston and his girlfriend," Marshal Polanski says as they continue deeper into the mix.

"What they say is certainly true," Polanski says as they take their time walking between the fans, "That the women dress to kill."

"The smell of barbeque is tempting me," McGraw says as they move past a group of sorority girls in short dresses and cowboy boots, most standing but a few sitting on a couch in front of a suspended sign with huge letters *Delta Gamma* painted on it.

"Too bad you aren't wearing your Stetson," Roark says, smiling. "Those Delta Gamma sorority sisters would go crazy over you."

He shrugs. "My luck—no perks in this job."

They laugh.

Eyeing the food, Polanski says, "The buffalo wings look mighty good, too."

"I'm sure one of the coeds would be glad to give you some chicken," Roark says.

"Very tempting, but I'll pass for now," he says.

"Tommie Lee said the fans will clear the walkway when the Rebels come through, so they can be greeted from both sides of this walkway," McGraw says.

During this morning's meeting, the marshal divided the Grove into four quadrants and each officer was assigned a specific area. Tommie Lee and Buddy are to patrol the two north quadrants and McGraw and Roark have the two south sections across from Faser Hall and the Thad Cochran National Research Laboratory. Polanski will police all areas and remain in charge.

Polanski leaves them.

CHAPTER FIFTY-SEVEN

Lulu awakes from a long nap after having a run in the sheets with Max, who is still asleep with his back to her. She eases out of bed and heads into the master bath, which is as large as her bedroom in Atlanta. After bathing for an hour, she sits in front of the vanity applying makeup, then slips into a black dress she brought with her. She goes to the edge of the dresser, slides her feet into four-inch high heels, and moves in front of a life-size mirror on the door, turning her body from left to right, rubbing her hands down her hips. This should get me a drink with one of the Mississippi boys, she thinks.

She tiptoes through the kitchen to the back door and makes sure she doesn't slam it as she eases out of the house. The sun is bright, and the air is not too cool for a November afternoon. She is expecting it to change around game time, but the black shawl she's wearing around her shoulders should be enough for the evening. She makes her way to University Avenue and joins the crowd of energetic Rebels. *Max was right*, she thinks, *they really do dress up. Glad I brought my Sunday best.*

Ten minutes later she reaches the Grove, filled with rows and rows of tailgating tents. Fans are milling around and the music is so loud it is beginning to stir every muscle in Lulu's body. She's ready to do her jig right there on the pavement, but instead, she shuffles past tailgaters who are watching TVs, eating barbeque pork and fried chicken and holding red cups in their hands. She's never seen so many people in one place having such a good time. Lulu wonders what's in those cups. Half-way up the walkway, someone whistles at her and she waves and smiles, not forgetting to wiggle her hips, just a little. A nice-looking man in his forties, auburn hair, dressed in slacks, white shirt, bow tie and blue sport coat approaches her.

"You an Ole Miss alum?" the guy asks.

"No, honey, I'm just visiting an old friend who is a die-hard fan. I lost her somewhere."

"I hope you don't find her," he says with a big smile.

"Everyone calls me Lulu. What's yours, baby?"

"Jim Weeks."

"Pleased to meet you, Mr. Weeks," she says, flirting with her eyes and a strong New Orleans accent.

"Would you like something to drink?" he asks.

"Does the sun come up in the morning, honey?" she says, giggling like a school girl.

"Sure does, and I take that to mean, yes."

He ushers her into his tent. "Hope you like bourbon, Makers Mark," he says.

"Thank you, baby," she says, when he hands her a red cup, and she gives him her special Lulu smile. "I like it all."

She glances around the tent. It's filled with an array of foods. But Lulu isn't hungry. Booze is all she cares about for now. Several guys and girls are screaming, watching some sports program on the TV.

"Care for something to eat?" Jim says.

"Thank you, this is enough," she says, holding up her red cup.

He glances at his watch.

"The Rebels will be coming down the walk in about fifteen minutes," he says.

"Ya'll really like your football, don't you, baby?" she says.

"Nothin' better, ma'am."

Jim steps out on the sidewalk to look over the crowd. Lulu comes up beside him and stops in her tracks, almost dropping her drink.

"Something wrong?" her new friend says.

"Let's step out of the way of the crowd," she says, moving in between his tent and the one next to it.

She feels her face getting hot. The man and woman detectives Max pointed to last night are coming down the center walkway toward her.

CHAPTER FIFTY-EIGHT

Some of the tents in this area of the Grove have drapes at the front entrances and tables covered with fine linen, trays of cheese, fruit, and brownie kabobs. Large signs denoting Mississippi Mud Brownies and decorated Hotty Toddy cakes are visible.

"Seeing all this food is making me hungry, too," Roark says.

"Hold off," McGraw says.

"What? I'm not really going to eat now?"

"No. Over there," he says pointing. "That woman in the black dress and the guy in a blue blazer are standing between two tents. Her profile is toward us, but she fits the description given to us last night."

"She does at that."

"Let's move in closer," he says.

They maneuver between several fans and stand to one side.

"The guy in the blazer isn't Max," Roark says. "But I believe it's definitely her."

"She, it's she, not 'her'," McGraw says automatically.

"Noah," she says with loathing in her voice. "This isn't the time or place for correcting me."

He reaches for his radio and calls Polanski.

Polanski answers.

"We've spotted the woman who we think was with our fugitive last night. Is Officer Brian close by? We need him to make a positive ID."

"Is Kingston with her?" Polanski asks.

"No, she's with someone we think is an innocent tailgating fan."

"I'll contact Tommie Lee and have him get the officer over to you," Polanski says.

Holly inches closer.

Minutes later, McGraw's radio bleeps. "Yes."

"The officer's coming from town in a patrol car and will be here in a few minutes."

"Radio him to meet us at the entrance to the Grove across from that National Research Lab," McGraw says. "And how about letting the brothers know that the woman is in their area?"

"Roger," Polanski says.

"I'll watch for the officer," Roark says.

Five minutes later, Officer Brian pulls up to the curb. He jumps out of his cruiser and they usher him into the Grove.

"What do you think, officer?" McGraw says as they stand where she couldn't see them.

"She looks like the one I saw last night, but I can't be sure. Need to get closer."

"Hold on," McGraw says. "We need to get you out of that uniform. Your slacks will be okay, but you need to get a tie and put on a sport coat or jacket."

"My brother-in-law has a tent here. I'll see what I can come up with."

"Be quick about it," Roark says.

He nods and hurries off.

Earsplitting screams erupt. Roark spins around, almost losing her balance.

"What the hell?" she says.

"The Rebel band is playing on the stage next to Ventress Hall," McGraw says. "That means the football players are making their entrance. Keep an eye on the woman. She could give us the slip in this crowd."

"What do you think detective?" Officer Brian says, coming up behind him.

"I hardly recognized you, Brian. Get up there and see if she's the woman you saw last night," McGraw says.

The officer dodges the stream of players as the coach struggles to lead his team past energetic, back-slapping fans blocking the way.

McGraw pulls out his radio. "I don't have time to call Polanski," he says. "Attention, Tommie Lee and Buddy, there's a good chance the woman in the black dress could get away in this crowd if we don't keep an eye on her. She's with a guy in a blue blazer."

"Roger that," Tommie Lee says.

Minutes later, Officer Brian comes back. "She's gone, sir."

"What do you mean, gone," Roark says. "We just saw her a few minutes ago."

He shrugs. "I'm sorry, but she's no longer up there."

McGraw radios Tommie Lee, again. "Officer Brian says the woman has given us the slip."

"We're on to her."

Roark turns to Brian. "You race over to University Circle and I'll cover the street at this end by Ventress Hall," she says.

McGraw radios Polanski. No answer.

Fifteen minutes later, McGraw spots Polanski with one of his deputies and the West brothers, talking to the guy in the sport coat and their female suspect behind Brian's cruiser parked in front of Faser Hall. By the time he makes it across the street, the man in the blazer passes him, walking back to the Grove and the woman in the black dress is placed in the back of the cruiser.

Roark rushes over.

"What do you have, marshal?" McGraw says.

"Name is Lulu White. The man is just a fan and we let him go," Polanski says. "My deputy here caught up with them sprinting out of the Grove."

"I ain't done nothin'," the woman screams from the back seat.

Polanski leans in. "We just want to ask you a few questions."

He turns to the others. "We'll take her to the Lyceum; meet us there in a few minutes."

Inside the command center, Lulu is sitting at the table facing the marshal when McGraw and Roark enter and stand against the wall by the door. Tommie Lee and Buddy are in chairs on either side of the suspect.

"I ain't done nothin'," the woman keeps saying. "I came to enjoy the party before the game. I wasn't doin' no drugs or nothin' like that, just havin' a drink, and talkin' to a gentleman. That's all."

"Can I see your ID, Ms. White?" Polanski says.

She reaches in her purse for her wallet and extracts her driver's license and hands it to him.

Polanski reaches for it and examines it closely.

"Atlanta?" he says, but doesn't give her time to respond before asking, "Did you come to Oxford alone?"

"No, I came with a friend."

"Who is that friend?" McGraw says, moving to the table.

"Oh, someone I met in Atlanta."

"What do you do in Atlanta?" Polanski says.

"I run a boarding house my late husband and I bought ten years ago."

McGraw notices the frown on Roark's face. They both suspect Lulu is a madam. If nothing else than from her name, since it's the same as a famous madam in New Orleans.

"You know if you aren't straight with us, we'll find out when we run you," McGraw says to her.

He can tell from her eyes he hit a nerve. Her synapses begin working overtime. She crosses one leg over the other and back again a couple of times.

"You sure it isn't a brothel, Ms. White?" Roark says.

"I don't keep watch over the women that live there, detective," she says, yet not denying it.

McGraw winks at Roark, his signal for her not to pursue it, since they're after Max and not concerned with Lulu's activities.

"What is the name of your friend that came with you," McGraw says.

She frowns. "Max is his name, but I don't know his last name."

Roark asks Lulu to describe him.

"He's a big man, over six feet, has blond hair and blue eyes." Lulu seems reluctant to rat on Max.

"Any tattoos or scars?" Roark says.

She shakes her head. "He's got smooth skin and kinda good looking. Likes to wear sun glasses all the time, but hasn't since we came here."

266

"Where is he now?" McGraw asks. "We need to talk to him."

"I guess he's still at the house. He didn't want to come to the Grove. All he's interested in is his Rebels and that damn football game. He's bonkers over it. I came to have a good time and could care less about football."

McGraw notices Polanski glancing at him. He could be thinking that McGraw was correct in thinking that Kingston only came for the game.

"Does Max have a friend here who let you stay in his house for the weekend?" Roark asks.

She shrugs. "All I know is he rented it from someone. I don't know who."

"We'll need you to take us to the house and point it out," Polanski says. He radios a deputy to bring an undercover car around to the front of the building. He tells Tommie Lee and Buddy to escort Ms. White out to the car.

Lulu jerks her arm away as they ease her from her seat.

"What's this all about? What's he done?"

"We'll explain it when we talk with him," Tommie Lee says. He escorts her to the door.

"Don't you need a warrant?" Lulu says with sarcasm and the look of defiance.

Tommie Lee spins her around. "You better cooperate and change that attitude of yours. You can be part of the problem or part of the solution. Which is it?"

Lulu must see the seriousness in the Oxford police chief's eyes, because she raises her hands in surrender, perhaps afraid he'll lock her up. "Okay, okay, don't get your dandruff up. I'll cooperate." They turn and set out. Buddy follows them out of the room.

The Marshal turns to McGraw and Roark. "Give me a few minutes to call a judge in the federal building downtown to get a telephonic order."

They nod and leave the room.

Two marshal's deputies in a black SUV with tinted windows are parked at the front steps. The one in the passenger seat jumps out when the brothers bring Lulu down the steps, and he guides her into the back seat and moves in next to her. Polanski comes out of the building and tells the deputies to call him as soon as they get the address and description of the target location. The deputies drive off with Lulu. Polanski takes out his cell from his shirt pocket and calls the off-site tactical team station about a mile from the campus in the gymnasium of a high school that is locked up for the weekend. Polanski tells the commander to get his team ready to hit the house, and that he's on his way and will give him the address when he gets there. Polanski pockets the cell and turns to the Atlanta detectives and the West brothers. "Let's go."

Fifteen minutes later, Polanski, McGraw, Roark and the West brothers are in the school gymnasium, watching as the tactical commander briefs his team of twenty-five operators and two sniper teams, dressed in black military BDU's (Battle Dress Uniforms), tactical vests, radios with headsets, black Kevlar helmets and an assortment of special gear attached to their vests, including flash-bang grenades—diversionary devices that emit a loud percussion sound and one-million candle power light in a fraction of a second upon detonation. These hand-thrown devices will be used to temporarily stun and blind the fugitive, Max Kingston, giving the team crucial seconds to move in and control him before he can respond.

"Quite a sight," McGraw says. "This is the second time I've seen them prepare for a mission."

"Thrilling," Roark says.

Polanski gets a call from his deputies. "I got it," he says.

The team members are intently listening to their commander's directives with sober faces. McGraw knows these guys and gals are all business, and are confident and ready. Many of them are ex-military, either SEALS or Special Forces. He has a special place in his heart for those who have served their country and continue their service in police departments. After all, he's a former marine.

The briefing ends and the team does a walk-through and rehearsal on the gym floor. After ten minutes, the team leaders give the orders to load up and perform communication checks, testing their radios on a private encoded tactical channel.

Polanski reaches for his cell again. A minute later, he turns and says, "Let's load up; the warrant has been issued."

After Polanski gives the commander the address of the house Max is in, the tactical team loads up in minutes and drives off the school parking lot, heading toward the target location. McGraw and Roark ride with Polanski, while Tommie Lee and Buddy follow in the sheriff's unmarked car.

The lead car hits the campus and flows around the Circle, heading east over the bridge and continuing on University Avenue past Old Taylor Road.

"We're thirty seconds out," Polanski says to McGraw and Roark. The armored tactical vehicles slow and stop briefly, while the doors are opened and several operators step out onto the metal footholds on the sides of the vehicle. Then the driver resumes coarse to the target location. Several houses from where Max is holed up, the vehicles stop, the team pours out, and the operators fall in stack formation (one behind the other), while the other members peel off to positions at the perimeter. In unison, the entry team moves out, assault weapons in a ready position, approaching the house in one deliberate motion like black beetles in formation. Officers in the stack cover the house's exterior windows, passing off the cover assignment down the stack as they move within several feet of the front porch. The breacher, carrying a handheld battering ram, moves to the front of the stack and approaches the front door. The number-two man pulls open the storm door as the team leaders scream in a loud authoritative voice, "POLICE, SEARCH WARRANT." In seconds, the breacher hits the door with the ram with such precision it explodes inward into the foyer. Simultaneously, the number-three operator rolls a flash bang grenade into the living room. The explosion rocks the foundation. Smoke fills the house while team members pour through the front door. Inside, two-man team operators, like a gust of wind, flow throughout, clearing each room with precision. Every room is swept until the all-clear response is given by the team leader. The three-bedroom house is cleared in less than three minutes. The all-clear is given by the team leader and Polanski and the others rush up the porch.

"The house is empty. No one here," team leader says.

"That's just great," Roark says with regret.

The team leader turns to Polanski. "Deputy Marshal, we're out of here unless you need something, sir."

"No, that'll be all," Polanski says, disappointment in his voice. "Thanks for your help."

The shadows from Polanski and the others are longer now and in a couple of hours, darkness will begin to set in.

The team leader motions to his members, they gather their gear; exit the house, load into the assault vehicles, and pull away, as well-ordered as they came.

McGraw is amazed at what just happened. He turns to Tommie Lee and says, "That was really impressive; they make me proud of our country."

"Sure in the hell was," Tommie Lee says. "Never saw anything like it, except in the movies."

McGraw and Roark enter the house, followed by Polanski and the West brothers. "Let's hope Max left us some clues," McGraw says.

"Let's give it the once-over," Roark says.

They nod in agreement and fan out.

Five minutes later, they meet in the living room and Polanski says, "From all signs, the fugitive isn't coming back," Polanski says.

"I think he's gone to the game. It's after four, and the game starts at six," Buddy says.

"He's somewhere, but I'd bet a week's pay he's not at the stadium just yet," McGraw says.

A deputy rushes in with a plastic bag in hand. "Look what I've found in the trash can outside," he says, handing it off to Polanski, who opens it and looks inside.

"Partially used black hair dye," Polanski says. "He's changed his hair back to its original color."

"No surprise," McGraw says. "I told you Max was smart."

Polanski grabs his radio and calls Chief Walker, UPD. "Chief Walker, this is Polanski. We originally were told that Max Kingston was disguised as a blond but we now have evidence he's changed his hair back to its original black color. We're on our way."

He turns to Tommie Lee. "Can your deputies take Ms. White to your holding cell until we finish tonight?

"Certainly."

"Ms. White, you'll be in good hands until we can resolve this matter. You aren't in any trouble, but we want to hold you for a few more hours."

CHAPTER FIFTY-NINE

Max Kingston's arm falls into the empty space next to him when he turns over in bed, jolting him from a pretty good sleep.

He glances around, and calls out, "Lulu, you in the john?"

No answer.

"Lulu," he shouts, again. "Where are you?"

Again, no answer.

He glances at the clock next to the bed. *Christ, it's nearly three o'clock. He's to meet Ron in an hour.* He jumps out of bed, sprints into the bathroom in his shorts, looks in the mirror, and smiles.

"That stupid bitch thinks she's pulled one over on me slipping out to the Grove, but she's played right into my hands," he says.

He only bought one ticket.

"The way she flirts and wiggles that ass of hers, the cops will nab her, and she'll squeal like a pig to save her hide."

Gotta hurry.

He's pleased with himself for having packed everything in the SUV earlier this morning while Lulu was asleep and driven to his parking spot. He had been looking for a parking place at the edge of the campus where he could race out after the game, but most were taken. As luck would have it, he met this kid Ron knew in the Student Union yesterday morning where they were having coffee. He asked if they knew of anyone needing a parking space, just twenty bucks up front. Max jumped at it. He was instructed to come at seven this morning to Fraternity Row, behind the Sigma Nu house. He was suspicious that this frat kid was going to con him for the twenty, but when he got there the guy was in his car holding a spot behind the frat house for Max.

After shaving and washing up, Max gathers the bottles he bought at the drug store to change his hair back to black, throws them in a trash bag. Lulu would squeal if she got caught. She'd tell 'em he's a blond. He quickly slips into fresh underclothes, new black slacks, a white shirt, bow tie and a gray

270

sport coat. At the dining room table, he picks up his Ole Miss Hotty Toddy cap and goes into the kitchen. He reaches for the trash, opens the backdoor, steps out, locks it, and peers around the side of the building. No cops, but hundreds of fans are walking toward the campus. He dumps the trash into the green cart at the edge of the house.

Ron is waiting outside his fence when Max arrives. Ron's wife isn't going to the game, so he has invited Max to join him in her place. His tickets are on the fifty yard line, several rows up from the playing field. All Max could get online was a seat in the south end zone up in the top row.

"Hey, you're no longer a blond," Ron says.

"Yeah, I didn't like it bleached. I just did it for an old girlfriend."

"Ready for some eats?" Max says.

"Always," Ron says.

———————◆———————

"The game will start in about forty minutes," Ron says as they come out of the Student Union and head down the steps.

"I'm really looking forward to it. This is my first Rebel game," Max says smiling.

They cross the street and file in among the fans moving through the middle of the Grove, coming out the other end in front of Faser Hall. They pick up their pace between the buildings and through a parking lot, ending up at the curb across from the stadium. The Vaught-Hemmingway stadium looks like a big ship in the middle of a lake of fans. Ron and Max maneuver into the streaming bodies, being swept toward the main gate, narrowing into two lines that flow in between parallel bars. Ron moves into the line to Max's left.

Ole Miss students are tearing tickets and returning the other halves to fans. The lines are moving at a snail's pace because a student is looking into purses and bags as the fans pass through. Max stops dead in his tracks. Holly Roark is standing inside the entrance, behind the female attendant in the other line to his left. Next to her is a man that has to be a cop. Both are dressed to blend in with the fans, but that doesn't fool Max. He'd recognize her no matter what she's wearing. She glances in his direction, but is distracted. Those big, beautiful brown eyes of hers are a dead giveaway. Max steps behind two tall guys moving forward, keeping his head slanted away, acting as if he's examining his ticket. Ron has moved in front of Roark as Max comes within inches of his ticket attendant. *What a break*, he thinks. The guy tears his ticket and Max grabs the other half, rushes into the stadium and stops outside the nearest restroom just twenty yards away. Minutes later, Ron meets up with him.

"What took you so long?" Max asks.

"Did you see that pretty thing behind the ticket taker? Some guy ahead of me invited her to have a drink after the game, but she blew him off. I think she's security."

271

She sure is, Max thinks.

"That guy with her is a deputy with the University PD. I've seen him around campus a lot. Don't know why he's dressed like a fan."

"Do they always have this many cops at home games?" Max asks.

"Ever since nine-eleven."

Ron leads the way up the ramp, dodging students and alumni and moving between individuals already standing in long lines at restrooms and concession stands. The smell of liquor is strong on guys standing in the restroom line.

Two cops are leaning against the wall next to a pizza stand. They glance at Max. No way would they recognize him. He smiles at them, but they pay little attention to him, more interested in looking at the coeds.

Max follows Ron down the steps to their seats—one and two—next to the aisle on the fifty-yard line, several rows up from the field. Max moves into the number two seat and sits. *This is perfect*, he thinks, looking around. It will be easy to take off in a hurry if he has to; won't have to climb over a lot of people to get out.

The stadium holds 62,000 and it's filling up fast. The Rebels are on the field in the south end zone, limbering up and running through plays, while the LSU players are practicing in the north end zone. Max is surprised at how big the LSU players look up close.

Ron tells him that the LSU Tigers are unbeaten and the Rebels are having their worst season ever. "They haven't won an SEC game so far," he says. "We may get slaughtered tonight, but there's always hope."

Ron isn't too convincing on the 'hope' part. That's something Max doesn't want to hear. The players from both teams trot off the field and the Ole Miss Band, The Pride of the South, rushes out on the field.

Suddenly, two men wearing blue jackets with *Police* in large letters on their backs pass next to Ron and stop. Max lowers his head pretending to look at his ticket stub. The officers look around and then move down the steps and station themselves at the railing. Reality sinks in. Sooner than later, he could be caught if he doesn't play it smart. Officers across the way are coming down all the aisles, while a pair remains at the top of every aisle. Max's palms become sweaty and his breathing is increasing. He's beginning to struggle with his claustrophobia since he feels caged in. He turns his attention to the Ole Miss players on the field to get his mind off his anxiety.

Five minutes before the start of the game, Max looks around and across the stadium for Holly and McGraw, but they're nowhere in sight. Cops are all over the place and he has spotted two snipers on top of the Pharmacy Research building. All he can do now is sit tight, try to enjoy the game and wait until it's over to file out with the crowd to give him cover.

The Rebels race on to the field from the southwest corner of the stadium and the Tigers run out from the southeast corner. The crowd are on their feet screaming.

In the first quarter, the Rebels get mauled by the big defensive linemen of LSU and are unable to score. LSU puts up 21 points.

Max joins in with the fans screaming, "Defense, Defense!"

In the second quarter, the Rebels are stopped in the red zone and kick a field goal, but LSU lays on 14 more points, and at half-time they're ahead by 32.

"Where in the hell is our defense?" Max says to Ron, who is shaking his head.

"They haven't shown up yet," Ron says. "I hope they get their asses chewed."

Max's anger is raging. He didn't come all this way to watch his Rebels get hammered by these rednecks. With his fingernails digging into the palms of both hands, he's thinking how good it would feel to clobber a LSU fan, but they're across the way on the east side, screaming their heads off. The Ole Miss fans are quiet and looking around in a daze.

At half-time the players rush to the locker room and The Pride of the South rushes out on the field again from the south end zone, screaming and boogying onto the field in a rhythmic flow that covers fifty yards. This awakens the Rebel fans, who scream for the Pride. What else do they have to scream about? *Nothing,* Max thinks.

Ron stands and stretches, looking disappointed. He asks Max if he'd like to go back for something to drink. He shakes his head and Ron steps out in between two guys in the line heading up the steps. The two rows in front of Max have cleared. He scans the stadium again. This time he sees Holly and McGraw on the field directly below him. He wonders where they came from. Apparently they have walked the edge of the field checking the sections. Certainly, they can't see him. But he's exposed with the empty seats in front of him. She and McGraw disappear. Have they seen him? Are they coming after him? Max's heart is ricocheting against his ribs. Surely they'll radio the cops in his section, and in a couple of minutes a bevy of them will pounce on him. He's exposed like a sore thumb with all the empty seats around him. He jumps up, rushes to his right, staying in his row, tripping on a few feet. Luckily, he's able to maneuver through and ends up two sections away without much difficulty. The two cops near the field in his old section are rushing up the aisle and stop at the seats he and Ron occupied. They look around but haven't spotted him yet. The police at the top have rushed down to meet the other officers.

Max takes the steps up to the exit two at a time and enters the outer ramp packed with people milling around like they're lost. Police are all over the place. His blood speeds through his veins in overdrive. He's looking for Gate 8, which is close to the Kennon Observatory, where he hid his gun yesterday. He tells himself to calm down and heads off at a steady pace—not to draw attention—and doesn't look back.

Hordes of frustrated fans are converging at the gate, passing through in single lines. An elderly man in front of Max is holding up the works. He tells the young staff member that he wants to go out and come back. He's told that anyone leaving cannot return. The old guy says he's left his heart meds in his car. Max is getting impatient, but the other lines also are long and he's stuck in place. The attendant apparently feels sorry for the old guy and stamps his ticket receipt and tells him he can come back, but make sure he has that stamped part with him. Then he looks at Max. "We hear all kinds of stories from fans who want to get boozed up and come back in after half-time. What about you?" he says.

Max feels like socking the kid, but instead pushes past him. "I'm not coming back," he says in a coarse voice.

"Don't blame you," he says. "Our Rebs are getting an ass whipping."

Max flows outside with the crowd and moves in the shadows. A golf cart with a droning sound slows by the curb in front of the stadium. Holly is in the passenger seat and McGraw is behind the wheel. *So that's where they took off to*, he thinks. After several minutes looking around, McGraw starts the cart and it moves slowly in the direction Max wants to go. *They're smart. They've figured out he would rush out in that direction.* Max looks around. No snipers are visible on the buildings from where he's standing. They could be hidden and concentrating on the fans inside the stadium. But the street is well-lighted and heavily patrolled. The snipers easily could see him. Should he take a chance and race to his SUV with the Atlanta detectives heading in that direction, or should he dash across the street to the Kennon Observatory to get his gun? Finally, the cart moves out of sight, heading toward Fraternity Row. Max decides there's a big enough crowd that he could slip through without the snipers seeing him. The gun could be his saving grace. It's just across the street.

The back of the observatory faces the street, next to a parking lot. He races around the dark side of the building to get to the front. There's a cop on the steps. "Shit," he whispers to himself. *Would he recognize me?* Max wonders. He has to move fast. He'll take a chance, so he goes up to him and starts a conversation.

"We're getting our butts kicked," Max says. "I couldn't take it anymore."

The officer pulls out one of his ear buds and moves down one step. "You can say that again. This may be the coach's last year."

The screams from the crowd in the stadium are so loud they could be heard a mile away.

"Did the Rebels score?" Max says.

The cop inserts the ear bud and frowns. "Naw, they had a long run but lost the ball on the twenty and LSU is taking over."

"Shit," Max says. He takes a deep breath and shakes his head. "I didn't know this place would be locked during the game. I was told it would be open. I really got to get some water and use the john."

"It will be open after the game. You're supposed to use those in the stadium."

"I forgot my heart meds and went to my car. I'm afraid I can't make it to the stadium. And I really need water to take my meds."

"Just a minute," the cops says, pulling a set of keys on a chain from his pants' pocket. "I'm not supposed to do this, but make it quick."

"Thanks, man, thanks."

A few moments later, Max comes out. "I can't thank you enough, officer."

"That's okay. Hope you're okay."

"I'm fine now."

A patrol car pulls up to the curb in front. Max turns to face the building.

"Gotta go," the officer says. He rushes to the cruiser, gets in. They pull off.

The droning of the golf cart is approaching. No way can McGraw and Roark see him at the front of the building from where they are.

A guy dressed in LSU garb from head to toe is coming toward Max. "Howyu doin,' Reb? Oh, I guess you ain't doing so good, are ya?" he says, bursting into a belly laugh. "You guys are getting your ass kicked by a team that knows how to play the game. But don't take it to heart, you Rebs are doing the best you can for a high school team." He busts out laughing again.

Max is snorting like a bull ready to attack, and his hands are balled into fists.

"My brother is one of you Rebs. Bet he's cryin' in his beer in that Grove watchin' it on his TV. I'm fixin' to go over there and razz his ass a little." Again, the guy lets out that irritating laugh and walks away. The redneck has stirred up such a rage in Max that he catches up with him in the middle of the adjacent parking lot crammed with vehicles. Max eases up behind him, pulls the Glock from his waistband and slams it against the guy's head with such force his knees fold under him and he drops unconscious to the gravel lot. Max looks around, bends down to check the guy. He's still breathing.

"That'll teach you to talk shit about my Rebels."

Max races back to the stadium, where fans are still streaming out. He asks one of them what the score is. He's told that there's only five minutes left and the score is 52 to 3. LSU scored two touchdowns in the third quarter and a field goal in the fourth.

"Shit."

Max rushes with the crowd toward Fraternity Row. Cops now are everywhere, but they seem to be concentrating on the fans leaving the stadium, and haven't spotted him yet. He knows they're paying special attention to the men. McGraw must have told them that Max would wait until the game was over to come out with the crowd. *That smartass thinks he knows me.*

The Sigma Nu frat house is at the edge of the campus and only a block or two away. Once he makes it there, all he has to do is pull out from behind the house, go a short distance and make a left and he'd be on his merry way to West Jackson Avenue and then on to Memphis. He now berates himself for taking the time to go for his gun and not rushing off to his car earlier, because the traffic is now heavy heading off campus. "Stupid mistake," he says. "Shit."

McGraw and Holly reappear, coming from the west side of the stadium, this time moving quite fast, eyeing the crowd as they approach. At one point they stop. Max thinks they've spotted him. He has only one more block. He pushes his way through the thick crowd and gets behind a guy around his height and size, holding his breath. At any moment, Max is expecting a cop to grab him. The cart moves on. He rushes around the guy and gets behind two couples who are discussing the coach in disgust. "It's time for a change," one of the guys says.

The others agree with him.

After keeping in the shadows behind them, Max reaches his street, but is startled when flashes of light streak over them. More cops are moving in. The place is surrounded.

The moaning of the golf cart is loud.

It's becoming louder.

"Shit! Shit! Shit!"

Max breaks away and races down the street that runs alongside the first frat house.

That whining is closing in on him.

"Max," someone calls out.

That sounds like Holly, he thinks. *They've spotted me.*

"You'll never get me alive," he says in a whisper, running with all his might.

He darts between rows of cars behind the frat houses, making it through to the back of the Sigma Nu house where he parked his SUV. About half of the cars have already left, but no fans are in his lot yet. Max's heart is pounding and he's gasping for air. He drops to his knees next to the driver's side of his car and bends over with his face close to the ground. *They nearly got me.* He inches up and sees cops everywhere. They've cleared the area and fans are nowhere in sight. He sees Holly and McGraw in a cart stopped in the middle of the street directly in front of him. Max bends down again. He thinks about shooting off a few rounds into McGraw, the bastard that saw through him from the first time they met.

Streaking lights inch along his car windows, hitting the walls behind him. He hears the droning of more carts. They know he's behind the SUV. He has to make a choice. A couple of minutes go by, which seem like thirty. He hears Holly's voice shouting to the cops to surround the block.

CHAPTER SIXTY

"You think he'll come out shooting?" Holly says.

"I don't think so," Noah says, shining the beam of his mag-lite over the SUV. "He's not in the car. He must be squatted down next to it."

"Did you radio Walker or Polanski?"

He shakes his head. "Just Tommie Lee and Buddy," Noah says. "Anyway, we have enough deputies around here. We're covered."

"Oh, yeah, you know what's going to hit the fan," Holly says.

"You said you wanted to take him, right?"

"I did."

"Well, who needs Polanski or Walker? Max belongs to you."

"What's the matter, lieutenant, you chicken shit?" Max screams.

"Come out with your hands on your head, Max. You're surrounded," Noah shouts.

"Come and get me, McGraw. You gonna let your girlfriend do your job for ya? Send that bitch out; she'd look good in a drum. No bitch rejects me." He fires off a shot.

"I'm gonna take him. I need this," she says.

"He's yours." Noah says.

She places her Glock in the holster and grabs the mag-lite. She whispers. "I'm going to make my way over to the cars directly in line with his. I'll come over the hood and get a bead on him and take him out if he shoots at me."

"I'll keep him busy."

"Come out, Max," Noah shouts. "You don't need to do this. Give yourself up."

"Yeah, so I can rot in the pen or get the needle. No way, Marlboro Man," he says, still shouting.

"Give up now and I'll see what I can do for you."

"Here's what I think about that, McGraw."

Before McGraw can squat down by the cart, Max's hand comes over the hood of his utility vehicle. Two shots are fired. One round hits McGraw in the neck and the other in the shoulder. He goes down.

"Come on out and play, Holly. I've got something for you."

Holly moves slowly in the shadows like a cat, crouching, moving between cars and stops at the fender of a black Corolla, three car-lengths away from Max's car. She eases up just enough to see his silhouette. He's looking at McGraw. She bends down again by the fender with outstretched arms facing away from her towards the back of the frat house, holding the Glock in her right hand and resting it on the wrist of the inside of her left hand that is holding the mag-lite. She moves her arms ninety degrees to the left as she inches up over the hood in line with Max. She sees him, still looking in McGraw's direction.

"Come and get me, sweetheart," he shouts, and fires off another round in McGraw's direction.

"Roark flips on the flashlight and aims the Glock at Max.

His eyes become as large as saucers.

"Drop it!" she shouts.

"Never," he screams, raising an arm towards her and firing off several rounds that are not even close to Holly.

She fires two rounds. Max falls to the ground.

"He's down," she shouts to Noah.

She rushes to the body, kneels next to Max, who is bleeding from the mouth. He is mumbling something. The rounds had entered his chest.

"Not going to make it," he says looking up at her, coughing up more blood. "Tell me," he says in a whisper. "Did my Rebels score in the fourth?"

"What'd you say?" she says, moving her head in closer.

Max can barely speak now. "Final score of the game?" he says in a raspy voice.

"Final score, fifty-two to three, LSU," Holly says.

With a dying breath Max Kingston says, "Shit!"

Roark looks up. "Noah, where are you? Max is down."

She stands and looks in his direction. "Noah, you okay?"

"Been hit," someone shouts.

"What?" She races over to him. He's lying on his back next to the cart and two deputies are bending over him.

"He's been hit in the shoulder and neck," one deputy says. "We've stopped the bleeding. The EMTs are on their way."

She kneels down. "Hey, cowboy, talk to me."

The ambulance pulls up.

"Did you get him?" Noah says.

"He's dead."

"Good. Meet me at the hospital," he says as they put him in the ambulance.

"No way, I'm riding along."

CHAPTER SIXTY-ONE

Holly Roark has been walking back and forth in the hall in front of the ER in the Oxford Hospital for almost an hour. The EMTs said Noah was going to be okay, but she wants to hear it from the doc. She's having a hard time concentrating on anything else, and is not concerned about the berating she took from Chief Walker before him and Polanski left the hospital. Walker made it clear that Capt. Dipple was going to hear about their defiance.

The doctor comes out of the ER looking for Sergeant Roark.

"I'm Sergeant Roark."

He shakes his head. "Never had a patient like your Lieutenant McGraw," the doc says. "Is he always like that?"

"You mean a hard ass? Yes, he is, but we love him."

The doc smiles and says, "Well, if you're up to it, you can go in."

"He's going to be okay, right?" she says.

The doc nods. "He needs rest for a couple of weeks. Does he have a wife?"

"No, but I'm the next best thing," she says.

"He won't stay overnight, so if you are willing to be responsible for him. I'll release him."

"Scouts honor," she says crossing her heart.

The doc shakes his head again but this time he adds a smile. "I've got two comedians on my hands," he says, leading her to one of the stalls with its curtain closed. He pulls the curtain to one side.

"You have a visitor," the doc says. "I'll work on the papers to release him," he says to Roark, and leaves.

McGraw is propped up with two pillows behind him, still in his hospital gown, and wearing his cowboy hat. He smiles when he sees Holly.

"Well, aren't you a sight," she says. "I guess they'll bury you in that hat, cowboy."

"It's in the will."

"How in the world did you get your Stetson?" she asks.

"Polanski brought it. Guess he thought it would cheer me up."

She moves next to him and places a hand on his arm. "Noah, all kidding aside, you scared the hell out of me. I don't want to lose you, partner," she says. She knows her eyes are glassy.

"Aw, come on. You know I'm too ornery to leave you."

"That's not funny."

The nurse enters and stops in her tracks, as she gazes at Noah's hat. "Well, I guess you want to get out of here, don't you, lieutenant? But you're not dressed just because you're wearing that hat. You can get your clothes on once you've signed these papers," she says, placing them on his stomach. He signs three sheets and she takes them and turns to Holly and smiles. "The clown's clothes are in the bag on the chair. Stop by the desk and we'll give the cowboy the doctor's orders." They laugh.

"Thank you, nurse," Holly says. She gets the bag and throws it on the bed. "Didn't we do this once before? I seem to remember you had a motorcycle accident."

"I guess you're destined to take care of me." They laugh.

"Well, you're in a playful mood." Holly says. "I've never seen you like this before."

"I haven't felt this way for a long time." He pauses. "I've been thinking," he says. "The doc wants me to take a couple weeks off from work and then light duty for a while. I got a call from the Capt. Apparently, Polanski called him."

"Walker chewed me out for our insolence a little while ago, but Polanski was okay with us."

"The Capt. told me about it, but he's not concerned. Once he learned I was still alive, he wanted to know what the doc said about my condition. He agreed that we need to take a couple weeks off."

"Whadda you mean, we? I wasn't shot," she says.

He glances at his hands and then back at her. "I have to be honest. I asked him if we could take some time off together. Hope you don't mind."

"Why would you do that?" she says, hoping his answer is the one she's been waiting to hear. *You're more than a partner to me, Noah.*

"I just thought you would enjoy spending some time at the Circle M. I know Texas Rodeo and Mystery Lady took to you, and you've taken to them, too."

"Is that all?"

"Well... no. I'd like you to spend some time with me, too, since I'm going to need some care."

"Noah? You're making me angry."

"Oh, Holly," he says, holding up his hands. "I'm just jerking your chain. I've come to realize something...."

"Yes."

"How much you mean to me, and...."

"...and?" she says.

"I really like you."

"That'll do for now," she says, "now get dressed and let's get out of here."

THE END

A NOTE TO READERS

Thank you for reading my novel. I hope you've enjoyed reading it as much as I did writing it. Please remember in your prayers Mary Shotwell Little and all those who have disappeared and never been found.

As an author, I greatly appreciate any and all reviews on my books, so if you can take the time to leave one, I'd be grateful. Reviews help other readers find new books, and they're especially important to newer authors like me. Thank you for sharing your love of reading with others!

Every quarter I hold a drawing for a free, autographed copy of one of my novels. Please go to my website (www.robertamagarian.com) and sign up. In addition, you will receive quarterly newsletters and hear about any new releases. You can also follow me on Facebook: www.facebook.com/authorRam

If you liked Noah McGraw and Holly Roark, they will appear again in my next novel. The story involves a psychopathic graduate student in forensic science. When under pressure, the student begins hearing a voice urging him to kill. While Noah and Holly investigate his murders, he keeps an eye on them in the guise of learning to work crime scenes. Can this clever killer outsmart Atlanta's finest detectives?

ACKNOWLEDGMENTS

Writing is a lonely task, but having a team that brings life to the novel makes it all worthwhile. The author wishes to thank those who have contributed to this novel in many, many ways.

The detectives: Captain Scott Waldrup of the Alton, Illinois PD. Enjoyed our many meetings in our special writing den, and you teaching me how to think like detectives; Lieutenant Mike Isaac (ret) of the Norman, OK PD. Enjoyed learning about hand guns, police work, and working through your many suggestions. Both officers have been my guides in presenting step-by-step law enforcement that occurs when a major crime is committed.

Editing: Nancy Hancock, the consummate language scholar, eagle-eyed corrector, and best advisor a writer could have.

Cover design: Peter O'Connor, www.bespokebookcovers.com

Print Formatting: By Your Side Self-Publishing, www.ByYourSideSelfPub.com

Readers: My persnickety brother, Dr. Edward O. Magarian, and my Oxford and Ole Miss readers: Drs. Dewey D. Garner, Ron Borne, and Brian Reisetter.

Use of names: Thanks to those who allowed me to use their names in this novel: April Dawn and Brooke Tubbs of the OUHSC Dentistry College, and my Ole Miss friends Dewey D. Garner, Ron and Brian.

My family: Love you all.

The author couldn't have done it without you guys.

Thanks to all.

ABOUT THE AUTHOR

Robert Magarian is the author of two thriller novels *The Watchman* and *72 Hours*. In addition to his fiction, Robert is the author of two nonfiction essays on Amazon Kindle, *Follow Your Dream* and *A Journey into Faith* (amazon.com/author/robertmagarian). He lives with his family in Norman, Oklahoma. You can learn more about him at www.robertamagarian.com, and you can follow him on facebook.com/authorRAM.